GARRETT KOSIS

THE PIT

PART ONE

Published in the United States by Cloak and Candle Publishing Inc.
St. Petersburg, Florida

Summary: When the cohesive balance of Earth and Penumbra begins to crumble, the winter solstice summons the mages at the College of Adarius for a grand ceremony enacting The Pit and consuming five competitors in its imminent spotlight.

ISBN 979-8-9919684-0-9 (hardback)
ISBN 979-8-9919684-1-6 (paperback)
ISBN 979-8-9919684-2-3 (eBook)

Library of Congress Control Number: 2025901638

Edited by Robin Fuller and Aly Owen
Cover artwork and design by My Lan Khuc
Interior artwork by Tanner Yurchuck
Interior design by Jaycee DeLorenzo

Printed in the United States of America
First Edition March 2025

For Joel – remarkable friend and imaginative soul
You are the original mage, the flame to the candle.

To All New Prospects,

It is with great pride and pleasure that I congratulate you on your admittance to The College of Adarius.

Our team of Seekers search Earth and Penumbra for prospective mages like yourself. You have been selected to join the newest batch of students who share a similar gift to your own—magic. The magical potential in your body grants you exceptional abilities that we will channel and harness at The College of Adarius. I understand the choice of attending a fantastical school of magic in another world feels daunting. I applaud your bravery, and, rest assured, our campus's extensive resources and relentless commitment to excellence will never waiver during your college years or beyond. The College of Adarius depends most of all on the talent and competence of the mages assembled here, particularly our students. It is our firm belief that you will make important contributions to the magical world while attending our prestigious school. We are thrilled you have chosen to pursue this outstanding achievement with us, and we cannot wait to see what you will create beyond our campus in the future.

Penumbra and Earth are two halves of the same planet. They are separated by a small, middle realm known as The Veil, a mysterious dominion uninhabited by humans where only elementals, fairies, and other creatures can live. It acts as a barrier and gateway to either side. Penumbra is Earth's mirror image, often having the same biomes, environments, ecosystems, and atmospheres. It is as enormous and stunning as it is dangerous and erratic. You are among a select few who will experience it firsthand. The wonders of Penumbra are my home, and it is an honor to grant you passage to them.

In this world, magic is no myth. Elemental magic runs through your veins in the same way blood travels. It is the rarest gift of all humankind, typically showing itself in various stages of puberty. This means that an elemental, a creature-like manifestation of an element's pure energy, has slipped through The Veil and attached itself to you as the host to survive in adverse conditions. The connection between student and elemental can be unpredictable, but that is where The College of Adarius and your courage come into the bigger picture. When you agreed to join the Seekers and voluntarily gave a vial of your blood, you began a journey of intense training and studying that will culminate in the miraculous procedure of Bonding with that elemental.

The College of Adarius is unlike any school. Our curriculum will flourish the needs of the worlds and embrace the inner beauty of elemental magic. From unique teachers focused in evolution to dynamo instructors capable of growing draconic wings, our classes can provide all of the tools you need for success. Please note that while special events and phenomena can occur during your tenure, and representing your element in them is an honor, they will never detract from our goal of creating a safe and secure community for all mages. These events are intended to showcase the college's great athletes and young prodigies and prove that they are worthy of demonstrating their elements. Our beautiful, diverse campus blossoms with the most wonderful architecture and genius these minds can create. Phoebe and our transition team will help you with your luggage, dorm situations, class schedules, and orientation activities. All novice mages should make a note to stop by Central Command for any questions regarding your new life at The College of Adarius.

The campus you are about to enter sprouted from my small, mortal mind before the power of five natural elements exploded me from the inside like an overinflated balloon. Within this world, you will see fairy tales come true, fantasy become reality, and planetary differences become necessary cooperation. It is a unique gift that we share and that I am proud to teach. On behalf of the entire Penumbra sorcery community, it is my humble honor to welcome you to our College of Adarius family. Here you will discover magic is not only real, but it is alive and thriving.

For magic and majesty,

Adarius

Adarius the Saint
Founder

THE PIT IS A SERIES of exciting fantasy novels set at the College of Adarius where a magical battle royale decides the fate of two worlds. It includes elements of graphic language, violence, battle, hand-to-hand combat, blood and gore, depression, anxiety, and self-harm. Readers who may be sensitive to these elements, please mind this message and proceed to Central Command. Your schedules and dormitories will be assigned shortly.

O C E A N

NORTHERN FOREST

THE COLLEGE OF ADARIUS

IGHT
ASSLANDS

Dunnmore

Wild's
Edge

Mazara ★

SOCOLLA
SEA

★
Persaw

Uldarr

THE VOLCANO

E S E R T

T H U U M   M O U N T A I N S

T H E   D R E Z C O G

★
Gahari

HALITE
SEA

O C E A N

MAP ILLUSTRATION BY TANNER YURCHUCK

THE COLLEGE OF
ADARIUS

OLIVIA'S TOWER

VOID COURTYARD

WATER COURTYARD

AIR COURTYARD

FIRE COURTYARD

FESTIVAL OF THE ELEMENTS

EARTH COURTYARD

THE COLISEUM

THE STABLES

FESTIVAL MARKETPLACE

CENTRAL COMMAND

THE INFIRMARY

THE TRENCH

MAP ILLUSTRATION BY TANNER YURCHUCK

KIKU I

"Okay. Ms. ... Kiku Kaipan ...? Age sixteen, sound mage, yes?" Phoebe asked, clutching a clipboard and pen beneath an eager smile.

I nodded gently.

Phoebe was the friendly orientation girl who showed new students the college's main focal points. Her outfit was as bright and bubbly as her personality; she never shied away from vibrant colors or fabrics. I found Phoebe intimidating; something about her fervent demeanor felt suffocating. Although I enjoyed that enthusiasm, even if I wasn't able to match the same level.

"Great! So, this is your dorm. Your roommate is Zoe. Here's your key. We're so glad you're here at The College of Adarius, Kiku. Please enjoy yourself, explore the campus, and remember, if you need anything, I'm just a spell away!" She beamed and winked at the pun.

"Thanks," I whispered, squeezing the key between whatever fingers could find a grip on it.

Phoebe hugged the clipboard, spun towards the stairwell, and ascended out of sight. "Toodle-oo!" she hollered, voice echoing up to the second floor.

I took a deep breath and tried to slow my rapidly beating heart.

Room 3105 opened onto a modest living space with a couch, lounge chairs, a long coffee table in the middle, and colorful posters on the walls. Before peeking into the bedrooms, I glanced around the corner to the vanity at the end of the hall and the large bathroom next to it. All the doors were closed, adding to the suspicion that I was alone in the dorm.

Dropping the keys on the coffee table, I grabbed my bags and headed for the two bedrooms. I stepped back towards the nearest bedroom door and casually opened it.

"Oh, hello there! I was wondering when you would show up! Sorry, where are my manners? Hi. Name's Zoe Evelyn Oz. But, yeah, Zoe will do dandy," said the busy young girl who was unpacking shirts and pants onto her bed.

Glancing at my hands wrapped around bag handles, I nodded at her and gave a shy smile.

"Here, here. Let my help you with those bags—just give me one second." Zoe emptied the rest of the clothing from her bag before tossing it under the bed. She came over to where I was standing in the hallway, unrolled one of the bags' handles from my fingers, and led the way to the other bedroom. We turned the corner, and Zoe opened the door with her free hand, ushering me to head inside first. Effortlessly, she dropped the bag onto the clean, made-up bed, and I followed suit, loosening my fingers from the remaining luggage.

I reached out my feathery hand and properly introduced myself. "Hi, I'm Kiku. Sorry I didn't say it sooner. My hands were full." I spoke as tenderly as I could to give her a good impression of me and even added a little chuckle at the end for good measure.

"No problem at all. Nice to meet you, Kiku. If you need any help unloading anything, let me know. I've been in my room doing the same," Zoe responded with a light chuckle of her own and a smiling face.

"So, where are you from?" For a usually shy girl, I just blurted that right out. But there was just something about Zoe's direct friendliness that invited mine out. It was a relief to put a kind face to the name on Phoebe's registry. Her eyes were calming and brought out the same sensation in myself—a foreign feeling for an anxious girl.

She had my *Geography of Penumbra* book open to a chapter about the similarities between the landscapes of Earth and Penumbra. Zoe pointed to a picture of Australia, with her finger inches from the Indian Ocean. "Right ... there. A town called Bourke."

I could tell by her gleaming eyes that she was incredibly proud of that place.

"That must be why your skin is so shiny and tan! Spent hours in the sun all day," I said in a relaxed tone. All nerves from the orientation group of new teenagers were gone, and the fear of forced conversation disappeared with them. I felt comfortable here with Zoe now.

"You could say that, yeah," joked Zoe. "Or perhaps years of my mother watching to make sure her daughters had perfect complexions."

"Whatever it was, it worked."

"Thanks. You don't look so bad yourself," Zoe replied. "And where do you call home?" She scanned through my book to find a good picture of a map with all the countries.

"In a small town outside of Tokyo," I answered, pointing across her chest to Japan.

"Oh, Japan?!" shrieked Zoe. "I've always loved the architecture and plant life there! It's so beautiful and detailed—you could frame every moment as a work of art. Truly incredible. Though I've only seen it in pictures and books and museums. But you—you got to see it all in front of your face every day! Must be amazing." Before I could speak, Zoe interjected with another thought that crossed my mind: "Well, I mean, you *did* see it every day, until you came here ..."

Her voice trailed off, quietly disappearing into the silence between us. That was a very soft spot for me. Leaving my family and responsibilities back home to come to the college to pursue my "unique talents" was devastating. It had taken a lot of convincing from my parents and relatives alike to push me into following the Seekers' proposal. I'm still not quite sure that I had made the right decision. After all, I'd only been here for a few hours and had become immediately overwhelmed by a whole new world on the campus. I managed to hold back tears and pushed those emotions to the wayside as I looked back at Zoe's concerned face.

"I'm sorry," she said, "I probably hit a sensitive spot and overstepped some boundaries. I hope I didn't upset you ..." She softly set aside the textbook and retrieved another.

Kiku ...

Astonished to see her so visibly troubled, I changed my facial expression and stared at her. "You didn't upset me at all. My home is a lovely and beautiful place. So, you're right." I chuckled, trying to soothe the ambient tension. "You didn't upset me; I promise. Leaving home was definitely difficult, but you couldn't offend me if you wanted to."

The warmth of Zoe's rosy cheeks returned, assuring me that she was not bothered anymore. "I can understand that. It was a tough decision to leave my family, too. Coming from Australia, where I'm so used to the heat and the wildlife and the lifestyle and the people, to a place no one could imagine existed? It's crazy to think about. But it happened. So, I understand and feel those same feelings that you do.

Also, may I add that I'm so happy you're not an insane or boring girl! I feared that so much."

Kiku ...!

Suddenly, this college did not seem as beastly as it had earlier. I felt like I could tell Zoe anything and that we were going to conquer this mess together.

"Kikuuuuuu! Kiku! Hey, wake up, sleepyhead! We've got work to do!" my roommate hounded me.

I opened my eyes wearily.

"Zoe? Sorry ... I fell asleep, I guess," I stammered.

I quickly came to my senses, rose to a sitting position on the bed, and watched Zoe. She was glancing between her hand and a sketch pad while taking notes as she went.

"Wanna go explore? Like around the campus and such?" she exclaimed randomly.

Zoe had rosy cheeks and gorgeous, cascading hair so blonde that it looked nearly white. Her blue eyes gazed longingly into mine, making me feel welcome yet startled at the same time. Slightly taller than me, she was very pretty; her makeup and glowing face brightened up the entire room. She was awesome. Since our first semester began a few months ago, I got to know the lovely and friendly soul of Zoe Evelyn Oz, a name she bore proudly.

"Explore? Walk? Hike? I don't know. Let's ... let's just go outside! We've been in our dorms studying and practicing so much, it feels like we're quarantined. What do ya say? Get some fresh air with me?"

Her proposal sounded like relief, because I had been thinking of doing the same for the past few days, really. Yet I was still unsure. Small droplets of rain pattered against the window and created snaking rivulets down the glass pane. "I don't know, Zo. You know I'm not good with crowds. People make me wanna tuck into my shell like a turtle."

She could hear the anxiety in my voice and came to sit on the edge of the bed with me. "I know, Kiku. But it'll be fun! Just you and me. Two youthful, ambitious air mages out on campus. We'll go to Market Square, the lake, maybe The Stables, and so on. Plus, we can eat lunch down in the market, too. C'mon ... please?!"

Her begging was hard to resist. We mentioned putting aside the incessant magical practices and other studies for one day. But I never really wanted to do it. I feared that releasing the pressure, even for a few hours, could be detrimental to my success at the school.

When I had started as a novice mage three months ago, every subject was difficult. Don't get me wrong; I loved each of them for their unique approach, and I was fascinated by this new world of Penumbra. But each was a scary beast in its own right. Luckily, one of my classmates from Forest Safari class, Abraham, helped me transition from Earth schools to this magic college. Our wallflower personalities had found each other in Professor Leon's class, as both of us shared struggles and a childlike wonder for magic. Unlike my estranged sister, Abe had somewhat become a surrogate older sibling, attentive to my questions and caring for my well-being. We also shared the same initial thorn in our side: Alchemy.

"Yeah, okay," I yielded.

"Yeah ...?" Zoe paused curiously, rising to her feet and stretching out for a high-five.

"Let's go! You're right. I should explore more—WE! *We* should explore more," I said, more adamantly the second time.

Letting a subtle grin shine through, I raised my hand to meet the high-five before she leapt back towards her desk and gathered up the school materials. She quickly changed outfits, from casual to social, and bounced from her bedroom to one of the leather couches in the living room. In a matter of seconds, she was prepared and waiting for me to catch up.

"Um ... that was fast," I admired.

"I know. Get ready so we can go. I wanna be down in the market before the afternoon crowds get there." She laughed.

My outfit was much more casual compared to Zoe's: a comfortable hoodie to keep my head from getting wet, a pair of nice but not overly flashy jeans, and short, cute boots for warmth, as the winters here got very cold (from what I'd heard).

Flipping through the student handbook, Zoe rose from the couch and greeted me by opening the door. We shuffled out of the dorm and down the hallway towards the staircase.

"Told you that hoodie would look good on you!" Zoe chimed as we neared the doorway to the stairs. Heading down the small flight of steps, we heard the light rain outside the walls and slowly turned the corner to enter the outside world. Bracing for the chill of winter, I pulled the hood over my head and opened the door for Zoe and me.

We made a quick right turn, looping through The Air Courtyard, where the Elder statue of Eliza stood proud; around the lake, where the benches were wet and unusually empty; and across the savanna, where the low grasslands introduced the bustling atmosphere of the market. Damp sidewalks quieted the weather and shone in the peeking sun's rays. Zoe exclaimed with joy at the sight of the first booth as we entered Market Square.

There was nothing quite like the soothing pitter-patter of rain falling. As it bounced off my shoulders before splashing to the ground, I stood still, swimming in a sea of people. Being short was not easy when it came to sightseeing; I was always on the tips of my toes to get a glimpse of anything. But here in this expansive marketplace, I saw everything clearly. Little women passing out hand-crafted trinkets. Strange yet beautiful acrobats performing in a circle of cheering people.

Zoe and I noted the massive party being set up near the marketplace. Dozens of mages carried equipment and props into the open savanna. We debated whether it was possibly a circus or a temporary zoo the college was hosting as we crossed the threshold of the market. Alive and well, it was a glorious menagerie of booths, creative food and drink options, and curious people walking about. I remembered my mother teaching me about ancient dynasties and world cultures from all over Europe. Rapidly glancing from the Roman-inspired architecture to the Persian-style bazaar setup of the whole marketplace, I picked up on all the things she showed me. It was amazing to see them with my own eyes.

The sight of the market brought me back to orientation day, when Phoebe had introduced it to the new students for the first time. I vividly recalled her words: "Our market is a proud melting pot of world cultures and various locations! Here you will find the best delicacies and specialty items from across the worlds." I remembered everything about my first day, especially walking through the market and meeting Zoe that same evening.

"You remember the day after orientation? When you and I came down here to see what all the hype was about?" I asked, peeking my eyes out from beneath my hoodie's falling cowl.

"Of course I do!" shouted Zoe, throwing her voice back at me over the noise of the crowd. "It's when we became friends, and I bought you that awesome hoodie, which seems to be keeping you dry. So, you're welcome!" Her face beamed a wide smile as water dripped off her baseball cap. Most people were thrown off by her Australian accent, but I failed even to notice it anymore.

"Yeah. Thanks, by the way!" I shouted awkwardly, having to raise my voice for her to hear.

She grabbed my hand and wove us between clusters of students gathered around the entrances and huddled in the open spaces while talking and shopping with each other. Seeing many new faces, even familiar ones from some of my classes, forced my shyness to the forefront.

"Fish popsicle?" asked a tomato-cheeked, tunic-clad woman as she braced against the cold. "It's a delicacy from Italy!"

I stared curiously at the woman and the pale blue cube on a stick. It looked nasty, but I did not have the courage to tell her so. Not accepting no for an answer, she pulled one from the tray and handed it to me.

"No thank you, ma'am," Zoe interjected, yanking me in another direction before I could grab it.

I glanced back at the woman, and her eyes flashed a smile of stubborn disappointment. Her attention shifted immediately to the next boy walking past the booth.

"Not a disgusting fish popsicle, Kiku!" My roommate chuckled again, slowing her pace and nearing a small unoccupied table. "Let's get some real food—good food for a change! Wait here ..."

I nodded at her and took a seat.

Zoe quickly darted towards an array of food carts and booths and vanished into the traffic of moving students. Awaiting her return, I sat and watched the people nearby.

I recognized a few students, though never waved or said hello. The rain faded from a minor drizzle to a few drops until it gradually ceased altogether. Above the tops of the stands, a rainbow emerged from between the gray clouds as the sun shone brighter, breaking up the opaque sky.

The market bustled around me. Groups of girls gossiped at the tables behind me while sifting through their shopping bags and putting on fresh clothes. Boys talked of how to "get ripped in no time." A couple of them nearly lost their collective minds as they toyed around with spears and shields.

Thankfully, Zoe split the crowds and finally came into sight carrying two plates of food, a pair of sealed teacups, and a mysterious brown bag.

"Did you get enough?" I said sarcastically, snagging one of the wobbling plates.

"I hope so," Zoe replied as she set the rest on the table. "Care for a wild boar shank? Or would you rather start with the Takoyaki?"

"Ummm ... yeah, sure!" I replied softly, taking the bottom of the wooden stick she handed me. "You got variety, I see."

I took a bite of the boar shank. The curry gave it a smooth, spicy flavor that matched beautifully with the sea salt and smoked meat. It was interesting to my palate (different from my usual fare) and I finished the entire stick in a few bites and threw it onto the empty plate.

Zoe finished hers at nearly the same time, and we both moved on to a more familiar dish—the Japanese snack. There were a half dozen wonderfully wrapped Takoyaki on this plate. She held out her left hand over the group of them while her right reached down into her pocket. Excited eyes locked onto mine as Zoe brought out a pair of chopsticks.

"These should make it easier," she added.

"Thank goodness!" I shrieked.

I took a pair of chopsticks and dug into the Takoyaki. The pan-fried batter encasing the cooked octopus was delicious and tender. Seafood was very common in Japan (same for Zoe in Australia), yet we both agreed that this surpassed our expectations.

Taking a sip of the golden tea, I paused and collected myself before asking what was in the bag. The tea was sweet and tasted like honey served straight from the honeycomb. It was a delightful flavor, and I noticed that it also created a great warming sensation throughout my body, from head to toe. Zoe raised her teacup shortly after, following with a drink of her own before replacing it on the table.

"Whoa!" I said, startled. "This tea has some wild properties."

"I know, right?" Zoe exclaimed, running her fingers over her cheeks and forehead. "The barista told me that this tea is used by arctic civilizations during heavy winters to prevent hypothermia. Neat, huh? It's not *that* cold out, but still ... how could I pass on the opportunity? Now, guess what's in the bag," she continued.

"I honestly have no idea. Gimme a hint," I replied.

"Pastry. A layered pastry."

"A brownie? No, it's a cake!"

Zoe unrolled the bag to reveal an immaculate two-tiered white cake, iced with a mixture of decorative purple lilacs and green leaves. We broke it in half and each grabbed a slice. Without a care in the world, my lovely roommate shoved the entire piece into her mouth, dabbing at the mess around her lips.

"Go on. You can eat yours. No one's watching."

I glanced around us, seeing groups of people flocking in all directions of the market. Many had shopping bags, and others were eating food as they walked.

Little by little, I took bites of the cake and wiped my face after each one. I was not as dangerous or adventurous as Zoe—but I loved that carefree attitude of hers.

We passed a cup of tea back and forth until it was empty and our stomachs were full. I walked over to the trash can and tossed in our garbage. Zoe adjusted her pants and jacket as I closed in on her.

"Where to next?" I asked.

"Do some shopping while we're in here? Might be a long time until we're back. Who knows?"

"We can do that," I agreed.

Zoe and I left our table and headed to the clothing booths and shopping stands.

"Good selection for lunch today, Zo."

"Why, thank you! I'm glad you liked it," she said. "I thought I'd honor our home countries with some seaside delicacies. A lot of mages were nearly puking when they saw me carrying the Takoyaki. I knew right away that they've never lived by water!"

I chuckled, as did Zoe. We split through the incoming crowds as I posed a request to her. "Look for a cute little boutique. I need a new journal, and those shops are the ideal places to find them."

"Yeah. I'll keep an eye out," she answered, darting her eyes from booth to booth.

After we traversed a row or two lined with delightful booths and prolific stores, Zoe found the perfect shop for me. It was in a segment of the market that resembled an Indian bazaar. These open-air stores carried everything from silk dresses to bedazzled knives to outfits fit for a queen, each one a part of the ideal emporium for everything a person could need. If I was ever going to find a new journal, it would be here.

I bobbed my way through the racks of clothing stretched into the walkway towards the rear of the store. Zoe stayed up front and occupied the vendor's attention while I browsed their book collection. Tucked away in a corner were many wooden shelves lining the walls. A row of thick, brown books sat on one shelf, with a leather-bound journal hidden behind them. A cherry blossom was pressed onto the cover. I could smell the sweet aroma of vanilla and almond as I picked it up and scanned through it. The pages were a faded white color, and a thin strap wrapped around to fasten it closed.

"This is it," I said, turning the journal over to admire the back.

Zoe left the vendor, and I called her over immediately to show it off. After a few minutes of me explaining the beauty of its Asian influence and plethora of open writing space, Zoe agreed that this journal was the one for me.

"Beautiful, yeah!" Zoe said.

I reached into my pocket and got out the proper gold as Zoe led me to the counter. She did most of the talking while I finished the sale and left the store. She was still discussing the meals we had had earlier with a vendor she'd met mere minutes ago. I abruptly pulled Zoe out of the store so that we could continue our campus excursion without spending the entire trip in one place.

Scurrying out of the shop and back into the marketplace, we whipped around the corner and headed towards the northwestern exit. I hugged the journal tight to my chest and trudged on.

"Never been to The Stables before," I stammered, locking my eyes on Zoe's feet.

"Neither have I," she answered. "But I know this campus pretty well! I've been studying more than just those books, Kiku."

"Apparently so."

As we broke through the market's chaos, someone yelled for Zoe's attention. True to form, she flipped around to face the person, waved and said hello, then redirected herself back to the path ahead. It was crazy. Students wandering through the halls always greeted her. Girls in our classes who had only talked to her one time would later say hi in the hallways. And random strangers (random to me, at least) would pick her out of the crowd and wave with a loud hello. These situations always baffled me because Zoe was a such a sweetheart. If it were me, I would have sprinted back to the dorm room and hidden behind the bed until they were gone. Yin and yang, huh? I laughed to myself, no doubt looking like a loon.

"You alright?" my roommate asked, politely concerned.

"Fine, yeah. Just laughing at how you say hello to literally every person who recognizes you!"

"C'mon, let's go to The Stables. I read that there are dragons and bears there! That's a wild combination, right? You'd think they would kill each other if they're in the same place for too long."

"Maybe. I don't know," I replied.

The sidewalk forked once we left the busy marketplace. A massive, extravagant stadium with vibrant blue banners draped along the top was far ahead to the right. To the left wove another path to The Stables. Zoe led the way, talking about how they were used and what other animals were available.

The Stables sat in a small clearing by Central Command, a stopping point just before the Northern Forest. I read that it had been converted into stables from an old water mill that used ocean water to power the facility before the college ever existed—in fact, before the rest of the world was formed. Now this beautiful stone structure utilized the same two-story building as a renting stable for eligible students to travel Penumbra. It spread between the meadows of mowed grass in a long stretch of stone as far as my eyes could see.

"Pretty wild, isn't it?" Zoe asked.

In a row of box stalls were two brown bears alternated with two horses. Against their own nature, the two carnivores were relaxing in their areas, calm and collected.

"How is it possible?" I asked, looking at the animals tied to wooden posts.

"If I remember correctly," Zoe began, rummaging through her brain for the answer, "students need one signature from a guide or a professor and one signature from the stable master. Once they have both, they ... just ... rent a mount for the day."

"That's great and all, Zo. But I meant, how do the bears not eat the horses alive?"

"Ask the stable master. I have no idea. You'd think they would, right?"

The horses were nibbling on buckets of food, and the bears circled around, looking for the best spot to take a nap. Each stable was blocked off from the next by a wooden fence and a locked gate. The stable master was nowhere to be seen, though Zoe walked the length of The Stables to find him.

My roommate transformed herself into a caricature of the Forest Safari guide, Leon. I smiled at Zoe and locked eyes with one of the bears.

"Bears and horses are too boring!" She laughed. "Wanna see more unique creatures—ones we don't have on Earth?"

"Sure," I replied.

Zoe gestured to some stone stairs and started a slow climb to the upper level.

"We're not going in, are we?" I asked, puzzled, suddenly feeling queasy about venturing too close to the dangerous animals.

"Not unless you want to."

"I'm good."

Suddenly, frantic shouts rang out as we approached the main door. Amidst the man's rapid shrieks of terror, the ominous sound of growling and wings flapping roared from inside. Through the cracks of the windows, Zoe pointed out the sharp talons and wings of a drake. I also noticed the majestic wings of an eagle. She quickly pointed out that this beast was *much* larger than the average eagle. The stable master looked to be having a very difficult time corralling the two flying creatures.

"A drake and a griffin," Zoe interjected abruptly.

"So ... the griffin is the eagle-looking one?" I asked.

"Technically, part eagle and part lion ... but yes!" The thrill and excitement in her voice was overgrown. I abruptly hushed Zoe, hoping to stay silent outside The Stables. Not alerting the stable master or the animals inside was my main priority now.

Zoe decided to get closer and gestured for me to follow her lead. I planted my feet on the ground and adamantly shook my head. Zoe neared the stable, inches away from the alarming rattling within. It sounded like cracking wood and hay bales being thrown across the room.

Watching from afar, I saw Zoe drag a wooden crate to the wall and position it underneath the window. She grabbed ahold of it and hoisted herself up to see what was inside. Her ears popped back slightly with anticipation. Stationary at the crack in the stable wall, Zoe flicked out her hand at me and snapped her fingers, calling me over to witness it all for myself.

"Pssst!" Zoe threw her voice to me. "Come here. Check out these beautiful creatures! They're ... breathtaking." Her eyes remained fixed on the happenings within the walls.

Unsure, yet intrigued, I eased my way to the crate and leapt up next to her.

The young dragon fell to the ground and lay in a circle in its stall. It had magnificent purple scales, which looked bruised. This drake must have had a rough adventure today with a student. A long, lengthy body with a blue underbelly shone in the flickering lamplight.

A pair of griffins were tucked into their pens, mirroring one another on opposite sides of the drake's stall. Elegant brown beasts, they slept soundly next to a dangerous predator. One mythical creature lying motionless beside two more mythical creatures? It seemed to defy logic and instinct. As we peered into the stable, the three of them slept calmly now, despite Zoe and I overhearing the creatures rumbling and tumbling around with the stable master just moments ago.

Frustrated by my own confusion, I broke and asked her. "Hey, Zo," I started, still watching the sleeping animals. "They're asleep now? But when we came over here, they were wreaking havoc. How does that make any sense?!"

"It doesn't!" shrieked Zoe. "That's the point, isn't it? It doesn't have to. This place is magic, Kiku. Things can change in an instant, I guess. I'm sure there's some rhyme or reason sometimes. But at the same time, maybe there isn't."

"Yeah, you're right, I suppose. Head back to the dorms? My anxiety is starting to kick in just standing here." I checked my hoodie pocket to make sure the journal was still there. It was. I brought it out and held it in my hands.

Zoe hopped off the crate with a quiet thud. "Time to roll!"

I took one last look at the drake and griffins before stepping off too. They looked gorgeous and deadly at the same time. I clearly had a lot to learn about The College of Adarius.

We started back toward the dorms and retraced our steps to the marketplace. Zoe and I avoided the hectic stores and crowds and snuck around the edge. The world felt much more familiar as the elemental areas and classroom buildings came into view. I was relieved. Being away from my studies and bedroom made me feel lost, and I was positive Zoe could tell.

"We'll be back soon, Kiku," she reassured me, her eyes glowing with a strange, inviting glimmer.

"I know. It's just—"

"Hey!" Zoe shouted. "Mason!"

She rushed ahead without me towards one of the benches by the lake. I slowly came up to Mason and Zoe, who were sitting on the bench together. Sneaking up behind her, I stood off to the side and kept to myself.

"Oh, sorry, where are my manners? Mason, this is my friend, Kiku. Kiku, Mason. He's in my Elemental History class."

"Hello, Kiku," he said briskly, then refocused on Zoe.

"Hi."

Mason continued, "Love that class. Yesterday's lesson about the different species of akiknaks was amazing! The stuff in Penumbra is literally wild. Fascinating stuff."

"Totally agree!" Zoe's eyes lit up at the mention of it. "We just went to The Stables actually, to check it out. You gotta go! There's dragons and griffins and horses and bears."

"I will for sure."

"You liked it too, Kiku, didn't you?" she asked, spinning around to look at me. Mason flicked his eyes to me as well.

I felt awkward and unsure of what to say. "Oh, yeah!" I flashed a quick smile before diverting my attention to the frigid lake. In nearly three months on campus, I had never noticed the gazebo sitting in the center. Linked with two nearly floating walkways, it sat comfortably unoccupied on the surface of the lake. Of course, on my way to class, my face was often buried in a textbook as I tried to pick up last-minute details, or I was with Zoe, studying and relaxing in the dorm. I had never seen it until now.

Zoe and Mason continued their conversation as I zoned out. They were going on about his plague magic abilities, or something like that. I tapped Zoe on the shoulder to steal her for a moment.

"I'm gonna head back to the dorm. I wanna start on this new journal and get some work done before Forest Safari. I'll see you back there?"

"Sounds good. I'll catch up with you later!"

Zoe smiled at me and reached her hand to the sky for a high-five. I lifted mine to return the gesture.

With this encounter out of the way, I started back to our dorm building and folded my arms across my chest, pushing the journal into my stomach.

Without warning, seemingly every class ended, every shop closed, and every dorm building released its students at the same time. The lake area rapidly became overpopulated. The flow of traffic ran in both directions with clusters of students passing around me. I panicked, holding the journal tightly and lowering my head to push through the masses. My eyes locked onto my shoes, and I watched each step as I was propelled forward automatically.

Little puddles of rain dotted the walkway before they were splashed on me as boys and girls sprinted past. Their shadows passed over me like a thunderstorm. I just kept moving, though, realizing that stopping even for a second would disrupt the flow. I hated confrontation; it always resembled a towering discussion with my mother back in Japan, which rarely ended well. She was hard on me as a performer of kabuki, a form of Japanese dance-theater. Being of a royal bloodline as well had put me in a constant spotlight. My family received rigorous scrutiny and speculation with an equal amount of praise and love. Having their shadow cast over me throughout my life had grown relentless. I used to participate in kabuki because I loved it so much—the other actors, the audience, the *kumadori* makeup. However, over my many years of performing with royalty attached to my name, it became a demanding routine day in and day out. I still enjoyed it very much, despite living at the college now, but the feeling of being in the spotlight had unfortunately changed.

Lost in my reverie, I picked up the pace—and bumped right into a large boy. Anxiety and fear flooded my mind. "Oh!" I muttered, dropping my journal and stumbling to the ground.

A group of girls laughed as they walked by; some other guys next to them joined in.

Embarrassed and unsure of what to do, I froze. I said nothing and did not move. The boy picked himself up and handed me my journal back. It was damp after landing in a puddle.

"Don't you know who I am? Take this back and keep quiet about it."

Reaching my hand out quickly, I grabbed the journal and held it close to my chest again. "You're—you're right. I should've been watching my step. I'm sorr—"

"Whatever," he interrupted, "just watch where you walk in the future. Novice mages on campus don't often piss me off a second time and have their social reputation survive. One simple rumor from me and my legions of devotees can ruin your collegiate career before it gets off the ground. I have a reputation to uphold, and puny Earthlings like will not stop Kamaul Metjen from achieving glory. It's very simple: Put one foot ... in front ... of the other."

I got a good look at his face. He was handsome and muscular, and his tanned skin glowed from his reflection in the water, which created an aura about him that attracted the eyes of open-mouthed teenage girls strutting by. He was tall, too—roughly Zoe's height. He had a wide smile and charming dimples.

Then his face abruptly shifted into a scowl, and he flexed his theatrics to create a heartbreaking act. "Mind where you're walking, troll! A king deserves a red carpet. Learn some manners! Keep your crap to yourself and step aside, little girl. Go 'head. Shuffle forward. Shoo, shoo. *Thank you very much*!"

He winked my way before rejoining the girls and boys waiting for our scene to end. They laughed and snickered again once he situated himself as the captain of the group. The five of them disappeared as swiftly as they had arrived.

I left the scene of the crime, stifling tears, and made a beeline for the dorm. I turned back to try to catch a glimpse of Zoe, but she was still deep in conversation with Mason.

Scurrying like a mouse, I made my way to the building and raced up the staircase. Only after I thrust open the second-floor door did I slow my pace.

The clock in our living room read 12:07. I scrambled into my bedroom, opened my new journal to the first page, and prepped myself for the best class of the week.

KAMAUL I

EVEN WITH NO SPECTATORS, an undeniable adrenaline rush from the prospect of sparring in the coliseum coursed through my veins. There was no greater pleasure than the dance of combat. The combination of hand-eye coordination and trading blows lit up my eyes like an inferno. It was a staple both in my household growing up and in Egyptian culture (at least that's what my father said). Throughout my childhood, my father had pitted my younger brothers against me, which often led to black eyes, bruises, broken bones, and arm slings. He claimed it was "a true test of character and leadership." However, Kamuzu and Kasto never held a candle to me, despite their best efforts.

I imagined the stadium full, the stone bleachers overflowing with a wildly cheering audience. Posters and plaques bearing my face were held up high for me to see—an ocean of Kamaul paintings and face cutouts wide-eyed and basking in one another's glory as the crowd chanted my name. *"Ka-maul! Ka-maul! Ka-maul! Ka-maul!"* The cheering echoed in my mind while I mindlessly scoured the coliseum in Nero's class. Nobody else existed. I was alone.

But, sadly in reality ... they did.

To my left was Bosamma, a volcanic mage with serious anger issues but no confidence to do anything with it. Second was me, a suave slag mage with unmatched potential (and a bit of a temper). I was succeeded by Solomon, a miniature echo mage who had probably gotten in the class with his gag-worthy teacher's pet forced likability. Next, barely standing on his own two feet, was Bosamma's equally aggressive twin brother, Baffy. Pike was last, whom I honestly paid so little attention to that I only knew his name because he was the newest recruit to the class. I stood on an invisible line among these four other students, like we were a military battalion preparing for war. In my eyes, it was only a matter of time before the other classmates were an afterthought. I had bigger muscles and significantly better battle knowledge than any of them. Plus, I was more pleasing to look at, and I could slice a pea in half before it hit the ground.

Baffy and Bosamma chuckled on either side of me. An expert-level mage and Nero's favorite punching bag, I eagerly watched the entry tunnel. Loud footsteps increased their tempo as one man's voice talked to another. Then their figures emerged from the tunnel's darkness, and all other conversation ceased as we collectively came to attention.

Life after coming to the college from Egypt had been such a drastic change from normalcy, yet Nero strangely made me feel right at home, almost like a replacement father figure. He had outfitted the dormitory to my Egyptian style, banishing the blandness by adding authentic artwork, small statues, and heirloom artifacts. Out the gate, Nero had helped me with my slag magic and gave me harsh criticism when necessary, which he deemed to be very often. Much to my confusion, it didn't make me angry or irritable; it was more like a specialist preparing his apprentice. Each adjustment and correction was calculated and never understated in its deliberation. His madness was unmistakable, but it was purposeful. After all, like a coach to a prospect, Nero and my slag teacher, Karnak, had suggested that I take this Gladiator class as an elective. Some students would take suggestions from other interested professors. When Nero made a suggestion, though, following it was typically in your best interest.

"Alright, insects, just like with the rest of the school, today's lesson has changed. I could explain Jackson's reasoning behind this change, but I don't care to ask him about it. Instead of an archery competition, based on last week's less-than-stellar results, we are whetting your whistle with a little student-versus-beast showdown. I've brought in Renner to conjure creatures for each of you to fight," said Nero, indicating the other teacher at his side. "*Do not* misinterpret my words. The dean may have altered today's plans, but my expectations have not changed! You pitiful pupils better put in twice the gusto as in our previous class, because that was a disgrace!" Spit flew from his mouth and landed on poor Pike's feet, and Pike's expression was an uneasy mixture of manic delight and deep-rooted terror. "I will first show all of you how simple this new task is. I imagine you're tired of hearing about these changes as much as I am already tired of talking about it. A brief demonstration to show you the proper way, then we'll begin at random with you guys."

Renner nodded and waved to us. He was stout with a gray beard, and somewhat taller than Nero, though it was by a very slight margin, as both professors looked small to me. His stern expression combined with Nero's scowl to create a visual tension indicating that these two did not get along with one another. Renner wore the typical boring wizard robes; Nero had donned black Roman-style armor with a white toga underneath and a bright red cape draped from the collar.

"Renner, start with any animal. Any animal—I really don't care," demanded Nero.

"As you wish," remarked Renner, concentrating on his hands.

"Beautiful. The sand is your playground," Nero said bluntly, peering into Renner's eyes. "I'm itchin' to taste blood. Though not my own! Not again, at least." Nero paused for the forced laughter of his class ... and was met with stunned silence. "Alright, class, try and keep your distance from the carnage. But make sure your eyes are glued to me!"

We all took a couple steps back and patiently watched Renner.

Nero, keen-eyed Gladiator professor and prolific master of wildfire magic, looked to the sky with a hungry smile. Wildfire magic had once been believed to be uncontrollable—an embodiment of untamable and unteachable pure fire energy. As one of the first professors of the subject, Nero was feared for his magical prowess and relentless personality. This unpredictable combination had helped him become the only teacher students hated to take classes with. Had you asked any wildfire mage in training, I would guarantee you that they hated their life. The same could be said of Gladiator classes, too, as Nero's notorious behavior cut deep into the soft-shelled students. Not me, however; those characteristics only increased my desire for his respect and admiration.

As if molding imaginary clay with his hands, Nero generated a blazing ball of fire between his fingers and hovered it above his palm. The fire burned white hot and streamed thin tendrils of black smoke towards the sun. He squeezed the ball tighter and tighter before launching it into the sky, where it exploded high above in a sparkle of light and pyrotechnics.

"Move in closer," he said, ushering the five of us towards him. Nero turned to give Renner a quick nod.

"Wait, Nero, you now want us to come towards you?" Pike responded.

"That's what I said, yes. It's a simple request, Pike. Do not make me repeat myself," the annoyed teacher answered.

A cold, sunny December sun warmed the dirt as we walked away from the coliseum's stone walls. Staying in the small group, I shifted to find the best viewing angle.

Meanwhile, Renner disappeared into the stands overlooking the stadium. From the balcony, the echo professor quickly engulfed the stadium in a cyclone of smoke and sand whirling in front of the class. However, hidden in the seething twister was an animal with large teeth curving back from the mouth. The four-legged beast's silhouette panted amidst the smoke. It stood nearly four feet tall and made fierce rumbling and growling sounds. Renner's hand motions ceased, and the cyclone vanished, revealing a saber-toothed tiger. It leapt into the center of the stadium with a menacing snarl.

Once its leopard-like, sparsely furred body landed, Nero's face shone in a gleaming smile. He cast a fire around the stadium's perimeter. In a yellow-orange flash, the blazing fire roared and circled the entire edge. Amid the heat, my mind froze. I became hypervigilant, anxious—and unhealthily aggressive. I felt the hot, burning sensation encompassing my entire body, like being burned alive. It was an inescapable feeling. This moment unlocked a memory, a haunting instant that …

NO! I refuse to relive that flashback! I refuse to feel those claustrophobic feelings again! I had suppressed them for years, and this ring of fire was not going to trigger them today! I was seeing my thoughts and hearing my own voice flicker in the flames.

Once Nero's fireball was extinguished, all of those feelings and emotions vanished along with it, coming and going as suddenly as his magic. As the memory faded, I regained my clarity and focused on the saber-tooth.

I watched Nero's cold eyes as he pursued it. The beast stood idle and glared back at him.

"Play the enemy to your strengths!" Nero shouted. His eyes locked on the saber-tooth's. I watched their pupils reflect in one another's like a jungle cat showdown. "A smoke bomb will disorient this Smilodon and allow me to track it with my thermal vision. Oh, and Renner, keep the upper torso of the saber-tooth for me to demonstrate with."

Huh? Like a fur puppet? I wondered humorously.

The comment made no sense to anyone except Renner, who seemed to understand as he consented to Nero's ridiculous request.

Nero cast the smoke bomb in his hand, throwing it down at his feet. A gray smoke cloud grew wide and dense in a matter of seconds. Meanwhile, the Gladiator professor and the tiger disappeared inside of it. Wildfire magic had very few attack spells, but a gifted mage like Nero could find ways around that and utilize those tactics to turn the tables in any fight.

Growls from the saber-tooth and shouts from Nero were the only things discernible through the opaque cloud of gray. The two dueled in a flurry of noises, which frankly could have come from either one. Then the dirt and smoke slowly faded away, and emerging from the cloud, Nero held the saber-tooth in both hands above his head like Atlas holding up the Earth. He had no visible damage or injuries.

"Now, during that smoke duel, something you could not see ..." Nero started, huffing and puffing under the saber-tooth's body mass. "... I used thermal vision to stalk the tiger's movement and track its white figure. I disoriented it and changed the momentum in my favor. If there is an advantage available, whether it be against man or beast, you *always* take it." He paused to catch his breath and readjusted his hands on the tiger's stomach. "Make the fight easier on yourself—never harder. Flip the scales in your favor. For instance, now this tiger is weak and disoriented enough that I can lay the final blow."

Nero reassured us that he was only tired because of the early hour, not from the tiger's weight. Whether or not these other simpletons believed him was up to them, but let me just say that his short stature and weak upper body *heavily* contributed.

Our professor let out a "controlled exhale" (as he had coined it weeks ago) before directing his eyes to the saber-tooth's belly above his head. Nero pulled harder and harder. A small incision was scorched into the flesh, from one end of its white belly to the other. Letting out a bird-like screech and somehow finding my eyes, Nero sliced the beast in half. With no blood splattered and no tendons severed, or anything left behind in the stadium, the saber-tooth's carcass dropped to the ground.

"Horrifying," Solomon said, dumbfounded.

"That was illegal to watch," Pike muttered, mouth agape.

"Incredible," I added, shaking my head a little.

Nero bellowed a hearty cackling laugh as Renner made the saber-tooth's body disappear. However, per Nero's request, he kept the tiger's upper half.

He addressed the class. Using the dead tiger as a puppet, he gripped the neck scruff in one hand and moved its mouth with the other: "Cast magic to your advantage. Fight smarter, not harder. Level the playing field. Lay the final blow when and where you can. Rip the heart from the enemy ... or, in some cases, rip the enemy in two." The scene of him reanimating the saber-tooth's body to tell us all this was a bizarre antic typical of Nero. A frightening man in more ways than one.

"Any questions?" Nero asked, holding out the saber-tooth's front paws to receive them. His voice had such determination that it could make a leader rally his troops, such emphasis that it could persuade a statue, and such severity that it could be the unforgettable last words of a man taking his final breaths.

With silence as his response, Nero continued to the next part of the lesson. He tossed the tiger torso aside at Renner, who erased it from existence before it could even touch the ground.

While the other students stood unblinking, I thought it was impressive. Seeing Nero outmatch an opponent with his wildfire magic was always exciting, like watching a warrior perform his signature move. And him burning a straight line through the beast's body and pulling it apart was insane. Nero was certainly a literal person, often making a joke about something only to do that exact thing minutes later. Truly an unhinged man.

"Great. Now, each of you will do the same. We call these 'gauntlets.' Simple as this: We start with one creature. You beat that one, then we'll move on to the second beast. Beat that one, and you'll face the third and final one. Old Gladiator teachers often used this as a way to improvise on the fly. Don't worry, Pike, or Bosamma, or Kamaul—if you're too weak to beat the first creature Renner sends your way, that'll be it for you. Simple as that: Win, and take it as far as you can go. Make sense?"

"Sir," Baffy ventured, "that's a lot harder than it sounds. Fighting random beasts with no practice other than what you just showed us?"

"You've been in my class since the start of the semester, right? You've been participating up to this point, right? You're still standing in my class, so this test *should* be a breeze. I only expect one of you to defeat all three enemies. The rest of you will probably spend the rest of the day in the infirmary, or the nuthouse, in my brutally honest judgement. Either way, I'm not expecting much from any of you. Just need to get a feel for where your weaknesses lie."

"Speaking of low expectations," he continued, "Kamaul, you're up first. Please prepare yourself for the first enemy while I escort the others to watch from a safe distance," Nero said, shepherding the other mages towards the stands.

I knew he was only saying that to get under my skin ... but it worked.

He pushed a wooden crate over to the edge of the stadium, leapt onto it, and pulled himself above the railing to the first row of stone benches. The rest of the class followed suit and sat in a line. All five sets of eyes watched me, displaying a variety of disgust, anxiousness, and interest. No doubt they were wondering how well I would fare against Renner's creatures. No need for them to worry, however, because I had no plans of spending an afternoon with Riley and Maggie, the infirmary nurses.

While they were both beautiful, they would only be seeing me on my schedule, not Nero's.

It was my time to shine—my time to prove all that I had learned so far in the college. As I had been here for more than three years, my magical knowledge had greatly improved compared to when I first arrived. This was my chance to warn the other students that Gladiator class would not be the walk in the park they were all hoping for, especially when it came to the student-versus-student duels later this semester. Nero needed to see that my physical combat and magic skills were equal forces of nature.

Walking over to the nearest weapon rack, I picked a battle axe from its peg and swung it around a bit. It had a thick wooden handle, stretching nearly twelve inches in length, but it was light enough to maneuver like a pencil. Topping the end was a sharp black blade. My handsome likeness looked back at me from the gleaming metal, but I was picturing a gory red paint job splashed onto its tip.

After choosing my weapon, I looked up at Nero, Renner, and my classmates to see if everything else was ready for beginning the gauntlet.

"Kamaul!" Nero shouted, still holding our collective attention. "Have your method of pain selected? Ready to begin?"

"Waitin' on you, sir," I replied keenly.

"Renner, conjure the first creature. Kamaul, do us proud in the school of fire."

Away from the seated students, Nero and Renner spoke quietly to one another. As they talked, I prepared to come out on top of the pack. I fixed my grip on the axe's handle several times with my left hand, trying to find the perfect hold. In the other hand, I focused my mind on slag magic. Everyone at the college knew the fighting powerhouse of a man I was, but Nero demanded to see my magic developed to its full potential.

With an abrupt exhale, I forced concentration and energy through my fingertips and out into the physical world. A fireball of slag launched from my palm. The power of it rocked the bleachers and left a black scorch mark on the stadium wall.

"Not my intention." I laughed to myself.

"Alright, Renner, let's get the entertainment started!" yelled Nero, making a grand gesture with his hands towards the empty coliseum. He was always one for showmanship, if that was not obvious already.

Renner stood up and focused his eyes on the space in front of me to cast echo magic. In another cyclone of sand, a winged creature spawned. I watched the smoky silhouette tower over me as dirt clods hurtled through the air like arrows. As the creature's form became more apparent, the surrounding smoke grew denser.

Squinting my eyes and covering my face with my free hand, I strained to keep an eye on the creature.

The winds slowly stopped, and the sand fell to the ground. A giant moth with yellowish-white fur stood proudly in the coliseum. Its brilliant red wings extended several feet on either side. The moth stared at me with expressionless compound eyes, and I narrowed my focus to only it.

A moth—really?! I thought, brushing my face off. *Treating my presence with no respect, I see.*

I glanced up at the stands to see the reaction from Renner and Nero. Renner, relaxing after sitting back on the bench, looked emotionless. Nero, on the other hand, leaned back against the row behind him, hands folded across his chest, and smiled with anticipation.

Not wasting any time, I charged directly at the moth full speed, tightening my grip on the axe's wooden handle. I let out a battle cry, flexed my muscles for the first swing, and pulled it above my shoulder. Gaining ground on the moth, I swung my axe towards its beautiful stomach. However, just as the tip of my blade grazed its tiny hairs, its wings clapped together and propelled the moth straight up in the air. A wicked gust tossed me aggressively into the dirt, covering my face in an orange tint. I sprang my upright and scanned the sky for the moth. Shaking the sand away, I found it hovering high above me. Its wings created a rhythmic ringing in my ears with each flicker.

Concentrating on the next slag shot spell, I directed my eyes to those wings. Nero had once told me: "Easiest way to take out an aerial threat is to eliminate its height advantage."

I aimed at the center of its left wing and launched a slagball. But that was ineffective; it simply wove to the right and returned to swaying idly above the stadium.

Frustrated, I flung another slagball at the opposite wing. The moth weaved back to the left as my spell shot past it.

Gathering itself, the moth abruptly beat its wings together in rapid succession, casting several sharp blasts of air at me.

Thinking on the fly, I looked straight at the ground and cast a defense spell. A black barrier rose from the sand to about shoulder height, wide enough to shield me from the moth's wind blasts. I ducked my head behind the shield as it blocked the moth's powerful gusts.

After the last attack rippled around me, I peeked my head above the stationary shield and watched for an opportunity to make my next move. I saw its next attack immediately: a bullet charge. With steady wings tucked at its sides, the colorful creature was hurtling straight for me. I quickly tossed another random slagball to the right of it, shifting the moth's momentum towards my dominant left hand.

I clutched the top of the shield wall and vaulted onto it.

"Wait for it ..." I said to the onlookers. "Wait for it ..."

"Now!"

Like a martial artist, I leapt into the air and performed a somersault (admittedly below average). Right as the moth's head neared my face, I swung the steel axe across its neck. Its body was propelled straight into the dirt at full speed, like a guided missile. The severed head lay spurting hemolymph, glistening in the dirt with a sweet blue color.

Nothing was more satisfying after a battle with a beast than seeing its life force spilled on your weapon. As I admired the blue goo dripping from the axe's blade, I sneered up at Renner and Nero for their appraisal. But none was given.

I wordlessly mocked the moth's efforts while laughing at the stupidity of it bull-rushing the Egyptian god-king Kamaul. My slag barricade and its body slowly vanished as Renner cleared the mirage in preparation for the next creature. He approached the railing of the bleachers and began casting another smoke cloud. The first fight had gotten my adrenaline pumping. This flight of emotions could only lead to Nero's star pupil (me) being crowned as today's sole gauntlet victor.

The sand cyclone whirled around in front of me once more as I moved back towards the center of the stadium. I reset my stance, eagerly awaiting Renner's next creation. Sand whipped past, and the winds dusted my face once again.

I watched as a new silhouette emerged from the shadows—a four-legged beast hunched over onto its front feet. As the smoke cleared, I saw Renner return to his seat next to Nero. The beast hunkered in the sun's spotlight. This next opponent was something I'd seen before, in my Elemental History class. Known as a subtropical moroddath, it was a species of giant monkey with pearl-white fur, large mammoth-like tusks, and curved ivory horns stretching out from its head. (Subtropical moroddath like this one had deep purple fur that counteracted their warm climate, whereas brown moroddath used mahogany-colored fur to keep warm in the frigid temperatures of theirs.) Capable of incredible strength and useful in traversing the more dangerous environments of Penumbra, the moroddath were often wrangled by huntsmen into the ultimate hunting companion.

The moroddath pounded its fists against the sand with a bellowing roar, rocking the stadium's foundations. Nero's expression suddenly changed, and I saw him leap to the railing and hang over the edge for a closer look. The beast's thunderous roar was like a summoning beacon.

Now standing on its hind legs, the moroddath pounded its chest and targeted me.

I held my axe steady with magic aimed dead center at the moroddath's head. It galloped directly toward me with intensity and anger. As it sped closer, I watched its mouth open for another roar, dripping saliva from giant teeth.

"BWWWWWWWARRRRRR!"

The ape's slobber nearly hit me between the eyes when I launched a slagball at its head.

But I had waited too long to fire off that spell, egotistically seeking the perfect time to do so. I felt that immediately, for it shot to the left, scorching a few moroddath hairs as it blasted through the air.

With a quick smack of the hand, the moroddath evaded my futile attack and whacked me backwards against the stadium wall. Hearing and feeling my bones crack and bend awkwardly was not the start to this fight I had gunned for. I tried to get back on my feet as quickly as I could, keeping an eye on the ape while it slowed and rotated around to face me.

I wiped the blood from my elbow with my sleeve and gathered my thoughts. A bloodstain tinted the moroddath's white fur near one of its mammoth tusks, displacing the hair like a river through a valley. Nevertheless, I saw no damage to the ape creature—which resulted in the frustrating conclusion that the blood on its face was my own.

This thing's gonna throw me around like a rag doll if I make dumb mistakes like that! I berated myself.

The moroddath charged again while I stood idly at the wall and thought about how to attack it. This attempt fared better; I shot another slagball at its head and rolled to the left. The beast barreled past me into the coliseum wall. Opposite us, I glanced over at Nero, who—not smiling or showing any emotions—remained fixed on the railing's edge. Stumbling back into the ring, the moroddath shook the rubble from its body.

Hair standing on end, I watched the head of the moroddath, eyeing up the curves of each tusk. I repositioned myself slightly to the right of its path, flipped the axe to my dominant hand, and held out my other to clutch a horn's tip when the time came.

With another ear-piercing roar, the purple-haired beast lowered its hands down to the ground and leveled its eyes back to mine. The moroddath's huge body rushed at me, toes digging deeper with every step for a better grip. I needed to grab ahold of its horns and get on top of it. I juked to the right and grabbed the nearest horn as the momentum yanked me to it. Lifting my leg onto its back, I held tightly to its horn and rode the beast like a bronco. It thrashed and bucked and tossed me around, but I clung on for dear life.

Modifying my grip on the axe with my right hand, I grabbed its blade with my left. Meanwhile, my thigh muscles tightened against the monkey's sides to keep me atop its upper back. Carefully inching up the neck, I got to the crown of the moroddath's head. It tried kicking its legs high in the air, leaping up and down like a bucking bull, but I continued straddling its neck. Switching focus now to killing the beast, I flung my axe between its tusks and across the woolly neck. With as much muscle as I could, I showed off my Egyptian power, forcing the axe back towards my chest. I felt the ape creature gasp for air, so I yanked harder.

I hurled out an exhausted battle cry, watching the veins bulge on my arms. *"RAWWWWG!"*

I held my grip stiffer, while the giant monkey lashed beneath me.

It mustered a wimpy whine and a small, gurgling roar. The dying sounds only drained it of those painful final breaths.

The moroddath finally stopped struggling and succumbed to the force. I released my axe's grip on its neck. Dropping to the sand, the moroddath took its last pitiful breath as I slid off its back and checked my hands for any blisters or bruises.

Catching my breath, I glanced over the railing at the onlookers and their immediate reactions. *Of course—same degenerates not paying any attention to the brilliance on display in the stadium. Oughta be taking notes, if you ask me. Wouldn't know a learning experience if it hit them in the face,* I thought. But their disinterested faces were not even on my radar once I saw Nero's expression—an aggravating assault of unfazed, unamused, and unenthusiastic.

I felt the unrelenting urge to press the axe's blade against his neck, the same way I had on that ape! If any other teacher or student passing by had witnessed these fights, they would have been swarming me like a true king and praising my efforts until the end of their miserable lives! But Nero? Oh, no—his expectations were so unbelievably high that dragons couldn't touch them!

Be realistic, Nero! You chose me first to prove my worth to the other four. Surely, you weren't expecting me to fail on the first go-round? But just like with my father... Never good enough.

"What? No round of applause, Nero? Worried that I'll beat your stupid gauntlet on my first try?" I shouted at him mockingly. "Nothing to add that I could've done better? You love to critique and nitpick, so where's the peanut gallery of reactions?" But electing to voice my displeasure foolishly showed my weakness as my exhausted breaths huffed out. I glanced down at my body to see the total damage done, but saw nothing of note, except the bulging purplish-blue veins of my arm muscles.

"What's next?" I gasped, panting in that instant.

Nero leaned over to whisper to Renner, eyes still locked on mine.

Without warning, one last cloud of smoke and sand swirled in front of me, clearing away the moroddath's dead body. And as the cyclone whipped around furiously, a new enemy appeared, a wavy shadow in the darkness. I was so consumed in the heat of battle that blocking out the sand cloud was subconscious. It was as though my brain and body were unfazed by anything but my target. I was on cloud nine now, riding high on adrenaline and bloodthirsty fury.

Renner's third creation didn't wait for the dust to settle before showing itself. Wild sapphire fur ran down the belly and underside of a gargantuan dragon, contrasting with the pristine opalescent scales covering the rest of its body. Talons sharper than a hawk's marked the ends of its toes, and the pointed snout of a snake stood out on its fan-like head, with pink frills shooting out diagonally. A generous array of spikes finished out the dragon's sleek look.

Pushing off the sand with its hind feet, the dragon leapt towards me. I tried to dodge, but its front left claw caught me before I could move, pinning me to the ground and slicing open a welt below my eye, warm and wet. I frantically blinked it open and closed to clear the blood from beneath it. I could feel it swelling up and disrupting my vision. I squirmed and wiggled to get out of its grip, but it only tightened its hold on my ribs. I saw the dragon's other front claw rise into the air and swing down toward my arm. I immediately pushed my body to the other side, and the smooth talon glanced down my shoulder.

Better than my arm, I told myself, wincing at the wound.

But this was not the pain of any normal cut. This one stung like hell, with an invisible toxin prickling its way into my bloodstream. Pure torment coursed through my veins and pinned my other arm to the ground, invisibly forcing my body against the sand.

I silenced the pain quickly while figuring out how to avoid a second poisonous scratch. I twisted my head to the left and looked next to the dragon's outstretched hand, where my axe lay a few inches out of reach.

As an incoming claw swung down from above, I shoved my hand between the claws and extended my arm to the base of the axe's hilt. Wriggling my fingertips, I managed to finally grab ahold of it. Then I punched my axe into the dragon's restraining hand, spilling rivulets of its pink blood on myself. With a dreadful, piercing screech, the dragon released its grip on me and abruptly retreated to assess the damage.

The now three-legged beast pointed its snout between my eyes and glared down at the scratch on my shoulder. I knew I had to fight the toxin's awful sting if I wanted to take this thing down.

Letting out a disgruntled sigh, I shot two slagballs, one right after the other. Both scorched small burn marks into the dragon's belly. I needed to avoid its talons at all costs; more of that toxin in my bloodstream could totally shut down my magic. Just casting those spells had worsened the poison's sting in each hand. As the dragon stumbled back after my second attack slammed into its stomach, I cast another quick flick of slag magic. This time I concentrated until the dragon's roar faded from my ears, and the painful sting slowed its pulse through my brain. Lifting my right hand, I created another obsidian barricade, rooted in the ground. The flurry of magic made my hands shake, and I felt a sudden numbness come and go from my fingertips.

The dragon fanned out the frills on its head and angrily hissed at me, and the spikes on its back quivered. My stomach dropped as I watched the beast regrow the severed hand I had sliced off. But glancing behind me, I looked down at the ground to see my trophy—one of the dragon's razor-sharp talons.

I smiled at its beady eyes and laughed. "A hydra! What an unexpected treat! Shall I take one of its heads this time?" I hollered at it, getting it riled up at me again and preparing for the inevitable attack. "Hercules took too long to kill one of you. I won't make that same mistake!"

To my excitement, Renner's hydra shot off the ground, hovering feet above my head. I yanked the barricade out of the sand and held it in my right hand like a warrior's shield. This trick I had learned from Karnak, my actual slag professor, during my second year. He tried and failed to teach it to other students, but they were too weak to pull it from the ground.

I held it close to my chest and whacked the shield with the axe blade. Swinging the barricade across my body, I clubbed the stupid beast across its face, throwing it into the stadium wall.

I snickered again, mocking it for thinking the toxin would be enough to subdue me.

"Don't play with your food, Kamaul," I heard a voice shout from behind me. "Finish it!"

Nero egging me on was the exact push I needed to deliver the death blow. I rushed over before the hydra could get back on its feet.

With expert force, I aimed the axe at the dragon's next and flung the axe with both hand. The weapon flipped through the air before it buried into the stomach of the beast and pierced its heart. The life wavered in its eyes right as the sun's rays changed from white to orange. I retrieved my axe and crawled over the scaled beast, sliding down its back.

Silently, Nero and Renner helped me over the railing and found me a nearby seat on the bench. Renner grabbed a moist towel from a folded pile and tossed it in my direction. Snatching it from the air, I kept my focus on Nero, who, true as the December cold that had returned, stood emotionless with his hands crossed, staring at my shoulder wound.

"Anything to note yet?" I asked with a sneer, hoping to get any kind of reaction from him.

Then he approached me. Bending over the bench, Nero whispered in my ear. "Wounded? Bleeding, after fighting a *fake* threat? Abysmal. An embarrassment to the school of fire. And no, you're wrong; I had you go first, Kamaul, to see how long you'd pout over your own failure afterwards." He paused to watch as the words bore into my chest. "Right on cue."

His words cut through the sting of the hydra's toxin and burned into my ego. No amount of anger I had towards the moroddath or the many-headed dragon matched the aggression I felt for Nero right now. Not backing down, I maintained eye contact with his cold, dark eyes. He shortly dropped my gaze and looked at the other students, whom I had completely forgotten existed until now.

"Solomon, you're next. Let's go," he said, gesturing with his head to the weapon rack. The short echo mage nodded willingly at Renner and jumped over the railing into the sand arena.

Dabbing at my shoulder wound, I suppressed the pain. I rotated the towel between that gash and the one below my eye. But I kept my eyes glued to Nero's back as he waited for the second student's gauntlet to begin. In a puff of frustration, I wrung out the bloody towel on the floor and let it lie in a small puddle near my feet.

Despite my impressive results, Nero was not wrong. I had let three imaginary creatures inflict damage on me. Three years of working with him, and months of Gladiator lessons on every battle tactic he knew, and I *still* took damage!

The dragon's toxin seared through me again, making my eyelids twitch. Blood still slowly leaked from the shoulder cut, but I ignored it all and leaned back into the bench behind me. I crossed my arms and glared at the back of Nero's head while imagining one of the hydra heads swallowing him whole.

AARON I

MARA'S YOGA CLASS SEEMED to fall into my weekly schedule at the perfect time, every time—whenever I needed it most or felt overwhelmed. Between struggling with my lackluster magic and the constant reminders of how out of place an underprivileged Penumbra boy was at this college, it often felt as though the walls were caving in on me.

Stepping into Yoga, I found an open space near the back. I laid out my coffee-colored mat, sat down crossing my arms and legs, and waited for the professor to enter the room.

There were many aspects of Yoga I enjoyed, one of which was our benevolent teacher, Mara. She was the epitome of a lovely soul. Her passion and determination rubbed off on most students in the class, especially me. With short black hair and a lithe physique, she was beautiful, and the sweat beading on her slightly tanned skin shone like a fresh polish. Mara used her kindness to be a great person, a friend to me when I needed one, and a symbol of the practicality of a simple lifestyle.

The class was crowded and tightly packed, as usual, with only a handful of remaining spaces for incoming students. As it was split evenly between male and female mages, it was a good mix as well. The one blessing that I noted immediately was the silence in the room. Typically, whenever you walked into a class for the day, it was so loud that you could barely hear your own thoughts. Not so with this class, however, as each day seemed to start with a welcome serenity. Greeting the last few stragglers, Mara beamed a joyful grin across the room. A large paned window stretched across the wall to the right of me and illuminated the students and their yoga mats with the afternoon sunshine.

When the sea of stress swept me up in its undertow, when the blizzard of burdens drenched me in layers of snow, when the avalanche of anxiety dragged me down the mountain, Yoga was my weekly saving grace, something I could count on to bring my mood up. It was a healthy balance of exercise and meditation that perfectly enclosed me in its world free from the worries of life.

"Morning, mages," Mara cheered, flapping her pink mat in the air and flattening it in front of the first row.

"Good morning, Mara!" I exclaimed with the rest of the class. I smiled happily as we all stood up to begin.

"Change of plans today, class. Originally, I had planned to use stone magic and create a rocky oasis here in the classroom. But with The Pit Selection Ceremony at the end of the week, we are now going to focus on channeling peace and calmness in situations that are the opposite. Another way we can manifest this energy is to think of 'silence among the madness.'"

Suddenly, as quickly as it had come, my relaxation fled. *Oh, great! The Pit Selection Ceremony? No idea what that is. But if it means Mara has to shift around her lesson plans, it cannot be good,* I thought.

A small murmur of conversation stirred around the room until Mara continued.

"Now, now. Nothing to fret over, class. I promise. Frankly, this change is really more of a change for me than for any of you. But never mind that right now, though. Let's get ready to begin, shall we?"

Mara turned her back to us, motioning for us to follow along with her movements. I pushed my legs out across the mat and watched Mara's motions to guide me. In a star formation, I leaned over to my right foot to touch my big toe, then over to the left to do the same. Mara instructed us to do this promptly and methodically.

We continued stretching for a few more minutes. Sunshine permeated the room with dense humidity and a bright white glow. Only a few clouds floated across the sky—white puffs of air that carelessly drifted parallel with the invisible wind gusts.

"One thing about today's lesson that has thankfully remained unchanged is our first order of business. So, let us begin with a sweet moment of meditation ..."

Her voice dropped off, and her grin changed to an uncertain frown. I could see the apprehension on her face, even down to the drooping of her eyes at the mention of our new Yoga agenda.

"Shall we?" Mara lowered herself down to her yoga mat and crossed her legs to sit down. The class followed suit shortly after.

"Gently breathe in and out. And again ... in and out. Feel the rhythm of your breathing take you to a world of bliss and serenity. Let the silence wash over you."

With great pauses for emphasis, Mara slowed her words to ease the anxiety in the classroom. An appreciated stillness consumed the class, until all I could hear was my own rhythmic breaths and the occasional footsteps outside the door. Soon, the other meditating mages scattered around on their own yoga mats became figures of my imagination, blending into the shadows.

"Breathe in and out. Quiet your mind and body."

Eyes closed and mind relatively quiet, I sat like Mara, my hands resting on my kneecaps. I felt the heat of the sun against my eyelids. I felt the class disappear. With each breath, the room felt more open. The mages around me vanished, and I became the only one in the room. Mara's soothing voice seemed made for my ears alone, and inside my busy mind was a place where she could do some serious work.

While we were meditating, I heard Mara move something into the classroom. It was heavy and rolled across the floor. I assumed it to be very large, as she maneuvered other objects to make way for this one.

"Awake now, please, mages. It is time for the next part of our class."

Staying in our seated positions, we all opened our eyes to join Mara.

A large golden gong hung on fine thread in its wooden frame. Next to it was a set of wind chimes dangling from a hook in the ceiling.

"I want to introduce the violators of your serenity: echoing wind chimes and a gong. Find the peace and calmness despite this noise. Center your focus on blocking out these sounds. Like I said earlier, we will be learning to ignore outside distractions and forging our minds into a temple from the chaos. Keep meditating and finding serenity while I ring the chimes and bang the gong." There was some hubbub and excitement once she mentioned the assignment.

"Now, return to a comfortable pose," she began after settling the raucous students. "Listen to your thoughts. Block out these sounds. Armor your mind from the gong and wind chimes. Find your inner sanctum, a place that belongs solely to you. Allow no outside distractions. Let's begin."

Mara took a step back towards the classroom's front wall. I followed her instructions and closed my eyes to discover my ideal inner sanctum.

"Once all of you have closed your eyes and found an oasis within your minds, I will try to disrupt it. Though this is not a game or a contest, feel free to challenge your own abilities. It might be good practice for your future."

Mara waited a little longer until everyone was settled before conducting the next part of the lesson.

"I will pose to you a series of thought-provoking prompts. Focus on your chosen retaliations as I play these instruments ... to the best of my ability." Mara chuckled, soft like the clouds in the sky. She let the final words sink in before moving forward. There was a long pause, then she readdressed the class. "Your first task is to think of stressful events here at the college. Class projects, independent studies, spellcasting, you name it. There are no wrong answers. A few minutes will pass before I instruct you to open your eyes for a new topic."

I took the subject in with open ears and dove into my thinking. Unfortunately, too many topics about the college came to mind. So, I narrowed it down to one and stuck with it.

Struggling at casting magic and understanding it. I know of magic from fairy tales and myths and legends. But yeah, actually having the ability in my fingertips has proven more difficult than I could have imagined. Luke says I'm about fifty percent on pace with everyone else, which sounds worse than he intended, I think. I just can't help but think I'm nowhere near where I should be; I'm falling behind the other novice students. Do you know what you get when you cross the compounding pressures of making your family proud with a lousy, besieged storm mage? Me. You get me, Aaron Dirge.

"Hold your mind to that topic. Really dive deep into those sore spots. Keep on it, ignoring my noises," Mara reiterated.

I don't even know if Luke, the great ice mage, Seeker, and esteemed Intro to Magic professor, can help me.

The room went silent. All the mages kept quiet and still. Even the smallest fly could have landed on one of our shoulders and we would all hear it.

Echoing off the window and walls, the gong made a resounding noise, ringing in my ears and immediately forcing me to open my eyes. I scanned the room to find other watchful pairs of eyes doing the same. More than half the class opened theirs as well, their gazes wandering around in frantic darts from one student to the next. Mara stood at the front with the mallet in her hand and looked to see how many students had popped their heads up to listen.

Mara, smiling innocently, placed the mallet back on top of the gong's wooden frame and spoke to the class. "I see that more than half of you allowed this distraction to disrupt your retreat. Not bad, but not great. For the second topic, I'd like to see the number of eyeballs looking at me cut in half. We can make it happen. I believe in all of you. Change your easy pose to cobra, and I'll give you the second topic once everyone is reset."

I stood up a bit and stretched onto the mat, flattening my stomach to it. Then I pushed my hands palms down and arched my neck bones to the ceiling, raising my eyes to meet Mara's. The rest of the class followed suit, and we all looked like snakes waiting for the perfect moment to strike. The cobra pose was rough to get into, but once you were content, it equated to an easing and satisfying move.

"Close your eyes again and calm your minds so I can share the next topic." She paused while everyone closed their eyes once again, but I was already looking at the insides of my eyelids before she could request it. "Next topic concerns the stress and anxiety of your personal life."

For what it was worth, my personal life had been a stressful topic at any point in my life. Pick a moment or age, and you would find some darkened cloud cast over it. Cracking down to give Mara the best fuel for distraction, I mustered up the most recent despair I could think of.

Feeling like less than other students. This ties into the whole "struggling with magic" thing, but there is something to it that's deeper than that! It's so frustrating and heartbreaking. The Seekers chose me to join The College of Adarius—chose me for my untapped elemental potential. But I've wasted it so far. Everywhere around campus is a big slap in the face; here, magic is as prominent as oxygen. I'm no further along than I was on day one.

Even more abruptly than previously, the ringing of the wind chimes did the trick. My eyes popped open. Again, I was not the only one looking back into Mara's eyes. There were many less students with theirs open this time, but that made it feel no less discouraging.

"Focus on those thoughts and the topic," Mara said, her voice getting closer to me as she quietly walked about the room. She had an unspoken gift for sensing one's deep personal feelings, even with their mind closed off. There was a slight breeze as she walked briskly behind me, weaving in between the rows of outstretched cobras. Mara and her light feet trotted to the front of the classroom. I closed my eyes again and waited for her. Hopefully, this third topic would be the lucky one, and I would finally be able to block out the noise. Not likely, though, if I knew myself.

Mara instructed us to open our eyes and assessed the lesson thus far. "That time things were ... better, I suppose." A pause relayed that that sentiment was not true. But she continued, "I know it sounds like I'm lying, but that was slightly improved from the first go-round. Some of you still opened your eyes at the wind chimes. Let's try a third prompt. And this topic is to think about things in your life prior to the college, whether that be three months ago or three years."

She wrapped her fingers around the bells to stop them from swinging. "Channel your life prior to magic, prior to spellcasting and potion-making. Maybe it was a simpler life that you miss. Maybe it was a complicated life you were separate from. Try to grab ahold of some feeling within that mindset and latch onto it. The noises this time will be louder than before."

Mara chuckled to herself and gestured for us to change poses. The gate pose, one of the more difficult for me to hold, became the new stance.

I got up to one knee and stretched out the other foot far to the edge of the mat. As I tried to rotate, my foot slipped off the mat, and I went sprawling. I quickly regathered myself. Pivoting my upper half towards the extended foot, I leaned over to the right and raised my left hand high up toward the ceiling. It was an awkward stance—a tricky one to maintain with something else on one's mind.

Technically cheating, I chose to focus on the transition from Dunnmore to the college. *Before storm magic and students with wands in their hands, life was ... simple. We lived in a small cottage in the Northern Forest. My father was a hunter, killing and scavenging animals to bring home for dinner. My mother was the cook and caretaker of the home. My younger sister and I worked all through the hot afternoons to make sure my mother had the proper ingredients and a clean house, and we set the table for every meal. We were poor—very poor. This college, however? Impressive stone buildings, students from countries and places I've never heard of, beautiful topiaries, a grand campus ... I never imagined that such a simple "yes" would become such a stress-inducing nightmare. There were events leading up to my decision that factored into it, obviously, but never did I believe magic existed—and that it would become my greatest adversary. I know it's only been half a semester, but I just want to make my family proud.*

A stern weariness set across my face, and Mara could see it.

Making her laps around the room, she struck the wind chimes in her hands. I fought against their resonant ringing, but it still burrowed deep into my brain. I felt the draft of air stop just as she paused at my back.

"Worry not, Aaron," she whispered into my ear. "Topics like this are intended to be hard. This is why we do them. Stay strong, Aaron. These are things we all struggle with. You are not alone in these mental hurdles. I have them, too. Just be yourself, and everything will work itself out."

I was irritated and down on my luck. But her tender voice soothed my pain and sadness, until she hastened to the front of the room and hit the gong hard. The chiming slowed down as well, but the gong's sound echoed off the walls. I tried to fixate on magic more, but the sounds joined forces and collaborated to break my focus.

Against my will, my eyes opened.

Discouraged, I let out a long exhale and looked around the class. Adding insult to injury, there were only a total of two mages with their eyes open—and I was one of them. What a miserable feeling. Nearly twenty-five students in my Yoga class, and yet I was the one who had failed all of the lessons so far.

Mara looked unfazed, thankfully. "The rest of you may open your eyes, and we'll get to the final distraction."

The class all came to attention with wide-eyed expressions of courage.

"Good. Our last topic will be a positive one! Think of that, huh? All those negative thoughts and emotions and feelings can be pushed aside, because the final topic I want you to think on is things you want to improve in yourself. It can be any aspect of life at all, and it does not have to pertain to anything you were thinking of previously. It can be brand new, if you'd like."

My mind began racing, flooding with things I could improve upon. I saw the flaws in my life readily, and I often could not think of a single example without compiling a list of others.

Improve my magic. With Luke's help, it shouldn't be impossible, right? Adjusting to college life isn't a walk in the park either, but time heals all wounds. Become the extroverted social butterfly instead of a dejected, outcast introvert. Change my whole personality? Uh ... On second thought, that does actually sound impossible. Then the small, minor issues. Replace my roommate, Duke, who is certainly less than ideal. Find someone to help me get over my ex. Did I mention that? Heartbreak was another factor in my acceptance to the college. Someone that makes me feel unique, someone that makes me happy, someone who loves me despite my flaws ...

I shifted the gate pose from the right to the left side. Barely getting into position, Mara rang the gong. Another resonant ringing echoed off the walls. I ignored it. It bounced off the large paned window and back to me, but I blocked it out yet again. Like a bee buzzing around a fresh flower, the ringing of the gong filled my ears. Foolishly, I lost track of the stance I was in and lost my balance. Returning my mind to the task at hand, I got back in the proper position. Though the noise had derailed my train of thought, I managed to keep my eyes and mind closed against Mara's distractions. I was overjoyed and content.

Next, Mara swept her hands across the wind chimes. They jangled loudly—nearly louder than the gong. I stayed the course and kept my eyes closed still as the trill of the wind chimes tried to burrow deep into my ears. The noise was incessant.

Ignoring it was nearly impossible, but I stayed at it. It seemed to knock me off balance again, though, and as I wobbled, I felt like the idiot in her class.

"Keep those positive thoughts in mind," Mara reminded us. "Ignore me and focus on your own ideas to improve whatever you believe to be a weakness."

With an invisible buckle, I strapped down the improvements and braced for more of Mara's musical talents.

Patience with new magic. Meet new people. Show my true colors for once and be proud of it. Embrace the changes of my new college life instead of fighting them.

I tightened the strap.

Magic. Someone new. Pride in myself. Embrace the change ...

The gong rang again. Mara hit the wind chimes as well, and the two merged into a festival of never-ending earworms.

Force your eyes to stay closed and keep at it. Lesson's almost over; then you'll be able to open them back up. A little bit longer ... I reminded myself, switching the gate pose stance back to the original leg.

Without warning, the gong and wind chimes finally dug their way too deeply into my brain, and I cracked under the pressure. My eyes shot open, and my mind went blank. To my horror, I was the only one looking around—the only one who'd cracked. So, despite my best efforts, I was not strong enough to ignore Mara's noise. It had become too much for me to handle, I guess.

I saw the disappointment on Mara's face. Even her rosy cheeks and innocent smile told me she was disappointed. She had reminded *me* specifically to think hard on these topics and do my best. Yet I had failed. I'd failed her, and I failed myself. The storm's next swell rose to new heights above me at the captain's wheel—and it would come crashing down soon.

Mara walked back to the gong to stop the gentle swing of it and wrapped her hands around the wind chimes. She took in a heavy breath and finished the lesson. "That will do it for today's lesson, students. Sorry about the last-minute change, but you all did great! I'm impressed at how well each of you did, with me and the college reworking my lesson plan. Think on those improvements you want to make. We'll work on those next week, channeling them into existence. I bid you all a lovely farewell."

She cupped her hands to the air and gestured for us to stand up straight. We bowed softly to her and one another.

"Oh!" she exclaimed suddenly. "Remember that this Friday is The Pit Selection Ceremony. It is mandatory, so you all *must* attend. Don't forget! I'll keep reminding you in the meantime. Anyways, have a great week, okay?"

The class was already packing up their backpack and yoga mats. One by one, I watched all the other mages head out of the classroom while I simply stood motionless, disgruntled by my lack of progress today. Before too long, I was the last to leave. I rolled up the brown mat under my feet and slung its strap over my shoulder. I kept my head high so as to not show weakness to Mara, but I think she noticed anyway.

"Aaron ..." she said softly, placing her hand on my shoulder before I could make it out the door.

"Yeah?" I turned to face her.

"I could tell you were struggling today. Something you want to talk about?"

I stood silent and did not respond, preferring just to look back at her.

"Look, Aaron, it's just you and me. Forget the belief that it's not cool to divulge your secrets to a teacher. You can loosen up around me. I was in your shoes at one point, too. I won't say anything, I promise. Is everything alright?"

I felt those feelings coming up, and my lip began to quiver. "Yeah. Everything's fine," I answered.

"Are you sure? I don't mean to be nosy or anything, but you were visibly upset. I wanted you to ignore the distractions I made but didn't want you to focus so hard that it brought you back to those harmful places. I'm sorry if I pushed it too far."

"It's not that, Ms. Mara ..." I stammered.

"Aaron, just call me Mara." She gave a light chuckle. Her smile was contagious, and I reflected it automatically.

"Mara," I started, "it was ... nothing. I work myself up too much about silly things I can't control. Don't worry about it. I'll be fine."

"I understand if you don't wanna talk. But I'm always here if you change your mind, Aaron. You don't have to, so don't feel obligated or feel bad if you don't. Stay strong out there. Things are difficult at this college. I can assure you, however, that every bad situation has a wonderful silver lining in store for you."

Her words were delightful and comforting.

"Thank you, Mara." I beamed.

I saw the genuine smile that mine brought to her face, and then I headed out into the hallway.

Against my wishes, my dorm was overflowing with more Duke than Aaron. My little paintings and random artwork on the walls had been replaced with abstract monstrosities, each absent of true creativity or purpose. The couches and lounge chairs were all his, too. Thankfully, the one aspect of the living room he had left alone were the potted plants on my side, to make it feel more outdoorsy.

My bedroom sat adjacent to Duke's, mirroring one another in every way. Still, he often reminded me that his was better. His room faced the main door because Duke thought it best that our visitors (of which we had none) see "the perfect example of a first year's bedroom first."

Donovan "Duke" Colwell had become my roommate the moment I walked through the doors of room 4017. He had peach-colored skin and short, spiked black hair. Hailing from "the great state of North Carolina," he saw me as an inferior and intellectually flawed compared to his genius. To be fair, he viewed everyone at the college that way. His white button-down shirt and ironed khakis completed his daily ensemble. The nickname "Duke" was self-coined, however, stemming from a wealthy background and an ego leagues beyond anyone else's. While his talents lay in alchemy and steam magic, his perfection had its flaws. Of that I could assure anyone who asked.

Duke's annoying personality aside, his prized possession was actually an elaborate alchemy table. Upon first glance, it appears as a wealthy, family-funded gift to their spoiled child to get a leg up on other poorer students. However, and perhaps as a dark silver lining, I knew this alchemy table had been stolen from another mage's dorm. He said if I ever told anyone, he'd burn all my textbooks in a roaring spectacle in our living room. I knew it might not seem like a serious threat, but to a mage who struggled with his lessons, the first-year textbooks were my only saving grace sometimes. Therefore, I had remained quiet on his post-class habits. I was not sociable, so this was second nature to me. Sadly, Duke's "charming" ambience scared away most students, too, which forced us to spend plenty of happily assigned fun time with each other.

"How'd your exaggerated stretching class go?" Duke insisted, yelling through his cracked door as I entered the dorm. "What simpleton would even be hired to teach that?"

"It's Yoga, Duke. I have it every week. And it's more than a stretching class. It helps you clear your head and think about life," I replied, closing the main door behind me. I hastily sped past Duke's room and directly into mine. Peering through the small gap of his door, I glanced at the thick, flowing tubes and cylinders of liquid. While the top of that table was immaculate, one could tell instantly where his priorities lay.

"Clear your head? For you, storm boy, that must be really easy!"

"'Storm boy' is a weak insult, Duke. If your brain is so big, how can you only manage to come up with the most pathetic nicknames?"

"Because my muscles make up for it!" he shouted as he spun to face me.

"Whatever you say," I retorted, slightly regretting the tone in my voice as the words left my mouth.

I twisted my doorknob and tossed my yoga mat over the bed. I started to close the door when a photo on my side table distracted me.

"Who's that?" asked Duke in a mocking singsong voice as he peered over my shoulder.

"Yeah, that's my best friend from Dunnmore, Matthew," I answered in a guarded tone. Matthew and I were close. He was the one who'd helped me make the decision to come to the college. I owe a lot to him. He had helped me through some tough times, too. So, I kept photos around to remind me of the people who had helped me accept this invitation. The photo of him and me beachside was a happy vacation memory, captured perfectly as we lounged in our swim trunks. The intense heat of the sun's rays had warped the coastline that day. Lying around on the beach, Matt stood up to take the photo and felt little beads of sand running down his legs. The fun photo was taken only seconds before he spastically began shaking the sand out while I tried not to laugh like a hyena and pee myself in the process.

My eyes darted back to Duke, who looked back at me with a scowl.

"Just a friend, Duke. Seriously."

"Whatever, storm boy," Duke retorted.

"Still a lame insult!" I exclaimed, slamming the door in his face.

"You would know lame!" He squeezed the words through the crack before the door closed completely.

Night was taking over the shift for the sun. I slid under the covers and lay flat. The photo stood on the table to my right, the side I preferred to sleep on. Longing to experience that vacation again, I thought back to heat on the coast. Everything at The College of Adarius reminded me of life before it. A world where my friend and I could race down the beach in our bare feet. A world where magic did not exist. A world that seemed so mundane and carefree.

I missed that world right now.

OLIVIA I

"Rotling pod ... Rotling pod ... I swear, if Tarik ever touches my stash again, I'll introduce him to a rampaging plague fiend, or wrap his hands in barbed wire. Maybe then he'll understand to keep away from my private cabinets. Ah! Here we go," I muttered to myself, working the gray pods into a fine dust with the mortar and pestle and dumping the particles into my roaring cauldron. The Rotling goblin tribe lived in a nasty, swampy underwater cave system, so it was difficult to steal seed pods from them.

The cauldron was a gift from my boyfriend, Tarik. Or at least, I think it was. If I am remembering right, today should be our one-month anniversary together. Most students at the college hated me, avoided me around every corner, and rapidly left the room when I entered. Having someone stick around for more than a few minutes was nice—even if my loner personality kicked in sometimes, and I wanted to sneak away from his company. Either way, one thing I am positive of is that I did not get him a gift ...

Bubbling in my cauldron, the green viscous material suddenly turned red with the addition of the dust. I stared into the boiling liquid, but I was focused on something else. Unevenly chopped black hair lay loosely at my neck. I had begun cutting it myself after my last visit to the college's salon. The hairdresser had closed their doors in my face when they saw me walking towards the shop. I wasn't even going to get a haircut; I was simply walking by.

Thinking of the salon and being in class today, I recalled another distressing memory. During my novice year, I found myself lost in thought and shortly fell asleep. Sleeping was not as normal for me as it was for other students, because whenever my eyes closed, I traveled into the Bad Place, a nightmare realm of shadows, fearsome creatures, and my darkest imagination. Look, I realize it was a silly and simplistic name, but I had been just a toddler when I came up with it. What do you want from me?

I couldn't remember how I woke up from that classroom nap, but I did. To the class's horror, after I resurfaced from that realm, I brought a friend back with me into my Alchemy class: a semi-decomposed, mummified (but somehow very much alive) mastodon. Needless to say, the creature frightened the students, destroyed the classroom, and nearly crumbled the whole building to the ground. The Alchemy professor, Nic, finally killed it, solving everyone's problems—all except mine, however, as I had run crying from the room. That day in class changed my life at the college.

I began to tear up at the memories. Though I was content and fortunate to have a tower to myself, seeing people stare and then look away after I made eye contact was still painful. Letting my "gift" control my emotions, I quickly wiped the tears away. Because of that incident in Nic's class, nobody saw me anymore. They avoided me at all costs. But *I* saw them, and I felt that rejection. That silence. That fear.

Even the Elders were afraid of me. Who else on the entire college campus was given their own secluded place to live in anyways? Not kidding; this was a true tower, a giant obelisk on the edge of the void area, away from the rest of the students, so I could live "comfortably and stress-free," as Marrick had so lovingly put it. Heaven forbid anyone should evoke the wrath of the freak disguised as an orphaned teenage girl.

Throughout my four years here, it had been difficult to think of a time when I was not living on the campus outskirts. I couldn't complain too much, though. My tower was my home, and I liked it. It was paradise compared to that hellhole back in Russia I had been exiled to by my so-called "parental units." I swear, once I graduate and leave here, I will make them regret abandoning me. I was not crazy. I was strong; Marrick showed me that. Elders didn't intermingle with students often. He reminded me that I was wanted, and that there were others like me. He took care of me, even when the other Elders disagreed. They feared me, just like the student body did. Marrick, the Void Elder, had this tower built specifically for me, and I was thankful. Without him, I would not have been here today.

"All better," I said aloud, dabbing at my cheeks and drying the tears. The black circles faded as my eyes returned to their natural focused state.

A single blink would take me away from reality and into the nightmare plain that haunted my very existence. Unlike other mages in nightmare magic, I could not stop going to the shadow realm. Whenever my eyes closed, whether to blink or think or sleep, I was instantly taken away to a place where demons and spirits called home.

After the mastodon attack, the college blamed me for the damages and the indisputable fear it created in the other students' lives. So, Marrick put an enchantment on my eyes—one where I was now unable to close them at all. This allowed me to go about normal life with them open all the time. To this day, I would still say that his unique enchantment on my eyes was the best gift I have ever received.

The boiling liquid had turned sanguine. I wandered over to my apothecary cabinet (also a gift from Marrick), which was full of potion ingredients stored on shelves and in drawers.

"Where are my screaming scarabs?" I asked aloud, pushing aside numerous boxes and bottles. Everything from roots, berries, seeds, and bark to dried insects, skin, and organs were staples in my kit. It was fully stocked, of course, because I took great pride in keeping it full. In fact, I harvested most of the ingredients myself. What I could not find, catch, or grow, I would buy from suppliers—or anyone who wouldn't run screaming when they saw me coming.

"Ah, here we go!" I muttered, clutching a small wooden box with a sliding lid. Back at the cauldron, I pushed it open, snatched out a fat black beetle, and looked at the box in disgust.

"Only one?" I said, holding the squirming insect. "Guess I'm going to the forest today. Might as well get the essentials while I'm out. Check the drop point, too. People owe me gold." I smiled a wicked grin. "As soon as this is done ..."

I tossed the beetle into the pot. A horrendous high-pitched wail emanated from the liquid, which was slowly turning amber as the beetle tried to escape its scalding grave. With one last shriek of terror, the husk of the bug sank into the soup. It changed, now bright gold, and slowed into a soft simmer. The scream of the scarabs was always my favorite part of this potion.

As I grabbed the vials and apothecary satchel, I heard a rattling at my door. As there were only two people who knocked on my door and were not afraid to travel the staircase to do so, I knew who it could be.

"Hello? Who is it?" I asked cautiously.

"It's Marrick," replied the visitor.

Sporting a shy smile and a nonchalant look, I turned the knob and opened the door. "Oh. Hey, Tarik. I knew by the voice that it wasn't really him."

My lack of reaction astounded Tarik, who was disappointed that his surprise did not work. I leaned in to kiss him before quickly pivoting, so his lips touched my right cheek. Kissing on the lips was too personal and made me afraid to let someone get too close to me.

Closing the door, I ushered Tarik inside and hung his coat on the nearest hook.

"Marrick usually drops off the allowance. Never actually comes here to do it," I said.

Tarik handed me an odd book on old void magic. I laughed under my breath. It was an inside joke between Marrick and me that the allowance he gave me every week should be hidden and disguised from the others. So, he had hollowed out an ancient tome and used it as a box to give me the presents discreetly. Marrick once told me, "I removed a chunk of this book's pages because you already know all the information inside! Might as well put the rest of it to good use."

When I took the book from his hands, I got a clear look at Tarik's benign face. Lively green eyes looked back at mine. He had spiked brown hair, which usually resulted in a few strands falling over his forehead. It was cute, though, the way Tarik's perfect hair always seemed to fall just in time for him to see me. His lips felt soft on my cheeks, despite a fine beard poking me wherever he kissed me. I laughed aloud as my tired eyes drifted away from Tarik's.

"Thank you for the cauldron, Tarik." I smiled at him while walking Marrick's book over to my shelf of ingredients and setting it down.

"The what?" Tarik replied, strolling over to sit on my alchemy table.

"This cauldron?" I said, pointing to it, confused. "Didn't you buy me this cauldron? I know it's our one-month anniversary, and I'm sorry, I didn't get you anything."

"I'm flattered that you remembered our anniversary, Olivia." He showed a kind smile, but quickly let it wither away into a frown. "But I didn't get you that cauldron. I did get you a gift, though! I swear. It's just not that. I bet you'll like his gift better than mine."

"Oh," I began, "I'm so sorry, Tarik. I really thought this was you."

"That's alright. Do you want me to get my gift?"

"Sure. In a minute," I answered, retrieving Marrick's book from the shelf. I opened the cover and checked its contents. There was a small pouch of a thousand gold, my weekly allowance from Marrick. I made plenty of gold from my own business, yet he continued to deliver a pouch of it. I removed a small black rose from the book and set it atop the highest shelf with the others. Dozens of flowers—I was never sure where to put them.

At the bottom of the book was a piece of parchment paper, folded in half. I pulled it out and unraveled it.

Dear Olivia,
Your eyes were truly opened to the world four years ago. It was a gift where no thanks is ever needed. The gratitude is all mine, regardless of how cold you are to me. Enjoy the new cauldron. Hope all is well.

— Marrick

I slipped the note into my pocket and turned back to look at the cauldron past Tarik. It felt like I was looking at it for the first time. On tiny legs, the large cauldron sat in the middle of my alchemy table and took up a quarter of the space. It had a deep basin and a pair of sturdy handles on the sides. The bright gold liquid boiling inside offset its cast iron color.

From the corner of my eye, I could see Tarik's blurry face and the glow from the cauldron. Then it hit me.

"Anniversary." I said it loud enough that Tarik definitely heard it.

"Yes. Our one-month anniversary. As in dating? You know, boyfriend-girlfriend? What happens when two people like each other and want to spend more time together?" Tarik interjected.

I couldn't tell if he was being sarcastic or serious.

"Yeah, I know what dating is, and I already said that I remembered that."

"Okay. Look, I get it. Marrick and you are close. I'm just ... trying to get that close to you, too." Tarik hopped off my table and walked over to grab his coat, only he did not pull it off the hook. Instead, he reached into an inside pocket and took out a pink wrapped box. He walked over to my bed and set it atop the pillow. Giving me a short nod, Tarik went back over to retrieve his coat and pulled it over his shoulders. He reached for the doorknob before turning back to face me.

"I hope someday I mean as much to you as he does. I'm trying here, Olivia. I just want you to see that. Happy anniversary." Tarik let a fake smile shine between his dimples and shut the door on his way out.

"Anniversary," I muttered again. "Such a silly thing to keep track of."

My eyes darted back and forth from the cauldron to the wrapped gift Tarik had left on my bed sheets. Heading over to my bed, I picked it up, untied the white ribbon around it, and opened the top. Inside was a black pearl necklace with a yellow citrine pendant.

"A necklace with an ugly yellow gem?"

Frankly, I was not that surprised. As much as Tarik liked to showcase his affections for me and wanted to be there for me, he didn't know me very well. I do not wear jewelry; in fact, I hate jewelry. If he really knew me, a necklace would never have crossed his mind at all.

I was disappointed. This was the reason I liked being alone. This was the reason I preferred my secluded tower, compared to bouncing from orphanage to orphanage in Russia. People feared me at every turn. It made me question Tarik. I cared for him, enjoyed spending time with him, and loved to nitpick at the little things about him. But a necklace? It seemed like a stretch. The idea of not knowing what to get his girlfriend led him to default to jewelry? *Wrong choice, Tarik.*

"Today has been just full of surprises!" I shouted, knowing no one would hear me. Switching my mood, I wandered back to my cauldron and inspected its bubbling contents.

I grabbed my cloak and apothecary satchel. Cold fresh air was what I needed to get away from the memories of my past. Shoving a few extra vials in my bag, I glanced back at the necklace hanging on Tarik's usual coat hook.

"Tarik," I said to the necklace, "I think it's time I check on my clients and Cal to see how the day's transactions went. Travel to the woods and catch up on some work."

I guess I'm not really a "good girl." I make money where I can. Not like I needed it, though. Marrick has a fascination with me, and I admit, I like the attention. Besides my weekly allowance, I got by selling potions. Some of those potions—created and handmade by me, of course—were legal; others ... not so much. I sold potions and elixirs to whomever will buy from me. The college would have looked down on that kind of sale. But it doesn't matter, because what they don't know won't hurt them. Better that way, too. I keep to myself, and the college won't have to worry about their freak zoo animal anymore.

I had other jobs, too. Occasionally, I would work for the Elemental History professor, Tori, and conjure creatures for the class to examine. It's not my favorite thing in the world, but it helped the class—and I got a real kick out of scaring them. Tori was very lenient, so I could create whatever monstrosity I wanted, and she'd use it for that lesson.

My least favorite job was the one Marrick personally asked me to do. The way he cared and looked after me made it challenging to say no. This job, however, offered me no choice whether to accept it or not. My nightmare magic was strong and profound; thus, the college required me to remove harmful and highly dangerous elementals (known as revenants) bound to potential prospects. Sometimes a student did not bind well with their elemental, and if the elemental wasn't removed, it could injure or even kill the student—or worse, assume and take control over their human form. So, I was brought in to remove it from the student by using my "gift." It was never pretty—like watching someone's soul being torn in half—and it felt like playing the role of executioner at a trial. The prospect was never the same afterwards either ... if they even survived. But the balance had to be preserved, and we couldn't afford a rogue elemental freely stalking their way around Penumbra. Thankfully, this job was rare, and the Seekers usually found other methods to do it.

Cloak wrapped around me, I slung the satchel's leather strap over my shoulder and left the tower. Being quiet was never necessary when I left for the forest.

I traveled down the flights of stone stairs to the bottom and opened the rusty, creaky door to the outside world. The main door to the tower faced the forest behind it, which ensured that nobody would see me come or go. It allowed me to avoid other people as much as they wanted to avoid me.

The Northern Forest was a large expanse of tall trees on the edges of campus—some of which very few people ventured into. Cal, my friend and client partner, was close to me near the entrance of the woods. Despite its location to The Void Courtyard, students eluded this forest in fear of running into me or catching someone doing business with me.

Checking around to make sure all was clear, I walked through the dampened grass. Living in Russia for the early parts of my childhood had adjusted me to the bitterly cold temperatures of the college. As the winds began to roar and howl between the nearby trees, I lifted the cloak's hood over my head and vanished past the tree line.

Once I got far enough into the forest, I ditched the hood and smiled at Cal.

How he was created is a fun memory rather than a tender one. On one of my nightmare trips while asleep (before Marrick's enchantment), a conniving fiend had attached itself to me. Once I realized this, I knew I had the upper hand and struck a deal with it. Instead of banishing the pathetic thing back to the shadow plains, I discussed my proposition: It could stay in Penumbra only if it agreed to work for me. The fiend agreed, and I brought it back into the real world. However, what the creature did not expect was for me to bind it to a willow tree. The name Cal came from an old roommate of mine at an orphanage. The boy there, Calvin, had been the only one who befriended me, for he was caring and unafraid. The fiend spirit got a place to live, and I received a loyal employee. Plus, I always got a kick out of seeing the willow tree with an animated face on it, which probably scared the pee out of any student who saw him.

"Nightmare magic really is a gift," I said to Cal. "Has everyone paid their tabs?" I skipped the last few steps to his stump, and pressing on a certain knot, opened a large hole just below his face.

"Yes, my lady. Everyone but that funny blonde girl who always talks to me," answered the tree's creaking voice.

Pulling out a sack of golden coins and placing it in my pack, I resealed the hole and looked Cal directly in what appeared to be his eyes.

"Why does she talk to me, Olivia?" Cal's voice sounded laughably worried. "Your other buyers run in terror when they see my mouth move. But why not her?"

"She's an odd one, yeah. Don't worry about her. She'll pay when she's ready." I giggled.

He was describing Emilee, my insect supplier. She was a bizarre one, for sure. Emilee wasn't afraid like everyone else; she was too interested in her insects to care. I had confronted her once about why she was not intimidated by me. Her response was: "I've raised things from tiny eggs to maturity that are scarier than the likes of you; you're just a girl. You don't lay eggs in people's ears, and the larvae don't chew their way out. A few select species drip acid from fangs or stingers ... Olivia, you're just a girl, like me." A strange smile spread between her cheeks before she proudly walked back into the forest.

I liked her. She was one of my favorite clients—always on time with her deliveries, and she often paid well enough for an additional tip. Despite his innocent fears, Cal liked her, too. I agreed on the freaked-out part, though. Bubbly, talkative, and fearless, Emilee was the last type of mage one would expect to be a customer of mine.

"Very odd, indeed," wheezed Cal.

"Expect more drops within the week, Cal. Oh, and do me a favor ... Please humor Emilee. She is the best supplier on the entire campus. It'll really liven her spirits up. Mine too. You never know—she might surprise you one day," I said as I began to walk away from the base of the tree.

"Olivia!" shouted Cal, elevating his voice over my footsteps.

"Yes?"

"Your other deposit hole. On this side of me ..." Cal's eyes slowly creaked down to his right to indicate my outgoing sales. "Tarik passed me on his way back to class. He left a gift for you."

"Another gift...?" I sighed, somehow both irritated and delighted. "What is it? Did he say anything about it?"

"Nope." Cal chuckled. "He woke me up, tossed a folded bag into the hole, and walked off. Didn't say a word. Strange."

I walked over to Cal's left side and pressed the knothole to access the compartment. Though it was usually empty this time of day, there was a brown paper bag crumpled in the middle. I pulled it out of the hole and reached inside.

"Frazzleberries?" I said after peering into the bag and taking a deep whiff. "Where did he get frazzleberries? *How* did he get them? They do smell wonderful!"

"Wonderful? Olivia, you think the smell of garlic and swamp water is wonderful," asked the enchanted willow tree.

"It's my kind of wonderful, Cal! And frankly, I'm touched that Tarik knew I liked them. I've never told him. Never came up before ..." I smiled at the plump orange berries. They hung like grapes on a thin brown vine that was wrapped in an oval shape at the bottom of the bag.

"You know, he really does care for you, Olivia. I see it in his body language, and I'm a great judge of character. I attached myself to you, after all, didn't I?"

"That's true, Cal. You're a very intelligent ... tree."

"I'm more than a tree, Olivia. You know that."

"Yes, you are." I placed the paper bag in my satchel and threw it over my shoulder. "Please keep a look out for tomorrow's potential clients. I hear we might have some first timers!"

"Will do, Boss."

I pulled the hood over my head and gave him a nod.

"Oh!" Cal shouted again, heaving his voice over to me. "Side note about Emilee: If she threatens me again with rhinomites, we're going to have an issue!"

But I was already passing through the parted leafy entrance by the time he finished. All I did was laugh to myself at his comments as I restarted the trek back to my tower.

As I inched up my head a bit to check my surroundings, I glanced up at my tower home and saw a familiar shadow in the window—a face that I had known for my entire college career.

I continued walking up towards the tower, opened the door, and headed to my room. Once I got far enough up the staircase, I removed the hood and slowly twisted the knob.

His body was entirely invisible. But like the classic character from the H. G. Wells novel, his male figure was loosely covered in cloth bandages. The whole shape of him was not covered, but a majority, where one could only make out his hands and feet. Seeing several layers of cloth wrapped around his head, I knew immediately who it was.

"Marrick? Hi. Can't be good if you're visiting me personally," I stammered, tossing my cloak aside and placing the loaded satchel at the base of my alchemy table.

"You know why I'm here, Olivia. I don't need to tell you." Marrick's voice was sharp and stern. It seemed curious that he was sitting in my room, on my bed, unannounced, but I realized he would not visit like this if the circumstances were not important.

"Another binding?" I asked, folding my arms and standing in front of him.

"I care about you, contrary to what you might think. I watch out for you to protect you. Believe me, I am aware that you are strong and independent. But I brought you here, and I want to make sure you're safe when you're here."

"Marrick, I've told you several times that I'm fine. I can handle myself. You don't need to check up on me anymore. I'll report it if anything goes haywire."

"The roses are for you, Olivia. The gold is so you never go hungry or become afraid of losing out on the college's experiences." "I know that!" I hollered, my voice louder than I wanted. "But I don't appreciate you spying on me like this. If you said I can handle myself and the situations I put myself in, then why spy on me? There's no need. I care about you too, Marrick. But I'm old enough and strong enough now that I don't need you monitoring me like I'm a rambunctious teenager!"

"Olivia, stop," he retorted.

"I'm sorry, Marrick. But I don't appreciate surprises like this. I don't know who sent out the memo about me liking surprises! First Tarik, now you. Who's next? Are the rest of the Elders coming by to 'check up on me'?" I mocked with air quotes—something I knew would irritate him.

"I am sorry. Please forgive me. I saved you from Russia that day after the fire, and I only wanted to protect you, to be by your side. Sometimes I get too carried away by those feelings. Please forgive me ..."

Calming down, I sat down next to him and looked in the direction of his forehead. "It's okay. I get it."

"So ... big day of anniversaries for you. Four years ago, I opened your eyes to the world." His head flicked over towards my potion cabinet, and he looked at me for an ironic laugh. But I was not ready to give him that yet. "And happy one-month anniversary to you and Tarik as well. I know you make that boy very happy, and I can see in your eyes that he does the same for you."

"Thank you, Marrick, for those sweet sentiments," I replied cynically. My lack of enthusiasm and quiet response led to a few moments of silence as we sat on the bed next to each other.

"To answer your question ..." he began, rising to his feet. They were wrapped tightly in open-toed sandals, like a mummy's. "Yes, the Seekers and I need you for another extraction."

I sighed, slowly looked at where his face would be. "So ... what's wrong with the kid?"

ABRAHAM I

Like a blooming lily, the leaves of my palm thatch roof drooped over the edge once I pulled the hidden lever. Their vibrant green colors shone against the sky. Looking out across the forest, I was encapsulated in its solace, tucked away from the campus and other students. Easily my favorite part of the whole house, the crow's nest sat at the highest point and was only accessible by a single ladder—a hidden bungalow modeled off adventure books and exploration journals. The inside felt like a deep dive into my subconscious. Most of the bookshelves were lined with novels from my father's collection. Only the classics, of course: *The Call of the Wild*, *Treasure Island*, *Swiss Family Robinson*, *Don Quixote*, and *Tarzan*, among others. But now pale, white holiday lights were strung across the railings, and beanbags and throw pillows lay in the corners.

Those last ones must be Emilee's additions. They could only be from my loving girlfriend.

With my arms on the railing, I welcomed the dawn of fresh blue sky and chilly winter breezes. I often stood up here and forgot the world existed.

My adopted father, Roy, worked as an architect. When I had gotten older, I joined his team. With his expertise and my creativity, we curated an incredible business together. Building treehouses for families in our neighborhood planted the idea of collapsible roofs. Now the concept had been given its own organic twist, thanks to yours truly. Although, as I looked back on it now, retractable panels were probably not the most practical thing in Washington, DC.

As the sun tipped its cap to me across the tree canopy, I pushed the lever and closed the palm leaves like butterfly wings to reform the roof. They rustled lightly as they met in a pyramid shape.

"Hello, everyone!" I announced to the towering giants nearby. "Great start to the day, huh?"

I laughed and slowly descended the ladder, noticing imaginary smiles forming on their trunks.

It still blows my mind that I can actually talk to plants—trees, bushes, flowers, moss, algae . . . you name it. If it's flora, I can communicate with it. I'm basically the Aquaman of the forest. While I may not exactly be well-versed in the specific emotional turmoil of poison ivy, I can sense plants' feelings, sensations, and passions. Though my elemental magic is germination, this ability to talk to flora is unique to me.

Dusting off my sweatpants, I rounded the outside of the house, marked a few spots that need repainting, and walked onto the porch. I slid open the glass doors and entered the kitchen.

Immediately, I noted the silence. There was an absence of running water, which usually echoed within the house. On a mission, I sped through the open-air dining room and came to the living room (the source of the silence). The winding river was jammed with loose twigs gathered like a beaver dam. Easy fix. I cleared the blockage and listened as the sound returned to the trickle of a gentle stream. Cloudy blue water rushed around the table and sofas.

"Ahh, yup. That's better." I nodded.

Getting the river in my house had taken a mix of innovation and magic. The college's forest had no real rivers or streams. For the college, it was just a dense, populated grove of trees that functioned as the great barrier between the campus and the outside world. But with the help of an old witch and her crystal, we had found an underground aquifer and tapped into it. She jammed the diamond-shaped gemstone into the ground, which then pumped the water to the surface like a fountain. I formed a small pond around the upwelling and created a synthetic river throughout the property. It took some time to purify and refine the water entirely, but that witch had helped me get fresh water to my house. A glorious feat!

The beautiful sound of nature was comforting—almost like ... second nature. (A little funny, right?) There was so much to learn from it, too. But many of the students preferred to stay indoors and ignore its splendor.

My reverie was cut short by the pitter-patter of footsteps. Guessing who it was, I turned towards the noise and saw a young woman trying to hide behind a wall—poorly. She was pretty close to me; kudos to her for her sneakiness. One hand was stretched out at my face, holding a daddy longlegs spider. Her efforts to remain hidden were cute, if hilariously obvious.

"BOO!" she shouted.

"Aaaah!" I shrieked, staring right at her and faking fear.

"I've got eight legs, and I love my boyfriend. What am I?"

"Very funny, Emilee," I answered, watching her walk towards me. The arachnid was uncomfortably close to my nose.

"Scared ya, didn't I?" she taunted, pulling the spider away.

Sweet blue eyes welcomed me into Emilee's warmth. Silky blonde hair flowed down her back, and her pale cheeks blossomed with pink in the cold weather. Raised in Washington, DC, I was accustomed to it and prepared to manage the college's winter. But Emilee? Not so much. She wore an orange Texas Longhorns sweatshirt (her parents' alma mater), fleece yoga pants, and thick woolen socks made for snowshoeing. But those eyes of hers ... They pierced through me immediately, like no one's I'd ever seen. It had stopped me dead in my tracks the first time I met her.

"No—*he* did!" I laughed, nudging at the spider, whose legs flailed in the air.

"Okay. Charles, say goodbye," Emilee whispered, holding it towards my mouth again.

I backed away. "You *named* it?"

"Yes, I did! So what? Wanna give him a kiss goodbye?"

"You? Yeah, anytime. That thing? Uh ... I'll pass."

She frowned at me before setting it gracefully on the floor, watching it scurry across the stone. I kissed her lips and wiped away that sad, cartoonish frown.

"Wouldn't it have been funny if you actually *did* kiss Charles?"

Her laugh was obnoxious, yet adorable.

"Hilarious." I chuckled. "But please don't name these creepy-crawlies."

The sun's beaming rays peeked between the trees and through the window. Quiet and peaceful mornings like this one proved to be the best time for work.

Emilee's eyes and hands fell to her sweatshirt pocket. I knew by the look on her face that she was planning another trick or gimmick.

"Nope. Not gonna happen," I said, grabbing her wrist and bringing it safely into view. "You aren't gonna sneak into your pocket, pull out a scorpion or a beetle or something, and drop it down my shirt! Nope! Not fallin' for that again."

"Bleh. You're no fun!" she mocked, sticking her tongue out at me.

"What brings you by?" I asked kindly, rushing to the kitchen to fill my tea kettle.

"Just came to chat and see how you're doing. Shocked not to see you in the garden. You practically live there now."

"Very true. But today I found myself lost in the majesty of the forest from my crow's nest—which now feels like as much a part of you as it does me. Probably due to the interior design work you did up there. Throw pillows, beanbags, lights strung up ...?"

"Abe, I'm sorry. I—I just wanted to have a touch of me in your bungalow ..."

"Honey, it's fine. I'm kidding. I love it. It looks nice." I grinned at her.

"Well then, I'm glad! I was hoping you might."

I started a fire in my cast iron stove and placed the kettle on the burner. Watching Emilee, I admired her natural beauty as she took in small details of the home.

"So, how was your visit to Olivia's ... drop spot? Get what you need?" I asked.

"My *friend* Olivia, that is, Abe. We're friends. You can say it. It's not weird. Olivia and I are friends. Ask her. She'll agree. And everything went fine. I got what I needed; she got what she needed. Perfect teamwork. We have a good system—*as friends would.*"

"Uh-huh, I'm sure," I sighed. "She's still pretty odd."

"She lives in a tower alone because people bully and judge her. It fits her whole ... vibe. Plus, I talk to bugs as if they're humans. And you hear the emotional problems of plants like a therapist for the earth. So, don't judge, Abe. We're all weird."

"Good point," I answered begrudgingly.

"What's the plan today? Where's your head at, babe?"

"Well," I began, pouring the whole kettle into a large mug, "I'd like to touch up the chipped paint I just noticed on the side of the house. Work on the pulley system to propel water upstairs. Reinforce the interior wall panels in the bedrooms. But first off, my plan is to tend to my garden. Two weeks in, it looks decent. But the irrigation system I tried isn't cutting it anymore. Plus, I want to add another few rows of plants while they're fresh in my mind."

"Sounds like a busy day." She chuckled softly, turning off the stove.

"And what about you? Come by just to scare me with your eight-legged freak and hide behind my furniture?" I joked, taking a few long sips of delicious tangerine tea. My newest batch is a culmination of previous taste tests with added hints of cinnamon and nutmeg. Setting down the mug, I wrapped my arms around Emilee and tilted my head to hers.

Her cheeks flushed red. Eyes as blue as the ocean looked up at me.

"Noooo. Honestly, I just wanted to stop by and see how you were doing. I have to get to class soon."

Soft lashes, curled fashionably and accented with mascara, matched the grin upon her lips. We had been dating for two years, and I still saw her as lovely as the day we met. Nature and Emilee shared equal parts of my heart (though she might have argued otherwise).

"Well, thank you for coming over. I'll be here most of the day, if you wanna grace us with your presence again. So, swing by if you get bored."

"I'm never bored, Abe. But I'll keep that in mind."

My hands held tight to her thick sweatshirt as hers wrapped behind my neck. We leaned into one another and kissed. Eyes closed with the flowing water flanking us, Emilee and I held it for a few seconds, then pulled away.

"By the way, no bugs in my pocket. Only this ..." She reached into her pocket again and slid a note onto the dining table. "But you can't read it yet. Wait 'til I leave!" Emilee winked at me and disappeared out the sliding glass door. I slid the note into my pants pocket.

Watching her walk away, I soon zoned out, trying to subdue the nagging in my head telling me that the room's wall paneling was uneven. Upon first glance, the exterior looked like a wild mishmash of various types of wood: mahogany, birch, oak, and redwood, just to name a few. For me, however, I knew the true meaning behind how each board had been chosen and which shades and textures were used.

When I began it last year, I never realized how big of a project it was. However, this two-story house had become a glorious masterpiece. It was a mountain of a project, no doubt. But with Emilee's help, it had made the past eighteen months fly by. She followed this dream with me and worked as my sidekick, occasionally voicing her frustrations with my fading focus in my master-level classes.

The first floor had five large rooms (kitchen, dining room, living room, family room, and foyer) and two smaller ones (bathroom and mudroom). Being the living quarters, the second floor held the master suite, bathroom, study, and private library. Staying here a hundred percent of the time allowed me to focus constantly on ways to improve the whole place—making it more self-sustaining and waiting for my gardening labors to bear fruit. Still, never fear, the list of tasks I must complete seemed to grow by the minute.

Emilee said my home was "like the Swiss Family Robinson treehouse on steroids, built by an obsessive eco-freak." And frankly, I couldn't have put it better myself.

Strolling by the river in the family room, I stared in annoyance at another unfinished project: the water pulley. The idea was to create a cable system of tiny buckets to bring water to the second floor, yet it had not moved in several days. The wheel didn't turn properly, as it was caught on a snag or something. And the cables were not strong enough to support the weight of the bamboo buckets. You see, fresh water throughout the house would only *be* fresh if I fixed this and got it up here. Until then, it just sat here, an unchecked box on my to-do list—AKA a thorn in my side.

"Not today, Satan! This water system stuck in purgatory will not distract me. Nope. I must tend to my plants and flowers. That was my original task this morning." I shook my head, trying to avoid it, but my eyes kept returning to the contraption, like that pastry you know you're not supposed to eat. "*You* can wait 'til tomorrow ... or at least tonight."

I overheard the towering giants gossiping about possible options for fixing it.

I am sorry, friends. This project can wait! I told it, and now I am telling you.

They shrugged and drooped in disappointment.

But hold onto those thoughts, 'cause I will need some assistance when I do decide to fix it.

"'Geez, Abe, you're so smart and so cool!' Why, thank you, Mr. Pine Tree. 'Abe, you're such a great and skilled mage!' That is very kind, Ms. Conifer. 'Talking to plants and trees is not lame at all, Abe!' Of course it's not, guys. No one thinks that!"

I walked through the washroom and into the great outdoors. My eyes beamed at the brilliant, patchy lawn in the backyard. It was developing well, but honestly, there was as much brown in it as green. Nevertheless, I thought about how charming it would look someday and kept on towards the garden.

The birds were singing, and a gentle breeze whisked by my ears. The sun warmed my skin. The sounds of the world created a lovely song for me to walk with. Happy as a pig in mud, I hummed a tune in rhythm with nature and walked around my garden to the storage shed. Unlocking it, I retrieved a hand trowel, rake, and shovel from the wall rack, and a pair of gloves from the bin.

Reminiscent of Decembers in DC, the chilly weather brought a challenge to my house project. Thankfully, it was no match for me, an innovative environmental genius. Earlier this year, back in February or March, I had realized this place was unlivable unless I could find a reliable source of warmth. To acquire rare and foreign woods during construction, I would make deals with professors: I brought them rare flowers and plants, then they provided me with the materials. It was a simple trade, where each of us got what we wanted. However, during one of these scouting missions with safari professor, Leon, I was tasked with finding visciri, a small red flower whose petals were highly sought after for potions and medicines. But what I learned about this plant was that it absorbed heat from the sun and transferred it through the flower into the root system, creating extreme heat underground.

With a cluster of just four or five visciri, the area inside remained hot like the dunes of a desert. So, I gathered roughly twenty-five of them and planted a perimeter around the entire property. During the summer months, these visciri flowers made no difference in the ground temperature, but in the winter, they kept the dirt deliciously warm, transforming the property inside into a toasty little biome.

"Isn't it beautiful out here? Some might argue it has more charm than magic," I said to an imaginary audience.

Like an extension of my softer side, the garden was a delicate array of young plants and green leaves. It was the start of something new—something I'd perhaps been missing for a while. Among the tiny petals, there was a delicate ambience within these rows. The whispers from the vegetable plants sang in harmony with the flowers. Despite seeing nothing more than a few single stems, I listened to their newfound tune. The pressures of being a perfectionist often suffocated me within the walls of my home, but I felt more at peace out here with the seedlings.

No, my youthful, yet-to-be bloomers, I am not losing my mind! Thank you! Do not criticize your maker! It is perfectly normal to get excited over flowers and baby vegetables.

I knelt on the ground, took my hand trowel, and tapped the base of each stem. Maybe an inch or two tall, they looked like sprouts of asparagus sticking out of the ground. With a full packet of seeds, this row of tea plants would eventually become impeccably trimmed baby trees. The first sight of that would be glorious, because growing my own tea leaves opened the door for limitless creations.

Tea plants required a lot of water and warmth. While visciri flowers solved the temperature issue, I had tried a plethora of irrigation systems to deliver water properly to each row. Currently, my garden used hollowed bamboo with holes poked in the bottom to act as PVC pipes. The water traveled nice and smooth. Having tried rickety raised sprinklers (a half-hearted thank you to Ivanka the witch for those), along with a horrible attempt at braided rivers, I would take the success where I could!

The next row from left to right was carrots. These orange vegetables had slightly raised soil compared with the other plants, with sand added to help with irrigation. My imperator carrots would hopefully grow into a tiny forest of fireworks, where the veggie was the rocket and the leafy plumage was its light streaking in the sky.

I walked the line and trimmed extra leaves from each plant while listening to the gentle trickle of water into the soil. Not much trimming, though—just enough to match their shape to the rest. Early afternoon sun warmed my skin. The trees shivered as their branches danced in the chill air. The strangely comforting balance of warmth and subzero had just begun.

Peas and asparagus were next in the inspection line. Both had made little progress and mirrored each other's sprouts. Adequate water, dripping slowly even as it sped down the hollowed shoots, was supplied by the bamboo canals. After two weeks, the pea plants had grown from seed into a single green stem with a single green leaf. A row of them looked like the cover of a children's book on gardening for beginners. The asparagus, on the other hand, looked like little worms poking out of the dirt. This pair of vegetables required very little attention or maintenance on my end.

Next came the rows of flowers. The first one, native to Penumbra, was called screaming maw. While the name was rather aggressive and sounded like a horrible curse, it appeared to grow similarly to a calla lily—a long, thin stem with matching leaves on either side. The shopkeeper I had purchased the seeds from said they would grow into beautiful crystal-clear flowers. When a breeze blew through their petals, it sounded like delicate wind chimes. While therapeutic to the ears of humans, its tone warded off pests and bugs. Planting eight of them ought to do the trick for the garden.

Unsure of how to maintain the screaming maw, I left them alone.

The soft song of the flowers echoed more in this half of the garden as I moved to the lavender and hyacinth. Personally speaking, I was not familiar with these two in the slightest.

The lavender stems resembled small emerald-colored corals popping out of the dirt. They were all uniform and had a sweet herbal aroma. These would bloom nicely into purple delights, and the growth—compared to the veggies—would be more notable and dramatic as time went on. Much the same, the hyacinth seedlings had become a line of little artichoke-like corals. Their smell, however, was robust and almost spicy, like a strong perfume. The combination of lavender and hyacinth was lovely, which invited me to travel between them. I inspected each one, clipped extra stems if necessary, and ensured that the bamboo was working as intended. Once all was in order, I took a step back and smiled at the garden as a subtle gust of wind slid under my sleeves.

But the tedious inspection of these existing plants was not the topic of today's mission. No, no! That was simply a product of a perfectionist amateur gardener. The true goal for the day was to plant the remaining seeds: roses, which require no introduction; honeysuckle, which smelled like sweet, sweet nectar; magebloom, whose purple flowers produced red berries perfect for the young tea aficionado in me; and kypraxi, a type of mangrove tree that created sap said to be one of the most powerful substances in Penumbra.

"Now the real fun starts. Time to put the trowel and shovel to work!" I exclaimed, sounding like a coach preparing his team's comeback at halftime.

Gardening tools in hand, I knelt on the warm ground and started scooping dirt from the first marked spot. With the shovel, I created a small crater, only a few inches deep, before moving to the next location and doing the same. I went one by one, making a symmetrical row of twelve pre-dug holes. Then I pulled out my packet of rose seeds from my pocket and dropped one in each. Finally, I filled the holes back in, adding in some planting mix.

"I hope they turn out great, too, guys. I am equally excited. So nice not to be alone in that!" I laughed with the forest.

Connecting a series of bamboo shoots to the existing canals, I continued the water flow to include the roses. While I was at it, I followed the zigzag between the rows and completed the full circuit to hydrate the entire garden. My father always told me to think proactively, so here's to you, Roy! The quiet sound of rushing water filled the air, drawing another satisfied grin from me despite the dropping temperature.

"Winter is here, everyone! Bundle up, please. Don't let those faces freeze with a frown!" I hollered aloud.

I dug more starter holes for the honeysuckle, which had been shockingly difficult to get my hands on. As with the roses, each hole was of an equal depth, dug single file. I planted the eight black seeds and covered them all with planting mix. Once they were in the ground, I stood up and went to the storage shed to grab wooden stakes. This particular honeysuckle was flowered arching shrubs that could overtake their environment like grape vines. Now, I'm sure most gardeners would have preferred to avoid such an invasive species, but I was not most gardeners. I was betting on the tasty fruits they produced.

In the penultimate row, I knelt in the dirt and began excavating two holes at a time. Magebloom flowers required more space to grow, hence the four-inch depth between the seed and the surface.

Suddenly, as I shoveled deeper into the dirt, I hit something hard. The force of it stung my hand. I couldn't make out what it was immediately, so I dug more around the spot. With sore hands covered in grime, I ripped through the dirt with my fingers and trowel.

Eureka! After burrowing like a gopher, I discovered what it was. I pulled out a strange stone artifact and set it upright. It was a raven. Its folded wings and sharp talons were intricate and realistically detailed. Roughly seven inches tall, the bird showed impressive craftsmanship, yet ... Hold on. This raven idol had five eyeholes carved above the beak rather than the usual two. I imagined its beady little eyes summoning my attention. I couldn't look away from them. As if in a trance, I was trapped in their hollow gaze.

"What *are* you ...?" I puzzled, picking up the stone sculpture and glancing between the eyes.

Yes, yes. This thing is something else. Certainly random to find a many-eyed raven in your garden—but why is something telling me it wasn't random for me to find this? This idol is ... bizarre. It also doesn't feel like it comes from the college. It has ... an aura about it that captivates my attention and holds me hostage.

"... And why are you in my garden?" I asked it, twirling the stone around in my palm.

I held the raven tightly and squeezed it. It was lightweight, but durable. The stone was rare, something I had never seen before. It felt ancient—maybe even prehistoric. Sure enough, it was hard as a rock.

I dusted off the remaining dirt and watched my feet carry me away from the tilled rows. Leaving the garden tools behind, I strolled to the house with my hands clasped on the idol. With soil on my sweats and all, I stared into the raven's devilish eyeholes. I could almost see them blink like real pupils, piercing ones, tilting their curiosity at me. I pictured this creature alive, with a lustrous black color, shaggy feathers, a thick, bearded beak, and iridescent plumage at the tail. Its eyes ... I stared into them as I would a human's, and I sensed each one equally glaring back into my soul. They would have been fake, of course, made of ancient stone or whatever. But I couldn't shake the feeling that they looked as real as my own.

"*Right?!*" I said to the surrounding trees, who shared in my fascination with the idol. "It's so different! It's ... special. I can't place why, though. Like ... why was it in my garden? How long has it been buried there? What does it mean? Where did it come from ...?"

Trunks contorted with anticipation, the towering giants nearly split in half with laughter after I walked face first into the washroom door. My mind was wandering, my head was lowered as I peered at the raven in my hands, and my legs were strolling forward automatically. I felt like an idiot now, and the eavesdropping flora were not helping.

Save your sorries! It—it is admittedly pretty funny, I thought to them, chuckling to myself as I picked up the idol. *It's alright to laugh. Humbles me a little bit. I'm easily preoccupied, I guess.*

I shook the shame from my face, tucked the idol under my arm like a football, and twisted the door open. Mind racing over its curious allure, I envisioned its daggering eyes watching my every move as I headed into the kitchen.

AARON II

As the sun glistened through my window, I addressed the sun with half-opened eyes and a weary groan. The only thing worse than my storm magic situation was waking up in the mornings. In the Northern Forest, my father hunted for pheasants and wild game before the sun broke over the horizon, so that usual wakeup call was a reaction to my father's shooting. Even the rooster's crowing gave a better welcome to the morning than Duke's mumbling or his reused glass tubes clinking against one another.

I pushed the bed sheets aside, knocking the textbook from Luke's class to the floor and flipping past the pages I'd left it open to in the process. I closed it, placed it in my bookbag, and got dressed. The clock showed 6:38 when I rubbed my eyes to squint at its hands. As if that weren't bad enough, there was a vulgar smell seeping from Duke's bedroom into my own. It smelled of pond water and sulfur.

Gently turning the doorknob, I quietly walked through the crack in the doorway and into the bathroom. A stream of freezing cold water spurted from the faucet and over my hands. I splashed some of it on my face and blinked a couple times as I looked in the mirror. It had been a few minutes since I awakened, but I still felt groggy and miserable, nonetheless.

Shaved and square-shaped, my face looked average. It was hard to tell whether I had acne through my flickering eyelids. I dipped my hand in the running water again and tried to slick down a few long hairs sticking up on the top of my head. I forced a simple smile onto my face, but it sunk away as I retreated back to my bedroom.

After tossing a few more books into my backpack, I slung it over my shoulders and rapidly checked the clock behind me: 6:44. I stepped out of my bedroom and closed the door—silently, I might add, because I didn't want to trigger Duke's supersonic ears. Anytime he was "working," bothering Duke was the rudest and most inconsiderate act you could ever commit against him. Despite living with him for three unfortunate months now, I had only seen him practice his steam magic twice: once when I was coming back from a class, when he cast vapor on himself and scared me after I opened the door, and the other when he tested a geyser spell on a new "bioluminescent chemical" he was working on, which shot the shiny teal water into the air and all over his bedroom floor.

Meanwhile, Duke was hovered over his alchemy table. I wondered if he ever left it. Every morning when the sun rose, and every night when it changed into the moon, there was Duke, bent over the stone slab and attending to whatever bubbling concoction he was making. Today he was working with a sludge-like yellow liquid in a large basin and a trio of test tubes, each with markings scratched on them. With broad shoulders pushing the limits of his T-shirt, Duke crossed his arms across chest and stared at the basin.

"Can't sneak out that easy, loser," he shouted into the living room.

Dread washed over me. His door burst open as Duke's bedroom fully opened to me in a disturbing glow; he nearly ripped it from the hinges.

"I'm just trying to get to class on time, okay, Duke?" I protested.

"Bundle up, buttercup. It's bitter cold and snowing outside. But since you're a storm mage, I'm sure you know all about the weather." He leaned against the wall while judging me as if from a mountain peak.

"Like I've said since the day I met you, Duke, storm magic does not control the weather! Just go back to your cooking, or whatever you're doing in there." That sounded more hostile than I had intended; it made me nervous the moment I finished speaking.

However, amidst my stupidly worrying about what I'd said, some textbooks fell from my unzipped bookbag. Duke dragged one of them towards himself with his foot and bent over to pick it up. It was the one I needed for Penumbra History class, the first class on my agenda today.

"Duke, c'mon. I need that for this morning ..." I panicked and glanced at the clock: 6:50. "For this class in ten minutes! I need that back, please."

"Don't be nice, Aaron. It gets you nowhere. Now to teach you a lesson ..." Duke flipped through page after page, looking for a good spot to stop. Nearly three-quarters through it, he began tearing pages out, ripping them one by one from the seams and letting them fall to the living room floor. "If you need something desperately, like a textbook, don't let it fall out of your unzipped backpack, dimwit. I'll take these pages as payment for your brain's inadequacy and send you off. Please don't bring your shoes into our dorm later today either. Dragging snow, mud, and crud into the dorm looks ugly. It'd be a pain for you to have to clean the floors, too." He threw the book at the couch and snapped, "You're gonna be late, by the way." Then he slammed his bedroom door.

I ran over to the pages lying on the floor and stuffed them behind a couch cushion. Trying to keep my worry under control, I ignored the clock's ticking, slipped my shoes on, and left the dorm.

There was a drastic temperature drop the moment I set foot in the hallway. I felt the rush of wind send goose bumps shivering over my body, and I felt like Duke might have had a valid point about bundling up. The December winds at the college were minor most of the time, but the snowfall and ice during the first week gave it a lovely white layer of beauty. Winters in Penumbra often brought my family very close together to stay warm because our fire was not large enough to keep the whole cottage above freezing. Somehow, despite the college's sturdy stone buildings, those bitter drafts of snow still whipped down our hallway.

"Hey, Aaron!" hollered Sparrow from her dorm down the hallway. She was fumbling with a stack of notebooks. We shared the same Penumbra History class. Each morning, when my foot would barely step over the threshold of my dorm, there was Sparrow, short and sweet, but very annoying and talkative. She would always invite herself to join me on the walk to class, and I would always say no. Sparrow was persistent, though, so I never walked to class alone.

"Hi, Sparrow," I replied, looking at the floor in fear of making direct eye contact with her. I started walking down the hallway with my head forward, focused on the staircase at the end.

"Walk to class with me? We're going to the same place, you know! Who am I kidding?! You've never walked alone. Silly me! We walk together all the time!" She ran to catch up with me, despite my race to the stair door.

"Sure," I replied, emotionless.

"Great! And you know it's cold out. And it's probably gonna be snowing if it's cold out. I love snow! Don't you? My roommate can't see out the window from my room, so I cast reflective armor on myself, and then she can see the snow's reflection as it falls to the ground. It's basically like a glass case around your body. Pretty cool, right? I thought so, too! One of the first spells I mastered."

"I didn't sleep well, Sparrow. Can you just please ... not talk so loudly?" Gripping the straps of my backpack to brace against the cold, I pushed the stair door open with my foot. Meanwhile, Sparrow kept talking about her roommate's love for crackers and jam (home life back in a place called Greenland) and comparing the college's winters to that of her birthplace. Most of it ran together in one long monologue I tuned out for.

"Sure thing. I'll be very quiet," she answered in an outdoor voice.

I was certain it would be a long walk to the classroom building.

A relief for my underdressed self was not seeing billowing snow as we emerged from the stairwell and into the outside world. Sparrow was overly prepared, on the other hand, with enough long-sleeve tops on to keep the whole school warm.

My brown hair fell above my eyebrows and kept the top of my head warm. I clasped harder on the leather straps of my bookbag and bowed my neck to push forward against the winds. Sparrow never failed to disappoint as she continued talking about Greenland and the summers there ... or something along those lines. The cold was making my brain hurt trying to ignore her, so I had to listen.

"Summers only last the blink of an eye. One moment, you wake up and see blue skies for miles and miles and miles. Then, *bam!* The snow has returned to cover the hills of greenery in a fluffy marshmallow coating. BUT, the weather and stuff here in Penumbra is awesome! I love it, even when other people are complaining about it."

It was odd, because at the exact moment she mentioned people complaining about it, I was about to chatter my teeth and whine about the frigid temperature.

"Well, we're almost there. Dig your feet into the ground and push onward ... to Penumbra History! You know what blows my mind? That hologram of Adarius teaching the class. Like, the literal founder of the college teaching us? Oh, who am I kidding—everyone knows that! He's a legend. But how do they do it? Do you ever wonder how they created that hologram?"

The only thing I was wondering was how I could cast a storm to make Sparrow—or me—disappear. She was a sweet girl, and I could tell from her unplanned morning walks with me that she was passionate about a lot of things and a lot of people. However, I could not determine whether that was her best quality or her worst.

"Sparrow," I began, pushing my voice over the howling winds, "I like to go into class after you do. I prefer to sit in the back and not be noticed."

"No problem, Aaron. I always go in first, so you can enter whenever you want to."

I subtly smiled back at her while pulling my shirt closer to my mouth. I hunched my shoulders and hunkered down tightly into myself. She pulled open the door, and I allowed plenty of space between us before entering myself. I lingered behind as several other students took advantage of Sparrow's kindness and breezed their way into class. Once everyone else went in, I thanked Sparrow with a nod and let her go into Adarius's class.

I sat in the same seat every time—near the window against the far side wall. The seating order never changed; no one bothered to switch places. In front of me always sat a shy girl from Japan, who rarely raised a hand to answer any questions. But, as the class's seating arrangements never changed, neither had this girl's itch for knowledge—she was always scratching her neck and playing with her hair to fight the urge to raise her hand. Funny thing was, she and I had never talked or anything; I don't even know her name.

Finally situated, I dropped my bag beneath the chair and removed the textbook Duke had sadly ripped the pages out of. In a miniature panic as I slid it on the desk, it occurred to me that the ones he'd torn from the spine could be the ones I needed today. I flipped the book open to those missing pages and scanned quickly to find out what my textbook now lacked.

Distracted by the revel of the professor, I wondered how the college created it. It must have been a mixture of several spells fused together between many instructors. Known as the Father of Magic, Adarius's hologram showed off his slicked-back white hair, a fading black beard, and keen eyes. He wore flowing orange robes with a silver lining, which flagged a cape-like attachment down the shoulders. His face was welcoming and knowledgeable. Adarius had the visual appearance of a loving grandfather but the bellowing voice of a noble commanding officer.

"We start with the creation of the Elders."

My stomach sank, my mind began to worry, and my heart felt afraid. I tried to keep positivity and hope in the back of my mind, but the fear of this unknown topic and my book's missing pages ruffled them again. Fleeing moments of bad luck snuck their way into my train of thought and instantly made me reconsider my optimism.

"Open your books to page 537 and get your pencils ready. Lots of notes and old memories to discuss today," Adarius began, showing a longing smile.

I lost focus and simply stared at Adarius, assessing how in the magical world he could stand at the front of the class. Projected into thin air, the hologram moved and talked as a normal human would. It was glorious.

"Today is our discussion over the creation of the five elemental Elders and their purpose at the college. Page 537. No time to waste," Adarius began.

The most he ever wrote on the board was the topic of the lesson, nothing more. Everything else was spoken from his mind, just like it happened yesterday. He was the most talented mage ever to live, and his lectures were nothing short of incredibly powerful.

I took out a notebook and grabbed a pencil from the depths of my bookbag. My nerves kicked in over my fear of the missing pages. Suddenly, the cold outside did not exist anymore.

"Of course," I said, opening my history book to the chapter Adarius requested. Yes, Duke had in fact torn out the pages I needed for today's lesson. Thus, I was forced to jot down every word Adarius spoke.

Scanning the room, I saw everyone bracing for his words with pencils and minds at the ready.

"Crazy as it is to believe, I discovered and mastered the power of every element. It's why people often refer to me as the 'Father of Magic', because I am the creator of natural magic and the first ever mage in the history of Penumbra. Still, I understood that having all these abilities at my fingertips would inevitably lead to my death. My brain could handle the elemental power, but my physical body could not. At that point in my life, death did not scare me—I welcomed it. The 'mental' power weighing on my physical body literally exploded me like an overinflated balloon. So, the Elders were born directly from various aspects of me. Now that's a little morbid ... so think of it like this ..."

He hovered at the head of the classroom while watchful eyes followed his movements. Approaching the middle, Adarius cast an orb of rainbow-like colors that floated up peacefully, pausing inches below the ceiling. "This rainbow orb signifies me: immense power, but too much to contain within its own restraints." With a snap of his fingers, the ball exploded like confetti into five distinctly colored orbs in the corners of the room: orange, gray, blue, green, and yellow. "A single orb of various colors explodes into different balls only showcasing one color. Much easier to manage in this way. Breaking my magic into smaller things—that is what the Elders are. They are the separation of a greater rainbow."

He smiled for a while and watched dozens of hands scribble frantically.

"Note the image you see at the top right of page 538. You'll see an illustration of the Elders in a group and how I envision them. Around campus and Penumbra, stories from the skeptics will tell you lies about how the Elders were formed, how they came to be, and how they appear. Hear it from the man himself. Marrick, the Void Elder, was created from my shadow; Magnus, the Fire Elder, from my rage; Kai, the Water Elder, from my sorrow funneled through a single tear; Terra, the

Earth Elder, from my beating heart; and Eliza, the Air Elder, created from my final breath."

I felt a misery waft over my face like a phobia. Creating pages full of illegible scribbles, everyone hurried their pencils to keep pace with Adarius's lectures. Like a balance beam, the class raced to jot down his thoughts while keeping their ears open for his next words. Curious as a nosy fool, I leaned over in my seat to peek slightly at the sound mage in front of me. Her notebook was blank, as she was too enthralled by Adarius to be bothered to record today's lecture notes. Meanwhile, my notebook only contained a few sentences.

"Like demigods of magic, the Elders are mighty powerful beings, physical manifestations of their elements. They are the literal source of power for their respective element, as they act as an energy bank where spells are drawn from. Here. Think of it this way." Though his words contradicted the tone, Adarius laughed lightly and chuckled while his eyes wandered the room searching for inspiration. "When you use your wildfire magic, Sparrow, you are draining it from Magnus. When you use your steam magic, Raven, it is drained from Kai." Adarius's soft gaze fell to the shy girl in the corner, who was clinging to the window like a wallflower and praying to be unseen. "Kiku, when you cast sound spells, you are summoning air magic from Eliza. But don't any of you worry. It doesn't affect the Elders at all. Their existence is to contain their element's magical capabilities with great prowess and responsibility."

I saw Kiku's back and shoulders tense up when Adarius called her name aloud. *Kiku.* Interesting name. It was nice finally to put a name to the smartest girl in the room. She had never spoken a word or even turned around to look at me, but I could tell by her mannerisms and behaviors that she was the smartest, even if she hid it very well. Raven, the eccentric short girl with violet hair sitting next to Kiku, seemed to know a lot, too. She looked at me funny sometimes.

"Unfortunately, the creation portion of today's lecture is over, as is the fun talk. Your textbooks go into further minute details on the Elders' obligations, hobbies, jurisdictions, and appearances. But I like to go off the book—lecture from the heart. We must discuss the Elders in the college's current state," Adarius addressed us sincerely. "All of you in this class are first years—all novice mages. The complexities of Penumbra's magic are nuanced to each. You see, our Elders are only hailed as demigods and almighty beings for elemental magic by this college and the surrounding magical community. Non-magical factions and peoples have their own such gods and do not believe beings like the Elders to exist. Despite those beliefs, our Elders are paramount in maintaining the balance between Penumbra and Earth.

It's time to dig into the tensions and disgruntles of the five Elders. Pencils and quills at the ready for notes. It's going to get serious."

Adarius knew how to pack a punch with his words, whether it pertained to nonfiction or nonsense. His pauses felt like an eternity, and his sentences carried the weight of urgency if he meant them to. No sentence or stanza was unimportant, which inflected more dread as I heard each one.

"Let's begin with present day and their ... discrepancies with one another. After all ... it is the reason I had to reshuffle the day's agenda."

The class's minor chuckles and scribbling of pencils on paper suddenly ceased. It was as though the bitter cold winds from outside had swept through the room like a shadow and frozen all of us in shock.

The uncertainty in his voice now led me to believe the worst. Obviously, I did not have the pleasure of knowing the Elders, but I feared any influential people having arguments with one another. I lived in Dunnmore under the authority of The Citadel, so I have seen the hardships and the brutality an authority can have on its subjects. Terrible scenarios flooded my mind when I imagined these tribulations coming from almighty god-like beings.

"Nothing to fear, of that I can assure you. It just means rebalancing things that need to be rebalanced."

Adarius left the center of the room and returned to the front. He drew a barely visible timeline above the class and marked intervals across it with his finger. Slicing through the sunbeam intruding from the outside, the timeline stretched from one side of the room to the other. At the front of the line, closest to himself, Adarius lit a green ball of energy, signifying the creation of the Elders. On the other end, he created a similar blue one, signifying the present day. Then he dropped his hands behind his back and clasped them together to continue the lesson.

"This timeline is not in any textbook; nor is anything else for the rest of this lecture. I suggest that all of you begin drawing it now. Do not just try and memorize the one I have created for you here. Draw your own and follow it."

"So, you now know of this point," Adarius said, gesturing to the green ball above his head. "This is when the Elders were created from my body's explosion, for lack of a better term. The College of Adarius was built and established just before my death, shortly before the green orb in our timeline. Everything from Penumbra's smallest humdrum town to Earth's finest grand cities moves forward in parallel. My college, however, was founded as a place not only to study elemental magic, but also to harness magic's full ability and maintain the balance of these worlds. Before I sought to control the five pure elements, it was my goal to learn about them.

That knowledge was then transferred to each Elder. They know the limitations, the power, the necessity, the danger, and the ominous futures of their element if order is not preserved. Watching the destruction of the balance is easy; forming and fostering ways to repair it is the challenge. The Elders must work *together* to continue harmony here on Earth and Penumbra. These worlds are intertwined with one another like tethered twins. Both rely on each other, sustain each other, and depend on each other for their own stability and success. Though it may sound like fairy tales and old fables, much of what happens here and what the Elders do affects life on Earth, too." He slowed his train of thought and glanced around the room at all the curious eyes. "Elders have existed for centuries. Now ... who can tell me *how* the Elders decided to maintain the balance?"

The room was silent. Nobody moved. Not a single hand rose into the air.

Kiku scratched her neck with the end of her pencil.

I bet she knows.

"Compromise!" a bubbly voice cried out.

"Oh, Sparrow. Magnus would be so proud someone else shares his love of quirky creations and tinkering, and I love your enthusiasm. But sorry, that's not quite how it's handled." He paused a moment before continuing. "Turn to the next chapter, class. Chapter Seven: A Coexistence of Two Planets.."

When Adarius uttered those final words, I felt a chill rush down my spine. The sternness in his voice made it sound dire and horrible. I watched the sun retract behind gray clouds outside. Something beyond the chapter title made the hairs perk up on my body.

Luck had shifted its eyes onto me when I turned to page 541 for the next chapter. For the first time this lesson, the textbook came through for me and showed me exactly what I wanted to see, and ...

It was blank. Flabbergasted and panicked, I flipped through the next ten pages or so. They were all blank, too. The chapter before it about the Elders was full of words, pictures, diagrams. But, after nearly a dozen white sheets of nothing, chapter eight goes back to normal with the title, "Extra Measures to Ensure Equilibrium: Exploring Other Methods of Balance Across the Worlds." An entire chapter in a textbook for novice mages called "Coexistence of Two Planets" is left blank, with no descriptions or letters or numbered pages or anything at all? What kind of person leaves an entire chapter out? Nevertheless, I could not tell if it was a stupid accident or intentional.

Suddenly, another howling wind slapped the windowpane next to me and made me jump. On top of paranoia, stress, and anxiety, I never realized that being a scaredy-cat would be added to that list. The feeling as goosebumps flushed through my bones and off my skin was like something out of a ghost story.

"Class," Adarius began, revisiting the center of the room, "I'm sure you've seen by now that your textbooks are strangely blank—white pages with no text. Trust me ... it's done on purpose. They aren't going to be of much help, if you can't tell that by now. So! I need everyone to close your eyes and listen to these next words as I speak them."

I closed my eyes in accordance with Adarius's instructions. It felt like the other day's Yoga class, only this time, it was far less relaxing and seemed to augment my stress rather than take it away.

"Imagine you're in an arena, the most exceptional landmark you can muster up. Thousands of excited eyes are watching your every move, and great gasps and cries are ringing out from the balconies around you. People chanting your name, rooting for you to win, seeing the pride of their element showcased by one select student. Now, open your eyes."

I emerged from the darkness of my eyelids back into the classroom's light. But the room had changed. Wandering eyes desperately looked around. The rows of desks and seats had been silently rearranged into a circle, with Adarius standing in the middle as the ringleader. Like a giant oval, the room felt entirely brand new.

"Resemble an arena?" he puzzled, with a gentle smile on his face.

A few students struggled to find the proper response, but the majority were muttering under their breath about the change in scenery.

Adarius continued, retreating back to the green orb at the front. "Once the college had its first fifty mages, Terra and Marrick discussed possible ideas to repair the broken balance. The pair of them brainstormed a fight-to-the-death spectacle between students, one from each element, in a competition of wits and toughness. The other Elders agreed and found it to be a suitable fit for ensuring equality across the pure elements and two worlds. This event gradually became known as The Pit. Five students are selected to compete in it. Four die, while the last one is crowned victorious and granted a wish. After agreeing on this tournament, the Elders were on wonderful terms with one another, getting along and compromising at each instance."

Adarius looked at the second interval on the timeline and lit a white orb of energy. This glowing ball of light quickly colored itself rainbow. "This orb resembles all of the Elders' unity—all colors of the elements blended together. For several years, The Pit worked successfully. The relationships among the Elders were good, and all of them agreed that The Pit was the best way to keep the balance and everything in order."

One student from the circled seats chimed in with a question, stopping Adarius in his lecture. "Why The Pit? Why did the balance only work with The Pit? What about it was so ... important? Were there no other ways to do it?"

"Other methods were like putting a cork on a volcano—temporary. The Pit worked successfully for two key reasons. One, its Selection Ceremony chooses five competitors at random—no rhyme or motive or bias. This method was thought to be the most fair and just because it lets fate choose who will compete for the elemental balance. Two, the deaths of the four losing mages fuel the Blood Pact Wish, which is a wish granted by the Elders to the winning element's champion. Their sacrifices give that remaining student the acceptance of the losing Elders. With the might of two worlds on their shoulders, the winning competitor is graced with making a no-strings-attached wish for how to restore the balance during the next four years."

He gestured to the third mark on the timeline and lit another orb. This one began as white light. But the color changed, and the expression on Adarius's face shifted from satisfied to disappointed. Now yellow, the ball floated in line with the others and seemed to hold the promise of wonder or peril. Adarius, a true man of theatrics, walked back to the middle of the makeshift arena.

"This next point in the college's timeline is unsteady, and where the sleigh falls off the path. It is here in our history where Kai and Eliza started to deviate from the idea of a student-versus-student bloodbath in favor of a more civil solution. They brought up a few additional ideas to the rest of the Elders, which we will dive into during a future lesson. In short, despite their later judgement, eventually all Elders decided that The Pit remained the best option available, and thus, it continued on."

His face turned sour. Adarius lit the next interval with a black ball of energy. It did not change from one color to the next; rather, he cast it as black immediately. A haunting and ominous aura came over the room. One could tell Adarius was disgruntled, even if he was just a magical hologram. Many students had dropped their pencils and allowed their notebooks a breather.

"A black spot in the college's history, tarnished by overflowing frustrations and disagreements. As their creator, this part saddens me the most. I seek only happiness and cooperation for the Elders. However, like a father saddened by his children's actions, I was disheartened watching from the shadows as they continued to fight ..."

Having a younger sister, I saw the same look on my father's face whenever we screwed up.

"Heated discussions, flared tempers, heavy conversations over even heavier subject matters ... It was during this black spot that *I* learned something about the Elders! Their lack of cohesion came to such a volcanic climax that Magnus struck Terra with a cane of blown glass, which left a nasty burn mark down her forearm. I learned that, while Elders are immortal, they can do damage to each other."

Adarius stared out the window. He looked lost and discouraged.

"When The Pit was introduced centuries ago, it was the only option, and the decision was unanimous. It was never a perfect solution from the start, but it was successful, nonetheless. During this dark period for the Elders, votes had split, which severed the favorable relationships they once shared together. Losing The Pit consistently every four years, some Elders were desperate to find an alternative solution. Terra suggested wiping humanity off Earth, as their incessant need to usurp each other and inevitably begin wars was shifting the balance on its axis haphazardly. Marrick agreed with the notion to remove humans from Earth and allow the planet to resolve its own issues. Then Eliza and Kai argued why change what isn't broken. Magnus joined in favor of The Pit to stick to it as the only solution, and more importantly, the only *guaranteed* solution. Long story short, when the time came for a vote on the upcoming Pit Tournament, the Elder votes were split: three in favor and two opposed. Majority ruled, and because no better alternative was agreed upon, The Pit was deemed the last resort and their only chance."

Nonchalantly, Adarius returned his focus to the classroom and cast a new orb, the last one before the blue orb at the end. This one was also black, thereby continuing a trend I did not like.

"Tense discussions continued despite carrying on The Pit blindly in the background. However, a new standoff moment arrived as Kai switched sides to be against the tournament. After several victors not being of his element, his ego had taken enough beatings. Without the majority, Pit tournaments ceased and other ways to solve the unbalance were put in place. Those better ways, however, faced the same result as The Pit, which ultimately then resulted in *more* hostile and ruthless arguments between the Elders. Earth was driven into chaos during this time. Wars, famine, natural disasters, environmental shifts ... The more suggestions posed by the Elders, the more unstable Earth became. Easily outraged and narcissistic, Marrick and Magnus almost killed each other in a verbal standoff that turned physical through lashing twisted new spells at each other. Despite honoring what little respect they had left for each other, this severe rift created a mess on both worlds, therefore leaving the Elders with no choice. The Pit, barbaric and sadistic in its nature, was necessary. Balance is *essential* for our worlds to remain in harmony. If you break that harmony, even for a *second*, worlds are thrown into helpless bedlam and can collide and collapse inward on themselves. Now, for my Earth folks, once The Pit restarted in 2008, it was the first time revisited since 1942."

Adarius finally presented the floating energy ball at the end of the timeline. Every mage's eyes followed his gesture like a flock of birds. His words seemed to cut across my mind like a knife; I could not look away.

"This brings us to present day. Since the last tournament, the Elders have remained at odds. Hostility and hatred are boiling over, and personal agendas override previous answers to the same problem. Tensions are running high and washing these conversations in the same, red-tinted friction as before. But, decisions ultimately need to be made. That parallel leads us to a familiar result: The Elders are desperate to fix the balance. Adding pressure on a paramount level, a Pit Tournament this year could be Earth and Penumbra's last chance before ..."

Adarius paused when he heard a knock on the classroom door, but he continued his lecture as he walked over to address who it was.

"It is the killing of students. It is a spectacle of blood and brains. But it is impossible to maintain balance without it. Trust me ..." His eyes fell off the class and stared into open space. "The Elders have tried." As these words came out of his mouth, he opened the door.

"Ahhh, Jackson! How nice of you to drop by. I was informing the class here about The Pit."

Jackson was the Dean of Students at the college. With combed brown hair curling at the neck, he had an old-looking face even if his body still seemed young. Scraggly hairs lined his chin and mouth in an attempt at a goatee. He had blue eyes and a friendly smile that warmed the room and invited everyone's eyes to greet his. Like Adarius, he captivated a room with his presence, and all the mages at the college loved him. It was as though he were one of us—a very odd yet comforting feeling, given he was the newest dean. His robe was a vibrant silver with gold trim. A silk cloak, its collar puffed up beneath his curls, was fastened below his goatee and flowed down to the ground.

"Nice to see you, too, Adarius. Thank you for informing the students of this year's event. It is critical, after all, that they learn about it now rather than on Friday."

Inviting himself in, Jackson waltzed into the room. "What a glorious display of magic!" He said while waving his hand at the timeline floating near the ceiling.

"Thank you, Jackson," Adarius said, checking the hallway before returning to Jackson's side.

"Call me Jax, please, Adarius!" he scoffed. "How many times do I have to beg … *ask*? Anyway, you and I have some impending matters to discuss. Matters I believe you know about."

"*Obviously*," Adarius joked.

"Is it alright to discuss these things in here? With the class?" Jax asked.

"Yes. It is quite alright. Elder tensions was a keynote in today's lecture."

Jax stood close to Adarius and kept his arms folded at his chest as he eyed the innocent class. "The Dean's Council highly advised against talking about it with you or other faculty members—or any person on campus, for the record. But I figured if any person could lend an ear, it would be you! Every mage is directly involved, so students in every class ought to know. Council's a bunch of grumpy, old beard-scratchers anyway. What do they know? It's fair to inform students about it, right?"

"It's fine," Adarius said, calmly dragging Jax with him to the closed door.

Curious about what the important news was, I fixed my eyes on Jax's mouth. It was difficult, but I think I managed, despite the dozens of pencils having lost interest in the pair and playing frenetic catch-up on the lesson notes.

"The winter solstice is this Friday. The Selection Ceremony is nearing. Is everything in order and prepared for their arrival? The Elders are going to be … present?" He raised his eyebrows and narrowed his eyes to meet Adarius directly. "I hear things, ya know? Playground's no fun when everyone wants a turn on the monkey bars at the same time."

"They'll be present. Not happily, I'm sure. But they'll be there. Everything rides on their shoulders, so, yes, they *will* be there. I'll make sure of it. I can use aggressive persuasion if it calls for it."

Adarius was suddenly adamant about the Elders attending this ceremony. Just minutes ago, he told us that they would never be caught dead in the same room together, let alone stand alongside the others. From my spot in the circle of desks, I sensed apprehension and uncertainty from Adarius. Something felt off. But I wasn't sure what.

"Good. I look forward to seeing them work together again," Jax replied happily.

"Wouldn't count on that, Jackson. We just don't need a dead Elder in front of all these mages."

"It's *Jax*, Adarius. Please! I ask one thing of you—*one* thing! Look, they'll be fine. I'll be there if the wheels start to fall off the cart."

"Oh, trust me, I'm afraid of that, too." Adarius laughed, though not a drop of candor left his tone. "*I* will be there to step in if they lose their place."

"Alright, well, I just wanted to check that everything is in order prior to the ceremony," Jax added coolly, which felt out of key for Adarius's stern face. "It will be flawless, as usual. This is my first Pit! If I may speak freely, I'm quite excited for the spectacle. I'm sure the students are as well—at least, if their blood isn't drawn from the cauldron!" He nudged Adarius on the shoulder and was met with a dejected sneer.

Blood? I questioned, looking at my scant pad of notes. For a couple of seconds, I sat pondering what that meant.

Jax quietly shook Adarius's hand and closed the door behind him as he left the room. I drew circles on the next page while my mind raced with inexplicable ideas.

My head pulled up from the notebook. Suddenly, while watching a strange scene of Sparrow poking holes in a voodoo doll with her pencil, a moment dawned me. When the Seekers came to get me at my village, they brought an empty vial with them. My college invitation acceptance was contingent on my providing a blood sample. They said it was "to determine my magical potential." However, after hearing Jax talk about student blood, I suddenly realized their true intentions. They must have a massive storage room with a vial of blood for every student! Great. It was harder to tell which was worse: the anxiety in my mind, or the gross, sinking feeling now simmering in my stomach.

"That's enough overload for today, class," Adarius said, clearing his throat. He looked at the floating orbs and raised his arm towards them. Opening his hand, Adarius reabsorbed the colorful magic and dissipated from the room. It felt empty without them hovering above us.

"Dismissed."

The encounter with Jax had clearly been unplanned. Adarius looked dreadful; the color had been flushed from his face. The physical drain was evident in his looks, hologram or not.

The class started packing up. Bookbags rustled on the floor as papers, books, and other items were loaded inside. The scraping of chairs felt obnoxiously loud, perhaps because I could still feel the tension from today's lesson and the dean's unanticipated arrival.

In a rush, I tried to scramble down as many quick notes as I could from the lecture. Looking at them now, I realized none of them made any sense; they seemed to run together in a muddled mess. I peeked up from my notebook, but the classroom was empty. All other mages had left, and it was just Adarius and me alone in the room.

I closed the partially blank textbook on my desk, stowed it in my bookbag, and pushed my chair back to stand up. I could hear the commotion of students bustling through the hallway as the other classes let out. With Adarius wiping off the board, I entered the streamline of students heading left and right. It was a horde of young mages, cluttering the halls without a care in the world.

Hugging the wall, I scurried down the hallway. Passing by vacant classrooms, I stuck to the edge and kept my eyes glued to what felt like an undulating floor.

"I don't want to see a fight!" came a shout from a nearby room.

"Won't be me sweeping up the dust when one of them crumbles!" another voice spoke out.

Curious, I retreated backwards to the room where I'd heard the commotion and stood silently outside the door. I sat down and opened my bookbag to make a show of rummaging through it aimlessly to seem occupied. Now within earshot, I listened.

"Art, what are we going to do now?" said the first voice. It was female and sounded frail.

"Amber ..." began the apparent Art. Calming her down, I assume. "There's nothing we can do. We have no power in the decisions of Elders. It's just ... what has to happen, I guess."

"Guess so," she replied.

"They're dangerous and powerful! Surely they can come to a more practical decision than this cruel act." Art's words were stern.

"If anything, Jax should be putting in some objection against this! I understand that Earth is dealing with global warming, famine, hurricanes, and shit, but is The Pit really the *best* answer?"

"You really believe our eccentric Dean can do anything here, Amber? At the very least, it better be a different element than water that wins. Unstable fucking disaster is what those mages are. Water's as unpredictable as the Elders are. Neither have been stable for very long," Art argued.

The way they were talking about my element struck a nerve with me. Not a big enough nerve for me to do anything about. But a nerve, nonetheless. I felt awkward sitting on the opposite wall while stupidly picking up the same pencil ten or fifteen times. Maybe the inconsistencies of Earth's water situations are the reason why my magic is suffering, and my lack of control over it isn't from my hands alone?

Fearing that I might get caught—or worse, what I might overhear next—I rose to my feet and rushed down the hallway.

The hurling winds outside roared against the exit door. I pulled the handle and embarked into the winter fury.

OLIVIA II

I WATCHED EVERY SILENT footstep his sandals made as he approached the door.

"Name is Isaac," Marrick said while turning the knob slightly. "A severe case. That's all the Seekers informed me about. You can solve the rest of the mystery."

Rising to my feet, I stood to see Marrick out.

"I don't want names, Marrick! Anonymous people. I just need to know what's wrong with the kid. Why do the Seekers insist on having you feed me information? Why can't they ever do that themselves? They need my help, yet they refuse to fill me in on things? Feels a lot like they're abusing my ability."

"Well, I think it's because ... because they are ..." he replied cautiously.

"Are afraid of me? Too busy? Don't care? Which excuse is it this time?"

"Yes. To all of those reasons. The Seekers, who occasionally need your help, are afraid of you and your magic. Very busy prepping for this mission. And Silas is a part of your team today, so consider a bit of 'I don't care' in there as well."

"That's pathetic, Marrick. If they need me to play bad cop, I think the good cops can ask me themselves! They're the all-powerful, omniscient Seekers—the sole mages capable of travel between Earth and Penumbra. And you mean to tell me they're too busy and scared to fetch their errand girl on their own?"

"They just don't understand you like I do, Olivia. They don't see you for the person you are. Unlike me. They never will. They see you as a prop in their missions. If Isaac were dealing with an elemental, they'd handle it on their own. But when it comes to a revenant, well ... They do need your help, Olivia. I wish that didn't have to be the case, but it is."

"Whatever," I said. "Did they tell you a time for me to meet them?"

"Usual time. After sunrise, I think. You need me for anything or—"

"Good day, Marrick. You're dismissed," I said irritably, waving a hand for him to leave.

"Okay. Good luck in the morning."

Marrick pulled the door shut behind him. The sound of footsteps hitting stone became softer as he traveled down the staircase.

"Wonderful," I said with a sarcastic smile that faded into disgust.

Wandering over to my simmering soup in the cauldron, I reached into the apothecary cabinet and pulled out a drawer of syringes. I learned throughout my years of Nic's classes that syringes were the easiest way to extract potions from a cauldron for transference into a vial.

Syphoning the golden liquid from the basin, I filled a half dozen tubes and grabbed a roll of masking tape from the drawer. I marked each one with a different letter and pushed them to the corner of the table. Then I leaned over my alchemy table to see out the thin window above it. A twilight glow of purples and blues gleamed across the treetops and cascaded into a beautiful color palette. A few waning clouds waved across the horizon before vanishing like a summer breeze.

"Guess I might as well wait until the sun finally goes down," I said, marking the last piece of tape. "Not like I can sleep or anything ..."

As I bent against the table, I thought about all the orphanages I had been in. It felt like a traveling circus, moving constantly as soon as things started developing nicely. The nurses who looked after me called it a circus, too, and most of them quit their jobs and left the country once I was assigned to their care. I felt like a walking plague—a freak of nature. Bouncing from institution to institution, my life had been a series of nurses and other kids hating me and wanting me dead. Some of the time, I wished them dead, too. I wanted to fear them as much as they feared me. But I was just a kid then.

"That's impossible, though," I said to the window. "Nobody will understand me. Not Marrick. Not Tarik. Especially not the Seekers or the college!"

Then, a dangerous memory interrupted my flashback.

I took the notebook from my table and took inventory of my ingredients. Jotting down the number of each item, I opened the drawers in the apothecary cabinet one by one and checked the shelves to see if Cal and my clients had fulfilled their orders. Once I counted what I already had, I opened the satchel and added today's deliveries.

"It was my parents' fault," I told the notebook. "They deserted me and left me in Russia! They abandoned me."

I pulled out the paper bag of frazzleberries from Tarik, the pouch of rhinomites from Emilee, and the pack of lakefin fish scales from a girl I didn't care to know the name of.

"I wonder why they never loved me. Is it because I was a mistake? Is it because I was a born with a defect? A cursed girl? Or maybe it was the fact that they had no idea what I was capable of and were afraid of finding out?"

I knew what resulted from their abandonment of me: living life in orphanages and group homes, never knowing who my parents were, and being shunned as a freak for most of my childhood. All of that had led to a revenant latching itself onto me when I was thirteen. An elemental is a literal manifestation of an element that lives in The Veil, and a revenant is a corrupted elemental that attaches to a young child's trauma or PTSD. More often than not, the child would die from such a connection. I, however, somehow bonded with mine. How? Don't know. Why? Don't know. But I do know that my *unique* abilities stemmed from that connection. Basically, I had been forced to make sense out of my life when others turned a blind eye.

I'd ask Marrick almost every day when I first arrived. His response tilted one of two ways: tiptoeing around the question without a direct answer or navigating the conversation towards a completely unrelated topic. Do you know how frustrating it is to try and piece together your life year after year, feeling like you take one step forward and two steps back? Which meant, once again, Olivia Virhorn had to explain everything herself!

Without realizing it, I had squeezed the life out of a single rhinomite, forcing its guts out through the eyes and sides of the bug. I sighed and tossed it in the garbage, then scratched out and updated the number I had written down.

A tear fell from my eye, wetting a corner of the page.

"No, Olivia!" I corrected myself while wiping at my watery eyes with my sleeve. "You can't think about them. It's too painful. Too sad. Move on. Think about the extraction. Make sure to clear your mind by that time. A busy mind will not help you or Isaac."

I crushed up the piece of dampened paper and threw it in the garbage as well. Not being able to sleep, I relied on the sunrise and sunset to keep my days straight. Glancing through the window again, I saw an orange-pink glow breaking in the night sky. Morning was coming to take away the final pieces of the black nighttime sea, and I knew what that meant.

"Nearly time," I muttered.

Adding the bugs and ingredients to the cabinet, I tossed in the notebook as well before closing it. I stared at the fading drops of yellow potion at the bottom of the cauldron, which would be gone by the time I returned.

I caught sight of a familiar glass case, hidden behind jars of severed ozeador tongues. They had been another gift from Marrick, on my sixteenth birthday, and his attached note read: *Olivia, now that you're sixteen, don't lose your tongue on me, or I'll take it from your mouth, just like I did with these ozeadors*. That note was in a drawer somewhere; I was sure of it.

I laughed aloud while sliding the jars over and reaching behind them. I pulled out the clouded glass case, covered in dust. It held the skeleton of a small dragon. On one of the first few nights before classes started, I was down in the forest and talking to Cal about how we were going to work together and what was expected of him. Behind a tree, I heard a weird sound. As I walked over to it, I saw this weird, wavy dragon flop out of thin air and catch on fire. The colorful, frilly fins and leafy appendages singed away, almost like a tree limb engulfed in flames. Nearing the burning creature, I picked it up and watched the last bits of its flamboyant body turn into a skeleton, shedding the layers into a pile of ash on the ground. Its magic was withering away into thin air; I watched bits of its energy vanish. The tiny dragon had burned up its whole body, from a seahorse-like beauty into a darkened skeleton. I carried it with both hands back to my old dorm and later that night, holstered it in an empty glass case I had lying around. It must have done something awfully dangerous or fatal to kill itself like that—a task that resulted in its magic evaporated.

Thinking fondly of its once great splendor, I put the case on the windowsill and let the growing light of the sun shine through the glass. I wrote on the case in enchanted black ink with a message for myself: *Never push the limits of your own magic.*

Leaving the case there, I chose a new state of mind and moved to the center of the room. "Been a while since I used my magic for work. So, I should make sure all is good with it. Out of practice for a little. Better see if I'm still as dangerous as the Seekers need me to be," I chuckled.

Looking down at my hands, I channeled the nightmare magic contained within me. I focused my attention on the floor. Suddenly, a black hole appeared a few inches from my feet. Long green tentacles rose from its depths and thrashed around, stretching up to my waist. There were nearly fifteen of them in the slimy group.

Unsure of whether they were octopus or squid, I watched as they flailed around and waved aimlessly in the air.

"Hello, friends!" I said to the black hole. "Good to see you again. Means my magic is still top notch."

I could hear muffled screaming deep down in the hole among the tentacles. Whether they were real or imagined did not matter. It was comforting to hear familiar voices. I simply sat down on my bed, leaned over my knees, and watched them in the open space. It was peaceful. They were so cool and unique. Watching them flail around felt relaxing to me. The tentacles lasted for a few minutes—long enough for time to pass.

But as all good things must end, eventually the tentacles lowered back down into the darkness. The black hole consumed itself shortly after and disappeared.

I looked up at the window and dragon skeleton again.

"Time to meet the Seekers." Walking up to the door, I turned the knob and quietly shut it behind me.

Once outside, I braced against the cold weather and traveled through the woods. Sure, there were sidewalks and paths near the water, easier ways to get to Central Command. But I preferred the woods. I liked them, and they liked me. Few mages frequented these woods.

Before circling the coliseum stadium, I looked back at my neck of trees and smiled, thinking of Cal probably scaring off the new day's morning deliveries.

I rounded the coliseum. It was a grand and extravagant structure of stone. I might have only been in it once or twice. Long and oval-shaped, the coliseum was home to duels and battles classes, all taught by Nero, of course. He would have to be dead before he let someone else teach those.

The college was eerily quiet early in the morning. In a couple hours, irritable, bubbly students would flock to their classes mindlessly like schools of fish. But come back at night once the sun vanishes, and the whole campus would be deserted. Many students used the evenings for studying and practicing their woeful magic. Without the true need for sleep, this time of day was my favorite, both here and in Russia. There was something comforting about being isolated in the world between the midnight moon and the sun's reawakening. Somehow, Tarik understood that, too.

I rounded the administrative building, established as the operations and orientation center for the college. I was never privileged to see it. Marrick had snuck me onto campus, forged most of my records so I could get accepted into classes (I was too young to attend legally), and built the tower for me.

While Central Command was not my official destination, attached to this building was the campus's ornate and beautifully-gothic clock tower. The college has a weird fascination with hidden locations, and its magnum opus was located beneath the tower's stone floor. It was home to the Seekers' debriefing room, which was used to discuss assignments, travel to obtain potential students, rescue mages lost in Penumbra, and meet up for the revenant-removing, Olivia-manipulating missions involving yours truly.

Rumor has it that the college used to house the Seeker HQ on the main floor of the two-story orientation building because they thought it was smart to show new students "the possibilities of magic, and what they can grow up to achieve." Frankly, I was ecstatic that the force-it-down-your-throat mentality was gone; it was a lazy way to showcase that. Magic is beautiful and creative on its own. We didn't need to shove it in people's faces to prove its worth.

"Olivia, you're late," whispered a woman's voice.

I picked up the pace and briskly walked through the door as she held it open. Closing it behind me, Aria's astute voice ushered me inside the clock tower. All stone steps and brass railings, the staircase traveled in a perfectly imperfect spiral up to the belfry. Aria and I walked to the gap in the center and craned our necks to look up the tower like a lighthouse. With the only walkable area being the one we stood on, the clock tower reminded me of a more elaborate and proper obelisk compared to my own.

Aria stepped to the side slightly and knelt to face the stone floor. My view was obscured as the Seeker dropped her wand to the floor and held it there. I listened keenly while she whispered a Latin spell. Abruptly, she rose to her feet, stowed her wand, and turned back to face my emotionless face.

"You know the drill from this point, right?" she asked.

"Not my first rodeo," I answered, disinterested.

We watched the floor quickly slide in half like a parted sea to reveal another spiral staircase, this one made of steel and traveling deep into the darkness underground. I led the way and eventually found the open Seeker HQ as I listened to the floor close above us. Aria took her final step into the room shortly after. Silas stood by the Beacon Board with his arms folded across his chest. Next to a cabinet of flares, scrolls, and syringes of serum, he awaited our arrival.

The pair of Seekers wore lavish suits: white slacks, white undershirt, and white suit jacket fastened at the buttons. A black tie stuck out like a sore thumb as the only article of clothing not resembling an eggshell. Well, that and the black loafers Aria and Silas had on their feet. From the shoulders down, both Seekers were dressed identically to each other, with the only exception being the individual's mask.

A Seeker's mask was their focal point, their coveted feature, distinguishable by all students. Each one throughout the history of the college had its own unique look. No two masks were the same. Aria's mask was a sleek burnt orange mask. It had two eye slits and two curled white waves near the mouth to represent the flowing sands of Africa. Silas's mask was modeled after a Venetian-style plague doctor with the look of a vulture's long face. It was also eggshell white with black eye holes.

"You're late. Almost lit a flare to rescue you two," Silas stated. His mask did not look in our direction but rather studied the Beacon Board.

Silas tapped his fingers to a small pad on the wall and spun towards the portal door. Rushing Aria and me along, he moved in front of the swirling mist. Normally this thin door blended in with the concrete background, showing scenic etched artwork, but whenever the Seekers called upon it, it would become a silvery-blue color and awaken from the wall. I watched the portal grow within the door's limits.

"Isaac. Seventeen years old. Tied up in an abandoned barn outside their village. We'll fill you in further when we arrive. Now, Aria, let's move!" His voice was intense with anticipation and concern. As his mask portrayed, Silas maintained a no-nonsense attitude on the job.

"Solving the mystery is what I do best, Watson. And let's be clear about things here: I am Sherlock on these missions. Since you drag me out of my tower—or I guess have *Marrick* pull me oughta my tower—I dictate how these revenant extractions go. Not you. You may get the tip-off, but I run the show from this point forward. Also ... *stop using names*! Leave it anonymous, please. It is a very simple request."

"Watch that ego of yours, kid." Silas laughed. "Seekers run the show on Seeker extraction missions. If Isaac weren't dealing with a revenant, you'd be cozy and warm in your obelisk, and the adults would handle the situation. It's true we need your help, Olivia, but don't get all high-and-mighty on us. I can knock you down a couple notches."

"Alright, alright. Focus, both of you! We're here to do a job," Aria interjected.

She and I walked to Silas's side, still keeping our distance from him as he finished the mission preparations. Then Silas nodded to each of us.

"Ready?" he asked with dour, narrowed eyes.

"Do I have a choice?" I scowled.

"Nope. Let's move!" Silas demanded.

"Ready, Olivia?" asked Aria in a quieter tone as she stared into the churning colors.

"As I'll ever be."

With her orange mask looking down at me, Aria grabbed my hand. I held onto it. Seekers didn't like to be kept waiting, so we were already in a crunch by the time I arrived. Silas kept a strict schedule, though I won't lie—it was very fun to poke the bear in the meantime.

Silas stepped through first, vanishing from the room and into the portal. Aria and I took a deep breath.

"Why does he have to be so unlikeable?" I griped, shaking my head.

"Just be glad he went first," Aria added.

The two of us walked from Seeker HQ into the swirling, blue mist.

We teleported to a snowy forest with thick beech trees and dense layers of snow on the ground. A light wind whipped between us. I had done plenty of revenant extractions before, but the tension it gave me never went away. With any mission, the kid's chance of death was extremely high, and the trauma affected everyone present.

I used to fear that these displaced revenants would latch themselves onto me, the next best target. But that was not the case, as both elementals and revenants can only have one host across their lifetime. They can survive in The Veil freely, but not on Earth or Penumbra without a human body to latch onto.

"Okay. See that red barn about fifty yards north? That is our target's location," Silas addressed us as he shuffled his feet through the deep white powder.

As the two Seekers set the route, I followed them out of the forest. They pushed on a bit ahead of me to where I could barely hear their stifled speech. We exited the forest into a sprawling meadow. After a couple minutes, Aria slowed to match her speed with mine. Per usual, I brought up the first thing on my mind.

"Silas won't be much help with this, so, I'll ask you: What's actually wrong with the boy?" I asked.

"Isaac is dealing with nightly fevers and bloodlust. The revenant latched itself onto him during his twelfth birthday, when he was searching the house for his presents and found his father dead in his parents' bedroom. His mother, Julia, remarried and moved on with his now-stepdad, Henry. Now almost fifteen, Isaac has developed hatred and resentment for both of them. As a result, his magic is untrained and unpredictable. Two nights ago, he tried attacking his older sister in her sleep. Thankfully, he was unsuccessful. But they believe him still to be incredibly dangerous and highly aggressive."

"Hmmm ... So, the mother was able to push forward in life quicker than her son. The parents do know there's a high chance of him dying, right? They know the consequences?"

"Honestly, I'm not sure. No, probably not. Silas will be watching over you as you work your magic while I comfort the parents. They'll be fine. Your priority is the revenant. We believe it to have almost full control of his body and soul, so expect Isaac to become uncooperative, hostile, and reckless. I'm sure you know all this by now, but it never hurts to reassure you. Be careful, Olivia. We are counting on you to help this poor child and extract the revenant. We'll handle it from there. Bloodlust, as I'm sure you are aware, is an addictive hunger that warps your minds' desires and cravings, forcing you to do things beyond your control. Expect the unexpected from Isaac."

"Yeah, I know. Got it," I replied, keeping my mind focused on the upcoming barn.

A pasture bordered by ranch-style fencing welcomed us to the farm. The rotting wooden fences ran long and far over the rolling hills, which covered several acres of land. Despite the large space, I saw enough to decipher a murder scene.

Silas jumped over the fence and pushed his way to a dead cow. The rancid smell of rotting flesh hung in the air. Sliced open across the neck, the cow's lifeless body was swarming with flies. It sat decaying in the pure white snow, painted in its blood.

"The kid did this. I can tell," Silas said, bending over to inspect the cow's neck and pointing at it. "This slice here—that wasn't done by hand. It was done with magic. No bruises or prints or points of contact." He sniffed at the air. "This was recent, too—only hours ago."

I wondered how reliable his sense of smell was with the mask on.

Aria's mask did not move, nor did my expression. Once the sight and smell of the dead cow hit us, we had known immediately that it was a victim of the boy's bloodlust.

"Safe to say he's in the barn, then?" I asked.

"Yes. As are his parents," Aria said as her partner regrouped with us. He dusted the snow off his pants (though you could not see it, honestly) and readjusted his Venetian mask.

The barn was made of uneven redwood weathered by the winds and climate of Penumbra's harsh winters. It rose nearly twenty-five feet from the dirt and was dotted with bales of hay along the outside. A thin tin roof topped it off.

We crossed out of the pasture to the barn door. Wild screaming and sounds of violence were coming from within.

"We'll do the talking. You watch his actions. Take note of what you'll be up against. We were told this is one of the most violent and sinister cases the Seekers have ever encountered." Silas pushed the rustic barn door open.

Isaac was tied to a rickety wooden post. The squirming teenager wrestled against the tension of the rope wrapped tight across his chest. His hands were hidden, no doubt restrained behind the post. His legs were yanked so hard to the post that they almost molded together. Cow's blood was splattered on Isaac's clothes, randomly splashed from his jacket to his sweatpants. The boy's lips and chin dripped with a telltale crimson color, which redecorated his teeth as he screeched in agony. Isaac's brown eyes looked haunted and desperate. They took notice of me and pleaded through silence to save him. But the wild thrashing of his body showed a different side.

Hiding on a haystack in the corner were the kid's parents. Julia was sobbing into her husband's shoulder as they watched their son cautiously with fear and defeat in their eyes. Once Aria closed the barn door, their attention darted to us.

"Hello," Aria said timidly, motioning for them to remain quiet.

Silas and I maintained our focus on Isaac, who was screaming at the top of his lungs. Words were not what escaped his mouth, for it sounded like a wailing banshee.

"Who ... who are you three?" his father asked reluctantly.

"We are a secret society of priests that deal with dangerous and possessive spirits. Our apprentice here—" Silas gestured to me. "—is the best chance your son has at survival."

"Please help!" cried his desperate mother. "I don't want that demon inside my boy taking his life!"

"We will do our best. There are no promises that your son will make it out of this alive," replied a stern Silas before wandering off to face Isaac head-on.

"Please. It's our son we're worried about. Whatever is inside him has taken over our Isaac. Please! You have to help us! We know the risks, but we have to try. For our son," Henry added.

"That's why we're here. We'll do what we can," Aria reassured them, placing her hand on Julia's shoulder.

Silas, his plague mask bowing to look in my eyes, pulled me to him and leaned down to my ear. I listened to his words, though my eyes never left Isaac, who was wrestling with the revenant.

"Isaac is gone, Olivia. I see it in his eyes, and I know you see it, too. We will watch over his parents to make sure they don't overreact or overstep. This is up to you now. Get that revenant out, fast. The boy, honestly, is not our priority anymore."

"You're feeding me details I already know, Silas. Please. I have dealt with these before. Let me just do my job."

Silas gave Aria a quick nod. "We'll be ready for it when it comes out. Be careful and protect your soul. You never know what these revenants are capable of ..."

His hand on the wand tucked in his pocket, he stepped off to the side near Isaac's parents. I took over Silas's previous spot, face to face with the raving teenager, then I shortly pivoted to catch four very different expressions staring back at me. Aria's orange mask was motionless. Julia's face looked terrified, and she wept into a handkerchief held by Henry, who bounced his eyes between mine and his son's. Lastly, Silas was resolute and strong.

I returned to face Isaac.

Suddenly, the thrashing and writhing ceased. His head, only supported by the rope across his chest and shoulders, drooped forward. His breathing slowed down to an eerie inhuman grunting. Then, Isaac flung his head upright and stared at me. Soulless white pupils glowered into mine. Menacing laughter erupted from the boy's mouth.

"Olivia Virhorn, orphan of Russia. Unloved by her own family," said a harsh demonic voice from Isaac's mouth. "Do you really think you can save young Isaac here? Maybe you can see the resemblance between you two now. Parents gave up on you, lost in your own mind, need help from ... an outside source, forced to fend for yourself. The desire to quench that insatiable hunger. This boy is mine! No magic of yours can change that!"

"Your parents don't believe you're still in there, Isaac, but I do. I'm going to prove them wrong and bring you back, alright? This revenant is using your body as a host, and I need your help to break the connection," I pleaded.

Isaac grinned with a sinister glare before cackling uncontrollably like a hyena on drugs. "I know what you are, Olivia! Your own parents abandoned you when you were a baby because you were a mistake. A mistake! Isaac's parents are desperate to save him now. But where were they when he needed them most? They abandoned him, like yours abandoned you!"

Ignore it, Olivia. Just get the job done. Forget everyone else in the room, I reminded myself.

"I'm going to get you out of there, kid. I believe you are still in there somewhere, and it's my job to get you out." The sincerity in my voice could not be mistaken.

"You can try," that raspy voice replied as it wriggled Isaac's tied hands behind the wooden post. "But even the boy's parents don't want him back. Look at them, cowering in the corner. They don't see their son anymore. They only see me! Those two imbeciles are as anxious to get rid of him as I am to have him! Just give him over to me ... It'll be easier on everyone."

I raised my hands and waved them in silky movements, diving into my magic and avoiding the fearful eyes behind me and the malevolent ones in front of me. In a room full of voices, I focused on the actual boy within his body and channeled the strongest void magic I had.

"Please help me," said a soft voice. This was Isaac's real voice, weak and worried.

"I will," I answered, looking into his brown eyes.

Isaac stopped moving.

"I didn't mean to attack my sister. It wasn't me! I didn't actually attack her. *It* did! It was ... this thing inside me! I can't control those feelings!"

Then, as if a switch had been flipped, I immediately saw the revenant's disgusted glare.

"Don't let the boy fool you, orphan girl! His own bloodlust is growing; I merely forced his hand. How much of his sister's fear is attached to me, huh? Be honest with yourself, Olivia: she only saw Isaac because he *wanted* to attack her. By the way, did you like our work out in the pasture? The cow's blood has sated his desire ... for now. But you know from experience that it will return ..."

Isaac spat in my face, a mixture of saliva and bile. I plunged deep within his spiritual body and saw two souls swirling around his heart, like a pair of sharks circling their prey. As I pulled at the revenant's grasp on him with my magic, I considered Isaac's face. He was lost in a body that was not his anymore. Something else had found exactly what it was searching for.

"Am I going to die?" Isaac asked.

"I don't know," I answered honestly.

"AAAAH!" Isaac screamed in pain, though I could not tell if it was my doing or the revenant's.

"Olivia!" Isaac shouted. "That feeling is coming back! I don't know if I'll be able to contain it this time. It's getting ... much ... stronger ..."

"Then don't try," I replied.

"Olivia ... It hurts. It's fighting back! I don't know if I can contain it much longer." Tears streaked down Issac's cheeks before he fell forward, body suspended by the ropes. But those tears were betrayed by a bellowing, hearty laugh ringing out in the barn.

"Try and try! As hard as you want!" The revenant cackled and forced Isaac's head to smile greedily up to the sky. "His bloodlust is coming back. The more he tries to suppress it, the more damage it will do. I will feed on everyone in this room!" Isaac's face spun to his parents and snarled before returning to its main target: me. "And frankly, I don't care how powerful and in control you think you are. You're wrong! The kid. Will not. Make it. Out of this. Alive!"

"Shut your forsaken mouth!" I shouted at Isaac, finding it hard to see the boy anymore myself.

Keeping one hand focused on the intertwined souls, I rapidly spun around and scowled at the pair of eyes attached to Isaac's parents. A yearning frustration burned within me, like the feeling I got when thinking of my own parents.

"Your fear and loathing of your son is not helping! He's still your son, you know? Don't give up on him so easily! That's what led you to this barn in the first place. If you had tried with Isaac prior to this point, you'd still be in your two-level cottage in the village, safely away from this farm miles down the road."

"That is not our Isaac! That is not our son tied to that post. It's something entirely different!" Henry retorted, foolishly believing every word he said.

"I told you, Olivia. See? His parents have deserted him already. Take their lead and give up yourself, because I'm not done with him yet. We have so much more to accomplish together. Sound familiar? But please, do keep trying. I look forward to haunting your nightmares as well." The revenant's white eyes stared at me, with Isaac's distant ones trapped behind them.

"I don't have nightmares," I snarled at Isaac. "I'm more afraid of people like that." My head flicked back to indicate the couple seated on the hay bale.

"I'll be dead after this, won't I?" Isaac said with eyes wide and red.

"You'll be fine," I reassured him while pulling harder on the beast within his chest.

"Don't lie to him!" screeched the hoarse voice.

"What's happening to him?!" Henry demanded.

"I don't wanna die, Olivia! If it means I get to live, don't remove this thing! I want to live!"

"What is happening to my boy?!" added a frantic Julia, who was holding her husband back from lunging at me.

"He's already dead, according to both of you!" I jumped in, thrashing my head at them.

"Olivia! You're fighting that revenant, not Isaac's parents. Please! Focus on the boy!" Aria cried to me, beckoning for my attention. "Isaac is fighting the revenant and needs your help," she continued, looking to Silas for a better answer.

"What's going on? You can get my boy out of there, right?" hollered Henry, directing his scowl at Silas's mask. "Right?!"

"Isaac, this is your mother. I know you're still in there. Your father and I love you very much, and we just want you to be safe. Please fight this thing as hard as you can. We believe in you!"

"You both once had your chance to be parents! He just needed you to listen for five minutes! He saw his own father dead. Dead! Not sleeping, not resting—dead! And you, Julia, moved on with this other man *much* sooner than your son accepted. So, this revenant within him, this trauma born from that day ... is your fault. If you knew him or cared for him at all, you would've realized Isaac was struggling long before that revenant attached itself to him! Now something else has taken over." I turned back to face the boy's scared eyes. "Isaac, listen to my words, not theirs. Listen to me when I say I feel your pain. I hear you, Isaac. I hear your hurt and your sadness. But don't let that beast inside you control you. Listen to my words ..." I reassured him.

"OLIVIA!" Aria shouted. "You have a job to do. Extract the revenant and save Issac. You are here to fight the revenant, not this boy's parents! His parents are not your own. Now, get your shit together, work your magic, and remove this damn thing! Do your job ..."

"Mom? Dad? You're here, too?" the disoriented teen asked, puzzled.

"It's almost out. This last part is the most painful. Do you understand me?" I said, snapping at him to return his focus to me.

Isaac looked hopefully at his parents before I forced his head to meet mine. "Okay. Yes. Yeah, we understand you," he replied fearfully. White eyes inched into view as the brown ones rolled back in his head.

"Not good at all if he is saying 'we,'" I admitted.

"Wha—what do you mean?" Julia stuttered.

"If you don't know the significance of your son using 'we' to describe his own mind, then perhaps you are more lost than he is. It means he's already succumbed to the revenant's grip ..."

He nodded rapidly, sweating from his long, wavy hair as he wept.

Screaming a battle cry and draining my own energy, I pulled with all my might. Soon, I began sweating as well, and I felt the dark magic within me slowly becoming weaker.

I shouted.

Isaac shouted.

"What's happening? Will someone please answer me?!" screamed his father.

"Will someone shut them up, please?" I demanded. Focusing on Isaac's eyes behind the revenant's white pupils, I watched Isaac horrifyingly alternate between the two.

"Olivia!" Aria snapped.

The barn started to shake and rattle on its foundation. The creaking wood felt as if it were loosening at the bolts. Screams from Isaac and myself echoed inside—the only sounds I could hear.

I yelled.

Isaac yelled.

I yelled.

The revenant yelled louder.

Our three screams merged into one enormous screech, until mine was the only one left.

I suddenly stopped. The barn went quiet. I refocused on Isaac's face. My body was now as exhausted as his. His head was drooped forward again, hanging by the highest strand of rope. His body, to my horror, stood motionless.

Looking down at my hands, I noticed strands of black coursing through my veins. These were the dark magic that burns in my blood and marks the source where it had come from.

"What ... what is that thing?!" screeched Julia as she pointed behind the wooden post Isaac was tied to.

I stepped away from the boy, wobbling slightly on my feet. Still staring at the top of Isaac's head, I prayed for a response—any response. But none came.

Behind the post, rising from a pool of blood, was Isaac's revenant. It had no body up until the torso, which was so tight that I could see every rib and muscle pulsating beneath the thin red skin. Long biceps stretched nearly to the floor as bucket-sized hands clawed their nails at the dirt. It had no face, either—just a wide mouth of sharp teeth dripping blood and drool.

"Get the boy down from there. We'll take care of the revenant!" Silas shouted while drawing his wand and directing Aria to flank Isaac with him. Aria went left of the wooden post as Silas moved right. The pair cast simultaneous blasts of bright light at the creature. It shrieked and howled before imploding into bubbling liquid, which soaked into the muddy ground.

Meanwhile, looking as though she would faint, Julia leaned back against the haystack.

"I'll watch her," Aria said, making sure the revenant was completely gone, then joining the mother to keep her upright. Julia placed a weary hand on the hay bale and breathed prayers to herself.

I stood against Isaac, holding his back with one hand and his head with the other. Henry rushed over to undo the rope. Silas assisted. I staggered back a few steps and watched the two men lay Isaac's body on the ground. Julia broke free from Aria's restraint and rushed to her son's side.

"We need to move soon," Silas whispered.

"I agree," I said.

"Our job is done here, Olivia," he said, grabbing my shoulder and pushing me towards the barn door. "The balance is in order, and it was the kid's decision. We must disappear before they start asking questions."

"I know! I get it," I insisted.

Aria understood and followed his lead.

The two pushed ahead of me once I wiggled loose from Silas's grip. I stood at the barn doorway and watched the rest of the scene play out.

"Isaac? Isaac, please answer! Please don't do this to me! Please, Isaac! I love you!" Julia's screaming and crying became so frantic and surreal that it was nearly inaudible. Feeling for a heartbeat, Henry's hands lay on Isaac's chest. Yet we all knew he would not hear one. "My boy! He's my boy!"

"That's not what you showed him a few minutes ago!" I chimed in.

"You need to leave! All of you!" Henry screamed. "Ha'thar has no place in his new world for you! You're all demons! You killed my *son*! You killed my Isaac." He launched over his son's body at me.

"And you need to feel something for once! Now that he's gone, maybe you'll realize you should have jumped in sooner. At least one of us is at peace, knowing that the job has been taken care of."

Julia fell onto her son's chest and simply wailed.

"Get out of here! *NOW!*"

Turning from the dreadful sight of Henry, Julia, and Isaac's body, I walked away from the barn. I knew their dread and sadness had come too late.

Just like my parents: They quit trying when the going gets tough. So much easier to call for help than to answer the difficult questions yourself.

I sped up to catch up with Silas and Aria, who were waiting at the edge of the forest as I weaved around the dead cow and hopped the fence. I rejoined the two Seekers and continued walking at their side with my face bent down to the perfectly white snow. I saw so much red blood and brown dirt that the snow felt like an illusion.

We soon came to the teleportation spot where we had first arrived. With Silas to my right and Aria to my left, they each raised a hand towards a pair of trees. Their hands met in front of me before they traveled in a circular motion over the ground. Another portal opened out of thin air and formed a swirling silvery-blue mist between trees.

"You could have been more understanding in there, Olivia. Those parents lost their son today," Aria said empathetically.

"My parents lost their daughter seventeen years ago. Their choice, not mine. That boy's parents lost their son tonight. Their choice, not his. Isaac needed help, and they didn't help him, so he turned to the revenant for comfort. These things find you at your darkest moment and show you the light. And look, I moved on, and I turned out fine. So will they. Clearly the mother at least is able to move on pretty quickly."

"Time to head back to the college," Silas said, blankly watching the portal.

He and I eyed each other simultaneously.

"You're right," Aria said timidly.

With their hands in mine, the trio of us stepped into the portal.

KAMAUL II

THREE NURSES HUDDLED AROUND me in my hospital bed. Heather I recognized, because I had seen her ... Ignore that. The reasons for my familiarity to her are better left unsaid. Nevertheless, the youthful British poison mage grinned sympathetically at me. To her left and right, Heather introduced the newcomers, Mason and Maggie, who glanced over my wounds while no doubt mindlessly planning a course of action.

"Hello again, Mr. Metjen," Heather said sweetly, rotating my shoulder and lifting it for the other nurses to see.

"Easy!" I groaned, looking between the three. "Easy with those hands, unless you want to lose 'em! But yes, hi."

"Another difficult Gladiator lesson?" she muttered.

Heather knelt to inspect the cuts along my shoulder blade, where the blood had dried. Scabs were beginning to form. Maggie and Mason proceeded with the usual questions and prep work. Their poison colleague obviously held the reins during surgery; she was quite talented and had graduated with top honors about nine years ago. She and I had come to know each other a little too well, but I never made her job any easier.

"Mason," Heather said, ushering him behind me as she put on a pair of gloves. "You stitch up this one." She motioned for Maggie to do the same on my cheek. "Maggie, you're on the cut below his eye. I, on the other hand, am gonna remove the toxin. Report was of a 'mysterious hydra venom.' So, this oughta be a fun time for our favorite Egyptian."

She winked at me. I mocked the niceness and glared at her two henchmen.

My eyes redirected immediately back to Heather once she pulled her wand from her hair clip. Flowing brunette hair rippled down her purple scrubs like a waterfall. She fixed a few straggling pieces at her ears and reworked it all into a squishy ponytail. A long, slender birchwood wand, similar in color to limestone, was held delicately in her hand. It was magnificent, and I made a point of recalling its craftsmanship whenever she used it.

"This is going to sting, Kamaul. I'm sure you know that, as this isn't your first rodeo with poison removal. But it's procedure to go over it each time. I'm going to extract it from your shoulder wound while Mason is sewing it up. Are you ready?" she said softly.

"Lovely wand, by the way," I said, ignoring her spiel.

"I am well aware. But thank you," she answered, sadistically placing its tip at the claw mark.

Maggie finished stitching up my cheek with black thread and cut the excess with a tiny knife. Mason, however, was out of sight, which infuriated me. I only trusted Heather to treat me—not these newbie fools. Still, the feeling of her wand touching my fresh wound blocked out my annoyance, and my eyes darted down to watch.

I focused my discomfort and frustration towards Heather for the duration of the toxin removal. Meanwhile, the other nurses took a step out of the way.

Her wand glowed pale white, then its light began to illuminate brighter; I watched every moment of the process. After a few seconds, a slimy tar-like goo streamed out of my shoulder and absorbed into the birch wand's core. The toxin infused the wand with midnight black until the final drops soaked in. With a light whooshing sound, Heather flushed out the poison and returned her wand to its original shade.

Bones and muscles tensed inside me as I fought the poison's grasp. Heather lifted the wand and tucked it behind her ear like a flower. Then Mason hurried to me again and began hastily stitching up the wound as fresh blood oozed from the once-dried area. Small thread was woven into my skin in my peripheral vision while Maggie soaked up the dripping blood with a wet rag to prevent any of it from splattering on their precious floors. Heather's medical staff was not as tender as she was; they put great pressure into the patchwork.

"How you feeling?" Heather asked, tossing her gloves aside and observing Maggie and Mason.

"My face should answer your question pretty well," I retorted.

"Excellent." She chuckled nervously. "Well, good, 'cause that was a nasty infection. Anyone other than yours truly wouldn't have been successful in removing it."

I could tell she was clamoring for a compliment, so I obliged. "What a magician you are, Heather!" I beamed jokingly. "So talented. So one of a kind."

"Aww, why, thank you, Kamaul." She grinned, cleaning up the rest of the mess and sending the other two out of the room to dispose of it.

"Keep some of that blood on your floor." I winked, sliding up to a sitting position on the edge of the bed before standing up. "It's worth more than any vial the college has in their files, you know."

"Oh, Kamaul ..." She sighed, shaking her head and keeping her arms out to catch me if needed. "How wonderful you would be if you weren't a pretentious, selfish jerk. I'm glad Dahir and your followers like you, because while I love our regular visitations, I'm not as much a fan of you personally."

"Missing out!" I gestured as if to mark the conclusion of a final act.

"Ehhh ... no," she added matter-of-factly. "I'll just wait and see you tomorrow. You're the most frequent customer I have."

"Ha ha!" I snarked, rubbing the fresh stitches on my cheeks and shoulder.

"Go back home, Kamaul. And keep an eye on those in case they bleed. If they do, I need you back here ASAP, 'cause it means the infection has returned."

"You got it, boss," I replied. "Noted every word of that."

I strolled out of the hospital room.

"Looks like I get the last laugh," Heather yelled after me. "I sent Maggie to tell Dahir the same thing. Because I know you, bud, and I know you don't do anything anyone tells you to ... unless its Nero."

"You're annoying. I'm leaving!" I taunted, turning the corner and moving out of earshot.

Making a couple lefts and rights, I arrived at the lobby, where my followers were anxiously anticipating my entrance. Dahir, Mina, Gillian, and Samara walked in a cluster as I silently joined them and pushed through the infirmary's exit.

Samara and Gillian were two peas in a pod—inseparable even when I was not around. Samara, a tall blonde girl with great sense of fashion, had joined my group after a Gladiator event during my first year. She was dating Elias at that time but dumped him shortly after and fell in love with me. I do not fall in love with anyone, so I livened up to her company instead and simply let her know I was not one to date. Gillian, on the other hand, had an ear-piercingly annoying voice that drove holes into your brain. She was a few bricks short of a full load, if you know what

I mean. Nothing against her at all, though; it was good to have a die-hard sidekick attached to your hip.

Mina was the interesting one. She had actually become a Kamaul groupie by way of Dahir. A pixie-cut-haired curiosity, Mina became friends with the girls, yet kept a close eye on my best friend. Ankhor Dahir was his real name, but I usually called him Dahir. He didn't mind it. He was one of the few people in the college from Egypt who knew about life there and how difficult our transition was. I had come from wealth, and he from poverty, but that didn't faze either one of us, as Dahir and I connected almost immediately. Eventually, it molded into this friendship we have now. Despite his charm and incessant nosiness, however, I never confessed to him about my true past: the path to my father's crown, an arranged marriage to Taira, and my perfect departure from that mess. A little tick in him brought it up once in a blue moon. Poor Dahir, though; he'll never know a thing about it. No one in my collegiate tenure had even gotten the slightest clue at my hidden truths. Better off I keep it that way, too.

Samara ran her fingers over my shoulder stitches. I instinctively brushed them away.

"Those are fresh, Samara!" Gillian interjected, talking down to her. "You can't just run your fingers over a healing wound. That's what makes it hurt."

"Uh, thanks, Gillian," I added awkwardly. 'You sure ... know how I'm feeling."

"Does it hurt, Your Highness?" Mina asked, peering at my cheek.

"Of course it hurts!" I yelled, feeling minor rage burning hot in my heart. "But I can manage. I'm stronger than the average man, after all."

"You're right, Kamaul," Samara stammered. "That's—that's why I touched it. I-I knew you could handle the pain." I heard the uncertainty in her voice and saw the fragility in her bones.

"Nice save," Gillian whispered, not so quietly.

I gestured towards where we were heading and headed off around the elemental areas.

"Baffy and Bosamma said all three of those creatures you fought looked tough," Mina said.

"To them, I'm sure they did," I interjected.

"Yeah, Mina. Kamaul took the whole thing as a light jog, thank you very much," said Gillian. She and Samara were flexing their muscles and swinging imaginary swords in the air.

Evenings at the college were often breathtaking sights. A rose-pink horizon overlapped with the black night sky. Most nights featured a thin layer of mist tucked below the moon's shadowed rays. Quiet and relaxing, these nights had become one of the premier examples of why I stayed at the college.

As the female groupies walked slightly ahead of Dahir and me, we slowed down once we hit The Fire Courtyard's Elder statue and talked about the rest of the Gladiator events while letting the ladies carry on ahead.

"I need to go back!" I started to tell Dahir as I watched the moon come out of hiding. "I miss that class already. I miss that rush of battle. I miss the adrenaline in my veins. I need it, Dahir! I really need it. Makes me feel alive!"

"I get that. It's your comfort zone—your palace of carnage. You'll be back next week," Dahir replied with a lighthearted chuckle.

"You know the feeling of your brain salivating at the thought of killing something? The hunger kicking in as it charges your adrenaline ... The bulge of your biceps tightening around its neck for the audience's pleasure ... The satisfaction of slicing its tender little throat ..."

"I guess so?" Dahir shrugged. "I love being in battle; don't get me wrong. But I'm personally more of a mage warrior than a combat one. But that last part about the ... uhhh ... slicing of someone's throat and stuff? That's all you, man." He laughed as his eyes glanced over the Fire Elder statue of Magnus. I laughed, too, playing off what I'd said as a joke, but knowing it was serious.

We caught up with the girls. The group of us was heading to Market Square, a central hub for food, drink, and shops. It was a glorious maze of delicious foods, blacksmith booths, and designer shops. The market served as the meeting grounds for every mage and often served as the place where students of different elements could come together. Unlike during the day, evenings at Market Square seemed to exist only for those who couldn't bear to be in their dorms at night. Normal operating hours brought in a majority of the students. So, my crew and I always flocked to it after that time for the best deals and more intimate shopping sessions.

"Looking for anything in particular, Pharaoh?" Samara asked as she scanned the store facades for valuables. Mina's eyes seemed to follow exactly where Samara looked, just with a slight delay.

"Best armor and weapons gold can buy," I answered.

Dahir laughed. He knew my answer before I even opened my mouth because it was the same response every time we came down to the market. Clothes and food only lasted for so long until you moved on to something new. But weapons have a life of their own. I wanted to build an arsenal of the most powerful, unique, and damage-inducing axes, swords, knives, spears, and whatever else I could find to put in my dorm. I wanted a magnificent portfolio of steel-crafted creations for blood and mayhem—an ever-expanding history of combat over the ages.

"What weapons are you lookin' to buy?" asked Gillian. She and Mina acted out scenes from my Gladiator greatest hits, where I took down the walking meathead Bosamma with my bare hands, bested Solomon in a typical yet laughable Roman shield-sword fight, and fought in a crazy slag-versus-wildfire after-class session between Nero and me, in which I held my own for longer than he gave me credit for. Of course, nobody in this group had been there to witness the glory in person, so I had to reenact each one like a play.

I made them stop acting like fools when Samara and Mina began bowing at Gillian's feet. Doing that for me was one thing. But for each other? It just looked dumb.

"Ladies, get ahold of yourselves!" I hollered. "Let's divide and conquer these booths and seek out the best fighting equipment they have. Remember, two key things when picking out items for me: how much blood will it shed, and how good will I look wielding it?"

Hopefully taking mental notes to relay to the girls, Dahir grunted his approval. "Matter of fact, Mina, why don't you come with me?" he said, reaching out a hand for her to hold. "We'll search for armor and stuff, while the three of them look for ... whatever Kamaul's fiery heart desires."

Mina gladly took hold of Dahir's hand, and the two strolled off towards the south side of Market Square, a location known for shields and helmets. He flexed his arms to bulge against her hand as it wrapped around his bicep, and the pair turned the corner and went out of sight.

Gillian, Samara, and I traveled in the opposite direction towards the more lavish and luxurious booths. These were owned and operated by graduated fire mages who followed the blacksmith legends before them and forged greater weapons each and every day. Of course I knew other elements existed at the college and across the worlds and blah blah blah, but they were all frail in comparison to the great power of fire magic. I refused to believe the five natural elemental bases were equal, as I had seen firsthand the mayhem and destruction fire could truly inflict.

Heading to the first booth, I greeted the overjoyed blacksmith and peeked at his selection.

"Kamaul!" shouted the man from behind the counter. "My new favorite customer! The big spender himself! A man of money and mystery."

"You don't know me, peasant!" I hollered. In the blink of an eye, the entire marketplace disappeared, and silence fell around me. I only saw myself and the weak salesman. "You know nothing of my life in Egypt. You'll keep to your own business if you know what's good for you!"

The vender took a panicked step away from me and began aimlessly figuring out something to put his mind to. I kept my eyes on him, though, and let the fury blaze through my gaze.

"Kamaul," said Gillian, trying to soothe my anger. "Don't mind this man. He doesn't know what he's talking about. Time to move on, huh?"

"Allow me to be hostile if I want to, Gillian! I will calm down when I'm ready," I exclaimed, shifting my eyes to her pale skin.

"You're right, Your Highness. It was not my place to speak up. But believe me, if you may: This laborer is not worth it. Use that anger towards something that warrants it."

"Fine," I agreed bluntly.

I gave in and simmered down. I honestly had no clue as to the vendor's name; nor did I know how he knew mine. Good word travels fast, I guess.

The stout, overly friendly salesclerk wandered the store while chuckling to himself and nonchalantly peeking out from behind items to see what I was looking at. Like a hungry cat patiently stalking its prey, I glanced behind me every few seconds to see where he adjusted himself to. His eyes never focused on Gillian or Samara, which I found irritating and a poor business decision. I might have an eye for glamor and bone-crushing weaponry, but the ladies had nice taste of their own.

"How much is this?" asked Gillian, pointing to a bronze longsword.

Gentle and giddy, the man replied with an outrageous amount for such a mediocre weapon. "Six thousand gold."

I howled a hearty, disrespectful laugh that echoed around the shop. Oddly the vendor let out a chuckle, too, trying to hide the fact that he was ripping people off. Gillian and Samara stared at the salesman yet remained silent. Instead, they looked for my assessment of Gillian's choice of weapon. My facial expression blatantly showed that I was not impressed. Taking the hint, Samara gestured for Gillian to follow her, retreating from the booth towards the next to avoid the vendor's laughter.

Turning around to leave the booth after the girls, I spoke one final piece of advice to the friendly salesman. "I wouldn't give you the sandal off my foot for that garbage sword."

Ignoring the annoying smile on his face, I left the booth, shook my head in disbelief, and caught up with Gillian and Samara a few shops down the row.

"That sword was pathetic," Samara said.

"I agree. Move on, though. Next store!" I encouraged.

"Wonder if Dahir and Mina are having any luck?" Gillian asked.

"Hopefully, 'cause we're not having any so far," I added.

"Before we go into the next shop, what kinda weapon are you looking for, Your Highness?"

"Anything that looks good with my hands around the handle. Looks good coming down on an enemy. Point to anything you like, and I'll let you know my thoughts," I clarified as we entered the next stand.

I turned to the left, opposite of where the blonde and brunette headed, and immediately loved this one's selection compared to the first. Then, I saw it—something that finally caught my attention for the right reasons. A thick, polished wooden handle curved down from the steel axe head. Beautiful, wavy orange carvings were etched into the silver blade. It looked to be from Earth, too, based on the design and markings. Perhaps Norse or German? Big and grand, the battle axe hung on the wall amidst weak, feeble swords and knives that shined in their gleam and reflection.

"That one," I said. "How much?" "Unfortunately, that axe is already sold," spoke a soft, kind voice from behind a rack of armored shields. She must have known instinctively which battle axe I was talking about, because she couldn't see me nor it. "Sold this morning actually," she added, coming into view shortly after.

"Already sold? Then why is it still hanging on the hook?" I asked unpleasantly.

"Wanted to show off the prized possession someone bought at our shop," replied the proud shopkeeper, who was putting away more shields as she spoke.

"That makes no sense!" I shouted and pivoted around to stare deep into the woman's eyes. "How much did you sell it for?!"

"Nearly seventy-five hundred gold."

Her voice was so tender and gentle, despite my rising temper, that it made me furious.

"I'll buy it for eight thousand right now. I have it. I'll give it to you."

"Sir, this particular axe is already sold. I cannot sell it again," she replied.

"Far too cheaply, and not to the right person. You'd be selling this wonderful craftsmanship to a person who actually knows the value and beauty of it—not some scumbag who wants to flaunt a new purchase. Sell it to me, the king of Egypt."

"King of where? This is The College of Adarius, sir. No Egypt here." She snuck around me and conveniently grabbed the axe off the hook before heading over to the clerk's counter. "But you're right. If this axe is sold, it should be off the shelf, off-limits. I'm sorry, but this item is no longer for sale."

"I wish there was something I could do or say to change your mind ..."

Gillian and Samara came around a corner to catch the action.

"I really am sorry, Mister ... uhhh ...?" she started, prodding for a name.

"Kamaul, pharaoh and king of Egypt, like I said. But you can just call me Kamaul ... or the highest spender in your store's history, when I purchase that axe for a price of your choosing. Eight thousand gold? Nine thousand? Make it ten thousand, if you want. Gold is not the issue. Not being in possession of this exquisite weapon is. So, what do ya say?"

"I say, unfortunately, I can't sell this axe to you, Mister Kamaul. We already sold it. I agree, it is beautiful and exquisite, as you call it, but it's already been claimed."

I could tell she wasn't selling it to me, so I needed to up the charm. Based on Gillian's giddy expression of excitement, I knew she was ready to see it cranked up to eleven as well. Samara blankly modeled her face to match Gillian's anticipation.

"Tell me how a proud, attractive saleswoman like yourself can turn down such a generous offer. Seriously, name your price. I am willing to put it on the table." I leaned on the counter and flexed my upper bicep in her direction as she turned around from pricing items.

"As impressive as that is, I still can't do the deal. I truly am sorry. I can't disappoint the person who already bought it." I could tell she was torn between the two buyers; thus, I had to amp the charm meter a little bit higher to convince her fully of my proposition.

With a simple snap behind my back, Gillian briskly walked up behind me, dropped a bag of coins into my hand, and wheeled around the racks of hanging swords to rejoin Samara. I snapped my fingers again, and Gillian came running up to the counter and tossed another coin bag onto it. I tried to sway the blue-eyed, redheaded vendor behind the counter and maintained eye contact with her each time I laid a bag down.

"Tell me when to stop. Or don't ... Doesn't matter to me. I'll lay out my entire worth of gold until you sell me that battle axe. Something's gotta give here, miss." My tone was pleasant.

I snapped once more, and Gillian rushed back to me to drop another bag next to the others. Three bags of coins now sat in a perfect line between the shopkeeper and me.

"I'll stay here all night with you. When closing time comes, I will walk oughta here with that axe in my hands."

Four bags on the counter.

"Not even close. I know. But we're getting there," I insisted.

Five bags.

I flung my right hand in the air towards the suspended axes and daggers. "You can close if you'd like. The amount of gold in these bags is enough to purchase every weapon hung up on those walls."

Six bags. Seven ...

"Look at that. *Seven* bags of gold. Seven thousand in total. Too little for that stunning craftsmanship, if you ask me. Can't imagine cheating a lovely saleswoman like yourself out of making *another* great sale." I winked at her and tipped my head towards the counter.

"That is a lot of gold," she sighed and smiled.

"Could be even more!" I exclaimed.

I snapped rapidly a few times as Gillian and Samara dropped three more bags of coins.

"Ten thousand gold! Shall we make it more? I'm not trying to get you in trouble, honestly. Just hoping you'll sell that item to a better buyer and make something extra on the side. What do ya say?"

"Okay, okay. I submit." Laughing, the vendor dragged the heavy pile of bags closer to her and put a hand out to stop me from throwing more onto the pile.

"Ten thousand gold it is, then?" I asked, thrilled.

"Yes. But don't tell anyone. I'll just act like it was a canceled sale and that the next highest bidder gave me a better offer."

"You, miss, are an elegant, graceful woman and are going to make a killing one day. I swear it. Pleasure doing business with you. In fact ... keep the rest for your troubles. No problem at all. Think of it as a small thanks from me to you." I tossed my remaining coin bags onto the counter and began to walk towards the axe.

"Pleasure doing business with you, too ... Your Highness."

Pulling a small scale from under the counter, she gently weighed each bag for the correct amount. Knowing it was already perfect, I watched the wide grin spread across her face, and a pink tint shone in her cheeks as she blushed with embarrassment.

"If you keep handling business like this, and looking this gorgeous doing it, I'll be here every day to take product off your hands."

As she shrugged and giggled, the rose in her cheeks turned to a vibrant red as I lifted the battle axe from its hooks and towards Gillian and Samara. Lightly smirking, the ladies were shocked that I had been successful in my endeavors. They started walking out of the booth while I followed with the new prized possession in my grasp.

Mina and Dahir appeared from a booth next door and joined up with us.

"Find anything of value?" I asked with a dangerous grin.

"I see you did," Dahir answered.

"I sure did. Had to do a little bargaining, but eventually got my way. Ladies, why don't we call it a night? Early start to tomorrow instead? Let Dahir and I discuss some manly battle stuff with my new weapon." I tried to say it as politely as I could.

"Totally," they said in unison.

I gave them all a quick nod goodbye while Dahir hugged Mina, then the three girls turned to face the market's exit. Dahir and I waited for them to get out of view before wrapping around westward in the direction of the fields.

"What do you think of Mina?" Dahir asked, glancing down at the axe's intricate markings.

"Not my type at all, really. But she's a sweet girl, and interesting to talk to, I suppose," I replied, confused.

"I meant for *me*, Kamaul," Dahir corrected, staring out at her in the distance.

"Well, I'm not going to go for her. She's all yours." I chuckled.

"Wanna go out in the fields and try out your battle axe against my ice magic? A little target practice session?"

"Been waitin' for you to ask, man!"

As we walked past the rows of stores, I watched the vendors roll down the drapes in front of their booths. All the shops around us had closed for the day. I knew at least one fine vendor had made a massive profit this evening.

Squeezing our way through the closing shops, Dahir and I made it out to the open fields.

"Yo, Kamaul!" shouted Jett's voice, erupting out of Market Square. His shoes pounded on the grass as he fervently neared us.

I spun around to face him while already knowing this interaction would end like our previous ones. Several bloody noses and bruised bones had often resulted from our other encounters with each other. His heavyset figure made him an easy target, but a balanced attack of punches and muscles matching mine equipped him with a powerful arsenal. He had sun-bleached brown hair and a mustache that brought your eyes to the scars on his neck and chin. While a few of them were tributes to my fists, the rest were from brawls with his father back in Calonia, a large city-town in Penumbra.

"What do you want, Jett? Bored of stealing candy from the novices already?" I taunted, standing my ground as he approached.

"I have a problem with you, Kamaul."

"Shocker!" I replied sarcastically, eyeing his overzealous physique. "And what might that be?"

"You stole that axe from me, earthling! So, listen loud and clear ... " Jett hollered through gritted teeth.

Earthling.

I tuned out after he said it; a repressed anger thrummed through my veins. *Earthing?!* I hadn't heard that term in long time, and older students refrain from using it altogether ... But, oh, if Jett wanted a fight, I was itching to start one now. Earthling was a heinous slur used by students native to Penumbra against those of Earth origin. It basically inferred that we were tainted meat, imposters at the college, inferior to anyone actually born in Penumbra ... as if it honestly makes a fucking difference! It's a term anyone would take offense to. Some, like myself, took matters into their own hands to resolve such heresy.

"You stole that axe from me, Kamaul! I purchased it from Dana's shop—fair and square. Then Your Arrogancy waltzed in and stole it! You think you're some sort of king here, Kamaul, but you're not! Not in fucking Egypt, and not here. Now, I plan to take it back."

"Watch it, pal!" I snapped, firmly pressing my face to his. "You want more scars for that growing collection on your neck? Well, if you really want a repeat of last time, I can arrange that."

Dahir inched a step between us and tried to squeeze me away from Jett by placing his hands on my shoulders to walk me backwards. But I pushed him aside and got back in Jett's face. He puffed a loud snort onto my lips like an angry bull. I nearly dropped him to the floor and cut his knees out from under his fat—

"Kamaul," Dahir whispered, now hidden to my left. "You just left the infirmary. Don't try and go back there. He's not worth it, and you know that! C'mon, man, let's just head back."

"Aww. Listen to your jester. Listen to the puppy barking for your attention," Jett provoked.

"Shut up, Dahir!" I flicked my words at Jett, but he knew they weren't directed at him. "I can handle myself, thank you very much."

"I doubt that," Jett intervened. "Run along now, Dahir, and let the grown-ups talk."

Mumbling angrily to himself, Dahir scoffed at the two of us and moved out of sight.

"You. Me. Coliseum. Right now. A little magic-versus-melee duel. I'll even let you use my axe. That way you at least get to sample it before I officially add it to my arsenal," Jett growled.

"Deal!" I shouted immediately, barely allowing him to finish.

With my blood boiling and adrenaline playing my muscles like a fiddle on fire, I turned away from Jett and held the steel axe tight in my palm. I was so hot at the moment that my fingers felt like molten lava against its handle.

Jett, Dahir, and I walked silently around the market and soon arrived at the coliseum. Typically, a short break between confrontation and battle dimmed my burning desire to rip the other's head off. Not this time, though, because I'd bought that axe just as fairly as he did! He had waited too late in the day and trusted that it would be there at when the store closed. Big mistake, pal, and I'm not as easy a bargainer as the chick at the shop.

Being back in the coliseum's grand presence gave me a warm sensation. We had a love-hate relationship with each other: I loved standing in its glory and hated losing that spotlight. Thanks to Jett, I was about to be back in the limelight again, and he was about to leave on a stretcher.

With his wand, a custodian was hosing off the bleachers under a trio of floating lanterns. Water sprayed onto the stone as he shuffled through the empty stands. Blind to anything around him, the man jumped out of his skin when Jett and I yelled for his attention. He looked at us, dumbfounded, and we told him to beat it. I instructed him to leave the floating lights behind.

The water spraying from his wand slowed from a stream to a trickle. He packed up his cleaning bag and trudged down the stairs. Once arriving on the sand, he looked thoughtlessly at us once more, then disappeared out the opposite exit.

An issue arose, however: The dean had created a pair of sturdy, locked chain-link fences at either entrance of the stadium. While the custodian was given keys, the three of us were not so privy. Thus, climbing them became the obvious option. Jett and I scrambled up before leaping from the top onto the ground. Meanwhile, Dahir inched up the chain-link barricade and flopped down at my side. His face looked stubborn and sluggish, but I playfully elbowed him in the arm and assured him that everything would be fine.

"Great, now you two morons can duke it out in the playground. I'll judge the match honestly and stand idle until a winner is crowned. Have at it, I guess. Kill each other. See if I care," Dahir said blandly, not even acknowledging Jett's and my existence until he found a seat on the freshly cleaned bleachers.

The crescent moon perched high in the night sky. A dim array of stars steadily appeared across the darkness.

With an audience of one, the decay mage and I marked a spot to start the duel and glared at one another. As with any proper Kamaul and Jett battle, we began with a slew of insults.

I looked at my shiny new plaything and ran my fingers down it. "This thing is magnificent. Shame the only encounter you'll have is your blood on the blade. I'll leave it on afterwards in your memory."

"Quite an ego you have, Kamaul. Acting like you're a god and stealing things from us 'peasants' with your bags of gold? Guess that's one way to prove your status. How many legions of followers do you have? Ten? Twelve? Twenty? Oh, wait ... poor King Kamaul only has a total of four. Four people trapped in a lie you convince them is reality."

"Jealousy's not a great look on you, Jett. I appreciate the concerns, though. I'll remember to tap you when it comes time to write my memoir someday."

"I'm an expert mage. Just learned how to cast my ultimate ability and can't think of a more opportune time to test it out. Good thing Dahir is here to help you off your ass when I knock you onto it. Your image is everything, Kamaul, so I promise you don't get smacked around too bad."

"Alright, cut the sweet talk! Let's get tonight's entertainment started! Dahir, you say when," I shouted as I swung my axe around in the air with comfortable satisfaction. Seeing the anger in Jett's eyes over a weapon he had lost and me holding that very thing in my hands manufactured a photogenic moment of pleasure.

"Now!" Dahir shouted suddenly.

Before I even took a step towards him, Jett placed his hands on his shoulders, illuminated his collarbone area in a greenish hue, and created tree bark armor. The rough brown texture encased his arms and upper body. The magic took little energy, and the brutish boy quickly aimed his focus at my axe. I accepted the challenge, twirled the steel toy in my fingers, and grinned feverishly at Jett's jagged armor.

"Don't get yourself killed!" Dahir yelled, nearly out of earshot. He sounded like my father—and I hated that man.

"Thanks for that, but please shut up and allow me to focus."

"You wish." Jett smiled.

"My wishes are always granted, Jett." I beamed.

With a bloodthirsty fire in my eyes, I sprinted at him with my axe held mighty in both hands. The dirt kicked up with the vibration of my feet pounding on the sand. A rush of adrenaline roared in my veins. The desperate feeling of combat encased my body. The volcanic magma inside my heart jumpstarted my mind, like electricity on Frankenstein's monster. I felt free. I felt alive. I felt like I was where I belonged again.

"Come at me, Kamaul! See what happens!" Jett screamed, narrowing his eyes and sternly looking down on mine. He stood frozen in a mage battle stance and prepared for my arrival.

Grunting like a bear, I slowed down when I reached him and poised my feet in the sand to deliver the first blow. Jett blocked it with his armor. He spun around and slammed me in the ribs with a roundhouse kick, dropping me to ground. Instantly, I sprang to my feet and swung the axe towards his neck to avoid the tree bark protection on his chest. With a sidestep, Jett juked this attack, too, before abruptly punching me in the cheek. Another sucker punch to my chin, and I was flipped off my feet and tossed into the stone walls of the coliseum. The soreness was immediate in my ribs as I wiped the debris from my hair.

Jett looked on with a smile while Dahir shook his head with an "I told you so" kind of expression. He moved to the balcony's edge and peered down at me to assess the damage. "Kamaul, I'm telling you: He's not worth it! You're gonna end up in the infirmary again. You remember last time?"

"Of course I do, you idiot!" I squealed, grunting and grimacing as I gradually rose to my feet. "I beat him!"

"You left with a victory, sure. But also, a broken index finger, bruised knees, and a scar across your Achilles tendon. You remember that part, too, or does your mind only see what it wants to?"

"Now's not the time for words of wisdom, Dahir!" I shrieked, anger surging through my bloodstream. I darted my eyes to Jett, who aggravatingly stood yawning with his hands on his hips. "I can handle this myself. I have with everything else."

"If you say so," Dahir scoffed, exasperated. He fixed himself back on the stone bleachers before speaking again. "By the way ... he's winning."

That lit me up like Nero. But Dahir knew me and knew that it would. His words singed into my brain like a brand. I returned my attention to Jett's smug stance and redeployed for the next attack. Kicking off my sandals, I dug my toes in and gripped the dirt.

After a saber-tooth's howl, I charged at Jett, who proudly braced himself with a smile. My feet propelled me forward, clenching hard on each sand particle between my toes. The closer to Jett I raced, the fiercer my intentions became. He stood prepared and ready for me with eyes intent on the axe and hands awaiting their first spell.

Then, as I crossed the halfway point of the stadium, Jett slung a rot spell at me. I dodged to the left and gathered my footing, but it caught the thinnest edge of my right foot. I ignored that, held the axe diagonally across my chest, and bulldozed my bodyweight into Jett, knocking him to the ground. His tree bark armor cracked and shattered upon impact. As he slid across the sand, I dusted off my shirt.

I looked down at Jett, who shook his head in discomfort after the thud. The rot spell kicked in the moment I glared at his desperate reflection. While peering at Jett, I noticed the spell gradually taking effect. A black cloud of infection started to spread from the base of my foot towards my ankle, like a thunderstorm overtaking a sunrise. Putrid and pungent, small greenish warts and bubbling sores grew on my skin. I watched the rot harden into a crusty dry shell over the infected area.

Stupidly distracted by Jett's spell, I lost focus on him. Rummaging around for his wand, he still lay on the ground while his hands fumbled in the sand. Suddenly, he found it—and immediately thrust a blast of gray light at my face. From the tip of his gold-braided walnut wand, a massive stir of jergoli erupted and swarmed me. Though several feet away, the dragonfly-like bugs weaved menacingly through the air. Jergoli had no exoskeleton; their entire bodies were a visible skeleton—a ghastly sight when in groups called stirs. With split wings like a dragonfly and split tails like a moth, the jergoli hunted in these stirs to confuse their intended target. Harmless to me, the small horn-headed bugs clouded my vision from every angle and were ridiculously annoying. I swung my arms around to bat them aside and kicked my feet to avoid their heads against my leg hairs.

Meanwhile, amidst the swarm, I saw Jett rise to his feet, tuck his wand in his belt, and sprint at me. But by the time I braced for him, Jett had raced through the stir of bugs and straight into me. The jergoli divided and reformed behind him, so as not to assault their conjurer. I spun in midair and landed firmly on my chest. I turned my head to find Jett, but instead, I watched the jergoli vanish into mist. Then my sight was invaded by Jett's body standing over me, and he put his knee's weight against my upper back, pinning me to the dirt.

As I blew the sand from my mouth and pivoted my neck to face him, Jett pulled my right arm into the air. Stretching it out of its socket, the brutish decay mage pushed his knee harder into my vertebrae and knelt down to my ear.

"How weak you truly are, Kamaul. Three years later, and you still haven't learned to control your temper. How sad. Must be what happened to your father."

His words dissolved into a silent tension inside the stadium.

"You know nothing about my father, Jett! You lie!" I spat, blowing sand into my own mouth and eyes.

"Oh, no? I know all your secrets, Kamaul. You really oughta learn to keep your mouth shut and watch who you threaten. You're not a king here."

"You know nothing! Nobody ... knows about my ... past! Not ... even Dahir." Getting the words out while pressed against the dirt was uncomfortable and irritating.

"Admit defeat, and I won't spill your secrets to the school."

"Never! I will ... never submit to ... the likes of you!"

His weight increased on my back; I felt my bones nearly cracking under the pressure.

"Admit defeat, Kamaul! That axe is mine. Admit defeat, and I won't reveal your past!"

I spit blood and saliva next to my cheek. It didn't fly very far, but enough for Jett to see. "I spit on your threats. Do your worst. I'll never hand this axe over to you."

As I gripped it under my chest, I felt its cold steel blade against my shirt and the handle compressing into my hips. Rooting my other hand around for it, I kept close tabs on the axe.

"Just admit defeat and end this silliness—or I will break your arm. Believe me, Kamaul, I will!" The threat rang in the air as Jett pulled my arm further towards him.

"No! I ... will not. I do not ... admit defeat! Go ahead! Break ... break my arm if you want!"

It was becoming harder and harder to breathe. Jett put his entire weight on my back.

"You want me to break your arm? Really? Kamaul, the god-king earthling, wants me to break his precious arm! Fine. It would be my pleasure ..."

Fixing his grip on my wrist, Jett shifted around above me and yanked with more force to try and pull it out of its socket.

"Admit defeat!"

"No!"

"Kamaul, don't be an idiot," Dahir snapped. "Jett is *actually* going to break your arm! Don't be cocky! Just give him the axe."

"Dahir ... stay out of this! I don't need ... your motherly advice ... hounding me on what to do! I got this. He won't ... actually break my arm ... He's too much ... of a coward!"

"Coward, huh? Okay, Kamaul, I'm giving you to the count of five, and then I'm snapping it in half. You want to be prideful? Then pay the price. See if I care."

The smile in his voice seeped into my ears. Sand coated my face and mouth and hair. I grunted and grimaced as I tried to squeeze out from under him.

"Five ..."

"Not ... happening ... Jett!"

"Four ..."

"Ahhh ...! I'm not ... giving you this ... axe!"

My chest was compressing against the ground and making each gasp of air more difficult.

"Three ... I'm not kidding, Kamaul! The axe, or your arm?"

"I can ... manage ..."

"Two ..." Twisting my arm and forcing his foot into my shoulder blade, Jett pulled his hardest yet.

"Fine! Fine! I submit ... The axe ... is yours."

I hardly got the words out when Jett released his knee and stood upright again. I flipped over to grab at my throat. The steel axe lay at my side in a cushion of hard sand. My chest was tight and sore. My back ached, and I knew a footprint was stamped into my shirt. Wheezing and gasping for air, I eventually caught my breath. Dahir leapt off the balcony and rushed to my side.

Jett, who simply brushed off the bottoms of his shoes, twirled the axe in his hands. He grinned ear to ear as he looked at Dahir and me.

"Pleasure doing business with you both. Thanks for the axe, Kamaul. Is that two times out of three I've whooped your ass in a fight? Yikes. Better luck next time. Try someone smaller. Nice to see you again, Dahir. Take care of your friend. He looks a little worse for the wear."

Jett ran for the stadium fence, climbed to its peak, and jumped off to head towards the fields.

Dahir helped me while I stumbled to find my footing in the sand. Arm sore. Chest in pain from labored breathing. Back aching from that man's ... weight. I felt worse now than I had after the Gladiator class.

The foulest part? I was so frustrated to lose that axe!

"Let's head back to the infirmary. Maggie's not there, but you need to be."

"*Let's head back to the infirmary,*" I mocked, clapping my fingers together.

"Look, man! I'm here to help you. I told you this was a bad idea. Yet you refused to listen, and now we have to go back to see Heather! Who's fault is that?"

"Fine. But I'm not saying I lost."

KIKU II

PROFESSOR LEON WAS ABSENT from the room when I arrived in class. I sat down in my usual seat among the eleven other students. I unzipped my backpack, reached for my new cherry blossom journal, and plopped my bag to the ground. Looking upon the pink flowers, I simply smiled. Each blossom reminded me of those glorious trees that painted the parks and sidewalks of Japan. I imagined the sweeping, subtle aromas of magnolia and vanilla.

Breaking into my tranquility, a pair of slightly muffled male voices outside the classroom caught my ear.

"Yes—yes, I will remind them. Right when we get back, yes." The man paused as the other spoke. "Okay, yes, will do. Tomorrow morning, Pit Arena. I will remind them ... Yes ... Yes, alright ... You, too. Have a great class."

Our professor finally slipped into the room and closed the door behind him. With a quick sigh, Leon grinned widely as he strolled behind his desk and laid down his military-style leather backpack. Leon was a short Hispanic professor from a wilderness location in Spain, though not a place I had ever read about. Binoculars hung from his neck, a blue bandana was tied around his neck like a cape (just in case the journey was perilous and windy), and a safari cap was perched on his head. Everything about Leon's ensemble screamed "extravagant tour guide starter pack." Beyond his goofy yet charming nature, he was very environmentally focused, and I loved him for that. Unlike gung-ho teachers like Harper and Nero, Professor Leon often packaged his ideologies in a caring façade.

I felt a surge of adventure when he addressed the class.

"Mount Yarrich, keystone of the Qwalx Mountains!" shouted Leon, his pupils darting around the room. "It's just your typical, unreachable, predictable peak within a mountain range, like several others stretching across Penumbra. HOWEVER ...!" He paused to scan the captured eyes of the class, and a serious look took over his face. "To us, there is something special about Mount Yarrich. But I know what you're thinking ... 'Professor Leon, who cares about this place?' You tell me, my anxious little subjects. Who knows what significance Mount Yarrich has to the twelve of you? Anyone?"

Taylor, whose know-it-all status proceeded her, raised a hand nonchalantly and answered, "It's the location of our safari expedition today."

Leon launched himself atop the desk, crouched like a goblin, and pointed his finger at her. "BOOM! Exactly, Taylor. Thank you! Pencils out, everyone. Let's quickly go over the expedition details so the real escapade can begin."

He paused, then returned to standing. There was a ruffling sound across the classroom as everyone prepared for the notes session.

"Our safari location today: the Castara Forest, a profound tropical forest located at the base of boring, old Mount Yarrich. I anticipate we will see many species of wild animals, plants, mushrooms, fungi, and anything else it might reveal to us! Specifically, we are looking for the—take notes, now!—the molten-horn stag. This graceful, rare species of elk has antlers made of molten ore, like an erupting volcano. Fascinating creatures! I have never seen one before, and when I began researching new spots, I found this place. It's known as a breeding ground for molten-horn stags, so I'm hoping to see one in person. You'll have to make like a banana and keep your eyes peeled!"

He paused shortly to allow the scribbling pencils to finish. I did not take any notes, however, because Leon had already covered these same details in the first Forest Safari class earlier this week.

After a few moments, once our ready eyes returned to Leon, his face lit up with childish excitement. "Okay, *mis protegidos*. How many trees can you plant in an empty forest?"

We answered in unison: "One ... because after that, it's not empty anymore!"

The class let out a collective pity laugh at this sad joke; it was the same one he told prior to every single scheduled safari expedition. He used it to segue into how we as mages should take the initiative and help the environment in any way we could. His follow-up quote was often ...

"It all starts with one. The dominos will fall into place from there!"

Yup, right on cue. I chuckled to myself, staring at his waving hands.

Leon lightly scoffed as he pivoted around to write out the safari procedures, protocols, and expectations on the chalkboard. Most students zoned out during this part of expedition day. While I had explored an untapped daring side of myself earlier today with Zoe, I stuck to the status quo and followed Leon's lead by scribbling down his written list line by line as he simultaneously spoke them aloud.

Like a microcosm of everything Penumbra had to offer, the classroom was brilliant, and shared by all of the individual safari classes. Various posters, showing some places visited by mages, hung on the walls. Youthful photos of our safari professors when they were students dotted the top left wall (Laura, Vladimir, Preston Parx, Silvia, and lastly Leon, whose painting portrayed an exuberant, youthful smile marked by dimples and braces). Underneath were inspirational quotes about how adventure could start anywhere and eager minds could propel a hobby into a career. The most interesting part of the classroom was coined the "exploration gallery," a wall completely covered in detailed student drawings of animals, plants, insects, natural structures, landmarks, gorgeous views, and even a sequence of pictures documenting the growth of a Pegasus, from foal to adult. I stared at the realistic white stallion art as Leon's muffled words bounced off the chalkboard.

"*Psst*! Kiku. How are you today?" whispered an affable voice behind me.

"Huh ...? What?" I said, startled, my chin slipping off my palm as I rapidly turned to see who the culprit was. "Abe! Don't scare me like that. Heart nearly beat out of my chest for a second. But yeah, I'm doing well. This class is my happy place."

"I know." He smiled. "It's one of mine, too. Leon may be a loon sometimes, but he never fails to find some exotic locales."

"How are you? What do you think of the Castara Forest? Ever heard of it?" I asked.

"I've been great! And oh, yes—been there, too. It's beautiful! I used a griffin to scope it out last week. The Poison professor, Woodson, told me about it, and signed off for me. The mountain setting brings out unique critters in the forest. It's lush, lively, and colorful. Very picturesque, in my opinion. Leon scouted a good one for you today." Abe grinned and winked at me.

"Wonderful!"

"Hey, can you ... bring your backpack with you? I need a helping hand with some ingredients. I'll take care of the pouches, bags, garden clippers, and other stuff. Just need a backpack to fit it in, and conveniently, yours is the perfect size. What'd ya say? Do it for me?" he asked.

"Well— no pun intended—you're lucky I'm feeling more adventurous than usual. So, sure. Why not? *But* only if you keep me company in the back of the group! On the last safari we went on, to the Wornia Waterfall, you weren't even in class, Abe!"

His excited face fell flat. "I know, and I'm sorry. I was with Emilee, working on my house. Lost track of time and missed it. I talked to Leon, who filled me in on the details and gave me a couple assignments to make up instead. But yes!" Abe made a lighthearted salute to me, which fizzled away some of my anxiety about more rule-breaking. "I swear to hang out in the rear with you, make stupid comments about Leon's stupid comments, and point out niche plant life that he will definitely overlook."

"No salute needed. It's okay. I get it, honestly," I said as he dropped his arm. "So ... how's your house comin' along?"

"Emilee would say that it's all done—has been for weeks. But for me, it still needs a few final touches. That's why I need you and your perfectly sized backpack today, Goldilocks. The more ingredients and fruits I gather today, the more materials I can trade with these professors."

I admired the twinkle Abe got in his eye when talking about his house. Though annoying to some people, this project was all he talked about recently.

"Aside from confusion over how you worked out those deals, that sounds amazing!" I exclaimed, just as Leon turned back to face the class.

"Everyone get the procedures down? Notebooks full of safari protocols I've reiterated for the hundredth time?" he questioned as he loaded the leather bag on his desk with textbooks, an extra set of binoculars, a field guide (probably homemade or workshopped), several pairs of sunglasses with different lenses, and a flask.

Watching him pack up his bag made the entire classroom burst into fits of laughter.

"Mr. Leon, do you happen to have an extra pair of underwear in that bag, too? In case you wet yourself in excitement?" asked Atlas, a bearded evolution mage, as he snickered to himself.

"As a matter of fact, Mr. Stevens, I do! I brought a pair for you, too—if you ever decide to grow up!"

A brief moment of silence fell over the room, drowning out the laughter and allowing the communal embarrassment for Atlas to settle.

"OHHHHH, wow, bro! Skipper Leon just heckled you right back! I would take a lap if I were you," heckled Philip and a couple other boys.

"Calm down, everyone. No need to get your vines in a twist. Mr. Stevens lobbed a joke my way, and I simply swung it back at him like a Spanish striker. Can we move on now, please?" Leon's voice showed sincerity and resolve, but the smile and lifted cheeks exuded the opposite effect.

"Love to," interjected Abe from the back row.

Shocked to hear his voice during a classroom session, I whipped around to see if everything was alright.

"You okay?" I mouthed to him.

"Follow me," he whispered back.

I shook my head in disregard and returned to Leon, who was already wearing the zipped backpack and adjusting the straps for "optimal walking condition." Staring forward, he mimicked an obnoxious boat skipper strut and walked in place, presenting himself as if he were the best ever to move on their own two feet.

Leon instructed us to leave our seats and rejoin him at the Teleportation Door while he walked over to a tall cabinet and opened it. Pulling out a chest, he brought it to his desk, retrieved a key from his jacket's front pocket, and inserted it into the lock. After the lid popped open, Leon reached inside and pulled out a dark green doorknob. He then re-locked the trunk and replaced it in the cabinet.

Meanwhile, at the door, we stood awaiting Leon's arrival. The other mages crowded together in a small huddle, with Abe and I positioned firmly off to the side. Holding the doorknob in his hands, Leon walked between the rows of empty desks and split the cluster down the center. He came into the group as the other students reformed the circle behind him.

The class went quiet. Leon's eyes focused on the blank black door. Our collective eyes watched him place the green knob in the slot and wiggle it properly into place. A glimmering effect cascaded over the door's blank face, transforming it into rustic polished mahogany.

"I never get tired of seeing that," I whispered to Abe, who was putting his empty plant pouches in my backpack.

"Magic can do some incredible things. It makes beautiful, unnatural effects in the natural world. But remember, what goes up must come down." His eyes stared into my soul, but somehow in a comforting way.

"What'd you mean?" I asked, taking my attention away from Abe and back to Leon.

The safari professor lifted his binoculars off his neck and unraveled the string. He pushed the two lenses together and flipped them into each other, shaping them into a telescope. Leon stuck a few fingers inside the singular lens cap and lifted them out, holding his signature bamboo wand. "Before I create the doorway, is everyone ready for our adventure to the Castara Forest?! If not, sorry, you're in the wrong class." He grinned.

We nodded our heads and watched his wand's magic.

"I mean that everything magic creates, it can equally destroy," Abe explained quietly. "I don't mean to be a downer ... just something to keep in mind."

"Very supervillainy, Abe. I always keep that in mind. But thanks ..." I smiled briefly before zipping up my backpack.

Leon held the tip of his wand pressed against the mahogany door's surface and wrote out the exact destination on its surface. He continued writing until the final stroke carved the name *Castara Forest*. Despite nothing happening to the dozen of us behind him, Leon spun around like an owl on a pedestal and put the binoculars back around his neck; they had somehow returned to their normal state.

"Vámonos!"

The class's enthusiasm swarmed closer to Leon, and it felt as though the room were collapsing into a small bubble. The inscription vanished into the door.

Adjusting his pith helmet, Leon grabbed the knob and took a deep inhale. He twisted it leisurely, building the tension. Then he pulled it towards us, and we formed a single-file line and readied for the march through it.

The Teleportation Door opened to reveal an expansive view of lush greenery, overcast skies, and a small hiking path festooned with twigs and fallen leaves. Warm, humid air flooded into the classroom as Leon led us through the doorway. Tree trunks curved into sight from the edges. Colorful squawking birds flew by, and small bugs began to crawl into the classroom as a gentle mist flowed in from the distance.

"Welcome ..." hollered the overenthusiastic safari guide, "... to the CASTARA FOREST!"

Randomly, Abe's hearty laugh echoed behind me. The other classmates turned to give him questioning looks. Floating in his own world, he said, "I was hoping he would finish that sentence with '... to Jurassic Park!'" He chuckled, nearly crumpling to his knees.

Leon had no idea. I couldn't help but laugh, too. Seeing Abe react this way was too ridiculous not to.

When I turned around to see where we had entered the forest, there was no evidence of a door or classroom. In fact, everything behind us was shrouded in mystery by a dense layer of fog that fell across the ground and rose all the way to the peak of Mount Yarrich.

Meanwhile, Leon explained the significance of our expedition today.

"We are making history today, team, as the first safari to explore the Castara Forest. Consider this a bucket list place of mine—one previously thought to be mere fantasy, never reality. But dreams do come true, everyone! Of course, first and foremost, I need to remind all of you about our off-campus safety protocols before we journey into the forest's splendor. We will be walking single file on our hiking paths. We are to stay on those hiking paths together as a class—no veering off or wandering on your own. So, the way you're lined up now ..." He gestured across the class with his pointer finger. "... is the way we will return. Taylor at the front, and Abraham at the back. Next ...!" Leon pulled out a folded guide map of Penumbra and pinned it up against a nearby tree. He took the top off his pen and circled a random location. "This marks where we have arrived, and where we will depart from the forest. Now, if you will all turn you attention to ..."

Leon walked along the line of students and arrived at the rear with Abe and me. Behind us and off to the side, Leon pointed to a large tree with a wide trunk. He noted the five interlocking circles reminiscent of the distinctive Olympics symbol carved into it.

"... this tree here. It marks our classroom's doorway—the same doorway we just used to get here. If anyone gets lost, falls behind, gets injured, is bitten by an animal, or any other type of unique accident, all thirteen of us will meet back here. Understood?"

Along with our classmates, each of us nodded in agreement.

"Then onward!" he shouted, marching his way back to the front. Once he reached it, Professor Leon whipped out his field guide and held it open in his hands as he walked. Inching along the dirt path like a long, crawling caterpillar, the students followed after him with a bit of space between each one.

I glanced down at the trail, with its foliage jutting up from the forest floor. Hanging palms and leaves created walls of green on either side. We passed over loose rocks and damp spots of dirt that stuck to my shoes. The Castara Forest was a massive jungle; the view in every direction was dense trees and mist hovering around the forest canopy. It smelled of exotic flowers and recent rainfall. It was beautiful and serene as a few tropical birds called above my head.

I heard small rustlings in the leaves behind me, and I spun around to look. "Okay, Abe, what are you looking for?" I asked, locking my eyes on the crushed tree limbs and fallen twigs squished into the mud.

"A plant called scarlet trillium. It has three red petals and a thin brown stem. Usually found in a cluster. Finding one should reveal even more clusters. Like a banana, I'm gonna need you to keep your eyes peeled."

"Wow. Yikes, Abe. Quoting Leon to help you? Hmmmm ... I'll do my best," I said gingerly.

Leon made a quick left turn and ventured down a forested slope. The exposed beige roots of the towering trees created a natural staircase. As we followed his overly cautious instructions of one student per step, it took us a few minutes to reach the flat trail again. As we went, he rattled off bird species, types of trees native to Mount Yarrich, animals we might expect to encounter, and even some edible fruits we could pick along the way.

The safari continued dutifully along the trail for nearly a half mile before Leon abruptly halted the line. We approached an opening in the brush. The wacky professor pulled his binoculars to his eyes in an instant. I broke formation from the other students and wrapped around Leon's right side to get a better look.

After he found the source of a peculiar sound, the short man quietly waved his hands to gather the students in a tight circle. I peered through a pair of trees and pulled the branches aside.

"The umbral fox," Leon said. "This charming mammal lives primarily on mountainsides and in valleys."

I finally caught what he was looking at. Off in the distance stood a white-and-blue-striped fox on a mound. In search of a small fish, its eyes darted across a rushing river. Bearing a long, flowing tail like a bushy feather, the keen fox fluffed its rear. It also had a pair of pointed ears and the seemingly sharp pink horn of a stag beetle. The umbral fox looked odd but majestic as graceful breezes ruffled the fur on its back.

"Everyone, remain quiet," Leon whispered, retreating from the trail's opening and allowing other students to get a better view of the animal. Abe waited for the last few to get their turn before approaching the space. He took out a pocket-sized spiral notebook and drew a rough sketch of the umbral fox with its pose perfectly reflected in the river.

"What is it doing?" asked Allie.

"It appears to be scouring the water for food, probably to feed its young. These foxes often collect and store fish in their mouths like a stork until they reach their dens. And take note of this! That umbral fox has a horn. Which means what, class? Look at your notes, if you must."

No one answered. The echo of Leon's voice awoke the sleeping toucans and parrots.

"It means that this one is a female. Only females have horns; males do not. Hence, it's looking for fish. A mother fox's instinct is to find food wherever possible for her young kits."

Bright rays of the sun glowed through gaps in the tree canopy, which forced Leon to retrieve a pair of sunglasses from his bag. He strolled down the trail a bit further and motioned for everyone to reform the proper line. Abe and I partnered up at the back again as Professor Leon restarted our safari walk.

"How are classes going?" Abe asked as we wound around bends and past hills of sliding dirt.

Stretching my strides over an uprooted tree, I carefully watched every step and answered, "It's going well, honestly. Thanks for your help. My nemesis is in the same class as you, but Zoe and I tackle 'em together. Zoe is the magically superior one, and I'm the textbook one. We complement each other pretty well, so it makes class assignments easier."

"That's awesome. Good to use teamwork when you can."

"We thought so, too! I do struggle with alchemy, though. Something about it just ... just doesn't click for me," I added.

"If you need any help with that, I can try, if you'd like! Emilee is better at alchemy than I am, but I'll do my best. How did your Penumbra History exam go on Monday?"

"Oh, that? It was a breeze. Thanks for the pointers on that, too!"

"Great! They helped me on mine, too. Figured you'd be able to follow my chicken scratch."

Abruptly, Abe stopped and yanked me aside. The rest of the class continued marching along the path and under low-hanging palm trees behind Leon.

"Abe! Wha—what?! What are you doing? Trying to get me killed?! We're gonna fall behind, we're gonna get lost, we're gonna get caught, we're gonna—"

"Hey. Just ... wait here a second, okay? And look ... over ... that way!" Abe took me by the shoulders and spun me around to face the opposite direction. Launching his arm past me, he pointed down at the ground beyond the trail's edge. "A brambleback. Ugly little thing."

Abe was talking about a fat porcupine-like critter with briars on its back. It had the claws of a large rodent and the head of an ugly goblin. Completing the terrifying image were bulging black eyes. Stubby, angled legs rapidly wobbled it out of sight between figs and bushes.

"I see where it gets the name. Yeah ... gross. I agree, it is an ugly creature. Soooooo, why did you point it out to me?" I snickered, secretly happy that he did.

"Better catch up now; Leon's about to take roll call. If we hurry back, he'll never know we left, and you can maintain that perfect attendance record," Abe teased, gesturing for me to pick up the pace to get back to the group.

I briskly walked the trail ahead of him, down the small slopes and up the mounds until the last student finally came into view.

"Perfect timing," Abe chimed in, bringing up the rear.

"So, there's a nice little flower patch coming up here soon if my map is correct," Leon called. "We're gonna stop there to take a brief water break, let everyone catch their breath, and then we'll continue." Leon fixed the strap of his safari hat and lifted the binoculars over his head.

The class and I approached the colorful groupings of lilacs, trilliums, and other flowers before each finding a spot to rest. I noticed right away (and pointed out to Abe) that the ingredients he was looking for on his personal scavenger hunt were found in this area.

"Abe." I nudged him. "Right here. Hidden behind those weird bowl-shaped ones. I'm pretty sure those are the scarlet trilliums you're after!"

"You're right!" Abe exclaimed, unzipping my backpack and pulling out his clippers from the smaller pouch.

"Very sorry," he said, soothing the flower as he trimmed a few petals off the top and placed them in a clear bag. Other students shot him confused looks.

All the materials went back into my backpack before Abe zipped it shut.

I watched him take out the oak wand from his sock and flick a quick spell at the same flower bed. Slowly, the stems he had cut began to regrow their respective petals, brighter and fuller than ever. He casually strolled past the hydrating students and leaned against a tree. Abe looked around at the quiet scenery and began twirling the wand in his hands, as if he were foreseeing a question in my near future.

"Yes, Abe?" I rolled my eyes at him.

"Oh, nothin'. Nothin'. Just thinkin' ... Uh ... what would you say about a little shortcut with me?" he asked enticingly.

"Abe ..." I sighed. "You know how I feel about breaking the rules ..."

"But it's *not* breaking the rules, Kiku. Think of it more like a side quest on this grand adventure. We'll meet back up with the class before you know it. Leon won't even notice we're gone. Trust me."

"I don't know ..." I stammered.

"Think on it. Let it simmer in the ol' noggin. I'll ask again once he takes count of everyone. The spot I know splits off from the hiking trail about a mile or so further down."

Staying quiet, I slid the straps off my shoulders and set my backpack on the dirt. I took a sip from my water bottle, then placed it back inside. "You're a bad influence. I want to see what Leon has in store for this bucket list location. *But,* I also wanna follow you and see what undiscovered secrets you know about that our professor doesn't," I sighed, watching Abe fiddle with the wood of his handmade wand.

"Alright!" Leon announced, cutting through the side conversations. He silently counted all of us. Once he noted that we were all still present, the line converged at the end of the trail's opening. Leon reassumed his position at the front and wrapped the binoculars around his neck.

"Could be fun. Might see something *really* rare, if we're lucky. Never know. That's the beauty of my detours," Abe joked, joining the line to leave the caboose for me. "But okay, okay, look ... All I'm saying is that you'll see me cut through a bunch of overgrown ferns and hanging vines. Follow behind me and see where it takes us. That's all. If you don't, I'll see ya back at the meetup location and tell you all about the cool stuff I saw on my journey. I need certain berries that are difficult to find. It would be so much easier if I had an extra pair of eyes to help me."

Abe was nearly begging at this point, which got me thinking. It was a normal occurrence for him to invite me on a "friendly detour" during Forest Safari expeditions. I always rejected his offers. I was nervous about going exploring off the beaten path, but more afraid to get caught. Seeing the marketplace in all its bustle and excitement was actually quite fun. Frankly, I wished I would have pushed the idea of yesterday's college outing sooner. Zoe was a good guide—and I knew Abe would be the same.

Perhaps today is the day for Abe as well, I thought, completing the safari line as Leon started walking again. The other students and I inched along the muddy path behind our professor.

"No, sorry. I can't," I whispered to Abe. My feet stumbled over a few jagged rocks.

"If you say so. But should you change your mind," he replied, walking backwards briefly to face me, "all you have to do is follow my lead."

The lush, vibrant forest setting was peaceful, and gentle gusts of wind added to the ambience. While he was a biased tree lover, Abe had a point: Being amongst nature in the real world created an unmatched feeling compared to being at the college—a surreal sense of misplacement. But in a good way, you know? Like the way you could ignore the problems of life and put your mind at ease, away from the constant pressures and stresses that magic could produce. This Castara Forest invoked all the beautiful wonders of Penumbra, which Abe had been trying to show me. I finally understood what the germination mage had meant when he said, *"Penumbra's mystery and sensations elevate the senses and calm the body better than any Yoga instructor can."*

I had never truly felt it until this moment, though. Something about the Castara Forest brought it out of me.

The sun's beaming rays permeated the sudden lack of canopy, and we were sweltering in the grueling tropical humidity. Our hiking trail abruptly came to a halt at the edge of a rocky cliff. Peering over it, I could see that the trail continued down a slanted ramp.

Then, off in the distance, I noticed it. I caught sight of the one animal Leon wanted to see on this safari expedition. It was visible far off across the treetops and appeared blurry as it leisurely strolled on a grassy terrain. As I watched its every move, I tapped Abe on the shoulder and pointed it out to him. His eyes lit up, and he begged me to alert Leon myself. I shook my head frivolously against that idea.

"No, no. I can't. You tell him. I don't want to be the focus. You do it."

Abe sighed and slouched his shoulders. He approached the professor. "Now, Leon, before we take on this slippery slope of mud, take a look out in the distance. Below that mountain, there's an animal I think you'd like to see."

Hearing this, all the other students suddenly shifted to a spot on the edge of the cliff. A loud murmur of eagerness erupted from them as each one crowded near Leon to get a look.

It was the molten-horn stag, standing in the middle of a meadow and staring at us.

Soon after, another one appeared from beneath the tree canopy. The pair of stags tilted their heads, looking at our group.

"Look how graceful they are!" Leon stammered. He struggled, fighting through tears of joy. The muscular safari guy with his military backpack and homemade forest map let a single tear fall onto the cloth of his bandana. "Truly breathtaking nature in Penumbra. This is what I live for, everyone: seeing a rare animal in the wild, in its natural habitat."

We stared at the bright molten horns of the elk-like creature.

"He's actually crying." Abe chuckled by my ear.

"He is, yeah," I replied softly, wanting to laugh as well, yet having simple admiration for such a visceral reaction. "It's pretty wild to see a man's dream basically come true in your presence. Like, right in front of our eyes, Abe, a creature Leon's been searching for since he became a professor! Super cool to be a part of."

I smiled at Abe. Then a profound emotion hit me as my eyes darted between the pair of stags in the distance, Leon's face, and Abe's expression of peace, inspired by the beauty of Penumbra. It was remarkable.

Leon set down his backpack (a little close to the edge, if you asked me) and removed a spiral-bound sketchbook and colored pencils. Doing his best Bob Ross impersonation, he used the bag as an easel and sketched out the scene: two molten-horn stags against a leafy green backdrop. I was unsure if Abe was mocking the professor or feeling inspired himself as he took out his own notebook and pen to draw the pair of rare animals.

After a few minutes of them recreating the moment on paper and the class losing interest in the stags, Leon tore the page out of his sketchbook, stuffed it into his vest pocket, and dropped the pencils back in his leather backpack.

Soon, we began the trek down the side of the cliff. The slope began rather steeply, and I nearly fell down a couple instances. But the entire walk from top to bottom was shorter than it appeared, and it took only minutes to reach the flat path again. We all formed a circle down in the valley.

Professor Leon stopped for a quick moment to re-count all the students before continuing on. His laced boots were covered in mud and tiny broken twigs.

"Wonderful! Thirteen for thirteen. No one has decided to ditch us. Of course, you all know by now, I *wood* never *leaf* a safari trekker behind!"

The forest and classmates alike groaned together at the awkwardness. I, however, chuckled a little, equally out of pity and genuine laughter.

The single-file line became more broken and elongated the deeper we marched into the heart of Castara Forest. Abe slowed the pace around the next few bends until he and I were out of sight from the rest of the class.

"Abe? What are you doing?"

"My shortcut," he answered, spinning off the dirt path, lifting an overhanging branch out of the way, and ducking under it.

"Abe ... I'm not sure," I hesitated.

"Kiku, my young apprentice, just trust me. I'll be your personal Castara liaison for a moment. With me as your guide and the plants as mine, we'll be with you the entire time. You'll help me find these berries, see things off the beaten path, and maybe learn a thing or two along the way. Plus, I know how smart and capable you are; you can hold your own if this detour goes hairy. One thing I need to ask of you, and it's rather urgent ..." His arm was beginning to shake under the branch's weight. "Please make your decision quickly here, 'cause ... aaah! ... I'm not holding this forever."

Without saying a word or thinking on it any further, I hunched over and slipped under that branch. I turned around once he dropped his arm and let the branch thud onto the ground.

Abe nodded and walked on as the leader, pushing tree limbs out of the way and avoiding puddles when he spotted them. I followed, mimicking every step he took.

"Oh, lovely—lavender berries," said Abe.

"What?" I murmured.

"That's what Tyson said to look for. She showed me a photo of it in a textbook and used that description. So, keep those two L's in mind during our search: 'lovely' and 'lavender.'"

"Good way to remember, I guess."

"How's Intro to Magic going? Luke's a pretty good teacher. Smart guy for sure."

"*Ugh!*" I exclaimed. "It's so frustrating, that class. But he's good, yeah. Cute, too."

"You sound like Emilee." Abe chuckled, parting long palm fronds in our path.

"Most girls feel that way, Abe, c'mon. But yeah, he's a smart guy. I understand everything he's saying. But I can't actually use the magic, though, because I'm not a year two journeyman mage yet. Then there's Charlie, of course—a quirky old professor whose classes never have a dull moment. Scared me pretty good on the first day of class, if you remember! Using a hologram conjuration of Adarius to teach Penumbra History is insane, yet I find the class difficult to follow most of the time. Worst part of all these classes is the no magic rule. Feels like handcuffs."

"I get that. I felt the same way when I was a novice. It's like someone showing you a lollipop, then pulling it away when you reach for it."

I smiled at Abe, inspecting his messy hair and knowing that every word was sincere.

"How's expert-level magic treating you?" I asked curiously.

"Anxious for graduation and The Binding at this point. I've mastered every spell, except my ultimate. Emilee's got her bug thing. I've got my plant thing. Our house is relatively finished. It's livable. We usually just have fun together on campus, or somewhere in Penumbra. Magic has definitely changed my life for the better, though."

"If you think you're the bee's knees, tell me, then: How do you actually cast magic?"

"Like attack or defensive magic?" he wondered.

"Either one."

"Empty your mind. Close it off to outside noises and internal monologues. Think about the spell you want to cast. Visualize it, imagine it, feel it. Then close your eyes and release that energy. How you cast it is up to— Kiku, wait a second ..." Abe put an arm out to stop me. "Look there!"

Confused at first, I looked above his hand to a spot roughly thirty feet in front of us. Crossing the bumpy terrain of Abe's detour was a strange animal mindlessly eating nuts off a fallen tree. It was an odd creature, bearing a goat's body and color, an outstretched giraffe neck and blue tongue, and the velvet antlers of a small deer. I asked Abe if he had ever seen an animal like this one, but he simply shook his head. With Abe's arm still in front of me, we cautiously started walking down the path again while locking our eyes on the animal's peaceful demeanor.

"It has no idea that you and I are here," Abe shushed as I overheard the sound of a cascading waterfall nearby. "I haven't a clue what this ... thing is. No idea if it's friend or foe. So, if we're quiet, we can glide straight past it."

"Alright," I whispered.

Abe lowered his hand and moved one step at a time.

The creature poked its head into the muggy grass and removed a cluster of smashed fruits. Its tongue slithered under leaves to find the hidden ones. We slowly closed the gap between us until it was mere inches from me.

Suddenly, its head jerked up from the ground, and it gawked at Abe. My focus switched between his brown eyes and its cocked head as I wondered which one would make a move first. Abe, getting closer as we kept moving in, gently and gingerly reached out his hand to try and touch it. Its body stayed motionless by the trees. As the tips of his fingers grazed its furry neck, the animal sprinted off to the right, springing deep into the unknown regions of the Castara Forest.

"Crap!" Abe exclaimed, frustrated yet satisfied. "I knew it would run away, but I figured I might as well try."

"It was close, Abe." I exhaled. "I'm sure you were looking at its eyes." I started laughing hysterically, and Abe joined in shortly. "But ... its eyes were wandering in all directions but on yours!"

"What an odd-looking creature, huh?"

We giggled some more.

Dropping the smile and focusing on the path, Abe asked for my backpack and continued walking while unzipping the largest pocket. He took out an empty bag and the clippers. "The flowers that I need should be up here. Just a bit further."

I nodded as he handed my backpack to me.

As the late afternoon sun beat down on us, a dense humidity fell inside the forest. The hike now felt hot and tiring.

"Wait," I started, "didn't you find those flowers you were looking for earlier? The scarlet trillium?"

"The scarlet trillium is for Aria, the stone professor, who needs them for an upcoming project. Not sure. These are separate. They're for a different teacher."

"Hey, Abe," I said casually, "you know where we're going, right? The plants wouldn't lead us into, like, a ravine full of human skeletons, or a waiting hyena pack ...?"

He howled with laughter. This was concerning as well—almost more so than his not telling me where we were going. It felt like something a maniac would do, leading people like lemmings to their grave.

"Seriously, though ...?" I added.

"I trust the plants and their intuition and knowledge of this place. I listen to their warnings and directions. I know how selfish and crazy it sounds to say that. But that's the truth. The rumors on campus are true: I am that nature-loving, plant-speaking Tarzan boy who people think belongs in the nuthouse." His tone was serious and slightly somber. "It's okay. Those words don't hurt at all. But I am sorry that I can't share their thoughts with you, so you'll just have to trust me. And, oh, by the way, there are no hyenas here, Kiku. Not really their favorite place for hunting." He shrugged, wishing I could hear the plants.

"I do trust you, Abe. Really. I think your ability is one of the coolest and most unique attributes a person can have! It's incredible! Wish I were that lucky ..."

"You're luckier than you think. You have all this potential in you! I see it. Just wait until you get a real taste for magic. You are going to be a wise, powerful mage one day. With the young brain you have and the knowledge you carry, you won't need luck."

"Potential, potential, potential ... I hate how often and carelessly that term is thrown around here! My parents used to say it to me, too. Probably just to rub it in my face along with my sister's successes."

"Sorry. I forgot how much Phoebe drives that home. They certainly don't shy away from the demands of being a mage in your first year, do they?"

We trudged on around an old stump, whose tree lay broken in half on either side of our path.

"KIKU!" Abe shouted. "Kiku! That's it! Those are the berries I'm after!"

I instantly panicked but looked up to follow his focus.

"Wow ... The materials Woodson's gonna give me better be top tier for this. We're gonna have to risk more than our lives for these stubborn little guys."

I could not see the berries, or anything resembling a lavender leaf.

Without warning, Abe took off at a sprint, bobbing around trees and over bushes. Forced to follow, I began sprinting, too. I tried to mirror his movements as best I could, but he was quick. Before long, we were far away from anything resembling a trail.

"'More than our lives'?" I paused.

We came to another opening, where a small stream flowed at a gentle pace, and moss-covered rocks and branches curved towards us. In the middle rose a giant greenish-brown tree with roots wandering over the ground like octopus tentacles. The area around us was covered in a collage of shriveled leaves, additional cracked twigs and sticks, and little weeds poking from under the uprooted limbs. It looked like a scene from an old fairy tale.

"We need to climb this tree. This big one right here," Abe said nonchalantly, breaking the silence.

I abandoned the idea of scoping out the area and eyed up the tree. "Do *what*?" I questioned.

Remaining silent, he pointed with his eyes to the subject of this detour and began climbing the tree's thick trunk. I leaned my head back to see it fully. Like a cluster of bubbles stuck together, the berries hung from a tiny plant several feet up. They were teal at the base and changed into a deep lavender at the bulb. I mentioned to Abe that they looked like bigger versions of boysenberries.

"Barlimberries," he said, balancing on the roots.

I followed his lead, walking blind with eyes fixed on the tree's canopy.

"They're called barlimberries because the vines they grow on travel towards the clouds! Usually, these berries like cold weather and freezing temperatures, but Woodson said heat-loving barlimberries are favorites for special toxins. However, until you blend them or crush them into jam, they are safely edible and delicious ... So he says, at least. I need a lot of them, too. But ..." Abe lost his train of thought as he hugged the tree trunk and squeezed his way up it. This tactic quickly failed, and he fell back to the ground. He pointed above his head and gave me a friendly smile. "This is where you come in, Kiku. You're small and agile. I need you to climb this tree. Only thing I'll ask from you. After this, we'll retrace our steps and head back to the safari group."

"Oh, shoot!" I exclaimed. "I completely forgot we were still in class. You promise?"

He chuckled through his teeth and gazed at the purple barlimberries dangling in the breeze. "Time flies when you're havin' fun. I'll be at the base here to catch you, *if* you fall. But you won't. I'll hand you the pouch to put them in. You'll climb up the sturdier branches, pick as many as you can see, plop 'em in the bag, toss it back down to me, and ease your way back down to the forest floor. Simple, right?"

I knew he was trying to help, but my eyes were fixed on the height they hung from, an uncomfortable level off the ground. With a deep exhale, I agreed to his idiotic plan and scouted out the best course up this behemoth.

He handed me the carrying pouch, which I tucked in my pants pocket.

After some hesitation, I reached my arms up to the nearest branch and hoisted myself up. My balance was wobbly, nearly toppling me back to the ground. I leapt to the next branch with my hands out to brace me. Jumping to the next few like an awkward frog, I managed to get higher than I realized ... until I looked down. Abe stood far below, moving his lips, but I didn't hear any words. My mind and body froze as I suddenly felt my weight shift too far left, then too far right. My balance was fading, and I would soon fall. I was too far off the ground and would certainly twist an ankle or break my foot. Another deep exhale led me to reach out to the next adjacent limb and pull myself atop it.

I kept carefully climbing up the tree's torso. The world from this new viewpoint became clearer and more open. I could see miles and miles into the distance. I was nearly to the berries.

A trio of jumps and leaps led me a quarter of the way up the tree's height. After stupidly looking down again, I realized a fall from this height would break my arms or legs. The berries were too close for me to quit now, though, as I swung over to the branch closest to them. It was within arm's reach of their vines.

I pulled out the pouch and unsealed it. Despite the too-wide-for-comfort space, I extended my other arm and picked the first klakkioberry.

"Yes! Perfect. Just please be careful!"

"Yeah, no kidding, Abe!" I laughed at him in a panic while thinking it was an obvious and inane thing to say.

"Grab as many as you can. I need a minimum of twenty or so," he yelled.

"Abe! I know. Gotta be patient and wait for me to do it. Do you wanna climb up here? No? Didn't think so!"

"Keep picking. Doesn't matter how ripe or how purple they look. Remember to—"

"Abe, please!" I shouted, adding more berries to the growing bag. "Let me do it. If I wanted comments from the peanut gallery, I would ask for them! If I fall, you're paying my medical bills. So, don't take this the wrong way ... but please shut up."

"The infirmary is free, Kiku. Covered by the school!"

"Really not the point, Abraham!" I squealed, feeling my mind sidetracking from the mission.

"Right. Of course." I heard Abe move to a new location as twigs snapped under his shoes.

Counting the berries in the pouch, I shifted across my branch a few inches to reach a new vine.

Sixteen berries.

I grabbed the last four I needed (plus a few extras, just in case) and hollered down the trunk, "Alright, I got all of 'em. Here it comes ..."

Abe's head darted upwards at me, and I dropped the full pouch to him. I was unsure whether the berries would get smashed, but he caught it with both hands cupped like a basket. None of them were damaged, fortunately.

"Never again, Abe. Please," I stammered, short of breath. "Whew!"

"I won't. Thank you so much! I owe you one now," Abe replied, examining the lilac berries.

I was taking quick stock of my surroundings when a strange sight caught my eye. Downstream, I noticed an injured animal lying on a rock with its body and feathers soaked in water. But it clearly wasn't dead yet; little talons were twitching on its front claws.

I yelled for Abe's attention while raising one hand over my eyes to shield them from the sun and using the other to grip the nearest branch like a tree frog. "Okay, time to cash in that favor. Abe, wait. Look there! What's that ...?"

ABRAHAM II

Kiku immediately began her descent of the tree before I even got the chance to chime in. I was in the process of examining the individual barlimberries in the bag when she yelled to me.

"What's what? Where?" I stammered, shifting my focus to catch a view.

"There!" Her cry echoed so loudly that I feared it would attract an unwanted predator.

Kiku reached lower on the branches while simultaneously calling for my attention. "The injured bird ..." she said, carefully placing her feet on each limb as she went. "On the rock over there!" Her fear of heights must have subsided, replaced by these new cries of concern about something else. "The rock by the river. Can't you see it?"

"Ehhh ... Wait! Yeah, I do." I paused. "At the stream's end over there!"

"I hope it's still alive ... Hard to tell from here," Kiku added, voice cracking and eyes puffy. She neared the bottom, and her balance wobbled as she stood on a single tree limb. Poised like a squirrel rearing to jump, she leapt (well, more like awkwardly fell) to the ground. She gathered herself and sprinted towards the bird the moment her feet hit the ground.

I hurriedly stowed the berry bags in her backpack and chased after her. I ran quickly, crushing leaves and twigs under my shoes. Whispering soft apologies to them under my breath, I finally closed the gap.

Terribly sorry. On a mission. I hear your groans! And I will plant more of you when I return to campus.

Far from where we had picked the berries, the bird was a good ways downstream. Once I matched Kiku's pace, I pulled her arm back and motioned that we should be much quieter, in case its attacker was still lurking around. Naturally, she gave me a dirty look.

Water rippled around the stones as we crossed the flowing stream. Warily approaching the bird, I restrained Kiku to reach it first myself. She looped around me, placing the wounded animal between us.

"Is it ... is it dead?" she gasped, holding her hands over her eyes, yet peeking through her fingers. Her tears were heartbreaking.

"I ... don't know, honestly. But it doesn't look good," I said.

Camouflaged by the texture of the rock, the bird was difficult to see. It was small, roughly the size of a pigeon, with its head drooped to the side, closed eyes facing us. Rose-colored blood was drying on the underside of its damaged wing. I wondered how Kiku managed to spot it from up in the tree. Perhaps the bromeliads surrounding it had caught her attention.

"How did you—"

"Tell me there's something we can do, Abe! C'mon, I know you know how. Bring it back to life! Can't you use a seedling spell or something to heal it?!"

"Okay, A, a seedling spell only regenerates health for *me*. And, B, it doesn't bring anything or anyone back from the dead. Only necromancy deals with that madness. But what I need is for you to calm down. Please. Panicking won't help us."

"Calm down? Calm *down*?! Abe, this poor thing is dying right in front of us! How else do you expect me to act? I'm not one to ignore it, like the rest of our classmates."

"Well, I can't concentrate with you ... frenetic next to me. Magic may not be the answer. Please, just relax a moment, and let me see what I can do ..." I tried to be soothing and easy, but I feared it came off another way.

"Just ... please, do something! Anything," she begged, sniffling.

I sniffed at the bird to see if it was a recent attack, but only sensed the smell of nature. Running water. Moss on the rocks. Humid air. The delightful aroma of trees inhaling carbon dioxide and exhaling oxygen. The bromeliads seemed tense and frightful in their flowers.

You're afraid? Afraid of what? A premonition of death? Is this bird dead? Magic won't save it if it is—neither of ours, at least. Plus, I didn't intend for my "shortcut" to take this long. Gotta be heading back soon. I'll figure something out.

I retracted my hand from its wounded wing. A feeling of guilt washed over me.

Life remains in this bird, doesn't it? I have a feeling of that as well. That's what I was trying to tell Kiku, I thought as I bent to the bird's side.

Kiku bent down next to me and observed it. I put my arm on her shoulders to ease her pain.

"It's not dead, thankfully. The plants told me that we can save it. It's going to be okay, Kiku," I reassured her, hugging her shoulders tighter and looking into her eyes. "We're gonna save this animal. I don't know how, but we are. They're telling me that there is still life in it. But we *must* be careful. We have no idea whether human interference will be more detrimental than helpful."

"We're gonna save it?" Her cheeks shone in the sunbeams peeking through the tree canopy.

Then it let out a whimper—a simple yet heart-wrenching cry for help.

"We're gonna try to," I corrected. "Again, I am not sure how. But you and I are going to try. If there is life inside, we will help it."

While I refocused my eyes to Kiku, she kept her eyes on the bird's wounded wing, blood painted on its armpit. I felt her sorrow, despite knowing nothing about it. But I felt it, nonetheless. I wanted to help the animal with all my might—for its sake and for hers.

I lifted my arm from her shoulders. Kiku's arms were frozen at her sides, and her expression of hope gleamed at me. I saw something in her eyes like whenever Emilee spotted a cute new bug for her collection. A glimmer of optimism was palpable between us now.

The bird released another light whimper, more aching than the first.

"It's bleeding from a—"

"We need to take it back to the college," Kiku interjected.

"Huh? We need to *what*?" I flicked my head to the bird, then back to her. "Take it to the *college*? You're joking."

"No, Abe, I'm not!" She was suddenly petting the back of its tail, as if forgetting all previous concerns.

"Be careful, Kiku! We still don't know anything about it. And how do you propose we do that?"

"I don't know! But what choice do we have? Abandon it forever? Leave it here, helpless, and hope that its attacker doesn't return to finish the job? Let it die on this rock?"

"Look, I agree that taking it with us is one possible option. But is it the best option? I mean ..." I sighed, glancing around at the vast forest. "Life is all around us—plants, insects, apex predators. Who knows what we'll encounter if we try to take it back? You really wanna take that risk? There's still blood on its body. Odds are that the attacker will be on the prowl and catch a whiff of its alluring scent."

"I'm not sure, either, but we gotta do something! Waiting here and arguing about what to do is just wasting time. By the time we decide, it'll be dead for sure!"

"Okay, okay. Let's say, hypothetically, I am on board with taking it back to the college. How do we do that? What's the game plan here, Kiku?"

"I don't know, Abe! You're the expert mage with all the magic and stuff. Brainstorm something. I can help, but not much."

"Maybe ... maybe we put it in your backpack? I'll take out the bags with my stuff, and then we'll put it at the bottom. The bird will be okay in the bag. It won't bump around too much, and no one will notice anything. We'll just act normal until we get back to the safari. Then ... we'll decide what to do from there."

"Okay! Yeah," she replied.

"Yeah?" I echoed, satisfied.

Something about this bird is not like the others. It's unique. I've never seen a species like this either. I can't put my finger on what's different, but the orchids, ferns, and flora around this river bend are telling me this injured bird is special. And you guys are right! Kiku's right. This is not a fight I'm going to win, so it's gonna come back to the college with us.

"Yeah. Let's save this thing!" she said, looking at me in admiration. "Here ..." Kiku released the straps from her backpack and gently set it down near the stream. Then she soothed the bird's agony by gently stroking its wing. With each brush, she began to sing a lovely lullaby.

Stunned at what I was witnessing, I knelt next to Kiku. Listening to her harmonize with the running creek, I and the Castara Forest sat by and watched the scene unfold. Kiku's voice was light and nurturing:

"Life is tough, my little dove.
But with the moon and the stars above,
I will keep you in my arms
And away from harm.
There's no need to weep.
Rest your eyes and go to sleep."

"Where ... where did you learn that?" I murmured, looking at Kiku endearingly.

"It was a lullaby my mother used to sing me to me when I was younger. My father was royalty—a very important person in Kanazawa. Sadly, this meant he was also the target of nasty accusations and hatred. Those kids in my school were brutal with their words, not pulling back any punches. Hurtful and terrible. I came home some nights crying, confused about why people disliked him so much. So, she would sing this song to help me sleep. Glad you liked it, though."

"I did. It was touching," I added, glancing into Kiku's kind eyes. "It seems to have worked, too."

"I think so," she added softly.

"I didn't know you could sing."

"Neither did I." She chuckled, pivoted, and looked into my eyes.

I gestured at Kiku to open the backpack for me. Careful not to disturb the bird any further, I picked it up with both hands. Lifting it over the bag's lip, I tucked its wings in and lowered it to the bottom. We heard a light murmur as its stomach twitched up and down.

"It's sleeping," Kiku whispered.

"Yes, it is," I replied, carefully replacing all the bags underneath it. It was dozing softly, undisturbed by the berries as its mattress. "I thought it was dead at first glance. I wonder if your song or your soothing voice woke it up?"

It did. The lullaby of Kiku snuck into its ears and breathed new life into it. Like I told her before, magic works in inexplicable ways sometimes. The plants were right. This bird was certainly dead! It had to be. Yet ... it's sleeping in her backpack as we speak. Doesn't make sense, yet here we are.

"Must've. Alright, let's go," Kiku concluded hastily, brushing off my puzzled expression.

Listening to my better judgement (and the directions the plants offered), we started the trek back to the main hiking trail. I quickly stopped and splashed some water on the rock to wash away the splatters of pink blood.

Our path opened up to the left of us. Meanwhile, Kiku lightly lifted the backpack onto her shoulders. Following the river back, I walked ahead of her.

"Hey, Kiku ... your lullaby was sweet. Very charming. I can tell it meant a lot to you. Lucky that you had a mother to share that feeling with," I said quietly.

"Yeah," she replied uncertainly. "It does mean a lot to me. Makes me think of her."

"Nice," I answered solemnly, beneath the lively sounds of birds squawking. This moment reminded me of when I was a kid, trying to survive in the wild on my own.

"Oh, Abe ... I ... I'm sorry. I didn't mean to—"

"Hey. It's alright, Kiku. I know you didn't mean to. Sometimes those moments of my childhood spring up when you talk about how fortunate you were as a child. And I don't mean that in a cynical way, honestly. It's just ... my real parents abandoned me in the Amazon. No mother, no father. I remember everything in life after the age of, like, three. So, *my* birth mother never sang me songs, or tucked me into bed, or kissed me goodnight. My *birth* father never showed me how to fish, or how to write, or how to behave properly." I sighed. "All I had was the forest and its plant life to keep me company. Hearing you talk about your relationship with your mother makes me think of things I missed, not having a real one myself. Not your fault. Not mine either."

"I know, Abe. And I am sorry. Of course I didn't intend to bring up bad memories from the past. But ... I mean, you had Roy, didn't you? He helped in some ways, I'm sure."

Bless Kiku. Her sincere tone was endearing, like a curious kid.

"Yeah ... he did. But he's my adopted father, Kiku. It's not the same."

"Abe, I know you loved your birth parents. And I know you love Roy, too."

"Well, I don't know if I loved my birth parents. Clearly, if they had felt that way about me, my core memories would not have *begun* in DC. If they did, it was in a much different way than yours. They gave up on me before I really ... even knew 'em or could remember 'em. Otherwise, they, not Roy, would've been the ones wishing me luck at The College of Adarius. And don't get me wrong: I would not be the man I am today without him. He showed me a life I never knew existed for someone like me. Took a chance on an Amazonian 'Tarzan' orphan when every other person ran away. Just can't help but wonder, you know? What would Abraham Morrison's life look like if his birth parents had stuck around? What would he do with his life? Where would he live? Would he still attend the college? A lot of question marks, ya know?"

There was an interesting silence that befell us.

"Hey! Look! Found him on my backpack," Kiku added awkwardly, showing me a tiger-striped caterpillar on her index finger. "But it doesn't matter, Abe. You're here, at the college, months away from graduation. Whatever way you wanna look at it, I think you were always destined to be a student here, to find your destiny with magic. Abe, being a Tarzan of the forest, a man of nature, is one of the coolest things I know! To say that I am friends with a former survivalist of the wild is ... wild! Pun intended! You are one of the bravest and most thoughtful people I know. You're the confident one, Abe. Don't second-guess yourself, okay? Leave that to the self-doubting pros like me. I don't like this swapping of roles."

"Kiku ..." I laughed heartily. "I knew you were special the day we met. Gifted student. Selfless person. Kind soul. Caring animal lover and magic admirer. It's a blessing you had a mother to remind you of that when you were young. I can't believe I just got a pep talk from a sixteen-year-old wizard. It should be the other way around! But anyway, thank you. We keep each other in balance really well."

She laughed with me, both of us sharing the same emotions, if from different backgrounds.

"C'mon, enough deep talk. Time to get back to the group." I smiled.

We stayed close for a while afterward, but I must have lost her when we were forced to jump over kapok tree roots, thick and weaving, like a pair of dueling vines.

"Feel heavier? Want me to take over?" I asked, waiting for Kiku to catch up.

"A bit heavier, yeah. Not much, though. I can manage," she answered, stepping carefully around a fern's spiky leaves.

I ducked and wove around the trees jutting into our path. A brown worm crawled along the trunk of a fallen palm.

We walked for a quarter mile alongside the deep parts of the Castara Forest. Knowing the way, I followed the shortcut back to Leon's preferred hiking trail.

"Hey, Abe ... Why give me the bird? Make it my responsibility?" Kiku interjected. "What made you change your mind? Why did you ultimately agree to bring it back to campus with us?"

"Because I want you to be its adopted mother. I saw the way you cared for it, soothed it, sung to it. It was like second nature to you. I don't want to separate that connection by doing it myself. Watching over this recovering animal will take away the stress of your classes and remind you of the beauty of Penumbra. You'll help it heal and watch it grow. It will attach itself to you, and the two of you will conquer every obstacle that comes into your path. This bird and you will lean on each other when times get hard."

"Wow ... I don't know what to say," she replied.

"Say 'thank you,'" I added lightheartedly.

"Right ... Thank you, Abe. Hopefully I can do that. I have no idea what any of that means, really. Still, I'm scared I won't do it right ..."

"Sure you will! You just did at the stream. Without even thinking about it, your natural instincts told you what to do. Don't overthink it, and just be yourself. Everything will work out how it's supposed to."

"If you say so," she said, unsure. "I'm glad you have faith in me, 'cause—"

"Because you're the perfect candidate to heal this injured bird!" I laughed. "There is no better person to do it. Honestly. You and Zoe can do it together, even."

I made an abrupt swerve to the right between skyscraper trees and disappeared behind them. Kiku followed in my tracks. The two of us continued on through the deep jungle terrain for the next half mile. The aura of humid air and the muddy tracks were comforting as we trekked back to Professor Leon and the rest of the class. Kiku did not know the route these plants shared with me, so she stayed close to me. A real trooper. I appreciated her trusting me this much. It probably felt like walking blindly into darkness while praying not to get lost along the way.

Suddenly, I heard the prolific sound of Leon's voice and quickly thought on my feet. I came to the nearest tree and broke off a branch. Carving one end of it against the trunk, I sharpened it into a dagger. Kiku stared in shock. I smiled at her as I held it across my chest. It looked more like a spear, honestly.

"Sorry," I whispered back to the tree.

"What are you doing?" she asked.

"Just trust me."

"Okay ...? This is another one of those 'follow my lead' kind of things, isn't it?"

"Yup," I said, dragging the stick across my arm. Blood dripped from the incision and trickled down the side.

"Why did you do that?!" she exclaimed.

"Shhhhh!" I held a finger to my mouth. "They'll hear us. Hurry up and tear a leaf from that kousacane tree over there. The healing properties will make the wound look like it happened a while ago."

"Okay ..." Kiku answered, grabbing a leaf and handing it to me.

I wiped the palm over my wound. It acted as a sponge, absorbing the blood and cauterizing the incision. The leaf remained a perfect green color, and I laid it back on the other branches of the kousacane tree. My fresh cut had now turned into a dried scab.

Still in awe, Kiku pushed ahead of me as we began walking again. The light conversations of our other classmates soon traveled into our ears, revealing that we were not far behind. A few feet ahead of us was a dense fern blocking the path.

"Wait ..." I paused. "Let's check on the bird before we meet the others."

She dropped her bag in front of me as I bent down to retrieve it. I gently pulled out the ingredient bags and took a peek at her bird. It was sleeping soundly, snoring gentle and sweet. The injured wing was still damaged, caked with dried blood, but the animal was not in pain anymore, at least. Replacing the bags inside, I zipped up Kiku's backpack again and lifted it back onto her shoulders.

She pushed the leaves aside and held them for me as well. The path opened up back to the main safari trail.

"Hey, I know this spot!" Kiku exclaimed, pointing to the cliff to our right—the same location from which our class stopped to look at the molten-horn stag. We had returned to the halfway mark of the Castara Forest trek. I took the reins as the leader and made a left onto the hiking trail.

I walked the familiar path, following the voice of Leon and our classmates. They seemed to be discussing creatures they had found on the safari, some of which Kiku and I were there for, and others that we missed. Kiku and I approached the end of the line and joined the rear.

"—has been one of the most exhilarating safaris we've ever taken!" Leon said.

We secretly followed behind Atlas, who noticed Kiku and me behind him.

"Where've you been?" he asked. "Leon was spooked for a while, but I covered for ya."

I showed him the gash on my arm. "Appreciate that. I got cut on a branch. Stopped to take care of it. Kiku, actually, eased the bleeding and healed the wound. We got a little lost along the way. Just took the nearest forest opening ... and here we are."

"Yikes!" exclaimed Atlas. "Pretty close to what I told him, actually."

"Good cover." I smiled, turning back to see how Kiku was doing.

She looked horrified.

Staying quiet, I mouthed, *"How're you doing?"*

Kiku shrugged, staring ahead with hopeless eyes. "I'm scared someone will find out about my ... new pet," she answered, darting her eyes between me and the backpack.

"They won't. Just trust me. You'll be okay. No one is going to know," I reassured her.

"If you say so ..." she sighed.

The class circled around Leon, who had stopped in the next forest clearing. He began another head count of students. It was at this moment that I realized he never knew Kiku and I were even missing.

"Still a perfect score! Thirteen for thirteen! You know, the forest can be a labyrinth of hidden routes and dead ends. Glad to have everyone here in one piece. Seems like ... Wait, Abraham, you're injured?! What happened?" he exclaimed.

I showed him my arm.

"Ouch! Some plants are more aggressive than others, I suppose. Everything alright? Looks to be recovering nicely. Who tended to it? Did you take care of it yourself? Actually, that's a conversation for back in the classroom. Just glad to have all our peas in a pod. Onward we roll!"

"Guess so. Yeah, it's healing on its own now." I laughed.

There was an awkward silence as my laugh filled the empty space.

Then I heard a light whimper coming from Kiku's backpack.

"What was that?" asked Leon, spinning around to see the reactions of his class.

"Don't know," answered Taylor and Philip.

"Sorry!" I added sharply. "That was me. Just ... still in a little pain. Rubbed my gash accidentally."

There was another quiet moment following my confession.

"Alrighty, then! Let's return to the meeting spot and put this safari to an unfortunate end." Leon fixed his binoculars, which had gotten tangled around his neck, and prepared himself for the last leg of our hike.

Walking on the safari path, I turned again to see how Kiku was doing at the caboose. Her expression had improved, but not much. She still looked genuinely concerned and uncertain about taking care of the injured bird. I thought back to what the surrounding plants had warned me about. *This bird is special. We have never seen one like this before.* Never seen it before? A new species? Foreign animal not native to the Castara Forest, but from an outlying region? How'd it get here, then?

I nearly slammed into the back of Atlas, who suddenly stopped with the rest of the class at something blocking our trail.

"Class, we are seeing everything today! I tell ya ..." Leon began. "Do you know what kind of animal this is?!" His hand stretched out in front of the two girls closest to him.

"Isn't that a—"

"Hush for a moment," Leon interrupted, gazing at the beast.

Quietly crossing the safari path was a wolf-like animal with burnt-orange fur and a white stripe down the middle. It had piercing green eyes and the tail of a tiger. However, the focal point were the glossy insect horns on its head and the sharp, jagged spikes jutting out of its back. With its bizarre features, the creature was extravagantly unique.

"That, everybody," Leon said, pausing for suspense, "is a kasunine."

"A what?" asked a louder classmate.

"A kasunine."

His wide-eyed expression infected the rest of us, who were mostly clueless as to what we were looking at.

"We need to remain unseen and unheard, because these creatures are known to become aggressive whenever they feel threatened. Let's ... let's take an alternate route around it, actually. As outstanding as it is, the kasunine is dangerous and powerful. C'mon."

Leon whisked his hands for us to follow as he ventured off the trail and deeper into the forest brush. The line shuffled along in his footsteps like a military training regime. I could tell right away that the group of us leaving the kasunine's sight was a bad idea. If it was as intelligent and dangerous as Leon said it was, then surely its predatory instincts would come out, and it would spot an obvious group of clumsy humans fumbling through the brush. Nevertheless, I followed his lead.

Half in hesitation and half in cowardice, our single-file line grew more separated as we walked. Space opened up between my classmates and me, with Kiku falling further behind. Every eye was locked on the kasunine, who stood frozen in the middle of the hiking path. Its ears and snout pointed up into the air, like a stray dog catching scent of food. Horrified, I sensed that the food it was smelling lay asleep in the bottom of Kiku's backpack.

My fears came to life as Kiku's screams echoed in my ears. I frantically turned around to see what had happened. The kasunine had sprung over the hedge blocking our class and pinned Kiku to the ground, its paws holding tight to her arms. Its sharp claws were digging into her sweatshirt.

"AAAH!" she screamed. "ABE! Somebody! *Help me!*" Her cries were muffled under the kasunine's weight.

The class immediately pivoted to face us and ran back to where I was standing, inches away from the scene.

"Oh my goodness!" Leon called, his tour guide persona dropping away instantly.

Panicked and horrified shouts erupted from our fellow classmates, most of whom barely knew that Kiku existed, let alone wanted to put themselves in danger for her.

"Leon, what do we do?!" Bosamma yelled.

"How do we help her?!" Iris cried.

The kasunine flicked its head at Leon and snarled, slobber drooling from its grimy canine teeth.

"Everyone, calm down! Kiku, remain calm as best you can. I will help soon," Leon stammered, clearly flustered and unsure.

Easy for you to say, pal, I thought to myself. *But GI Joe here is right, Kiku: Remain calm and quiet. Sudden movement could be fatal. Think of purple orchids and passion flowers. That always puts positivity in my mind. Then again ... I've never had a hungry kasunine pounce on my sternum.*

I quickly took out my wand and hid it under my sleeve.

"It's after something in her backpack!" one girl shouted.

"Don't move, Kiku!" I interjected. "It's after the seeds I put in your bag. Keep it under your back."

Hope she got the reference!

The kasunine tightened its grip. It sniffed around her neck and shoulders, trying to reach the backpack underneath. Small streams of slobber trailed across her clothes. Baring its teeth, it pressed its snout near Kiku's face. Her nervousness made me dread its unpredictable movements; anything could spook it to kill. I had to act quickly.

Leon began flipping his binoculars into a wand when I beat him to the punch.

Sliding my wand from my sleeve to my hand, I held it out in front of me and closed my eyes. I channeled my magic and cast a thin vine snare, which became a whip. My wand became the oaken handle. Made of interwoven vines, the whip felt like leather in my hand as I grasped the end of it.

I swiftly cracked the whip to the right, away from Kiku and the kasunine. Its eyes narrowed at me, and it snarled in anger. Scowling with glowing green eyes, the wolf-creature then directed its focus to the vine whip.

I cracked it again at the dirt.

"Vine snares can become whips?" Moose asked.

"When you're this close to graduation, they do," I responded grandly.

The kasunine stood erect on Kiku's chest. Its claws released from her arms and shoulders. It sniffed at the air between us. Leon, meanwhile, corralled the students off the safari trail and out of harm's way, whether from me or the animal.

Strangely, it seemed not afraid of the whip's mighty sound, but curious.

I drew my hand back further this time and whipped at the ground inches above Kiku's head. Luckily, her eyes were still closed from the amount of drool on her cheeks. Otherwise, the look she darted in my direction would have been more irate than anything seen from her today.

Knowing the magic would not last much longer, I hurled one last crack of the whip above the beast's head. It sprang from Kiku's chest and ran off deep into the Castara Forest. I exhaled in relief as I dropped the whip to the dirt and watched it disappear into the ground. I noticed the rustling of bushes where the kasunine ran through them.

"Kiku, are you alright?! Abraham, are you alright?!" Leon shouted. Suddenly, he wanted to make himself useful.

"Yeah, I'm fine," Kiku muttered, shooting him the look I was worried she would turn my way.

I slid the wand down into my sock.

"Are you hurt anywhere? Here, let Abe and I help you up, at least!" Leon said, reaching out a hand to grab Kiku's as I stretched one out to grab the other. We lifted

Kiku onto her feet. She dusted the dirt off her backpack, shirt, and pants before shifting casually behind me.

"Abraham saved your bee-hind there! What can I do to help?" the safari teacher added. "I'd stick with him, too. Guy's reputation as a mage precedes him." He nodded to me while hurriedly scanning her sweatshirt to assess the damage. A couple rips and scratches on her sleeves were all I noticed.

"Everyone else okay?" Leon addressed the waiting class. Then he turned to Kiku and looked for her response. "Kiku, think you're ready to go? Need a moment to gather yourself?"

Kiku nodded at him.

He smiled nervously in response and glanced over at me before ushering the class to reform the single-file line.

"Thanks, Abe," Kiku said. She was still shaking and rubbing at her arms where the kasunine's claws had dug in. Her voice was fragile. "You saved my life."

"You're welcome," I replied warmly.

"I could tell it wanted that bird. It smelled it." She lowered her voice for my ears only.

"Yes, it did. Good thing Leon is so clueless that sometimes he bobbles around waiting for lightning to strike," I whispered back.

Kiku giggled. It was good to see her in high spirits, considering the terrifying encounter. I realized she was holding onto my shirt. I felt protective of Kiku, like the sister I never had.

"Kiku," I said, lightly guiding her ahead of me, "You're okay. I'll be right behind you, so nothing comes after it or you."

As Leon restarted the safari hike again, we shuffled up to the rest until we were walking at a brisk pace alongside them.

"Perks of having a wand," I murmured.

I watched her ears twitch as she smiled.

Though she seemed to be in higher spirits than expected, Kiku's shirt was ruffled. Tiny holes were ripped into the sleeves. She kept rubbing and inspecting her arm, when I noticed a faint stain appearing.

"Kiku? You're ... bleeding!" I exclaimed faintly, soft enough so as not to freak her out.

"I know!"

"We have to go to the infirmary when we get back. The nurses need to look at those cuts. Are they painful? Want me to patch 'em up?"

"No, it's fine. I'll manage."

"Are you sure?"

"Yeah, I'm sure. Thanks, though. I just want to get back to the college and get this poor thing out of my backpack before another animal smells lunch."

"Well," I began, knowing I had to break it to her, "I'm gonna have to steal your backpack from you when we get back to class. I'll take the bird back to your dorm and brief Zoe on everything that happened—the safari, the seeds, the flowers and stuff, and obviously the injured bird. Your priority is to get to the nurses!" I pointed to the bloodstain on her shirt.

"What about the bird, though?" Kiku asked, stopping to face me now.

Leon and the front of the line were nearing the meeting spot.

"The bird? Like I said, I'll take it to your dorm and catch Zoe up on everything. I'll stay there until you get back from the nurses, too."

"You sure? You don't have other things to do?"

"Kiku, it's fine. I'm the one who invited you along on my detour in the first place. I'll take care of the bird situation; you head straight for the infirmary. Nowhere else ... Got it? Straight there to get that checked out. I'll debrief Zoe on the whole thing and meet you at your dorm."

"Alright," she mustered. "Thanks, Abe."

"Medical ward. I'm serious."

"I know, I know."

"Good," I said, watching the line separate into a circle around Leon, who stood at the tree with the five interlocking loops carved onto it.

Quickly, Leon did a final head count, and once we were all accounted for, he pulled the binoculars off his neck and pushed the two lenses together to form a single telescope. He darted his hand inside and pulled out a bamboo wand. Holding it against the tree, he inscribed the words *College of Adarius* in the center of its trunk. Placing the converted binoculars back around his neck, Leon stepped away and watched the magic happen. A familiar green doorknob appeared on the tree as the trunk transformed into a mahogany door. In a few seconds, the ordinary tree had become the Teleportation Door.

"Everyone ready?" he said, addressing the class. "I'm very *grape-ful* for you all, but it's time to leave the Castara."

As expected, there was an audible groan as Leon looked eagerly for an uproar of laughter. Abe chuckled at the awkwardness that followed.

Leon reached out for the knob and twisted the door open. On the other side was the safari classroom, filled with empty desks, plant and animal photos, professor portraits, and student drawings. Passing into the classroom, Leon again counted each student. Kiku, still scratching and dabbing at the cuts on her arm, crossed the threshold ahead of me. I was the last mage in before Leon finally came in and let the door close with a thud. I turned around to catch one last glimpse of the Castara Forest, but all I was greeted with was a plain black door. The living forest had vanished.

So long, friends. Yes ... Yes, I'll see you soon, hopefully.

As other students returned to their seats, Kiku immediately looked to me for a plan.

"Let's go." I nodded, miming at her that we should sneak out of the class together. I flicked my head towards the hallway and urged her to follow. Casually, I started to walk out of the room. Professor Leon was facing the board, unpacking his safari bag, when he noticed us.

"You guys going somewhere?" he asked confusedly.

"Yeah ... to the infirmary. Best to get her arm looked at right away. No time to waste. Sorry, Professor." I beamed, giving Kiku a wide-eyed stare and urging her to sell her injuries.

"Uhhh ... Please, Professor! I don't want any scarring or anything ..." She winced.

"Right. Yes. Okay, well, stop back by later for the last bit of notes today. Also, there are no safaris next week. Jax has required the professors to keep our schedules clear. So, that means lectures and bookwork!" Leon noticed our lack of a stellar reaction and chuckled to himself. "Yes, your uninterested and discouraged looks are suitable for such news. Okay, off you go, then!"

"I will. For both of us. And thank you for the heads-up, Professor." I nodded, rushing her to follow my lead again.

Despite the initial confusion, she came shortly after, visibly concerned about ditching class before the official end. I glared at her as she took a slight pause. Kiku gingerly scooted by the occupied desks, holding her arm with an exaggerated look of pain painted on her face.

"Let's go," I mouthed.

She sighed and stepped into the hallway.

"Okay. Now give me your backpack and head down that way," I added, noting the vacant halls and bracing for the mad rush of mages in a few minutes. She handed me its leather straps, and I pulled it onto my back. I could feel the shape and size of the bird against my back.

"Take care of it, please," Kiku said once I started walking her down the hall towards the air buildings. "Let Zoe know about everything. Tell her I'm at the medical ward and that I'll be home soon."

"I know," I answered before disappearing around the corner and hearing her travel in the other direction. I was happy to see that she was naturally attached to this animal, because that would be crucial in helping it back to health.

Briskly, I cut down the hallways, out of the building, around the lake and court-yards, and quietly snuck into the air dorms without being seen. Kiku's backpack was light enough to where I made good time during that fast walk. The halls were empty here as well, which allowed me to slow my pace and take my time reaching Kiku and Zoe's dorm. Kiku told me Zoe's next class wasn't until later this evening, so someone should be there to let me in.

I took a quick deep breath and knocked on their door.

No answer. I spun my head around like an owl to make sure there were no other students nearby.

I knocked again.

"One second!" came a muffled but chipper voice.

Whew, I thought.

"Who is it?" asked Zoe on the other side, nearing the door.

"It's Abe," I replied.

"Abe?" she said, puzzled, as the door opened. "Oh, hey!"

"Hi, Zoe," I said casually.

"Where's ... uh ... where's Kiku? She's not with you? Did something happen?"

"She's with the nurses, which is why I'm here, actually."

"She's in the infirmary?!" Zoe exclaimed, shutting the door behind me once I showed myself into their living room.

"Yeah. Incident with a kasunine."

"A what? How bad was it? Is she going to be okay?!"

"A minor incident," I clarified. "Nothing major. I told her to head over and see the nurses just in case it turned out to be something serious. She'll be right back once she's done. I'm sure of it. But the real reason I'm here ... is this ..."

I dropped the backpack gracefully onto the nearest couch and watched Zoe sit down. She peeked over me as I pulled out my pouches from within. Bags of seeds, flower cuttings, and other ingredients now cluttered the cushion between us.

"Okay. Now don't freak out," I said, fairly certain that she was going to do the opposite.

"Why?! Abe ...? What is it?!" she panicked, trying to get a peek inside the back-pack while I pulled the zippered ends tightly together.

"Okay. So, we found this poor thing injured by a river. I'm ninety-nine percent sure it is a female. I don't know ... Kind of a plant guy myself ..."

I pulled open the top of the backpack again and let her see the bird.

"Abe, are you serious right now ...?!" she gasped, before immediately whacking me on the arm twice—one for me, and one for Kiku.

KIKU III

I HARDLY FELT ANY different when the beaming rays of sun warmed my bedroom. Between the anxiety over today's ceremony and the wounded bird, sleep was out of the question. Despite the safety of our dorm, I feared another student finding out about her. Worse yet would be if Leon found out about Abe's and my little detour. What would happen then? Leaving a guided safari and harboring a secret wild pet without the college's consent? That could be cause for expulsion—a fate that had recently plagued nightly slumber.

My eyes watched the soft, silent breathing of the bird, who sat in a bed of folded hoodies. She was so beautiful and mysterious that I could not look away.

"I'm glad you slept okay," I whispered, resting my head on my palm.

An orange glow of morning sky crossed in from the window when Zoe knocked on my bedroom door.

"Yeah? Come in," I answered kindly.

Zoe twisted the knob and came into view. "Hello." She smiled.

"Hey."

I sat upright, moving so my body's shadow no longer blocked the sleeping bird. She had dark gray feathers—a magnificent color that looked like a calm night sky. The most amazing and peculiar part of her was the dual pairs of wings, one smaller set beneath the larger ones, like a dragonfly.

Zoe joined me on the other side.

I shifted around the sweatshirt sleeves to check on her wing splint. Created by Abe while I was in the infirmary, he fashioned a pair of chopsticks to prop the wing up in a normal position, wrapped it with self-adhesive bandages, then tied it off with medical tape. Zoe had mentioned to me late last night that Abe initially wanted to use metal pins to hold the bandages together but feared the tension would cause soreness and discomfort for the bird. I inspected the splint. It was holding up very well.

"How's she doing?" she asked, petting her back.

"Good, I think? Hard to tell; I've never had a pet or taken care of one. Let alone this rare species of bird. Your guess is as good as mine. At least she's sleeping and not whimpering in pain anymore. So, we must be doing something right."

"Well, she seems happy, Kiku. Takin' a liking to you, too! Can't believe she ... attached herself to you so quickly. That bird and you have already bonded. I can feel it."

"You sleep okay?" I asked, pivoting the conversation from me to her.

"Fine. You?"

"Not at all. Worried about her, getting caught, and Leon finding out that I snuck out during that expedition with Abe. My anxiety is getting worse by the minute, and the ceremony today is not helping. It's in, like, an hour and a half, and I am freaking out ... I don't know which stresses me out more: the fact we have an illegal animal in our dorm, or the possibility of being chosen to fight in a death match. Right now it's a toss-up. Like, what if we go to the Pit Ceremony, and then they decide to do a random dorm inspection? What happens th—"

"Kiku, the odds of you or I being selected are *so* slim. We're novice mages! The Pit hardly ever picks first years. We'll be the ones in the stands, cheering on the actual five competitors! You'll be fine. I think we have bigger issues right now," Zoe said, nudging her head at the waking bird next to us.

"How's the nest coming, by the way?" I asked.

"Oh, great actually!" she exclaimed, bolting into her room. She returned shortly, holding a pile of towels assembled in a bowl-like shape. These towels formed a comfortable base while a mixture of leaves, sticks, and dampened twigs reminded the bird of her familiar habitat in the woods. Zoe was nervous that the loose elements wouldn't hold well enough on their own. She had it cupped in her arms as she brought it to my bed and set it down.

The bird's eyes slowly flickered open. A pair of glinting black pupils captured Zoe and me in their hypnotic glow.

Waiting for her to awaken fully, we hoped she would notice the nest Zoe had made and immediately approach it. Yet she did not. She noticed it and looked at it, but never moved.

"Let's just put it on the shelf and move her to it. It'd be easier, I think," Zoe suggested.

"Alright."

I flipped around to check the clock: 6:22. Reaching for the bird, I gently lifted and held her in the air while waiting for Zoe to set down the nest. Those midnight eyes pierced through me in fear. She fretted and wriggled around in my hands.

I sung quietly to her. *"I will keep you in my arms and away from harm ..."*

"I heard that." Zoe chuckled.

"Shut up." I laughed back.

The bird and I met Zoe's eyes as she prepped and adjusted the new nest on my bookshelf. She then walked back into her room to get ready for the ceremony. I carefully slid the bird into it and set the hoodies back on my pillows. I checked for a reaction, but none showed. Rather, I heard something coming from her I had never heard before—a pleasant sound that normally did not come from a bird: She was *purring*. It was light as a feather but vibrated the whole nest.

"You like it?" I asked, lying on the bed and watching her. The sound was louder now, and I waited for Zoe to barge in and ask what it was.

I twisted my head around like an owl to recheck the clock: 6:28. An uneasy feeling created a hole in my stomach. The Pit Selection Ceremony was less than an hour away, and I had no idea what to expect. Who got picked? *Why* did they get picked? What happens if they win? If they lose, they die ... What if I got picked? What if one of the names read was my name, or Zoe's?

The pit grew, getting bigger and deeper in my stomach as the time rushed by.

I returned to the bird purring on top of my bookshelf. "Our bird needs a name, Zoe!" I exclaimed suddenly.

At that very moment, she popped her head into my room and agreed. "Absolutely right!" She was wearing white jeans tucked into warm fur-lined boots and a lavender sweater that covered her neck in a thick collar. Zoe's sense of style was something I wished I had the confidence to pull off.

"That's a really cute outfit, Zo."

"Thanks!" she replied, spinning around to give me a full view. "Wanna see something funny?"

"Yeah."

She spun backwards and leaned down to show me the sweater's tag. I pulled down the collar and noticed an odd *Z* written on it in faded permanent marker.

"Z for Zoe, I'm guessing?" I said, lifting it up and fixing it for her.

"Yup!" She giggled. "My mom was afraid she'd forget which one of us got what color. Alexandra got the blue one, Maggie got the gold, and I got the purple one. All of them have our initials on the tags. Not the first time she forget-proofed clothes of ours."

Zoe had told me a couple hilarious stories of how her mom actually confused her own daughters with one another. Mixing up which sport one girl played, who Maggie was dating, whose favorite food was what—stuff like that. My sister was several years older than me, so moments like these never really happened between us. And when she had left the family, I was essentially an only child, left to envy close sibling relationships, or funny ones, like Zoe had in her life.

"Speaking of names, perhaps it's time we gave our third roommate a name, too! Had any ideas on that?" she began, releasing the tie in her hair before redoing it.

"Yeah," I answered cautiously. "I've got nothing so far, though."

"Well, what does she look like? What kinda name fits a bird like this?"

"Sierra?"

"Hmmm ... no. Tetra? Nah. Lumi? Luna?" Zoe brainstormed, finishing her ponytail.

"No ... Hmm ... What name do you like, little bird?" I leaned down, waiting for the bird to jump at the next name that piqued her interest.

"Harmony?" Zoe suggested, shrugging her shoulders.

"Sonnet?"

"I like that one, actually. Think she does, too."

Her head was staring right at us. Glowing eyes blinked slowly at me and showed my smiling reflection. "Yeah. She does like it, actually. I can tell."

"Well, Sonnet, the newest official member of the best first-year dorm at the college, welcome! There will be many years of magic and majesty and kick-butt-ery around here. Better get used to it," Zoe announced with her hand in the air, like a leading lady belting out a monologue on stage. She shortly left my bedroom again and strolled into the living room for a glass of juice.

"Sonnet, huh? You like that name?"

The clock now read 6:51. I stood up from my bed. Kneeling next to Sonnet's new nest, I petted the top of her head and down her back. I leaned back on my other hand and stared at her some more. Sonnet had such beautiful feathers that it was impossible to look away. Despite the splint on her wounded wing, she still seemed so happy and content just to be alive.

"We will get you back to full and proper health. I promise. Zoe and I will make it happen—mark my words."

She purred in my ears as a response.

"Good. Glad you agree," I concluded, standing up to get ready for the ceremony.

I pulled out an array of pants, shirts, sweatshirts, fluffy socks, and other pieces to try on. It took a couple of tries and combinations, but I eventually found the one I liked best. I matched slightly ripped black jeans with a dark-red-striped sweater. After starting with dark combat boots, I switched to sneakers instead. Satisfied, I bid Sonnet farewell and checked myself out in the mirror before joining Zoe in the living room.

"Love the look, Keeks!" she exclaimed, taking a wide-eyed sip of apple juice.

"Do you think I should go with these sneakers, or my boots? Which one complements the look better?" I asked, twirling my feet to give her a glimpse of the whole outfit.

"Whichever, honestly. They'll both work great."

"Please, Zo. Help me out here ..." I begged. "Boots or sneakers?"

"Let's see the boots."

I rushed back into my bedroom and changed back into the brown combat boots.

"Okay, here's the boots," I said, showing them off.

"Oh, yeah. Definitely those!" she said, giving a thumbs-up and putting her empty glass in the sink.

"Ready to head to the arena?"

"Sure. What time is it?"

"Seven twenty-nine, I believe. Better to be early, right?"

"Yeah, I guess so," I said, very unsure as anxiety returned to rear its ugly head. "I'm gonna check on Sonnet *real* quick."

Peeking around the doorway, I popped my head in to see how she was doing. Her head was tucked between her wing and the edge of a towel, and she was snuggled up for warmth. I smiled at her and waved goodbye as her black eyes disappeared beneath heavy eyelids.

Meanwhile, Zoe opened the door to the hallway and called for me to join her.

"Be good. Don't do anything I wouldn't do. We'll be back to check up on you after the ceremony. Pray for me and Zoe that we don't get picked. Oh, shoot!" I exclaimed. I ran over to my bedside dresser, grabbed a plastic container of blueberries, and dribbled out a few in front of Sonnet. She simply stared at them. I figured they would be a safe and easy thing to eat. "Here's some berries in case you get hungry. Okay ... bye!" I frantically tossed the container back on my dresser and reached Zoe's side as she shut the door behind us.

She and I talked about the Castara Forest safari, what Sonnet was probably doing back in the room, and what was going to happen during this Pit Selection Ceremony. It got the gears running in my mind about all the uncertainties that awaited us in The Trench. From what Zoe told me (and from what I somewhat remembered from my research before bed), this ceremony brought every single mage at the college to the same place. If a student did not attend, they were subject to expulsion from the school. So, we were bound to run into mages from all different years. To make matters worse, I would not be able to sit next to Zoe, one of only two people who could calm my nerves, as we were required to sit in alphabetical order.

The dorm building was quiet and had a vacant feeling. We entered and exited the stairwell in the blink of an eye and began the lakeside trek to the arena.

"How long is the ceremony?" I asked as we trudged down the snow-covered sidewalk. A few inches lay atop the college landscape.

"My Alchemy professor said they vary depending on the Elders. Sometimes they take over an hour; others it's, like, maybe thirty minutes. So, I'm not sure." Zoe shrugged.

"They only pick one person from each element, right?" I asked as we walked into Market Square. The market was abnormally quiet as well. It was as if the college had been abandoned overnight. Unfortunately, however, the main walkway to the arena was cluttered with students, which meant the line extended nearly to the market's exit.

"Okay, Kiku, follow the yellow signs for our seating area. Follow the air symbols. That's where you and I will be," Zoe reassured while standing on the tips of her toes to see how many people deep the crowd was.

"Okay," I said, alternating between keeping my head down and aimlessly scanning the crowd.

Dominating the western vista of the campus was a massive arena built to hold the college's entire student body. It sat atop a plateau overlooking Market Square. A single, wide marble pathway draped with long banners that were embroidered with stripes and element insignias marked its only entrance. Swaying in the wind, the drapes splashed a rainbow of color against the arena's architecture of limestone and travertine. It was as ominous and imposing as the textbooks suggested, which gave grave accuracy to the rumors surrounding it of 'one way in but no way out.' Guess that's why they called the arena The Trench.

Inching along with the massive group, I followed Zoe towards the entryway, where a yellow banner painted with black swirls hung from The Trench's velarium corbels. We were now halfway through the line to enter the arena.

"How you doing back there?" Zoe tossed over her shoulder.

"Starting to panic," I replied, staring at the shifting people ahead.

"Starting?" she answered jokingly before turning around to see my blank stare. "Oh, sorry. Bad timing. You'll be okay, Kiku. It's not going to be either of us. It's probably not even gonna be someone in our year!"

I knew she was trying, but it was simply not working. My fear and anxiety picked up with every step I took.

"Not much further," I muttered.

The scene tucked inside the arena looked like swarm of ants scurrying around.

"Alright, Kiku," Zoe began, reaching her hand back to grab ahold mine. "We're up next. Might be the last time I see you until after the ceremony. Good luck and remember to breathe! I'll be experiencing the same internal struggle that you are. You are not alone, okay?" She laughed abruptly in an attempt to soothe my worries. But I'm afraid they were plastered on my face, too strong to be soothed.

"I know, Zo. Thanks for trying to help. I'll see you afterwards." I smiled, released her hand, and watched her approach the arena attendant.

Spinning to take in the students awaiting their turn behind me, I heard Zoe's brief interview with the faculty attendant. Then they admitted her, and I was next.

"Finger, please," said the attendant.

I lost myself in the sea of various mages flocking along on the marble path.

"Finger, miss," she demanded again.

"Huh?" I panicked, pivoting to face her.

"Give me your hand. Fingers facing up, please." The irritation and exhaustion in her voice were not missed.

"Yes. Sorry. Of course ... Here," I stammered, fiddling my hands around to place my fingers near the tip of her wand.

The tip of her thin silver wand illuminated as it touched my skin. Wildly, it seemed to light up the veins and muscles inside my hand. Her wand flickered and twinkled a couple times before the light dimmed out and faded away completely. The mage lifted her eyes from my hand and moved her wand beside my face.

"Name?" she said, her gaze flipping between the wand's tip and my eyes.

"Kiku Kaipan."

"Branch of magic?"

"Sound."

"Okay, Ms. Kaipan, you may enter. At the end of the tunnel, hang a right and head up the stairs. Enjoy the ceremony." She gave a quick fake smile at me before gesturing for the next mage to approach.

I exhaled and shuffled my feet as I walked down the seemingly endless tunnel. I then exited, rounded the bend where the attendant had told me to, and braced for the journey up the stairs. However, once I turned the corner, I froze, staring up at the hundreds of rows escalating to the top. There were so many students ... The longer I stood there, the more eyeballs locked onto mine.

The signs atop the tunnel railing read G to J and K to N. I walked far up the stairs and found an empty seat on the right-hand side.

"Excuse me ... Excuse me ... Excuse me ..." Keeping my distance so as not to bump anyone, I squeezed my way to the open space in the middle of the row and sat down.

My eyes widened to see the wild expanse displayed in the arena. The Trench had a similar layout and structure to the Colosseum in Rome, with stone grandstands elevated twenty feet from its dirt floor. A skybox for the Elders and private personnel was fixed at the top of the north side. I watched the tiers of bleachers fill up as more and more students funneled into the empty seats. Only a few spots remained.

It took a few more minutes until the entire arena was full of mages, for the Pit Selection Ceremony was drawing near. There was a joyous yet tense anticipation in the area around my seat. Most of the air mages were gossiping about rumors surrounding the possible contestants, the rundown of the ceremony itself, and the suspicion that we might even see the Elders in person. I tried to ignore the hubbub as best as I could. My own anxiety was only getting worse.

However, the silver lining in this whole ordeal was the severity of it all. No other occasion than The Pit could gather every mage in the college into one massive crowd. It was impressive. Terrifying and barbaric and drastic, but impressive, nonetheless. Four years ago, when the last Pit Tournament had been held, the surviving competitor and crowned victor was a water mage. Water had thus become the element of power and decision-making for Earth and Penumbra. However, as time passed and the worlds changed, the time had arisen for a new element to take over, even if it meant giving water a redemption opportunity. The culmination of these factors meant that a new Pit Tournament was on the horizon ...

Without warning, a deep, looming hum resounded from the Gjallarhorn, inviting all attendees to take their seats and silencing The Trench in an instant. And oddly enough, despite the assembly of unruly teenagers and young adults, it remained that way.

Hoping to see a familiar face, I scanned the other students to calm my nerves. Down to the far left of me, I spotted Zoe, whose hair was in pristine condition. She looked to be laughing softly. I only noted the back of her head and didn't recognize anyone else.

Then Abe caught my eye, as he was making a fool out of himself on the far side of the bleachers. He had found me somehow where I was hidden between a very tall boy and a talkative girl. I was shocked, but very happy to see him. Smiling a wide grin, he waved to me. I waved back, much to the dismay of the girl next to me.

Abe flapped his arms like a bird, then mimed singing a song, using his hand as a microphone. I clearly did not understand, because he kept doing it.

Oh! I realized with an audible gasp. *He's talking about the bird. Duh.*

I held out two thumbs up.

Clapping like a proud professor, Abe nodded his head. Then he mouthed the question, *"How are you holding up?"*

I shrugged and mouthed, *"Fine."*

His head tilted to the side in disbelief, and he folded his arms.

"Okay..." I began, miming the words. *"Freaking out a bit. I'm super nervous."*

"I understand. It's gonna be okay."

He motioned with his hands to draw a friendly smile on his face. I felt content in the arena now. Abe had a comforting feeling about him, which brought out a happier side of me.

That feeling vacated immediately upon the next echoing blow of the Gjallarhorn.

Picking up some of the loose snow on the floor and whisking it around the lower levels, a draft of cold air wafted through the tunnel walkway and assailed my seating area. Watching the skybox, I saw the mage hand the Gjallarhorn to Jax, the Dean of Students, before disappearing. Jax raised the horn, flipped it to place the bell against his mouth, and spoke into it, which transformed the horn into a powerful, booming megaphone for his voice.

"Good morning, students!" he exclaimed, loud enough for the entire world to hear.

Some of the student body responded to his greeting.

His robe was a vibrant silver with gold trim. A silk cloak fastened below his goatee and curled hair and flowed to the ground. Jax held the audience captive with his words and reveled in our attention.

"Welcome to the Pit Selection Ceremony!"

A roar of applause and cheers filled the arena.

"Calm down, calm down ..." he muttered, gesturing for everyone to settle down.

I, unsure how to act, sat frozen in my seat.

"Today marks the winter solstice, and the official start to The Pit Tournament! It is a glorious tradition, where five of our college's best mages compete against one another to have their element crowned as the dominant power. It will be a test of character, physical strength, magical prowess, determination, and willpower. Not to worry for the rest of you, as the Festival of the Elements will then commence on the grounds for you to enjoy, to celebrate this momentous occasion!"

Cheers and hollering ensued. Jax was clearly not his normal witty self, as he was in the classrooms. Rather, his tone was slow and concise, and the audience hung on every word.

"However, before we can announce the mages selected to compete, I must bring out the Elders and explain the process."

Murmurs rose to a crescendo at the news of the Elders. These mysterious, magical beings were remarked for their immeasurable power and foreboding presence. Students and professors rarely saw them, which added to the allure and rumor around their true existence.

Jax dropped the Gjallarhorn from his lips and kept it tightly at his side. Suddenly, five giants emerged and stood behind him. Their faces were clouded by the enchanted glass of the skybox.

"Professors and students of The College of Adarius, people of Penumbra, and the royalty of our world, it is my great pleasure to introduce to you the creators of the college ... the Elders!"

Outrageous, extravagant cheers swarmed the air of The Trench. There was so much excitement and disbelief from all the mages all around me. Meanwhile, I was frankly shocked that they even existed, let alone that we were seated in their company. While many professors informed us that they were not gods, the speculation around them shrouded each one in untouchable mystery and respect. They were immensely powerful beings, and the direct sources of our magic. Despite their faces being hidden by Jax and the shadows, this feeling of amazement was a very welcome surprise.

"Magnus, the Fire Elder. Marrick, the Void Elder. Kai, the Water Elder. Terra, the Earth Elder. Eliza, the Air Elder. We are blessed and grateful to you for joining us on this monumental day."

A small battle of which faction could chant the loudest broke out as each name was announced.

"Settle down, please!" Jax shouted, showcasing a serious look as he stood between them. "That is all I have for now. The Elders will take over for this next part of the ceremony. I will see you all later on." He methodically bowed his head, handed the Gjallarhorn back to his assistant, and left the skybox behind her.

The arena fell eerily silent, with the five Elders remaining perfectly still. Soon after, the petite assistant came hustling back into view with gloves and a giant black pillow. This time, however, the horn in her hands was replaced with a human skull.

The Elders rose from their thrones and approached the mage holding the pillow. One by one, they placed a hand atop the old skull. Jax's assistant stood in the center of the five Elders, very out of place next to their demanding and intense presence. They collectively lifted the skull into the air and held it above the cushion. As the Elders raised the skull higher, the atmosphere above The Trench changed dramatically into a dark evening sky with a sprawling array of twinkling stars, which replaced the morning's welcoming orange-pink glow with the twilight ambience of approaching midnight.

The soft chatter in the grandstands terminated immediately as every pair of eyes swiftly flicked to the skull, whose eyeholes gleamed with a bright white light. We watched it ascend on its own beyond the Elders' grip.

A group of maybe a dozen vivid stars suddenly descended from the night sky, swooped down towards the floating skull, and penetrated its illuminated eyeholes. In a flash, they then raced in a line to the center of the arena. Everything went completely black for a moment. Then, a flowing smoke trail slithered out the skull's mouth and hung in a giant cloud above the snow-covered ground. It was thin and nearly invisible yet growing in size as more and more continued to ooze from the skull. Gradually, the smoke cloud became denser and showed the stars once again. It was like a constellation's shape had been plucked from space and manifested at our collective eye level.

I saw the smoke fade away. The constellation formed a tall and stocky human figure on the snow. To my astonishment, the colossal man assumed the center of The Trench. Rising to the height of the skybox, Adarius had white hair, a fading black beard, and profound eyes. He wore dragging, orange robes with silver trim. Adarius had the face of a wise old grandfather but the deep, enthralling voice of a commanding officer.

"Hello, students and faculty of my college." His hands were folded inside his robe sleeves. "I invited you all this morning to partake in our coveted tradition, The Pit Tournament. I am certain that each one of you is tired of hearing about the rules and details, but let me repeat them one last time. In a few moments, each of the Elders will select one student to compete in their element's honor. These lucky students are then pitted against one another across a variety of challenges and battles. The first of these challenges involves the five Elemental Rites, one-day events based around a single element of nature, with randomized settings, creatures, and missions. Next will be the Labyrinth. As the maze has a mind of its own, this piece will test the mental resolve and strength of our competitors. Finally, once the tournament is down to the last two competitors, a hand-to-hand magic duel will ensue, and subsequently result in crowning the last student standing as champion and the element of power.

"But as for now ... Do any of you recall when you first accepted your admission to the college and were asked to give a vial of your blood? This is where that moment comes to fruition. The Elders will use a collection of those vials to select our competitors randomly. You'll see."

Using his hands as he talked, Adarius walked around the arena and spoke to the entire audience. "The Elemental Rites will begin exactly a month from today, on January 21st. The remaining Rites will continue on the 21st of every month thereafter, followed by the Labyrinth, then the Final Duels. It will be a grand seven-month tournament. And if you are not chosen to compete, do not worry; there will be plenty of excitement and activities to experience as part of our special tradition!"

He returned to the middle of the arena. "If you are selected, make your way to the main stage to be accompanied by your Mentor. This Mentor will be your tutor, teacher, Pit instructor, and mastermind for the duration of the tournament. They have competed themselves and were victorious—hence why they have been chosen to teach you. They will use their magical knowledge and past experiences to try to make sure you are the last man or woman standing."

"Now, with all of the details out of the way, it is my time to leave. Please redirect your attention to the Elders so they may perform the selection process and announce the five names to compete in The 248th Pit! Good luck, everyone!"

Adarius bowed to each section before dissolving into a thin cloud of smoke, which was sucked back into the skull. The stars faded away, and the glow of the sun gradually returned. The sky opened up to a lighter shade of blue, and the cold stillness within the arena returned.

Marrick snapped his fingers.

Instantly, the air was filled with little crystal vials of blood floating above the arena. They all looked identical to one another, just thousands and thousands of blood samples seemingly frozen in the air. I couldn't tell if it felt like a scene from a horror movie or a fairy tale, but both were unsettling. Was it actually the blood of every single student suspended midair ... right there? Again, terrifying, because it meant that mine was there, too, hidden among the thousands of others. It was, frankly, gross to think about it.

Meanwhile, in the skybox, the Elders stood huddled around a large cauldron. None of them made eye contact with one another and kept their gazes on the bubbling basin. Kai retrieved the Gjallarhorn from the assistant's pillow and whisked a single blood vial towards him. It floated across the sky, reached the center of the cauldron, and slowly poured its deep red contents inside. The Water Elder dipped the Gjallarhorn into it and blew on the brass mouthpiece.

Like an animated gust of wind, the now gaseous blood drifted towards the ground before sprawling out in the form of handwriting.

There, etched into the thin layer of snow, was the name of The Pit's first chosen competitor.

AARON III

A NAME SPILLED ONTO the snow like a signature, on display for the entire school to see. This name would become the talk of the town, an overnight celebrity. It was a name either doomed to their own inevitable demise, or immediately assigned to the history books. Whoever's name was revealed would be subject to the scrutiny of every eye in the arena.

As the blood settled, The Pit's first competitor was unveiled to be a novice storm mage from a poor little town in Penumbra—the antithesis of a popular kid.

The dean emerged on the main stage, which was centered the ground below. His smile was encouraging, if not also alarming.

"Aaron Dirge."

My brain had stopped working completely. I was frozen stiff in my seat and staring at the crimson blood painted across the snow.

"Aaron!" shouted an unfamiliar voice next to me. "Aaron, that's you! Go ahead! Jax is waiting for ya. How exciting!" she exclaimed.

Elias tapped me on the shoulder. "Yeah, man, that's you! Congrats, dude!"

I sat still. However, my body seemed to take over for my brain. Both arms pushed me off the stone bleachers. I exited to the right, dodged the legs of other students, and headed for the stairs. Luckily, the walk to the snowy arena floor was not far. I felt the attention of the entire college lock onto every move I made.

I followed the path from one staircase to another as I watched the blood signature vanish into the ground. Down a few more steps, and then I took a step onto the thin layer of snow. Now entering the arena itself, my body felt robotic, simply going through the motions. I saw only one person in the distance: Jax stared at me while my legs propelled me forward. But I wasn't there anymore; I was a ghost gliding above myself in a void of nothing. Seeming to enjoy my painful walk to the main stage, he stood like a statue.

"Morning, Mr. Dirge," he said indifferently. His hands were tucked behind his back as he greeted me, glaring at the markings my shoes made on the white ground.

I said nothing and stared into space. My entire body had been oblivious to the frigid air washing over The Trench, but goose bumps dotted my skin. The awkwardness between us led my eyes to wander aimlessly, and I noted the silent, serious look on Jax's face, and the remaining vials still suspended in the air. After mine was chosen, a great number of them had disappeared.

I looked around at the audience. Thousands of eyes pointed and watched me. Even I felt as though I were watching myself. It was an awful and uncomfortable feeling.

Meanwhile, the next competitor's vial left the space above us and drifted to the skybox. Magnus held the Gjallarhorn with both hands over the cauldron as the crystal vial poured itself into it. He dipped the horn inside and raised it to his mouth, blowing the blood into a mist-like form. Again, it drifted to the ground in the signature of the next Pit competitor, this one from the school of fire magic. My gaze followed the etching of blood on the white snow as the name appeared shortly after, captivating everyone in the final reveal.

"Kamaul Metjen."

A chorus of chanting and applause erupted around The Trench, much in the same way as it had when my name was shown. The students and professors cheered for this announcement.

Together with Jax, whose form and facial expression remained unchanged, I watched Kamaul walk down the staircase and towards an entryway onto the ground en route to us. Kamaul was a tall, muscular mage. He looked to be cracking his knuckles and proudly showed off a vibrant smile as he headed in my direction. Though not very big, he looked like a formidable opponent—one I would not like to battle in physical combat. That impression held strong when he reached Jax and me and greeted each of us with an abrasive yet alluring personality.

"Morning, Mr. Metjen," Jax said.

"Nice for you to meet me," Kamaul replied casually. "Sorry! Ha ha, my bad. Nice to meet you." He held out his hand to shake the dean's, but Jax kept his hands folded behind his back. Kamaul nodded and continued to me to repeat the gesture.

"I am Kamaul, rightful king of Egypt—but I'm sure that's not news to you." He grinned.

"It's ... A-Aaron," I stammered, cautiously forcing my hand to greet his.

As my fingers nearly reached his own, Kamaul pulled his outstretched hand away from me, sweeping it over his hair and behind his back—a juvenile trick often played by young children. "Oh ... yikes! Too slow! Hope you're quicker in the ring than you are with simple handshakes."

I stood awkwardly and scanned the arena. The applause had finally stopped when Kamaul came to stand to the left of me. His ego continued to wow the crowd as he waved, fist-pumped, and pointed to random students in the audience.

There's no way he knows who these people are that he's looking at, I thought.

The uproar abruptly faded, leaving the giant arena deathly quiet, with the whole student body focused on the two chosen strangers standing together.

I eyed up Kamaul again.

"Getting a good view?" he said, smiling and darting his eyes around to various girls in the audience.

"What ...?" I stammered, randomly darting my own eyes to different spots on the stage.

"You're staring at me. Are you enjoying the view?"

Kamaul still had not looked my direction.

"No, I'm not," I replied.

"I get it." He shrugged, turning to face me. "I am quite the specimen. And yes, I said 'rightful King of Egypt'—which is true, by the way! No, I do not take steroids. Yes, you should be intimidated. No, I won't feel bad for killing you on my way to victory." He spoke as if I had asked very specific questions.

"Didn't ask anything," I muttered, somewhat shocked at my own courage in saying something that bold. That was the moment I realized I was floating above my own body again in another out-of-body experience.

"Don't worry, kid. People stare at me all the time. Girls, guys, professors ... even salespeople and shopkeepers. I'm used to having audiences gawk at me. I suggest you get used to it, too, 'cause it's gonna be like this for the next six months ... or however long you last on the battlefield."

The thought of the upcoming tournament made my busy mind go blank as I stood next to Kamaul, a bulkier, more spray-tanned version of Duke Colwell.

"You're right. My mistake," I corrected, sighing and pivoting to face forward. I felt Kamaul's judgmental stare on me, then he shifted his attention to the arena.

I had never felt so confused in my life.

Eliza, the Air Elder, was awaiting the next crystal vial to go into the cauldron. Kamaul and I watched as it left the others suspended above and poured itself into the large basin. Lowering the horn into it, Eliza soaked up the blood and blew on the instrument's mouthpiece. The blood became a mist, flowing and drifting onto the snow in front of the stage before displaying the next person's name.

"Kiku Kaipan."

The echoing applause returned to greet the new Pit competitor. Kamaul and I waited.

Kiku? As in, Kiku from Penumbra History?

I rapidly scanned the surrounding sections of students until she made her way to the arena stairs. My assumptions were revealed to be correct once Kiku carefully stepped toward the stage behind Kamaul. Her footsteps were so faint on the snow that if I had not been watching her approach the stage, I would not have even known she was coming.

Eventually, she arrived on the main stage and greeted Jax next to me.

"Good morning, Ms. Kaipan," he said. His voice was sweeter this time.

"Hi," she answered meekly, trembling. Unsure of what to look at, Kiku's face was lowered to the ground. She walked past Jax and neared me.

"Kiku ... Hi, I'm Aaron. I sit behind you in Penumbra History," I said, hoping my greeting came off as friendly as I intended.

"Hi," she replied, monotone, just as she had for Jax. She had dark brown hair and was not very tall. She passed me and Kamaul before taking her place to the left of him.

"Nice to meet you, young lady. I know you're scared, and so am I. But one of us will win this thing. I know it." Kamaul's voice was kind and comforting, which did not match the man saying it. I hoped she didn't fall for the façade.

"I am, yeah. Nice to meet you, too." Kiku's face looked up at his, with wide eyes and an inviting smile.

It seemed I was wrong.

While it was a relief to have a second novice mage on the stage, my optimism disappeared into the snow like the blood. Thinking about the one class we had together, I remembered how knowledgeable Kiku was. Who knew how smart she was in other fields? Was she above me on this totem pole, with smarts I didn't possess? One thing was for certain: She was better at magic than me because, let's face it, there was nobody worse.

As I pondered my own shortcomings, I turned to see Kamaul and Kiku talking. He was sweet-talking her, charming his way through her anxious outer shell. She seemed more open and bubblier than I had ever seen her. They were discussing how to team up to beat the other three competitors, how to combine forces using combat magic, and how he'd be there to help her along the way in any way he could. But I saw past his egotistical prowess and figured he was luring her to her eventual death. I was too afraid to say anything about it to her, or to confront him. So, I ignored those feelings and let them talk on their own while silently eavesdropping on the conversation.

Returning my eyes to the skies above, I saw the rest of the floating vials. They twinkled slightly as the sun rose higher above the horizon. I felt horrible and confused standing next to two more talented students.

The next Elder approached the boiling cauldron to prepare for the announcement of the fourth competitor. Terra gripped the sides of the basin with both hands and stared into it like it was a brewing potion. With a quick flick of the wrist, Terra summoned a vial from the collection, which drifted across the sky and hovered above the cauldron, pouring itself in. She stirred the contents using the Gjallarhorn and quickly dipped it inside. She blew out the contents, and the blood mist again flowed down to the ground before revealing the next competitor's name in a crimson signature.

"Abraham Morrison."

Kamaul reveled once again in the spotlight as uproar and applause filled the arena. Next to him, Kiku got a light glimmer in her eyes when this name was announced. I, however, stood unfazed in a continuous mental loop of hoping this was all a sick fever dream.

More vials disappeared from the sky until only a few hundred remained.

Abraham approached the stage. He was taller and bigger than me (though not as muscular as Kamaul). Once he got to Jax, Abraham shone a pearly white smile with small dimples in his cheeks.

"Hello, Mr. Morrison," Jax greeted him. His hands remained tucked behind his back.

"Please, sir," he began in a pleasant tone, "just call me Abe."

Jax nodded, but did not respond, and gestured for him to find a spot along with the rest of us. Abe positioned himself next to me in line and spoke in the same manner—a warm welcome compared to Kamaul's boastfulness.

"Hello." He smiled at me.

"Hi," I replied, half-heartedly grinning back.

Lowering his head, Abe moved past me and on to Kamaul to the left.

"Hey, man, how you doin'?" Kamaul offered, beaming his intense eyes at Abe.

"Hi, Kamaul. Nice to meet you as well," he answered.

Kiku and I, on the other hand, simply watched them and listened to the loud cheering soften to a few stragglers.

"Best of luck to you, Abraham." Kamaul nodded sarcastically and mimicked Jax's gesture for Abe to continue walking down the line. Kiku and Abe talked to one another softly, but I was unable to make out any words. After a brief conversation, they faced forward with contented smiles.

After Abe found his spot alongside Kiku, his expression became stone, unimpressed.

The remaining crystal vials shifted closer to one another, creating a square-like formation of blood hovering above the center of the arena. Moving to the edge of the skybox, Marrick placed his palms over the edge and scanned the audience. It almost looked as though he were picking a specific student or seating area to choose from. That caught my focus, until I overheard a light argument between Abe and Kamaul. The fire mage leaned closer to whisper in Kiku's ear.

"I hope he isn't telling you lies about me," Abe murmured.

"No. He's not," Kiku replied softly.

"Someone is very jumpy! Don't worry about what I said," Kamaul interjected, speaking to her, yet locking his eyes on Abe. "Good to know in a fight to the death. I can't wait to see how many of your buttons I can easily push, tree hugger."

"I hope your skills are as notable as your massive head, Kamaul," Abe added.

"You won't last long enough in The Pit to find out."

Abe gently pushed Kiku out of the line of conversation and further back on the stage, fearing that something physical was incoming. "I don't have the patience for someone as dumb as you, Kamaul. Stay out of her way and stay out of mine. Best worry about yourself, because I won't."

"Wow!" Kamaul shouted, spinning around and catching a few students looking at them rather than at Marrick. "Tarzan has some bite in that bark! I hope you're ready to prove that on the field, 'cause I was born ready to prove myself. Shall we find out how good your magic really is?"

He shoved Abe backward. Though Abe did not fall, it certainly knocked him off balance for a moment.

"We love you, Kamaul!" shouted a group of girls behind the stage.

"Hear that?" Kamaul said, raising his arms in the air as if to stir up more excitement from the crowd. Despite just finding out that this guy existed, I knew right away he had no fear in the spotlight. "I already have some fans rooting for me. As for you? Where are yours? Does this little girl over here love you like my followers love me?"

"Keep away from her, keep away from me, and keep away from him!" Abe pointed to me. "And watch your tongue, Kamaul, unless you want me to strangle you with it." He then stepped closer to the fire mage until they were roughly just a foot apart from each other.

"I'm ready when you are," Kamaul snapped before closing the gap even further to the point where their noses were nearly touching. He shoved Abe again, this time harder and further back. With a jolt, Abe regained his footing and approached Kamaul once more. He drew his wand and pointed it at the fire mage's mouth.

"Try me!" Kamaul roared. "Let's see how tough you really are! Do it for Kiku. Do it for your pride. Do it for your school. Go ahead! TRY ME!"

Suddenly Jax got involved, pushing himself between the two. The arguing mages were forced to take a step back from each other when the dean inserted himself in the middle. He placed a hand on Abe's wand and lowered it to the stage floor. Jax was eyeing Abe, leaving Kamaul in the background to mock and provoke the earth mage.

"I love the enthusiasm!" Jax chimed. "That's exactly what The Pit brings out in our competitors. But save this for the tournament, gentlemen. There will be plenty of time to attack each other soon."

"You're right, sir. I'm so sorry." Abe retreated to his place on the stage and placed his wand in his back pocket.

"I hope so ..." Kamaul said, waiting for Jax's return alongside me and eyeballing Abe. Kiku fearfully moved between the two. Everyone could tell that she and I would have preferred to be anywhere else. To me, we were already on a lower tier than Kamaul and Abe.

Wonder who the final person will be? Can't wait for them to join this mess of misfits, I thought as the last crystal vial floated down from the sky to the Elder's cauldron.

Marrick grabbed the Gjallarhorn and dipped it into the boiling basin. The horn filled with crimson liquid before Marrick blew into the ceremonial instrument, which released the blood into the air as mist. It glimmered and sparkled as it traveled to the snow. The red leeched into the ground in front of the stage in a blood signature to reveal the fifth and final Pit competitor.

"Olivia Virhorn."

The stadium erupted in a massive cry—louder and faster than for any of the other names—at the naming of the void magic student.

Straight in front of me, a pretty black-haired girl traveled from the top of the arena's seating down the long staircase to the snow. She looked to be my height and was dressed all in black. The expression on her face matched the clothes, as she remained emotionless, seemingly unbothered by the attention from her name. I had feared for my life when I heard mine. Kamaul relished in the limelight for his. Kiku seemed utterly terrified at the showing of hers. Abe looked insipid at the sight of his. Yet Olivia did not seem to care about being called to the stage.

Stepping up, she walked right past Jax (who greeted her by first name) and the rest of us before quickly coming to stand beside Abe. He introduced himself to the new Pit mage, but she did not reply and instead looked at the back of her hand.

The Elders moved back into the shadow of the skybox, seemingly out of sight from the student body. Jax's assistant emerged from a hidden tunnel on our level and ran towards us. She was carrying (and balancing quite well) the Gjallarhorn on a cushion. Jax strolled to the stage's edge and retrieved it before sending her sprinting back to the tunnel.

Raising it to his mouth, Jax spoke into it, recreating the megaphone effect from earlier.

"Let's give a warm Penumbra welcome to our lucky chosen mages! Aaron Dirge, Kamaul Metjen, Kiku Kaipan, Abraham Morrison, and Olivia Virhorn. We look forward to seeing you all perform!"

He clapped alone until the audience joined in to form a chorus of applause. Once he stopped, the rest of the arena followed.

"Now, let me introduce the five Mentors who will be helping these students on their journey to victory. Ladies and gentlemen ... the Pit Mentors!"

More cheering and chanting reverberated through the arena.

Meanwhile, on stage, Jax brought the five of us into a tight circle. He dropped the horn to his side and spoke softer to us as the applause continued all around.

"Your Mentors will come out from that tunnel there." He pointed to the same one his assistant had disappeared into. "They will come up the stairs here and introduce themselves to you before standing behind you. We will get a few moments of the ten of you before the audience and other faculty members are ushered out of the arena. Then, we'll take you all to an area backstage and debrief you on the days to follow. So, once the Mentors come out and say hello, and the crowd gets a look at all of you, the Pit Ceremony will be over. All of your friends and all the other students will be directed to the festival grounds on the north side of the campus. You can meet up with them later, after our group discussion. Make sense?"

None of us said a word or moved an inch.

Jax moved away from us and brought the Gjallarhorn to his lips. "Bring out the five Mentors!" he exclaimed as he gestured to the tunnel.

The clapping had died out slightly once he made the loud announcement, but now it soared back into a great crescendo of excitement.

The other four competitors looked excited as well. Well, maybe not Kiku, who showed the same look of terror as me.

Who would be my Mentor? How would they overcome my struggles? Did I know them? Did *they* know me? Many questions flooded my mind as I blocked out the noise and focused on the tunnel.

The anticipation built as The College of Adarius waited for the Mentors to arrive.

KAMAUL III

STANDING PROUD FOR MY fellow students to admire my body ... Err, I mean standing proud *for my fellow student body*, I was their male Aphrodite. The excitement of the crowd imbued the arena with a sense of glory. However, among this line of anxious faces from the chosen competitors, their fragility and weakness dampened the mood at center stage. The Pit was intended to showcase the college's greatest athletes and young prodigies and prove that we were worthy of representing our elements all the way to victory. And, look, I know the school's curriculum touts the selection process as "randomized and by chance," but that is obviously bullshit. I, on the other hand, understand that each of us is carefully chosen to embody the spirit of battle and our element; these other sad excuses for competitors ought to have felt valiant and honored to be standing here alongside me. Maybe except Olivia—that crazy witch has a reputation even I don't tamper with.

"Mentors? Really? What kind of snowflake needs a Mentor?" I grumbled, crossing my arms and gawking at the others.

Honestly, I had sympathy for Jax and the Elders, who now had to rely on me to carry the weight of this weak group through The Pit.

"Can't you just keep it to yourself, Kamaul?" Abraham interjected.

Oh, that's right ... *My* new fellow competitors are the snowflakes in need of a Pit Mentor. Most of them now stared eagerly, waiting for someone to materialize from the tunnel, like kids on Christmas morning. All except Olivia, who spaced out and stared at the powdery snow on the ground. Their wide eyes betrayed their weakness and mediocrity. Abraham might act tough and forceful, but that was all an obvious ploy to seem bigger than he really was. It was also clear that he had a strange, sibling-type fascination with Kiku. Aaron is too feeble and fragile to be any real threat. The only wild card is Olivia—the one I'm actually unsure about. I'd heard of her before: the freak in the tower. Everyone seemed to be afraid of her for some unspoken reason, but I couldn't see it. Maybe in time, I will. I doubt that, though.

Kiku I recognized, however. She's the clumsy one who bumped into me the other day. Poor girl, too. Oof. With my reputation on campus, that moment nearly ended her social career before it had the chance to take off. Novice mages are easily persuaded and manipulated. It sounds harsh, but it's just the name of the game. I suppose I was being generous that day, but I certainly won't be as naïve in the tournament.

"Love to, tree hugger. But that's not me," I replied.

Jax walked down the small staircase of the stage and stood on the ground. He held his hands at the waist while he awaited the Mentors' arrival.

Giving a nod to familiar faces, I panned around at the student body. The whole arena was quiet. All of the students kept their eyes locked on the tunnel's entrance. Nice and silent, it reminded me of those sibling rivalries in Egypt, where my father used to pit us against each other.

Suddenly, the students and even many professors rose to their feet as the sound of footsteps echoed from the tunnel. A short older gentleman wearing glasses and holding a cane slowly walked out of it. As the arena roared (probably with some sympathy claps), he made his way to greet Jax. For an old fart, this Mentor moved alright.

"Hello, Charles, how are you?" Jax said, kindly shaking his hand.

"Please, call me Charlie, Jax. We know each other." The two paused and chuckled briefly before Charlie continued, "But I'm doing just fine, thank you. Splendid ceremony today, I might add. It might be something I've seen before." His voice was as tender and endearing as nails on a chalkboard.

"Charlie, it's a pleasure to see you again. Seems it's been a long time ..." Jax whispered.

Applause and cheering had died out, and Charlie's words were easier to hear.

"You just saw me this past Wednesday. Though, I agree: It is a pleasure to see you again and to be back in this arena." His eyes glanced around the familiar stadium as he waved his cane through the air. "Many good memories. Many heartbreaking ones, too. I watched enemies and friends die here."

Charlie's face now looked overcome with guilt. He released the dean's hand and solemnly ascended the steps of the stage. Grinning at each of us, the Mentor passed Kiku and stopped behind Abraham. The cane was positioned in front of him, and both palms cupped its handle. A feeling of adrenaline and sarcasm rushed through me.

"Hello, Mr. Morrison. Name's Charlie. I might look old, but don't let looks deceive you. I, too, have competed in this tournament, and lived to tell the tale," he said.

"Yes, of course, sir," Abraham began, turning to face him briefly. "I know I have much to learn, and I'm positive you will help me become victorious."

Charlie blinked slowly and nodded at Abraham, who followed suit and bowed back.

"*Pssst! Psssstttt!* Hey, Abraham," I whispered, leaning around the small girl between us.

He stood silent and faced the tunnel.

"Hey, Abraham!" I shouted louder this time.

"What do you want?" he replied through gritted teeth.

"I see they brought your grandfather here to help you. Good thing you're an earth mage, so crafting a walking stick for him or yourself won't be an issue."

Charlie interjected, placing a hand on Abraham's shoulder. "No, Abraham. We will prove him wrong during the events. Do not stoop to his level. Not this early, at least ..."

"Another success from an assist, tree hugger," I jeered. "Talk to me when you learn to handle your own problems. Can't wait to see how you eventually fend for yourself when you're all alone against me. Won't be an old man by your side in that duel."

I snickered, satisfied by the pot I was stirring. Getting under people's skin and watching their blood curdle was simply too much fun, especially for someone who had nothing to lose.

Gasps filled the crowd as two women emerged from the tunnel. The one on the left was middle-aged with dark blonde hair and a good set of muscles. The second had shiny black hair and was much younger-looking, with perfect and pale skin. Similar in height, they approached Jax at the same time before each bowed to him respectively.

"Kira. Joan. Nice to see you again. Looking forward to what you do with your chosen champions! Please, head up the stairs to meet your mages."

Without response, each one passed by Aaron and me until Joan stopped at Kiku and positioned herself behind her. Kira continued on to Olivia, then stood at her back with the same vacant expression as the student.

Three of the five Mentors had arrived for their mages. Now Aaron and I remained.

Completely unnecessary. I am my own Pit Mentor, I thought.

Then a stern-faced man embraced the sun's gleaming rays. He was wearing familiar Roman-style armor with his white toga underneath a red cape, and his eyes glowed with the fiery intensity only he could muster. A vacant and careless expression fogged over his face. Nero was now strangely becoming impossible to avoid, like a ghost.

Jax waited for him to get closer before reaching out a hand in a kind gesture. However, I knew Nero was not a fan of kind gestures.

"Morning, Nero. How lovely of you to join us," he said.

Nero said nothing, walked directly up the stairs, and stood behind me.

"Don't screw this up for me," he said quietly. His stern voice haunted me for a second as it flooded my ears and sank into my head.

"Trust me, I won't," I swore.

The other Mentor and competitor pairs talked amongst themselves. Muffled conversations and chatter filled the empty air while Nero and I fell perfectly silent.

With Nero standing behind me, I was uneasy. In the classroom, his attention floated from student to student, always critiquing and correcting their work. In the coliseum, he was masterful and unpredictable; he could verbally stab anyone at any moment. But in this moment? He was calmer, with a slower heartbeat. Gone was the wild persona he had displayed at the Gladiator lessons. It was replaced by someone I knew the face of, but I now feared his uncertainty more. Was he back in a setting he didn't want to experience again? Had the trauma of The Pit been too much for even the likes of Professor Nero? My ego told me Nero noticed all my new injuries and decided not to speak—the scabs on my cheek, the poison extraction scar on my shoulder blade, and the somewhat slouched stance due to my aching back.

An awkward silence fell over the arena as the college collectively stared at the tunnel while waiting for the last Mentor to exit.

However, like a mouse scurrying through a meadow of hungry cats, Jax's tiny assistant was the one to come out of it. She looked absolutely horrified and out of place, sprinting quickly to the dean. Aaron and I stepped a little closer to try to hear their muffled conversation as she spoke into his ear.

"Luke will not be joining us, sir," she said tenderly.

googly-eyed looks as I could. With a body like mine, in the condition I was in, it was impossible not to.

"C'mon, give the people a show! That's what The Pit is all about," I said to Aaron and Kiku.

"Hush," Joan whispered past a finger pushed against her mouth. "We aren't even in the trials yet. Save your breath. Control your pet, Nero, will ya?"

"Bite me, lady." I snickered before Nero whacked me upside the head and forced my focus towards Jax.

"Thank you to all for attending this morning! Another tremendous occasion to bring us together, The Pit breaks barriers and balances the world! To close out the ceremony, we will present a lovely demonstration, which will be performed by talented water mages. They will demonstrate wonderful sprites of illusion and natural beauty. Let us begin the finale, shall we?" Jax stuck two fingers in his mouth and whistled at the entry tunnel. "Please give a warm College of Adarius welcome to the Monarchs of Magic!" Jax's voice was much more jubilant, probably due to the exhausting ceremony finally drawing to a close.

The arena applauded and cheered as a dozen cloaked mages sprinted across the snow. They flooded into the arena, wearing black robes and holding gray wands. Dispersing into a circle, each one took their spot and pointed their wand to the sky. Quietly, Jax grabbed the Gjallarhorn and stepped out of sight.

The Pit stadium fell silent as their magic created an invisible dome above the arena, bubbling us inside the cool darkness. The sun's light went out, and the morning again vanished into evening. The wands' swishing gradually slowed down around me.

The light noise was broken by the deep, bellowing voice of Adarius, which grew louder and louder with each word. Though just a voice, his presence was dazzling inside the arena.

"The elements—the world's natural resources. Five channels of magic, each one special and necessary to life. After all, the elements are the reason all of you are here. They are the one connection each one of you has to this college and to nature. Your elemental magic is what makes you unique."

Suddenly, white strands of light leapt from the arena and disappeared from view, but the sparks never left the sky as they joined the darkness in the form of stars. This starry atmosphere produced a soothing and magnificent twilight while Adarius spoke around us.

"Our Pit story begins with the universe, a dense multitude of galaxies and worlds both known and unknown. In our world, this world, Penumbra and Earth exist in harmony as two halves of the same whole. This interconnected relationship is like a tango of nature and humanity. What happens on Earth affects life in Penumbra, and vice versa."

Aiming their illuminated wands at the ground, the mages split their magical strands into two balls of energy. One orb of blue light floated above the right side of the arena, and an orb of gray light floated above the left. They were drawn to each other like magnets.

"Ensuring the balance of nature between both worlds is where The Pit comes in. That dance and dilemma of how to find equilibrium on two planes is extremely delicate and complicated."

Both orbs swirled and moved towards each other.

"For nearly a thousand years, The Pit Tournament has selected a single competitor from each of the five natural elements. A fight to the death decides the winning element and crowns the champion. This event has proved successful each time and led to a roulette of different elements being in charge. Water was crowned the victor in the 247th Pit, as Luke washed away the competition. But the time has come to declare a new element of power."

In a flashy spectacle, the blue orb and gray orb collided, evaporating everything in sight. The stars fizzled away, and the arena went quiet again. After a moment of silence and total darkness, the subtle sounds of waves came alive. Then the ocean became visible. A sea of turquoise water and sea foam arose from the snowy ground and up to stage level. The sound of crashing waves softened once Adarius's voice returned.

"Under water's reign these last four years, Earth saw prosperity: limited droughts, flourishing ocean waters, and recovering coral reefs. Though the years started pleasantly, recent history has proven less fortunate. Melting glaciers in the Arctic. Tainted waters in poorer areas. Hurricanes and tsunamis wreaking havoc on coasts and ocean currents. While the reign of water started strong, it has not been smooth sailing since."

A rocky, discolored beach came into view, seeming arriving out of nowhere underneath the bleachers. As the waves weakened, we were swept ashore to see a coastal cemetery. While I imagined that the void students were losing their minds in a display of blank facial expressions and monotone cheering, the graveyard was creepy and repellant.

"While death will always be the final chapter in our lives, it should never be in vain. Let us please take a moment of silence for those lost in previous tournaments."

Fog blew across the ground, whisking and dividing between the gravestones. The arena held an innocent smell of chrysanthemums and roses. Like an invited ghost, this aroma brought me flashbacks to life in Egypt, the scent of similar flowers used for deceased loved ones and royalty. Many funerals were held during my father's tenure as pharaoh. Some planned. Some not. A painful stinging in my head ... came and went. I forced it from my thoughts, blinked my eyes rapidly, and shook my head to refocus on the passing gravestones.

"Thank you," Adarius said kindly.

The beach cemetery faded away as a chapparal appeared in the arena. The Majesties of Magic (or Maestros of Magic, or whatever they were called) shuffled their positions and took up a new place against the stone walls.

"On a happier note," Adarius began cheerfully, "by tradition, the Monarchs of Magic have dazzled us once again with their abilities and beautiful wand work!"

"*Monarchs* of Magic. That was it." I chuckled carelessly to myself.

"Tradition lives strong in The Pit! 247 other Pits have proven successful in balancing the natural world of our planets. So, the time has come again for us to find that harmony. Tradition is what this college is built on—what it thrives on! The tradition of magic. The traditions of nature and happiness and harmony."

A stream flowed gently through the small valley of dead grass, dirt, sand, and low bushes. Green-and-yellow brush lined either side of the stream. The shrubbery was quiet and peaceful as we listened to the water glide through the arena with a light breeze. It smelled calm, like a Sahara evening; the low-level brush and dead grass felt familiar.

"Sacrifice. The Pit is equal parts tradition and sacrifice. It takes courage and gusto to walk into the arena every day of the tournament. Each day could be the last, but that fight between all the competitors is a thing of glory and pride. We thank you for your valiant courage and sacrifice in this event! Your victory will lead to a greater balance in our worlds, so thank you, each of you! To those who will fight in it, you are now a piece of history."

A little breeze kicked up some tumbleweeds that rolled across the ground and bounced out of sight. The shrubs and bushes whisked along the ground as a group of birds flew above us.

"As per our Pit tradition, this year's tournament will begin with five Elemental Trials—one for each aspect of nature. An Elemental Trial is an environmental test held inside our arena. Magically created at random, these challenges will put the five of you face to face with new landscapes, beasts, weather, and biomes from our worlds. Don't ask for tricks from your Mentor, young recruits. Each year's trials are unique to that year; there is never a repeated task."

A freak rainstorm then rolled into the tranquil chapparal and poured buckets of rain onto the stands and the performing mages. However, despite the downpour, they remained at their posts. Everyone in the center of the arena was perfectly dry, as if a magical umbrella covered us all. Once the fog vanished, a dense rainforest with thick trees and vines in every direction surrounded us. A heavy humidity arrived, and the sounds of an exotic ecosystem came alive within.

"Balance is like a rainforest. Everything has a part to play in the grand scheme of things, and everything plays that part as it should. Like a circle, the balance of an ecosystem comes around and goes around, as does the balance of Earth and Penumbra. Our magic helps heal Earth's wounds, and its nature helps the Penumbra environment prosper. It's a healthy symbiosis, and one we play a bigger part in, due to our responsibility with magic. As with the once healthy rainforests, the time has come to reset the elemental balance."

The rainforest visuals hung around for a bit, with birds chirping and vines knocking against the tree trunks after Adarius finished. Raindrops fell from the canopy into the mud below. Winter was clearly absent in this humid forest, as the heat burned away the frigid temperatures of the arena.

All too quickly, as the warmth of the tropical humidity and heat soaked in, an icy wind blew in from the north. The mages' wands lit up with a bright blue glow as glaciers rolled across the arena. White slabs of ice froze around the stage as light snow dusted the ice caps and swirled through the tunnels.

"Which brings us to the glaciers," Adarius's voice continued, deep and sweet, echoing through the stone grandstands. "The vast openness of ice caps and tundra represents the clean slate brought on by a new Pit champion. Perhaps another element will be in charge and take the reins from water to bring us back into harmony with Earth. Or ... water will be crowned again, giving them a fresh opportunity to right their wrongs. Once again, I want to remind you that each of you, chosen or not chosen, is a part of history in this year's tournament! Thank you for joining us today, thank you for attending this college, and thank you for accepting the gifts magic has bestowed upon you!"

His voice blended with the blowing winds and was drowned out by the snow. As the gusts picked up, a loud silence filled the arena.

After we spent a few frigid minutes in the tundra, the blue lights changed back to white as the mages pointed them at the darkened sky. Twelve wand tips launched streams of sparking light. Each one exploded in a pyrotechnic shower of sparkles and flashing greens. Then a barrage of exploding stars, spirals, and fan-like shapes danced above us, creating rainbow smoke in the air. This dazzling fiery display lasted about ten minutes, with the glaciers gracefully reflecting the many colors. Thunder boomed and small flashes of light swirled inside the smoke as the scene became clearer and clearer before everything evaporated into the sky. The dozen mages stowed their respective wands, bowed to the stands, and then bowed to us on stage. They waved and blew kisses to the audience as each one trotted down the tunnel.

As they strolled out of sight, the audience erupted in ear-shattering applause, chants, and hollering. I loved the sound of that. Seeing their collective appreciation for great magic only boosted my resolve to win this thing. I could hear whistling and cheering from the water section especially. Aaron did not seem so frail anymore; he looked amazed and blown away by the Monarchs' display. I spaced out, hearing the chorus of bolstering applause from my fire section. Their uproar was intense. If they had enjoyed this pre-show demonstration, I imagined how they would feel watching the best elemental competitor take the spotlight. That would certainly be something cemented in the history books for eternity!

Professors and other faculty ushers popped up near the staircases of the stone grandstands. One by one, every row of students was guided back down to The Trench's entrance. In a few minutes, The Trench was emptied, and all that remained were us competitors and our Mentors.

Kira and Olivia started the walk backstage. The rest of us followed. The Pit ceremony had concluded, and Jax was waiting for his new Pit group to rejoin him for more debriefing or whatever. It made no sense why we needed to discuss more information, because after all, it was a simple tournament of wits and strength—a fight to the death. What more was there to talk about?

I quickly scanned around, getting a good glimpse of my competition, until my eyes met Nero's.

"Fun and games are over, Kamaul. These people are your enemies," Nero whispered.

"Believe me, I know ... and I'm ready." I grinned, following behind Joan and Kiku like a leopard stalking its next meal.

ABRAHAM III

"WELCOME IN, WELCOME IN. Alright. So, we have ..." Jax started, holding the door as the pairs passed through. "... the air duo ... the fire duo ... the earth duo ..."

Charlie and I entered the dark, quiet room following Nero.

"... the void duo, and the water solo."

Poor Aaron looked so out of place wandering in alone from the lit hallway.

The Dean of Students strolled in last, closing the door that latched into the metal frame. In a fiery glow, a few torches illuminated the room beautifully.

"Welcome to the debriefing room!"

Jax held the moment, waiting for a sudden uproar of cheers and applause, like it was another glorious Pit announcement. My Mentor giggled a bit to break the silence, but I think it was only out of pity.

It turned out that Jax's self-proclaimed "debriefing room" was simply his office in Central Command. The unusual lavender wallpaper matched the abundance of loose articles and artifacts. Among the disjointed chaos, a single desk and chair stood at one end. African masks were tossed in the corner on top of empty milk jugs. Chewed bubble gum was stuck underneath his messy desk of disorganized papers, unfinished origami swans, and an assortment of unwound baseballs. A painting of a dynamic tree giant hung by a loose thread on one wall. Paper lanterns collected dust on his leather chair, and ripped-out pages from cookbooks scattered the marble floor. Flannel sacks of Fabergé eggs and wooden chess pieces spilled across a thick walnut table. Frankly, Jax's office looked like a different person occupied it every day and never cleaned up their mess.

"Okay, yeah," he corrected somberly, "it's just my office. Not super special ... But I like to pretend that it is. So, welcome." His tone was still trying to convey jubilance even though it was masked by disappointment and random comedy.

"Jax ... This is ..." Joan began in a concerned tone.

"I know, I know. Jack of all trades, master of none. Am I right?" He laughed, scooting clutter out of the way to make a path for us.

Not what I would classify this as, I thought to myself.

"Oh, Jax ..." Kira voiced from behind Aaron. I looked to the left as she peeled back a loose panel of wallpaper to reveal lime-green paint. She pushed it back smoothly and attempted to reattach it.

Then Charlie cut in. "Jax, you think it's time to change the paint color?"

Everyone's eyes followed Jax around the room.

"Well, maybe? I don't know. But I just cannot bring myself to say goodbye to it. Kinda grown on me at this point." He smiled softly, scanning the lavender walls.

Jax lost himself when his focus caught the only picture frame in the room, a black-and-white photo of a woman in a wedding dress. She was standing alone with a rolling meadow behind her.

"Who's the woman in your photo?" Joan asked, kicking aside empty milk jugs.

"No clue. Gorgeous, though, isn't she?" he replied immediately.

"You don't know who the woman is in—" Joan began.

"I think her name begins with an S. No! A! ... B? Or was it an M?" Jax looked confused and scratched his head at each possibility.

"She is lovely." Kira nodded.

"That's so sad," I added, distracted at Nero and Kamaul's lack of attention. Complemented by their disgusted expressions, the fire duo were in quiet discussions behind the desk.

"So! Jax! The Pit. Tell us about it." Charlie snapped his fingers to refocus the dean.

"Yes! That!" Jax shouted, picking up a needle and a baseball to redo the brown yarn. He tossed the ball over his shoulder, which caused Nero to duck, instantly pick it up, and poise to throw it at Jax's head. "Oh, one quick thing before we jump down that little rabbit hole. Since you all are here, can you help me find the Muffin Man? Do you know the Muffin Man, or do you know if I know the Muffin Man?"

"This clown can't focus on anything! Look at his cluttered office! How do you expect to get any info out of him?" the fire Mentor screamed, throwing the baseball at the pile of African masks. They smashed apart and crumbled onto the marble.

"Hey! Easy, Nero!" Joan said scornfully as her face contorted to match his revulsion.

"Kidding, kidding! I've heard folktales and rumors of such a person, but I know the Muffin Man doesn't exist. He's just some ghost story you tell your kids to scare them into sleeping better!" Jax chuckled.

"Cut the act, Joan," Nero retaliated, rummaging through Jax's loose recipe pages and stuffing a few in his toga pouch. "You're not hardcore or anything special. If *you're* special, then we all are—and that can't possibly be true. So, Jax, I beg you with the fibers of my being to ... GET THIS SHIT OVER WITH!"

Charlie looked between Joan and Nero eyeing each other and found Jax's face, silently begging him to stay on track before the Mentors destroyed his office.

"Jax, your office is already a mess. Don't give us time to further the damage."

"Suppose you're right, Charlie. Thank you," Jax answered, casually pulling out a half-finished jack-o'-lantern from a shoebox by his feet. Kira split the onlooking group, carefully picked the pumpkin from his hands, and dropped it back into the cardboard box.

"You don't know how to carve, Jax. You're a draconic expert mage. You're the Dean of Students. You're The Pit Master of Ceremonies. Let's get back to that. Then I'll help you finish your projects."

"I'm not a carver? Are you sure? How did this magnificent pumpkin get started, then? I'm pretty sure I am, Kira."

Kira's cold façade dropped away as her eyes kindly met everyone's in the room and aligned us in an agreement to move on. She looked worried, like a daughter taking care of her aging mother.

"Okay, fine. Yes, thank you, Kira. A bloodthirsty saint you are." He performed a Victorian-era curtsy and tipped an imaginary cap to her. Jax smiled then brought forward the more serious face seen during the ceremony.

"Odd choice of words, but cool," Kira said, shuffling to Olivia's side.

Jax motioned for the nine of us to gather around his egg-and-chess-piece-covered walnut table. With one swipe, he cleared it and wiped it with a rag. Speckles of dust and food crumbs fell into the grains of the wood. Nero and Kamaul, of course, were in no hurry to join us, but later stood next to Charlie and me.

"What's up, Tarzan?" Kamaul whispered.

"Great. Now everyone take one step back," Jax said.

"Not my name. Don't care to answer," I retorted, favoring to admire the grain of the wood boards gliding down like winding rivers.

"Humor me," Kamaul added. "It's a cheat, right? Can't be allowed, I'm sure."

"What can't be allowed?" I answered, still not making eye contact.

"You talking to plants! That's gotta be cheating. I can't communicate with fire. Why should you be allowed to share middle school secrets with your tulip book club?"

"Wow. Your reputation precedes you. 'Communicate' is a big word for you. Lot of letters in that one there, buddy. But no, it's not cheating."

"So, you've heard of me?"

"Heard about how you lost to Jett over a battle axe. Heard about you and your posse bullying kids across campus. That kind of heard of you? Then yes, I know of you, false king of Egypt."

I twisted my head to him and saw that none of my words had entered his ears. Once I opened my mouth, he tuned out.

"Boys ..."

"You've heard about me. I've heard about you. That's how a rivalry starts," he warned.

"No rivalry, Kamaul. Don't include me in your life. At all. I stand next to you here, walk past you between classes, and cross paths with you in a select few other unfortunate instances. That's it. Passersby. That's all we are."

"BOYS!" hollered Jax, who slammed his fist on the table and reclaimed the attention of the room.

Olivia couldn't have cared less. Aaron looked hopeless, lost, and downtrodden. Kiku pretended to know me and not know me at the same time. Charlie, however, wore a frustrated look, like Roy used to when I forgot to clean my bedroom.

"Whatever you say, flower girl," Kamaul whispered to me, slithering his voice into my brain like a parasitic snake.

I stared forward, sighed, and smiled at Kiku. She held a vacant expression with her arms crossed against her chest and her head tucked down to her shoulders.

"By the way, Emilee is quite beautiful," Kamaul whispered. "Overlooked her once before ... But I won't make that mistake anymore. Should be able to charm her into leaving you." He winked in my direction.

I cannot let him get under my skin. But please, Charlie, switch places with me before I strangle this jerk with vines!

I nudged my Mentor on the waist and nonchalantly traded positions with him. Kamaul let out a hearty hyena cackle before shifting to a snicker behind his hand.

"Enough, Kamaul! Nero, control your champion." Jax hovered at the head of the table. "Time to get to it," he continued, bringing his wand into view. It was glorious, with an elvish white stem and gold-and-white etchings around its base, smooth and elegant. He gently tapped it on the wood surface. Our huddle watched as the table flipped itself over to reveal a giant sandbox. Once the rotation was complete, the glass cover over the maroon sand vanished. Jax submerged his hands in it. He oddly invited the rest of us to do the same, though no one jumped at the offer.

"Suit yourself." Jax shrugged, playing in the sand like a kid waiting for his parents to pick him up from the playground. But the intensity returned to his voice as he said, "But I now invite you to my miniature Pit Arena. This sandbox can show you what The Pit is truly like: what the arena does, how it behaves, and what moves it can make."

Joan and Charlie took note of it dutifully. Kira and Nero, however, kept their careless expressions, and their eyes peeled for the other's sudden movements.

Jax dusted off his hands with the table rag and stuffed his wand back in his sock.

"This sandbox is gonna show us what The Pit does?" Aaron asked dubiously. I was shocked and happy to hear him speak. He was soft-spoken and never looked up from the sand. Given he was the only one without a Mentor for the last hour, this must have felt so lonely for him.

"Exactly, Aaron," Jax replied generously.

"How's it work?" I added.

"My sandbox is enchanted with similar magic to the arena floor. It will show you in a rotating lineup what to expect from the various challenges. Think of it as a scale model of the actual event—a teaser for what's to come!"

"Okay, that makes sense," I replied, scanning the basic sandbox and looking for anything meaningful.

"Shall we begin?" Jax asked, glancing around the table to see the reactions.

Surprisingly, all nine pairs of eyes looked towards his own, including Nero's and Kira's.

"Uhhh ... alright ... I'm gonna begin by rattling off the non-event-related items, then move on to the actual Pit Tournament itself. Deal?"

We nodded collectively.

"Alright," Jax began, holding the edge of the table with both hands. He continued on while bouncing eye contact from every person in his office. "This tournament runs from January 21st, the day of the first Elemental Rite, until June 21st, the day of the Final Duels. Training periods begin tomorrow morning and run for the next seven months, with the 21st of each month as a Pit event. These event days will run from nine in the morning 'til twenty-one in the evening. However, they can be extended beyond that, if necessary. Training will take place every day, except Sundays, and will be held in your Mentors' respective facilities. As for classes and schoolwork, the five of you now have a choice: You can choose to do part-time training with part-time classes or drop out of classes to pursue full-time training. If you choose the full-time option, you will make up missed classes and classwork at a later date, to be decided by your individual professors. So, five Elemental Rites, themed to the five elements of nature, followed by the Labyrinth, and the Final Duels will decide the official winner. Any questions?"

Jax had run through this information fast. I picked up on what I could and branded it in my memory. Three of the other competitors looked even more lost than I felt. Olivia, on the other hand, seemed to tune out the dean's spiel entirely, zoning out as she stared at the sandbox like it was the windblown Sahara desert.

"No, I think we've got it," Olivia said matter-of-factly. It was the first time I'd heard her voice in a while.

"Good! Then on to The Pit events themselves," Jax concluded, retrieving his wand and swirling it above the sand.

Like vibrations of an earthquake, the small red particles floated lightly above the table's surface and hung there as Jax continued. He replaced his wand in his sock and gestured with his hands to create the sandbox magic.

"Now, this demonstration will *not* represent the actual Pit. Let me be very clear on that. What I'm about to show you is an *example* from a previous tournament. It will not be the same as what you will face, so copying and memorizing its pattern are utterly useless. Got it?"

The five of us nodded.

"Good. First ... was the Air Elemental Rite."

Like an aggravated orchestra conductor, Jax waved and swirled his hands above the sandbox aggressively. A wind moved across the sand, and soon the entire table was covered in a dusty haze before it all fell and unveiled the new display. Five sand figures stood in a circle around a spinning tornado. The characters split off in different directions and began creating bunkers and other defenses against the fake tornado's winds. Then the cyclone roamed across the sandbox in a fiery red funnel, seemingly prowling for each person. While I understood that this was only a model, the reality of it was sobering.

One unfortunate contestant's defense strategy was no use, and the tornado whisked them away. The four other characters stopped work on their defenses, and the entire tornado scene dropped back into the sandbox in mounds of maroon. Jax folded his arms across his chest.

Without the slightest hesitation, he moved on. "Next came ... the Void Elemental Rite."

Jax's hands traveled in similar motions as they had with the air rite. The dusty mist returned to cover the table's contents before it fell away to show a new scene. The four remaining sand figures all stood at one end of the box. Between them and the other side was a bubbling pit of swamp, or quicksand, or tar. One by one, each character used magic to make their way across it. The first jumped across giant blocks that appeared under their feet as they leapt. The second launched a rope up to a hanging hook and swung across, planting themselves next to the first. The third created a small trebuchet to fling themself over the bubbling river. But as they cut the cord to propel themself, their support structure collapsed under the pressure. The third figure plopped unceremoniously into the boiling pit and was slowly sucked inside, disappearing from the display. The final character simply teleported across it and arrived near the original two.

"Things can change in the blink of an eye, my friends," Jax said, whisking away the scene. "The Trench's dirt floor will change in front of the audience's eyes eight minutes before you all arrive on stage. So, they will see what it becomes, but none of you will know. This arena is an animal in itself. It becomes the sixth competitor, feeling like more of an enemy than the other players."

His brows lifted, and his eyes looked sincere. I could see the honesty reflected in them.

"Then ... the Water Rite came."

The red sand was shuffled in the dusty haze until it dropped back into the box and showed a new display. Now, suspended in midair between the office's ceiling and the sandbox, three sand figures swam in space. Their tiny hands and feet wove them under and over one another as they raced to a checkpoint of sorts. Then their opponent, an enormous worm-thing with a squid-like mouth and seaweed flowing from its back, appeared. It charged and attempted to devour the sand characters. Eventually, all three managed to swim across unscathed.

Jax extinguished this scene and stopped the demonstration, rapidly dropping the sand back into its box. Our huddle seemed intrigued and quiet, until a familiar jerk cut in with laughter.

"I'm sorry, but what is this? A kid's plaything, disguised as a scale model? Get real, Jax. This sandbox doesn't show us—"

"THIS SANDBOX, Mr. Metjen, is just a taste of what that arena is capable of!" Jax interrupted, indicating to The Trench outside the office door. "I am being nice and giving you a sample of what to expect. Listen—or don't. I don't care! But, Nero, will you please get a grip on your champion?! Perhaps his brain is too small to comprehend this simple demonstration!"

"Jax, that's enough," Kira interjected, firmly placing her hand on his shoulder. "This is not you. I know how much you love this sandbox." Her sweet tone and big eyes lit up her black pantsuit and her red heels that matched the sand. "But please, do not take it out on a student. Just because he doesn't share the love for it that you have does not make it wrong. Okay?"

"You're right. You're right. That was perhaps another dean talking." He chuckled awkwardly. "I apologize, Kamaul. That was out of character. But Nero, still ..."

"Kamaul, the clown of this college is right. Save your anger and energy for January," Nero stated.

"He just said that was another dean talking. What does that mean?" Kiku added.

"Ah! Wanna know something I don't share with just anyone?" Jax said, cheerful and chipper as if her question activated a hidden hypnosis trigger. The crowd of Mentors let out a disgruntled sigh but did not intervene. "I wake up every day and feel as if I'm trapped in another person's body. Like my physical body is my usual Jax self ... but my mind is elsewhere. A place I hadn't left it. In a water reflection, I see Jax, the same man in front of you now. But, deep within ... my mind could be Damian's. Or—or Trellow's. Maybe Ninham or Samuel. This is probably really confusing to you, but all of the deans basically share one brain. When one passes away, that brain is plopped into the next dean. Our thoughts live on beyond ourself, so every dean is interconnected like a—a hive mind type of thing. So, my brain has a million thoughts that are not my own. It is as exhausting as it sounds."

A sudden cold air permeated the room through the floorboards and lifted the tension. A foreboding atmosphere descended inside. Nero's dark expression fixed upon Kira's, and she returned the favor once her attention left Jax. Charlie and I stood silent, with Kiku watching as the Mentors' apprehension filled the room.

I kept my eyes on Kiku and saw the fear in her eyes as Nero and Kira shot looks at each other. Tucked away next to Joan, she looked horribly uncomfortable by the information overload, even as Joan rubbed her back for comfort.

Poor thing. She doesn't deserve to see this. This ... event ... is not for her. It's barbaric and relentless. Though I've never seen it, The Pit is a nightmare. Kiku has so much promise and potential! I fear that she will be turned away from magic's beauty during this tournament. Her and I might die in this goddamn thing! Not fair.

"Moving on," Jax continued, adjusting his robe and shaking out his hair, "the fourth event ... was the Earth Rite!"

Excitement was evident in his words as his hands swirled again above the sand, this time more smoothly and methodically. The red dust came and went to reveal another display for our huddle. The three remaining figures appeared, standing side by side as a handful of cyclops giants stomped towards them. Each step they took made the red sandbox tremble. The sand characters split and took on these cyclops in their own ways. Most of them were successful in the end, but one was not. The middle figure had finished off a pair of the giants but was crushed by another's massive foot. It lay smashed into the sand as the cyclops spun around to chase the remaining two.

"Finally ... came the Fire Rite."

I envisioned the smug smile of Kamaul's face standing next to Charlie. I did not need to see it; I felt it tap me on the shoulder, like a needy toddler whacking me with his toy truck.

Red sand dropped from the Earth scene and summoned up a new one, which was hidden one last time by the dusty haze of Jax's guiding hands. With just two sand characters left, they now looked isolated. Two small people stood in a corner of the box as Jax summoned a massive volcanic mountain that took up ninety percent of the table. Despite the task at hand, these final competitors were different. They held hands and trudged up the volcano together, dodging flying rocks and twisting around rivers of lava. There was a floating crown at the very top, where pools of lava bubbled below their faces. Once they made it to the top, the pair touched it at the same time, which allowed Jax's sand demonstration to come to an end.

"These Elemental Rites are randomized and spontaneous. The Pit does not even decide what event it will present until eight minutes before you all walk into the arena. You will know nothing going into each Rite, so prepare for *everything*."

The group of us five competitors was captivated by Jax's words, even Olivia. We were all riveted to the dean as he swirled up the sandbox again like a witch's cauldron. His eyes darted from Aaron's to mine, then to Olivia's and Kamaul's, and finally ended on Kiku, whose face would break a father's heart. She was clearly somewhat excited by the sand displays, but visibly disturbed and hating what they stood for.

A fight to the death involving a sixteen-year-old? That's brutal. But I'm going to help her as best I can. I think Charlie will understand that.

"The Labyrinth comes next. It does not matter if all five competitors are left, or two, or one sole mage in the tournament. It comes as scheduled."

Particles of red soared to form walls and corridors within the box. Constructing itself, the shifting sands assembled into a labyrinth, complete with moving paths, like the real thing. The walls looked sturdy and thick, with mounds of sand molded together and smoothed off to create the shape. One medium-sized space inside the sand maze remained still, where our two remaining characters stood holding hands and facing each other. Then they traveled in different directions and ventured into the maze as it changed every few minutes. Amazingly, both of them eventually made it out alive and hugged once they realized it.

"Then the final month of training commences. Whoever is left in The Pit will prepare for the Final Duels. This is winner-takes-all. And in our story portrayed here, love and majesty can happen during the event—which makes the ending all the more tragic."

His words floated around the room as he solemnly dissolved the entire sand scene, only leaving the two sand figures. The sandbox was smoothed flat like the office's marble flooring as they faced one another in a standoff position. For a few moments, neither character made a move nor cast a spell; they looked poised to end this in a tie. But The Pit wouldn't allow that, and it invisibly pushed them closer to each other. Like a sad Claymation film, the magic and gymnastics began once the two soberly cast spells at each other and performed acrobatics to flip or roll out of the way. Soon, one sand figure had the other pinned down, looking to deliver the final blow. The two touched hands one last time before the standing character struck down the injured one, burying the figure in the sandbox like the tide washing back into the ocean.

A strange and eerie kind of silence sucked the life out of Jax's office, with all nine of us in a variety of moods. Nero and Kamaul remained quiet, but not without loathing looks. Charlie kept his eyes to the sand as it reformed itself into haphazard red dunes. Olivia and Kira whispered to each other, pointing at unique spots across the table. But Aaron and Kiku stared at one another like friends drifting apart.

"And that's The Pit—not *your* Pit, per se, but The Pit nonetheless," Jax said slowly, breaking the silence and glancing around to get a feel for everyone's mood. "Alright ... Well ... That's all I have for you guys. Any questions about anything? The sand displays? The Pit? The classes?"

Silence.

"Oh, I almost forgot!" Jax exclaimed, eyes wide like he'd had a eureka moment. "I almost ... forgot to hand out ... your backpacks. These are only to be used during Pit events and are school property! So, no funny business with 'em!" He rummaged around behind his desk in a large cardboard box marked *Old Film Reels and Motion*

Pictures before throwing out five brown leather satchels. Lifting his head to face us, he handed each one out and then stood in front of us. "Alright! Now ... Are there any questions? Any comments?"

Silence.

"Then I'll give the floor to your Mentors. This is their first time with you. You can decide what to do amongst yourselves."

"That's it?" Olivia asked distastefully, glaring over her satchel, unimpressed.

"That's all I have for you, yes. Now the rest is between you and Kira," Jax answered.

"Wonderful," she said, rolling her eyes and leaving the room as her Mentor rushed after her.

Before reaching the door, Kira spoke to Jax directly, who was flipping the sandbox back into the regular table and replacing the chess pieces.

"Jax, I know you're going through a lot. Talk to me about it, will you? I can help. Really, I can. I know more about your situation than you realize. Understand more about it, too."

He nodded, but didn't respond, preferring to keep reorganizing his office's mess.

Nero and Kamaul left soon after, not speaking a single word to anyone else. But they made a left down the hallway rather than following the void duo to the right.

Aaron quietly followed Jax around the room while assisting with his cleanup and asking questions about Luke. Jax paused to answer the boy's questions before ushering him to the office door and pointing him in the appropriate direction. All that was left now were Charlie, Joan, Kiku, and me. Charlie drifted off to discover more, while Jax and Joan seemed to rekindle a lost friendship. They were laughing and smiling the whole time. I overheard Nero's name come up quite a bit in the course of their conversation.

Kiku held her arms close as I approached her standing by Jax's table.

"Hey. How you doin'?" I asked cautiously.

Her gaze was locked onto the floor. I was not sure if she even heard me or knew I was there.

"Kiku? You alright? It's me ... it's Abe. You wanna talk about anything?"

"No, Abe. I would rather not," she answered coldly—the polar opposite of how she typically acted.

"You can talk to me about it, if you want. I know this whole ordeal is a lot."

"Abe," Kiku retorted abruptly, "I'm fine. No, I don't wanna talk about it. I don't wanna be here right now."

The girl pulled away from my side and opened the office door to leave. Joan said a quick goodbye to Jax and chased after her. We could hear sobbing as their footsteps retreated down the hall.

"Jax, old friend, it was good to see you," Charlie said happily, extending his arms for a hug. But the dean was preoccupied, muttering to himself about a painting kit.

"Gotta finish that painting," he continued, holding brushes in one hand and yanking desk drawers open with the other. Charlie still hugged him from the back, then came over to me.

"Is he always this strange?" I asked.

"Only when he's in his office. The man is dreadfully confused and lost when he's not on campus. But he's alright. I've known Jax a long time, even before my time in The Pit. He'll be okay," Charlie answered, but he didn't sound fully convinced. "He was like this the last time I was in here."

My Mentor looked around the room at the many piles of stuff. "But c'mon, I think it's time we focus on you. Would you like to meet in my Evo classroom today? We can get started a little early and get to know each other better."

"Yeah, sounds good," I replied confidently.

I turned around to glance at Jax before Charlie opened the door. The dean yelled to himself about repainting the giant tree artwork as he held an egg with a spoon in his mouth and barely noticed that the two of us were leaving left at all.

"Oops! Silly nature monster. How did you get there? I know how to fix ya!" Jax hollered inside his solitary office. He took a paintbrush and put pearl-white paint in a tray, then began drawing stick-figure horses with obnoxious smiling faces. In crude brushstrokes, Jax created a childlike "masterpiece" that not even the proudest parent would hang on their bulletin board.

OLIVIA III

"This is honestly a waste of time," I muttered under my breath. I think Aaron and someone else heard me, but that did not matter.

Squeezing through the group, I quietly wove my way past Joan and Kira and down into the arena tunnel. I dusted off my sleeves and escorted myself out.

Listening to Jax drone on about classes and festivals or something, I turned the corner to the second floor, waved sarcastically like a princess at the admissions desk ladies, and headed for the exit out of Central Command. It was rough finding a way through the busy lobby and the hubbub of new recruits. I strolled out the front doors and into Market Square's nearest entrance until I was no longer able to hear Jax's annoying voice.

Just when I thought I was in the clear, I heard footsteps behind me as a female voice beckoned me. Needless to say, her voice dug its way into my ear cavities like a hungry parasite. Not that Kira was a parasite or anything—though maybe that was what I was trying to say.

"Olivia!" she called, her voice echoing down the tunnel. "Olivia, wait up!"

"Yes?" I replied curtly as I sped up my walk home.

"Wanted to say that it's nice to meet you. By the way, my name is Ki—"

"Thanks, but I know your name. You don't need to repeat it."

I rounded the edge of Market Square and followed the sidewalk around the coliseum.

"I'm going to be your Mentor for the tournament."

She was trying too hard. I could sniff out her pleasantries and forced kindness. "Great."

Kira ran ahead to block my path. Her hair was as black and smooth as midnight, gleaming with a light twinkle in the sun. Cherry-red lips and perfect peach skin completed her model-like appearance. She also outperformed my outfit with her coal-black pantsuit and heels.

"Look, Olivia ..." she began, the false sweetness in her voice cutting out. "You have a big head on your shoulders. Don't let that be the cause of your death. Show up for training tomorrow. I know you've got potions to make, or people to torment ... but I'd like to see you there."

"I'm fine," I said, sliding around her and moving forward. "I'll see you when I see you."

Kira might have spoken again after that; I really don't know nor care. I was focused on Marrick and why he had chosen my name from all of the other void students' vials. My thoughts were angry and aggressive as I shook Kira's hopeful wishes out of mind.

Keeping my eyes ahead, I trudged through the blazing sun. I played with my magic as I walked and created a tiny black ball, which I tossed back and forth in my hands. I had to stay distracted to prevent myself from unleashing demonic hell-hounds and faceless fiends on the ongoing festival. It would have terrified everyone there—and it would have been hysterical. Instead, I bounced this little ball of magic around so I could let the college enjoy their special evening.

The tower was finally in sight. It sat in the perfect location away from everyone else, which illuminated this haunted aura about it, because they were all afraid of me.

"A Mentor?" I said, heading up the stone staircase. "Who decided that I needed a Mentor? Was that another 'hilarious' prank on the part of Marrick?"

I opened my bedroom door and stepped inside. I felt relieved to be back in my safe space.

Remembering the deliveries from the past few days, I grabbed a couple vials from the alchemy table and my apothecary satchel. I then glanced at the ancient tome on my bed, sneered at it, and retrieved my cloak from the coat hook. I wrapped it around my body and stowed the vials inside my leather pouch. Leaving my room almost as quickly as I'd entered it, I closed the door with a thud. My footsteps on the stairs sounded even louder than usual.

After exiting, I slung the satchel over my shoulder and flipped the hood over my head. I don't know why; habit, I suppose. The entire college was at the festival, and those who were not were backstage at The Trench. There was no need to use the hood today.

"At least I made some money out of all this," I added as I begun the walk into the woods.

Once I got far enough into the forest, I ditched the hood and smiled at Cal, whose face awakened in the willow tree.

"Ahhh, how nice to see a friendly foe," his voice creaked.

"Tabs paid?" I asked, pressing on a knothole below his chin. I pulled out a few small sacks of coins, dropped them in my bag, and resealed the hole. Looking at his shifting eyes, I could tell something was bothering him. Or someone ...

"Emilee again?" I closed the satchel's strap.

"She talks to me, Olivia," he added. "Like she wants to have a conversation with me. Asks me how I am, tells me how she is, talks about school and other crap. I'm a nightmare spirit literally attached to a tree, and *Emilee* freaks me out! Think about that, boss: Emilee freaks *me* out. Is she as whacko as we are?"

"I fear she might be worse." I giggled.

"Worse?!" Cal panicked, his tree crunching with each contraction of his face. "We are the perfect team! I'm a talking tree. You're the freak of the school ... No offense!"

"Oh, none taken. And you're right. Heck of a team we make." My voice trailed off to the side as I became distracted by a small twig.

"It's not potions you're thinking about, is it, boss?"

He knew me well enough that I couldn't lie to him and get away with it. "Nope. Not even close," I said, vacantly staring forward.

"Life is not going to be the same after today, is it?" Cal asked, as if he knew about The Pit selections somehow.

"No, Cal, it isn't!" I fired back.

"Don't get upset with me!" he retorted. "I only asked a question."

"Not meant for you, sorry. You're just the only person nearby that I can yell at."

"I get it."

I began pacing in a loop around Cal. "Why me, though, Cal?! Seriously, there are two hundred void students at this college. So, why was *my* blood drawn from the cauldron?"

"I don't know," he creaked.

"Do you think Marrick planned it? Did he specifically choose my blood, my name, *me*?! You can't tell me it's just a coincidence. I mean, this has to be illegal or something! He can't just choose the person who competes in The Pit. It has to be random! Yet that doesn't explain how it's me. So, why me?!"

"I don't know," he creaked again, slower this time.

"What do I do now? Meet with Kira and watch her attempt to train me? That sounds awful. Fight against the other Pit champions? Fun, yet miserable all the same. Is this a test for me—something to prove that I'm still as powerful as ever? I don't get it!"

"Neither do I," Cal interjected, abrupt and stubborn.

There was a light rustle in the bushes near the forest's entrance—almost as if another person were coming. But no one was there.

"Somebody needs to answer for this! I should not be in The Pit. It doesn't make sense."

"Olivia!" shouted Cal, stretching the tree trunk to amplify his voice. "You're right. This doesn't make sense. You're right. It doesn't feel like a coincidence that you were chosen. And you're right. This doesn't feel like reality. None of it feels real, Olivia. But it is."

His voice softened a bit. I simply stared at him.

"You're going to be okay, boss. You're ten times more powerful than any of the other competitors that were chosen. I don't even know who they are or what they look like, but I already know you're better."

"Look, Cal," I sighed. "I'm not mad. Honestly, I'm not. I'm just confused is all. I'm the nobody ... the freak of the school, like you said. How is it possible that the chosen void mage is a black-haired orphan from Russia who lives secluded in an obelisk? It doesn't add up.""Perhaps some of your questions will be answered after all," Cal said, moving his eyes beyond, back in the direction of the sounds from earlier.

I spun around to look that way, too.

His figure was covered in loose cloth. Nearly invisible, Marrick strolled between the trees. I could always make out his head, wrapped in several layers of overlapping bandages. The feet and hands, on the other hand, were the more challenging parts to see.

"Hello, Olivia. Good to see you," he whispered finally as he neared Cal and me.

"Awkward ... Have fun, you two," Cal taunted, wrinkling his face back into the tree.

I charged Marrick as he got closer. I held my hand to his head, pointing it at his brain and preparing to cast a spell.

"Give me one reason why I shouldn't disintegrate your mind into madness right here, right now!"

"Because you can't, Olivia," Marrick answered, slowly aiming his eyes at mine. "You think it's a good idea to talk to me like that? Don't forget who brought you to this college in the first place."

My hand remained aimed at his head.

"I did not choose your name, Olivia. I did not specifically pick your blood out of the many. I summoned a random vial from the sky and drew it into the cauldron. But actually, yeah, I wanna hear this. So what if I did? I'm telling you I didn't—but what if I did?"

Marrick slowly inched closer to Cal while I kept my magic at the ready.

"Always have to have an advantage over me, the upper hand," I snapped. "You never let me do anything on my own. Classic Marrick. If you did choose me deliberately, I would say you're losing that subtle edginess and secrecy I *love* so much. It would be like holding a spyglass to my every move. And yet, how do I know you don't do that already? I don't! You just can't help yourself; you have to intervene in my life in every instance! So, choose me from the two hundred, let the cauldron decide, or close your eyes to the whole process; it doesn't matter. Your fingerprint-less hands are all over this thing."

"Olivia! Listen to me very carefully. I *did not* choose your blood," he answered, emphasizing every word and syllable. "Believe it—or not. It doesn't matter to me. But it's not true! If you want to blame me because you now have to compete in The Pit, fine. Do that. Do *whatever* makes you feel better. And if you have something serious to say, you'd better say it. I came here to check on you and see how you're doing. Instead, you immediately jump down my throat. Olivia, don't you dare forget who I am!"

"Whatever," I huffed, dropping my hand from his head and retrieving the satchel from the base of Cal's tree.

A very long silence fell around us, as both of us were too stubborn to speak a word. That is, until Marrick broke it. Feelings of dread and anger overflowed from him.

"I respect your gusto and aggression. It caught my attention in Moscow, and still has a hold on me to this day. But I am an Elder! You answer to *me*. Now ..." He paused, looking from Cal back to me. "How are you feeling? What does it feel like being a Pit competitor?"

"Oh, suddenly you're interested in my safety and well-being? Suddenly, you're on my side and rooting for me? No, Marrick, it doesn't work that way!" I answered coldly.

"That's not what I'm trying to do," he interjected. "I came to see you specifically for that! You're the one who aimed magic at my head—which we both know wouldn't do anything. I'm just trying to make sure you're not losing your—"

"Mind? Not losing my mind? And yet here you are, adding fuel to the fire. You want to make sure that I'm doing alright? Is that what you meant to say? Okay, fine. I'm angry. I'm frustrated. I'm confused. Are you happy now? Are those the answers you were hoping to hear? Hoping to come talk to me post-ceremony to see if I was doing alright? Was that the goal, Marrick?"

He stood frozen and did not respond.

"So, you are mad," Cal chimed in, chuckling, his voice so light that only my ears could hear.

"Zip it, you," I scorned. Then I turned my attention back to Marrick, who stood on the grass, feet leaving no markings on the ground.

"You say I'm old enough and strong enough to be on my own—yet you check up on me daily. You say I can handle myself—yet you stop by uninvited to see for yourself. Marrick, I don't get you! What kind of joke is this? You announce my name to the whole college, provide me with an unnecessary Mentor in Kira, and then come here to my place and my Cal to ask if I'm okay?"

No answer from him.

"If you have to come to ask how I'm doing, then you already know."

I bent down to pick up the satchel and slung it over my shoulder.

"Thanks, Cal. For the gifts and money, and for listening to me rant. I'll see you tomorrow night after training." My eyes switched to Marrick's face as I pulled the hood back over my head.

"*My* tower," he finally said.

"What?!"

"That is MY tower. And you'd better change your attitude, Olivia. This is a tremendous opportunity for you to correct how other students perceive you. Don't make a fool out of yourself. It's a great way to showcase your amazing talents, after all."

"'Change my attitude'? So, this *is* all a joke to you! I'm like a self-help mission or something for you, aren't I? You thought you were trying to help me, make me feel better about going into a death match? Because it really doesn't feel like that. Feels like you're tossing me to the wolves."

I walked right past him and didn't so much as glance in his direction.

Marrick spun to face me. "Olivia, you haven't even seen the wolves yet! Wait until training. Wait until Kira starts digging into how much more you truly need—the maturity and preparation you need. You think you can handle all this magic contained inside you? I'm here to tell you that you can't! But someday, you will! Kira and I will help you get to that point."

"'Maturity and preparation'? Honestly, Marrick, I need a break from you. You ... you're exhausting. But you know what? That's not even my call to make. So, before all of that, come to training tomorrow. I'll show Kira how little I need her help—and I'll show you how little I need yours, too."

Brushing by him and the tall trees, I made my way directly to the tower and yanked open the rusty door, hearing the creak groan through the empty area. The walk upstairs was quick, and soon enough, I was back in *my* room. It does not matter if Marrick believed it was his because I knew who lived in it and called it home.

A single tear fell on the floor as I hung my cloak onto the hook.

"No!" I yelled to the empty room. "Nope. No tears will fall from me. Nope. Not happening. Not today. I do not need my own sadness on top of Marrick's predictable lies, Cal's unwarranted sarcasm, and Kira's forced friendliness. She'll learn soon enough, though, that I'm not a huge fan of friendliness. And I'm not a fan of Marrick either right now!"

Wiping my eyes with my sleeve, I tossed my satchel on the table and pulled out its contents. The beautiful black cauldron awaiting me on the table made me feel exasperated. I reached up to the apothecary cabinet and double-checked my notepad to see what I needed. Leaning over, I read it silently:

Potion for Increased Adrenaline
    1 thyroid gland of a dragon, steel thistle, and ¼ cup of crude natural oil
Potion for Shinier Hair
    6 thorns of a rose, strand of caterpillar thread, and handful of blackberries
Elixir to Change Eye Color
    1 pickled eye of a drake, ½ jar of Kraken ink, and anchorweed
Potion for Flawless Skin
    Pair of siren cicada wings, 1 entire rock beetle body, shaven bones from a Guaibasaurus, and ½ of a Norem heart

Rummaging through the cabinet and shelves, I gathered the ingredients and set them down in an organized pile. I knew making potions would take my mind off everything else, so I ran over to my bed and pulled out a huge cardboard box from underneath. In it, I had several of my old cauldrons and brought three out. Holding them by their handles, I gripped them tightly and placed them on the table. I left Marrick's (the largest one) in the middle and spaced the others around it.

For the hair potion, I tossed the rose thorns into the far cauldron and dropped the blackberries in with my other hand. The potion turned a deep maroon color and smelled of sour fruit.

Once the boiling began, I swirled in the caterpillar thread in a circle while softly stirring the liquid. The deep color became a vibrant neon red, and I released the rest of the string into it.

"Okay. Now I need to remember to stir this one ... every ... three to five minutes," I reminded myself, switching between my notes and the boiling cauldron.

"Next one!" I shouted, feeling nervous now that I needed to work on four potions at once. I had done two at a time before, three sometimes, but never more than that. What choice did I have, though? These potions had been requested over the weekend. Obviously, me being selected for The Pit was not a part of that agenda, but I had to deal with that now as well. And with training for the tournament starting in the morning and probably taking all day, tomorrow was off the table for me to get any of these done. Who knows what Sunday would bring, and then, BAM! Monday would be here. I really did hate Marrick for putting this kind of pressure on me.

I quickly stirred the neon potion again and turned my focus to the next one. Grabbing two jars from the pile with one hand and a bunch of anchorweed in the other, I carefully dropped the weed in another cauldron. It immediately turned the potion into swamp water, thick and dense. I unscrewed the cap of the pickled eyeball and poured it in. It splashed and bobbed up and down before spinning as if on an axis, pointing its pupil to look me in the eye. Then the ink was poured into the potion, making it smell of raw fish and rancid ocean water.

"For this elixir, I need to ... add a single stem of anchorweed as it begins to bubble. Okay, so, for the eye color elixir, add weeds, and the hair potion needs stirred every couple minutes. Speaking of which ..."

Shuffling across the table, I stirred the neon one again, more intensely and aggressively this time. I moved back across to the eye color elixir and dropped in two more strands of anchorweed. Stressed, yet satisfied, I topped off both of those potions and turned to the final small cauldron to begin the third.

Searching for the steel thistle, I managed to find the box of dragon thyroid and the jar of crude oil. This potion required the ingredients to be added in a certain order, so I removed the slimy gland from the wooden box. Holding it far away from me, I kept an eye on it while unscrewing the lid from the jar of oil. Grabbing the open jar, I positioned both ingredients above the basin. I drizzled the oil into it and dropped the dragon organ in immediately after. Continuing to drizzle, I reached for the steel thistle, which was so silver that it looked light blue. One by one, the branches were tossed into the cauldron as I finished pouring in the oil. Both were done at the same time (as they were supposed to be), but somehow the potion inside became a pink color instead of orange.

"No. No, that's not right! How is it not right? I did all the steps the right way, in the right order. I have the correct ingredients. Wha ... What went wrong?!" I panicked, flipping through the pages of my notebook.

Suddenly, I noticed the hair potion was bubbling too high, and I rushed over to begin stirring again. I calmed down the contents, but it was still too hot and feisty. Thus, I stirred a little more moderately and tried to get every inch of the basin swirling on its own. I looked back to the pink elixir, eyes now darting between all three brewing cauldrons.

Stupidly, I had forgotten to add more anchorweed into the swamp-like elixir, which was also soaring to the top of the cauldron. There was not much left, but I tossed in more.

"Oh, damn it!" I exclaimed, realizing my mistake with the pink potion. "I needed to shave the dragon thyroid *before* I put it in."

I quickly slipped my hand into a lower drawer and pulled out a charmed spoon, which was impervious to extreme temperatures and stayed durable in contact with any kind of substance. Taking a deep breath, I lowered it into the pink potion, lifted the dripping organ out, and carefully placed it back in its box.

With the other cauldrons, I added in more anchorweed then stirred the bright potion. Returning swiftly to the dragon thyroid, I retrieved a razor from my tool kit and delicately shaved off its outer layer. After taking several strokes over the entire gland, it was properly trimmed, and I dropped it back into the basin. Thankfully, the pink color quickly changed into the appropriate orange.

Finally, I moved on to the most complex of the four: the Potion of Flawless Skin. This tricky gambit was another right-ingredients-at-the-right-time type of operation. If I got the order wrong, the potion would become a disaster, change entirely, and force me regather the ingredients all over again. Something tells me that Emilee would not be too thrilled if she had to deafen her ears again to recollect those cicada wings.

"Not going to let that happen," I said, dragging the beetle body and the Norem heart box towards the large black cauldron. The sealed box of shaved bones was next. The final ingredient to be added was the cicada wings.

Another pain of this potion in particular was its purpose: to give the user perfect skin, free from blemishes, bruises, acne, and everything else. It was an unnatural and unrealistic kind of effect—one that wouldn't last. Students who wanted this one were often chasing a boy or girl, trying to impress themselves, or showcasing to the rest of us that we were still flawed in appearance. Never a good reason. But clients' requests are clients' requests, and I must fulfill them, no matter their choice. All those students were paying customers in the end.

"Flawless skin," I mocked, rereading my notes before sliding the Norem heart from its box and watching it drop into the cauldron. A large splash of liquid leapt from the basin when it landed at the bottom with a thump.

I shifted back over to the others to add the last bit of anchorweed to the eye color elixir, then gently stirred the hair potion for a couple minutes.

Opening the box of bones, I had to take them out individually and gently lower them into the potion. Putting the fossils all at the same time would dissolve them too fast in the brew, without letting each one properly add itself to the mixture. Thus, the slower I put them in, the better their connection with the potion became. So, one by one, I gradually plunged the Guaibasaurus bones into the shiny silver liquid.

After the last one dissolved, I shoved the empty box to the back of the table and grabbed the rock beetle. Its shell was hard as ... well, a rock, I guess. I had to be careful adding this insect to the potion, too.

Once I plopped the beetle into it, I ducked my head under the desk as a small boom thundered over the table. The exciting thing about using rock beetles in potions was that their shells cracked under extreme heat and caused a mini explosion. I rose to my feet and retrieved the radiant cicada wings.

"Last piece," I muttered, dropping them into the cauldron. It glossed over like mercury, and the potion now shimmered with an iridescent effect.

I left to stir the hair potion a few times. Although the notes did not say to do so, I spun the adrenaline potion too, for good measure.

"I think they're all good to go," I concluded, peeking into each cauldron to check on its progress. All of them looked and smelled as they should. Not that I had any worries about them or anything; I've just never done more than three at a time.

"Now that I have the potions done ... time to rest my mind."

That thought gave me an incredible headache. While the potions boiled and bubbled on the table, I threw myself onto my bed and stared at the ceiling.

An ambient silence filled the space as I looked in the vanity mirror. Frigid air permeated the room as we shared a tense confrontation through its reflection. Cold and stern, my face straightened to meet a hollow gaze.

Shadowed by a hooded cowl hanging over its face, the fiend stood behind me, awaiting my response. Its hunchback arched in the air, with the shadow of darkness perched near my cheek. The rest of its body was hidden under oversized charcoal fabric, with its limbs bulging out from underneath.

"It'll suffice." I shrugged, pivoting my neck again to get a full glance. "Just a few more inches off the bottom oughta be fine."

The fiend grunted an inhuman response and reached over for the scissors and comb.

Sitting back in the chair, I flipped my freshly trimmed black hair over my shoulders and inspected the length with my fingers. It was not perfect by any means, but what choice did I have? Risk the angst and scrutiny of being seen in the market? No thanks. Since the incident at that hair salon, I had found several alternatives for cutting my hair. Doing it myself seemed like the easiest one, but after a single attempt, it was clearly out of the question. Then I tried Tarik, whose care and dedication to me figured to work wonder for my luscious locks. That failed, too, for his ... uhhh ... clear lack of hair-cutting skills became an obstacle in more ways than one. Thus, I had resorted to bringing creatures from the Bad Place into my bedroom and seeing which ones worked and which ones didn't—hence my current situation.

This particular fiend was an old hag, and her thin, weak legs slowly creaked across the floor with each step. From underneath the fabric, six arms, most of them ghastly and goblin-like, spread out in many directions. One hand held a pair of scissors. Another gripped a small hand mirror. Others bore combs and brushes. Though it was just a random, hopeful conjuring, the female creature had proved to be a surprisingly decent hairdresser.

Suddenly, the opening of my bedroom door echoed within the room. I spun around to face it.

"Hold on, Olivia!" Tarik exclaimed, slamming the door shut and immediately pulling out his wand. It was a beautiful ivory-colored one made of polished wood, so smoothly shaven that it gleamed like white obsidian. With woven red leather wrapped around its handle, Tarik's wand was roughly twelve inches long and was capped by a small crystal.

Seeing it, the hag shrieked like a banshee and tightened her grip on her hair tools.

I flung the chair against my vanity and leapt to defend the hissing hag, who lunged forward when it hit her lower back.

"Tarik ..." I eased toward him with my hand up, like a circus act taming a hungry lion. "I know what you're thinking, but I beg you not to—"

I was cut short by Tarik's wand casting a poison spell. Directed at the hag's hooded face, a dozen venom needles shot from the wand's tip and launched at breakneck speed. Not willing to risk a powerful toxin to the eyes, I stood firm next to the hag, but far enough away so as not to receive any unwanted impact. The venom hit instantly and dropped her to her knees, crippling each arm, and she dropped the tools in a clatter. Soon her rough grayish skin livened with a thread of glowing green before she disintegrated into a puddle of poison, which quickly burned a hole through my stone floor.

As the toxin sizzled on the edges of where the hag once stood, I darted my eyes at Tarik.

"You overprotective imbecile! Do you know how long that fiend took me to make?! All wasted away! The nice haircut I was *finally* going to receive is now only halfway done, because you panicked and destroyed my hairdresser! And my floor! All that time wasted!" I sighed. "Now I have to go at it again. Hmmm ... Maybe twenty arms this time ..."

"Oh, Olivia, I ... I thought you were in trouble! I was just trying to save your life."

"Yeah!" I scowled at him. "From something *I* made! Do you honestly think if that hag snuck into my room, she would've lasted more than one step before I banished her to the nether region? Live a little, Tarik. Please! Let me have some fun and a sense of normality for a change."

"You're right." He slumped onto the bed. "I'm—"

"If you say 'sorry,' I'm going to banish you instead to that same fate!" I retorted.

"Right."

Tarik was a sweet boy at heart, but sometimes that eagerness to be on my good side was frequently becoming the source of my frustrations. It was either that he was so eerily kind to me I wanted to strangle him or so distant from my ideas that I wanted to wring his neck. Either option could happen at any moment. Still, he was the only one who ever bothered to put in that much effort for me—even more than Marrick, on occasion. While I shook my head at the dumb reflexive things he did, I didn't forget any of them. What fun would that be?

Pushing my chair back under the vanity, I looked at Tarik again and forced a sappy grin. "Next time, at least let *me* kill the thing. It's more fun that way."

"Deal." He nervously chuckled.

"That for me?" I asked shortly after, noticing a small gift box sitting behind him.

Tarik and I sat while a light whistling sound sizzled in the middle of the room where he had vaporized the hag into a puddle of poison.

"Yup," he replied, smiling hopefully at me. "Stopped by your mail slot, as I always do ..."

My eyes flicked to him.

He cowered a little but held his ground. "You never have mail, Olivia. Not once since we've been dating. But ... today you did ..."

"I did? You're right; I never receive mail. Like, ever."

"Hair looks great, by the way. At least what's been done so far," Tarik added shyly.

Unamused, my hazel eyes blinked at this remark.

"So ... A lot of anniversaries this month, Olivia."

"Huh?" I stammered.

"A lot of anniversaries, ya know? Our one month, your four year with Marrick's eye enchantment, and your birthday."

His green eyes often created a lively and warm sensation over me when they gazed into my own. A genuine smile finally showed on his face. Tarik looked at me like no one else did—like no had looked at me. It was suffocatingly charming ... if very scary at the same time. At this moment, it was tough to tell if I wanted to see five goblin arms grow from his chest or hug him out of pity. Making him anxious over which one I was thinking did lift my spirits, however.

"Well, that's what happens when your family abandons you as a child, and then you jump from orphanage to orphanage until an Elder saves your life by bringing you here. No holidays. No special occasions. So, I was forced to create my own."

"No, no, I get it," he said tenderly, sliding closer to me. "Life forces you to adapt as it goes, and yours more than anyone's. I think it's awesome and impressive how you deal with obstacles when they arise. You are strong, Olivia, so it's not surprising that you've been able to traverse the difficulties of your life. That being said ..." Tarik paused briefly while pulling the box from behind his back and holding it out to me like it was from him personally. "Happy birthday, my little demon."

My little demon?

He had never called me that before. While at first it caught me heavily off guard and even felt insulting, I actually started to like it. Other students had called me "freak," "devil worshipper," and "demon" many times. But when Tarik said it, it made me feel loved and welcomed, as though someone truly understood my life. Thus, rather than scowling with my black eyes at him, I let a smile show and chuckled.

"My little what?" I paused. His face shrunk into an unsure look, as he was obviously afraid of how I would react. "I kinda like it. Thank you, Tarik. Nobody other than Marrick knows about it, so he must've told you, then, huh?"

Tarik nodded.

"Wow. So, he'll tell my boyfriend about today being my birthday, yet he can't even show up on the day itself to tell me in person? What a guy." I sighed.

"You know he means it, Olivia. The Pit is a complicated thing for him and all the Mentors. He's just busy right now."

"Whatever." I shook my head and redirected my gaze to Tarik's hands. "What's in the box?"

"No idea."

"Open it, then. Maybe it's a trap. Better you than me."

Tarik laughed uneasily, then turned away from me to hide its contents. He untied the ribbon wrapped around it. The box was fairly large and sat comfortably in his lap. Tarik opened the lid and tore away the paper stuffed inside.

In his hands was a folded piece of old parchment and a mask. The mask was an over-the-eyes masquerade-style mask like Zorro's, but it had soft straps laced to the sides. Glimmering gold trim lined its edges while a single black rose perched on the corner. More golden paint was slathered on the flower to create a subtle glint. Other than the vibrant trim and coloring, the mask was rather plain. The only problem was that it was certainly not a gift from Marrick or Tarik, which called my attention to the letter.

"Read it," I urged, curiously examining the mask in my hands.

"'Dear Olivia,'" Tarik recited, holding the top and bottom of it like a scroll. "'This is your grandmother, Vanara. I'm sure you have been told by countless people that you have no family left—no aunts or uncles, cousins, or siblings. Well, part of that is true. The other part—the hidden part—is me. While we've never met, I've maintained a close eye on you since you started attending The College of Adarius. You're a special girl, Olivia. Today is your birthday, so I feel it is time that I properly introduce myself. This mask once belonged to your mother. She often wore it to galas and balls while your father was courting her. It has a unique attachment to her, but she instructed me to send it to you once I felt it was the right moment. That time is now, Olivia. I know she'd want you to have it. Safe regards, V.'"

An emptiness filled the room. Tarik was too nervous to speak first. I, on the other hand, was too angry to do it.

Finally, I caved. "'V'? Who is this woman? I learn of her, and she signs off with a single letter—this Vanara?!" I shouted, rising to my feet and abandoning the masquerade mask on my pillows. Pacing in front of Tarik, I ranted, "Why now? Why announce yourself now? Why send a gift from my mother *now*? Where did she come from? Where is this woman? Where does she live? You know, I've lived my whole life by myself! I didn't need anyone then, and I don't need them now!"

Lovingly yet annoyingly, Tarik tried to be the water on my raging fire. He reached out a hand for me to hold, but the look I gave him would have made my nightmares slither back into their abyss. Awestruck and uncertain of what to do next, he sat frozen on the bed with both hands atop his knees.

I could feel my heart racing. With wild ideas flying through my mind, I snatched the letter from his hands and reread it a few more times.

"So, you've never heard of this woman? This Vanara?" he stammered.

"No, I've never heard of her! Did you not just hear what I said? Some lunatic claims to be a long-lost relative of mine, only to reveal the truth on my twentieth birthday with a letter and a mask? I don't think so. I think this is a scam, a joke! Someone really trying to screw me over by making me believe a lie that I know is not true. No one—and I mean *no one*—is alive in my family. Not people I know, or even people I don't. Especially not some isolated woman who claims to know my mother."

"I … I don't know what to say."

"I mean, why now? Twenty is not a special age. *How* does she know I go to school here? Did Marrick tell someone? Did *you* tell someone?!"

"Who am I going to tell, Olivia? I only talk to you and Marrick. Can't be me. Honestly!"

"I just wanna know … why today?" I flopped down on the bed while holding the letter in the air above my face. "And … and what's the mask for? I'm never gonna use that thing. Like, ever!"

"You sure are, Olivia," Tarik scoffed. "For the Masquerade Ball."

"What Masquerade Ball?" I retorted.

"The Ball? Big dance party thing for the competitors? It's like a gala in honor of you guys. Wait … I'm not technically in regular classes anymore, and I even *I* know that. Have you been paying attention at all during class these last few days?"

"No. That's exactly what I don't do in class. I prefer to tune out the professors."

Tarik could see my distress and distraction. He flopped down next to me on the bed. "Hey. Let's go out today."

He caught me completely surprised. I readjusted to a sitting position on the edge of the bed. Tarik quickly joined me and reached out his palms for mine. I reluctantly placed my hands in his and looked into those gentle eyes. Apprehensive and annoyed, I glared as he spoke.

"Today is your birthday. It's the first birthday of yours I've been a part of, and I wanna go out on a day trip with you." Confidence snuck through his words, but I was not feeling it.

"A day trip? Me, in public, with other people and students? Really? That is honestly the last thing I would consider doing on my twentieth birthday. I'll give you that it's better than jewelry, but still, no."

"Hear me out ..." Tarik said, his cheeks and eyes glowing with intensity.

I said nothing and remained still. His hands gripped mine harder.

After shuffling slightly, he pulled up a leg underneath himself and pleaded his case. "Not on campus. Way off to a place called Azuma Shores! A lush and quiet beach town on the southwestern side of Penumbra. It's off the beaten path, a place where no one knows either of us. Just me and you, enjoying the sun and relaxing the day away. Picnic on the sand, stargazing by the water—"

"I'm gonna stop you there," I interrupted, rising to my feet and leaning over the vanity. "What part of this dark, twisted tower of stone makes you think I'm craving time at the beach? What part of this black-haired, red-lipped, gray-sweater-and-jeans recluse wants any part of sunshine and publicity?!" I spun to face him once more, like a queen addressing her subject.

"I get it: You're not on board ... *yet*! Let me change your mind," he began. "So, like I said, this place is on the polar opposite end of Penumbra from the college. No students, no professors, no familiar faces. No Marrick dropping by unannounced. No spiteful eyes wishing you were back in the single window of your obelisk. Olivia ... the people at Azuma Shores have no idea who you are, or about your background or your magic—or any magic at all, for that matter! They don't know us—either of us! Tarik and Olivia from The College of Adarius will walk into that coastal town as complete strangers and leave as complete strangers. Also, the whole daytime thing? It's nearly noon, so it'll be nearing twilight by the time we get there. You'll barely notice the sun is out. Please, Olivia. Let me take this nonsense out of your mind. Take Kira off your mind. Take Marrick off your mind." He paused carefully. "Take The Pit off your mind ... Let it all go for a few hours. Just you and me."

Barely believing it myself, I snapped, "Fine. I do feel like a caged animal up here sometimes. Perhaps some new flesh would be nice to torture at the beach. So, fine, I'll go ... But if any funny business like stargazing or long walks on the beach or any other sappy, cliché things you can think of starts to happen, I will see to it that you personally fix the poison hole in my floor and enjoy a date of my choosing with some familiar fiends of mine."

"You mean 'friends'?" Tarik suggested.

"No, I mean fiends. You'll be enjoying a simple trip to my nightmare realm, free of charge."

"So ... you're in? You, me, beach town—a little date for your birthday?" he pressed, somehow ignoring my minor but genuine threats.

"Yes, Tarik. I agree to be tormented in the sun—"

"Ha! You're the best. Great! This would be kinda awkward if you'd said no."

Giddy like Cal whenever he saw me on the first day of the week, Tarik leapt off the bed, knocking it against the wall. He squeezed me so tight that I felt like I was going to burst. It was suffocating. I was glad to see him happy, but a hug? That was a once-in-a-blue moon occasion! Perhaps *IF* the date went well, I would *consider* a hug. But preemptively? Tarik was really testing my patience today, and on my birthday of all days!

"You won't regret it," Tarik exclaimed, racing to my bedroom door.

"Don't push your luck, poison boy. I can still change my mind," I said as I got up to apply a second coat of eyeliner.

"Oh, Olivia ... You talk a lot, but I don't know about that. I'm a pretty good void mage myself."

"Try me," I teased in the mirror, snarling at him as I finished my makeup.

"Can't scare me, birthday girl. I find your threats cute! I kinda like them. Just like I kinda like you." Tarik winked and nudged at the door, motioning for us to get going.

The pleasure and power in his voice were infectious, and not in a good way. His sweetness was a relentless poison, leaving a trail of optimistic acid on the floor and splatters of confidence on the walls. I gagged at the visual.

Once we left my room and started the trek down the stone stairwell, I followed Tarik's lead as he kept one hand on the railing. A curious question popped into my mind.

"How exactly are we getting to this ... Alakazam Shores place anyway?"

"Ah!" Tarik replied, voice echoing lightly down the spiral staircase. "That's also part of the surprise, my little demon."

"Wonderful." I rolled my eyes. "I hate surprises."

He pushed the creaky door open and held it for me as I crossed the threshold into the cold December day. A chill wind brushed between us, diving into my sweater and immediately making the thick, warm material useless. Despite going to a coastal getaway, Tarik and I were bundled up in long-sleeve tops and jeans. He wore a black beanie over his short hair, which illuminated the olive color of his eyes, and an ugly jacket that I was sure I'd told him looked great when he bought it. My ash-colored sweater and black jeans were a casual yet chic rebuttal against his beach idea and helped keep me warm against the temperature outside.

Trying to alleviate my hatred of being in public, I forced Tarik to talk about something other than me, The Pit, or our date. Anything at all ... which led to him discussing his teaching classes. Tarik had graduated a couple years ago and was in training to become a void professor. He was intelligent and charismatic, and certainly had the potential to be a better professor than any of the flounders I had watching over me.

"Going great so far! Second year now, so I'm starting to shadow the void professors. Yesterday marked my first week of working with Silas. And ... wow ..." Tarik trailed off as we wrapped the coliseum. "That man is wild. I don't know how he does it. Stoic. Stubborn. And strict." He turned around to walk backwards, with his face looking at mine with uneasy excitement.

"I'm familiar," I said, giving him the side eye. I knew all about Silas and his personality.

"He's the first one I'm training with directly, but I guess it's better to start with the hardest so it will get easier, right?"

"Right," I added carelessly. "Where are we going?" I interjected as his sneakers pivoted.

With the ongoing Festival of the Elements erupting in a chorus of loud music and sound to our right, Tarik thankfully continued on the path along the river, which funneled from the campus lake and wove its way around Market Square. He kept his feet at the edge of the water; I stayed more on the grassy banks.

"We are going to The Stables. I'm meeting someone there who can send us on our way to Azuma Shores! Trust me, Olivia, I've done this before."

"Done this before? Done *what* before? I don't follow ..." I muttered, cautiously stepping around a bouncing frog heading for the river.

"You'll see. Just hang tight."

"Whatever you say," I replied in a mix of angst and concern.

As the river picked up speed, The Trench loomed to our left. Dozens of element pennants hung from the top, swaying in the icy breeze. I felt a sudden chill course through my skin, and not from the winter winds. It was like an uninvited guest on our date—a ghost tracking my footsteps, no matter which direction they went. I didn't acknowledge it; the interactions with Kira yesterday threw it out of focus. That is, until now, when the imposing stadium hovered over me. My eyes scanned the massive arena, then flicked to Tarik, who rambled on about the difficulties of teaching void magic to ill-prepared mages.

"Olivia?" he said, stopping before The Stables entryway. "Everything alright?"

"Fine," I answered, brushing past his shoulder. "So, which one's yours?"

The sprawling stables were a massive two-story building. The large structure stood strong amidst the manicured grass and gravel. As I took in the windows and thick slabs of stone, I could hear the echo of pounding paws and scaled drake wings flapping inside. Flanking the building was a series of outdoor enclosures, which stretched into what looked like a sporting field. Bears huddled in the corners of their pens. Several pens were empty, as their animals were probably rented out for the day. However, the sheer number of occupied pens dwarfed those that were vacant.

The stable master was preoccupied by a scrawny teenage boy, who I suddenly realized was Aaron Dirge. I spied on him as he neared a horse stall. Like the forgotten child of a big family, he waited awkwardly and silently by a black bear enclosure as tiny hairs of fur blew around in the light gusts of wind. I refocused on Tarik.

"So, which one is yours?" I repeated. "The way you talk about it, you must have your own private pad here or something." My words were sharp and curious. While I was interested to find out more about Tarik, the more I found out, the less it made sense. Investing myself in other people was not a strong suit of mine; nor was I good at it, as I was never fond of growing attached to them. Still, there was something about Tarik that overcame my curmudgeonly ways. Perhaps it was his wit or his charm ... or the fact that he simply laughed off my threats whenever I made them.

He motioned around the stone building and towards a partially hidden gravel path beyond a group of towering pine trees.

"Yup. Private pen," Tarik said confidently. "Marrick has to sign me out anytime I use him, so he might be here," he added over his shoulder.

"Great," I grunted, heatedly staring at the bouncing black beanie on his head. That got my blood boiling again, thinking that Marrick would still have control over me even if I left the campus—a man who claimed to understand that I was a strong, independent woman, capable of taking care of myself. But he seriously couldn't help himself, could he?

"But he's busy today. Doubt he'll even be here," Tarik reassured me.

The gravel path weaved deeper into the pine woods and further neared the edge of the campus. Lines of trees seemed to pop up out of nowhere.

Then I saw her, standing with hands clasped behind her back. She wore a black leather trench coat, black slacks, and plum lipstick that lined an irritating grin across her pale face.

"I take it Marrick sent you instead?" Tarik began coolly.

A hangar tent erected between a clearing of trees behind Kira beckoned us, taunting me with my new desire to leave the campus. It was covered with long pieces of crocodile-green canvas, with arching pieces of wood marking the front and back. One wide door was cut into the near side, and a glass-thin, steel hangar door apparently locked the animal inside. There were no patterns or anything on the outside to declare who it belonged to, but the glimmer of lust in Tarik's eyes assured me that we had come to the right place.

"Yes," Kira replied. "He sends his apologies for not being here today. Other ... matters came up." She looked only at me, with the same fake smile she'd worn after the ceremony. I wanted to blast it right off her smug little face.

I followed after Tarik, thinking he would hold out his arms or his wand to stop me from lunging at Kira. But he didn't; he was giving me free rein to do whatever. I crossed my arms and glared at her like a schoolgirl ready to fight on the playground. Tarik kept his hands close to his waist and kept himself close to me, just in case.

"Oh, does he, now?" I said, mocking Kira's overly polite tone.

"Yes, Olivia. And ..." she began, holding my gaze with her irritatingly kind eyes. They blinked rapidly. "I personally just wanted to wish you a magical birthday."

My pearly-white smile was so exaggerated that it nearly cut from ear to ear. "Is that so?" I said through gritted teeth. "Tell Marrick to stick his birthday wishes where the sun don't shine. As for you, I can't wait to work together. I'm so excited to see how much you think you know."

I stepped closer to Kira with my arms still folded across my chest. The faux leather of her jacket offset her long hair. Despite the overcast sky, the sun reflected down her cleavage.

"I can tell we're going to be the best of friends." She stepped closer to me with slow, purposeful steps. "Sunday. I'll make two cups of cherry blossom chamomile tea."

I moved in, too, now within inches of smacking that smug look off her face. I matched her tone with the same teeth-gritting smile with my head tilted opposite hers. "And I'll bring little sandwiches and caviar. We can talk about our personal strengths, one-upping each other until our words become nothing but overly exaggerated, pointless lies, where the only true thing in each sentence is the jab hidden inside. We're gonna be such great friends! I can already tell."

Tarik jumped in and slid his way between Kira and me. Clearly, he could sense an unpleasant tension rising near the hangar, one that would probably result in blood magic and nightmare magic spells being shot across the trees like meteors. He was right to think so.

"Okay, ladies ..." He laughed cautiously, holding up a palm to each of our chests. "I think this quick interaction has come to a boil. Let's put a pause on all this and pick up tomorrow. What'd ya say, huh? Kira, you say your piece and leave us to our date. And Olivia, you keep your cool and stop with the pettiness. Yeah? Let's do that. C'mon."

He casually yet carefully eased me back from Kira's face as she stood with the same statuesque expression on her face.

"Tarik's right," she said. "Our friendship can begin blossoming tomorrow morning. Enjoy your date, Tarik. Toodle-oo, Olivia."

With methodical movements, Kira took her good ol' time walking out of view. I stood by Tarik's side with my arms locked at my chest. My fists were probably leaving marks on my biceps.

"I hate her," I muttered, quietly, but not enough to avoid Tarik hearing.

"Yeah ... Way to hide it." He shrugged it off and retrieved a slender silver key from his pocket.

"I would have fought her. Wait 'til Sunday! I'll show her how powerful I am. I can talk the talk and walk the walk!"

Tarik unclipped a few rabbits from a clothesline and casually held them at his waist. He suppressed a chuckle and approached the door to insert the key. Twisting it in the lock, he pulled the door open, and we entered.

A magnificent creature looked down at us. Its massive front talons were stapled into the dirt and dug sharply below the surface. The griffin had the golden body and proud hind legs of a lion, muscled and powerful in its stance. A tail twisted in and out of view behind the towering, feathery wings of an eagle. Their strength was unmatched as they pointed to the sky, perfectly parallel with each other, and opened narrowly towards the hangar's thin door. The head and neck of an aged eagle entranced me, like an explorer in unfamiliar territory. Steady pupils fixed upon my figure as Tarik's hand gently scratched what looked like a white lion's mane underneath a cawing beak.

The griffin was not happy I was here. It was relishing Tarik's presence, yet visibly distressed by mine. An unsettling mixture of its feeling safe under my boyfriend's soothing touch and the sweet nectar of fresh meat made the griffin look hungry, and my armpits grew sticky under the sweater. Still, Tarik nudged for me to reach out a hand. I was comfortable with creatures of all sizes and strengths, sure. But a griffin? *This* griffin?

Strategically, I opened my palm up for it to see and moved to its mane, a spot next to where Tarik's hand was. My eyes never left the griffin's, and its eyes stayed transfixed on my every movement. I could sense every muscle and bone of its being restraining it from making a midday snack of my arm; it could have bitten clean through my skin like it was an appetizer. It was profoundly strong and demanding as I inched closer. Meanwhile, Tarik gently whispered to it.

"It's alright. She means no harm. She's with me. It's alright now."

It was when I neared the neck that I noticed a dark spot under its left wing. Roughly the shape of a blotched bottle cap, it appeared to be a birthmark or scar of some sort—though it was difficult to tell, with the griffin bucking like a bronco when my hands grazed the tips of its fur.

"No, no, it's okay. She's alright—I promise."

The griffin immediately switched from an apprehensive beast to a happy puppy, tilting its head up so I could scratch its chin properly. I ran my fingers through the scruff on its neck. A soft whimper came from the griffin's beak, but quickly disappeared in the vast space of the hangar. Typical; I was hard-pressed to find a creature of Penumbra who did not enjoy my company. Tarik's griffin was simply being coy about it and trying to prove how tough it was.

"What's its name?" I asked kindly, scanning the mark under its wing more closely.

"Its name?" he echoed. "What do you mean?"

"Are you playing dumb, or are you genuinely confused?" I asked.

"I guess confused," Tarik replied, watching me touch his griffin.

"This is clearly your pet. Surely you must have a name for it?"

"A pet? What's a pet?"

Is he serious, or is he actively trying to achieve Kira-level annoyance?

"A pet is an animal you grow attached to, both physically and emotionally. You spend time together, do things together, and basically just enjoy one another's company. Share a bond."

"Oh, he and I do all of those things! I guess he is my pet, then," Tarik said, looking longingly at its eagle eyes.

"So, what's his name then? Spot? Chestnut? Silvertail? Shadowclaw?" I tossed out more names, none of which the griffin took notice of.

"Oh, so you give it a name based on its appearance? Got it. What about Ferret Swallower? Oooooh, maybe Person Piercer?"

"What?!" I exclaimed, laughing and hitting him in the stomach lightly. "No, you fool! Pet names are meant to be charming, or funny, or sentimental. Yours were awful. Let's go with Chestnut! Perhaps we can find a better one later."

From Tarik's side, I took one of the rabbits and fed it to Chestnut. His beak curved around the small hare and tossed it into the air before swallowing it whole. The griffin's eyes gleamed down on him in anticipation, but Tarik wanted to get a move on. "More food later," he told the griffin. The silent look between Tarik and Chestnut had the beast's neck bending to the floor so that we could mount him. Both of them were calm, and they shared an evident bond: Tarik sometimes being an insufferable optimist, and Chestnut being a magnificent, man-eating, carnivorous dominator of the skies. Meanwhile, an angry part of my heart latched onto those thoughts, bringing my smile to a frown once I straddled the griffin behind Tarik. This connection reminded me of my relationships. Holding onto his waist, I couldn't help but think of Marrick missing my birthday and not seeing us off at The Stables, and the horrible, forced appearance of Kira as his replacement.

"Would you like to do the honors?" Tarik whispered to me while holding tight to the fur on Chestnut's neck like reins.

"What? What honors?" I replied, visibly distracted. "I don't understand."

"Of opening the hangar. Chestnut's head is not an anvil; he can't bust through metal. So, we need to raise the door on our own. I usually do the spell, but today is your day. So?"

"Sure, I can manage that," I answered, focusing on the base of the hangar door. Raising my head slightly above Chestnut's bowed one, I focused my magic and shot a light gray mist from my hands. It spread across the base and created a dusty fog along the door's edge. The door began rolling up until it reached the top of the hangar. Tarik nodded at me and gently tugged on the griffin's neck.

"Alright, pal," he urged, crouching against Chestnut's soft, thick fur. "Here we go ..."

Excited yet scared about my first time flying, I held tight to Tarik's waist and dug my heels into Chestnut's sides. He sprang from the hangar in a single bound. In thunderous booms, his paws hit the grassy runway, like a lion racing after a zebra. The takeoff was smooth and fast, and we left the hangar behind as it dwindled into an anthill.

As we headed west, Tarik rose back to a sitting position and let the griffin float through the sky, coasting below the ceiling of clouds.

KIKU IV

ONCE ZOE AND I returned from the ceremony, I noticed a white wrapped box at our door. I picked it up off the floor as she opened the door.

"What's that? Something from the college?" she asked, tossing her keys in the bowl.

I quickly sat down on the couch and began unraveling the ribbon. Tossing the string aside, I popped open the lid and looked inside. Within the package were two things: a note written in pastel pink cursive on black paper and a gold-etched mask with musical notes painted on it.

"Wait ..." I paused. "Did you get one of these? Or just me?"

"Nope, just you. Must mean you're special."

"Why didn't you get one?" I wondered, lightly tapping my foot on the floor.

"Not sure. OH! Duhhhhh ... It's probably because you got picked for The Pit." Zoe rushed to my side as we read the invitation in unison.

"'Kiku Kaipan—'"

Her voice split off and yelled out an "OOOOOOOH," like I had been called out during class to go to the principal's office.

"Hush!" I retorted, not quite matching her overenthusiastic tone.

"Okay, okay. Not feeling jokes, I see ... Moving on, then!" Her attention focused back on the note. "'Kiku Kaipan, this is your Mentor, Joan. I am cordially inviting you to a magical night of mystery at the Masquerade Ball, tonight at 19:00. I have chosen a mask for you to wear as well.'"

"A ball?" I echoed, taken aback.

Zoe set the invitation back in the gift box and looked for my reaction.

"I'm not ready, Zo," I panicked, now rapidly bouncing my feet on the floor.

"But you will be!" she insisted, sitting down next to me and wrapping me in a big bear hug.

"But I'm not, though! I ... I'm not ready to be in the spotlight again. Or to go to a Masquerade Ball, or to be the center of attention at a college party. I'm not ready to train with a stranger or compete in a ... a death match! I'm just ... not ready, Zoe. I won't ever be ready either," I sighed.

"Then tell me—"

"First off," I continued, "these other competitors are smarter than me. Stronger than me. More experienced than me! I know Abe, yeah ... But ... but the rest are ... Olivia is so pretty, and so scary. Kamaul is strong and handsome, and I am positive it was him who threatened me the other day when I dropped my journal. Aaron is just quiet. And me? Well, I-I'm just—"

"An awesome and powerful girl!" Zoe exclaimed.

"I'm not, Zo! Can't you just be honest with me here?! I'm not!"

"I *am* being honest, Kiku!"

My foot was tapping louder on the floor, to the point where Zoe glanced between the books on the coffee table and the lamp next to us, waiting to see which one fell first. Darting my eyes from hers to my shoes, I gravely asked her if it was that noticeable.

"Don't think it's that bad, is it?"

"No ... Just being proactive is all." Zoe chuckled.

She rose from the couch and ran to her bedroom. "Let's start with this!" her voice echoed to me in the living room, followed by her return.

"How are you holding up? What's going through your mind right now? Don't give me anything other than actual emotions. Like, the ones going through your head at this very second." Zoe beamed her gorgeous smile at me—rather intensely, I might add. Pencil and pad in hand, she looked to me for a speedy response. "And ... go!"

"Well ... Ummm ... You're kinda putting me on the spot here. But I think all the other competitors are smarter than me, and more ready than me, and more confident than me. I'm scared. I don't think I'm good enough to be in this thing! I was terrified just going *into* the ceremony. Now, I'm completely panicking and freaking out. Zoe, why was it *my* name? So many other choices, but it was me. Why?"

Zoe was scribbling lines of notes.

"I don't know why the Elder chose you. But they did! And now, it's my job as the de facto best-friend-o to make sure you keep your head held high and your worries down low. So, that's what I'm gonna do!" She stopped writing and showed the notebook to me. "Listen well, Kiku Kaipan, because I'm going to blow your mind here."

On Zoe's notebook was a chart with our names on either side of it and titled *Pros of the Ladies of Room 3105* at the top. There were roughly a dozen little phrases on my side and a few on hers. My foot finally stopped tapping the more I focused on the page.

"What is this?" I wondered.

"Positive traits of you and me," she answered, shoving it closer to my face and scooching across the couch to set it on the table in front of us. She playfully nudged me on the shoulder.

"If you notice, there's only two on my side, and like, eleven on yours! Let's go through some real quick. Rapid-fire! Strong, independent girl? No argument there. Brilliant mind for magic? Check. Beautiful? Yup. Polite and proper, even to the scummiest mages? Yup. Capable of holding her own against the most dominant of sorcerers, including Merlin? Yes, ma'am. Should I keep going, or do you get the picture?"

"No." I chuckled back. "I understand."

"Good!" Zoe exclaimed, tearing the sheet from her notebook and folding it up. With a gentle calmness, she looked at me and tucked the paper in my pocket. "Keep this, so I never have to remind you how awesome you are," she added matter-of-factly.

"Thanks," I replied.

"Don't get all sappy on me now!" Zoe giggled.

Her laugh was infectious as I released my grip on the couch.

"Before I change clothes and head down to the festival, why don't we check on Sonnet?"

I had totally forgotten that we had an illegal wild animal living in my bedroom. I pushed off the sofa and flung my boots at the door. The growing level of stress was returning.

On top of my bookshelf, Sonnet slept with her head tucked under her injured wing. Her black eyes popped open and bored into me when I popped into view at the doorway.

"How you doin' in here?" I asked, taking off my ceremony outfit and changing into comfortable, existential-crisis-ready attire: sweatpants and one of Zoe's hoodies that featured a koala bear.

I swear, some way and somehow, Sonnet looked bigger than she was earlier. It was probably just my imagination. Yet I couldn't shake the feeling that it was true. I softly walked over to her and bent down to look into those piercing eyes.

In front of her nest sat the same blueberries I had left for her this morning.

"Not hungry, huh? Yeah. Can't say I blame you on that one. I'm not very hungry myself," I said, watching her dark feathers ruffle as she twitched her head.

"You know, Sonnet, I thought spontaneously adopting and housing a wounded bird would be the craziest thing to happen to me this week. Turns out I was wrong."

I knew I was talking to an animal who wouldn't respond, but it felt as soothing as talking to Zoe. Despite my friend's best efforts, I was still in my own head, wondering this, questioning that, and everything else in between.

Sonnet was purring gently in the nest. Zoe knocked on the door and entered my bedroom, sitting on the bed's edge. I was stroking the back of the bird's neck when she came in. "How's Sonnet doing?"

I touched her magnificent feathers. "I think she's doing well? Hasn't eaten anything, though. Her wing seems better, and Abe's bandage is holding up great."

In an effort to keep grave things like The Pit and the ball off my mind, I chose a textbook at random and flipped through the pages. Zoe moved to the floor with me. Sonnet hardly noticed we were there as she slept contentedly in her nest. Given the worrisome status of my brain, I would have given anything to have that kind of serenity. Even the flying unicorns and Pegasus dotting these pages could not break through the noise in my head.

"How long is their wingspan?" Zoe chimed, petting Sonnet's wings and looking over my shoulder.

"Huh? Oh, Zo, I didn't know you were that close!" I said frantically.

"Didn't mean to freak you out. I saw you reading about Pegasus and was curious myself."

"Yeah ... I'm not really reading it. More like skimming and looking at the pictures. Anything to take my mind off the—"

"Let's just not say it!" Zoe interrupted. "The less we say it, the less you'll actually have to think about it. We could focus on the ball instead?"

"No. Dancing, the public, spotlight on me, and just ... yeah," I answered.

"Okay ... Umm ... What about the training? Focus on all the cool new spells and magical powers that you'll learn!"

"It's a lot of magic. The idea and the methods I can absorb. It's the practice and actually doing it that I struggle with."

"Well, I'm sure Joan can help you with that," Zoe tried, turning to look at Sonnet.

"Yeah," I sighed. "I'm ... I'm sure she could. It would be ... uhhh ... good to learn all that stuff." My attention zoned out as I stared blankly at the pages. I wasn't sure what I was looking at anymore. "Look, Zo, I'm sorry. I'm super out of it. I'm not even sure what I'm reading right now. I have no idea what you asked."

"Kiku," she reassured me, "it's alright that you're stressed and worried about The Pit. Who wouldn't be? And I know it's gonna sound repetitive and boring and cliché, but you are going to be okay. You're going to win this thing, and then the three of us are gonna celebrate right in our living room! Since you now have a mask gifted by Joan, I need to go get one for myself. So, I am going to the festival in hopes of buying a really awesome one like yours. Wish me luck!"

"Good luck!" I smiled, finally glancing back at her and Sonnet.

"I'm going to change into something more suitable for this carnival-circus thing tonight, then head out to get my mask. Oh! I almost forgot ... Kiku, I'll be back here before six, so we can leave for the ball together. That way, we can get dressed, do our makeup, and present our masks at the same time! I'll meet you here around that time, alright? Deal?"

Zoe was rather persuasive and understanding. I nodded in agreement but kept watching Sonnet sleep.

"Good!" she said, bouncing out of the room.

A knock on the door sounded from outside.

"Coming!" Zoe chimed, rushing in mid-change to grab the door.

Tossing my book on the bed, I rushed to the hallway and popped my head out to see a familiar face standing in 3105's living room.

"Abe?" I questioned, shocked and happy to see him at the same time.

"Hello, Kiku. Hello, Zoe." He smiled, looking a bit exhausted.

Zoe welcomed him inside, then he and I took a seat on the couch.

"Sorry if I look tired. I just had a mini lesson with Charlie after the ceremony. Wasn't planned, but it went pretty well, all things considered. Real question is ..." Abe started, moving his attention from Zoe to me. "How are you holding up? I can imagine there's a lot running through your head right now."

Something about Abe's manner made his question feel much different than Zoe's, despite it being the exact same one.

"I'm doing alright," I lied, smiling at him.

"No, I mean ... how are you holding up? Scared? Nervous? Discouraged? C'mon, Kiku, you can't lie to me. How are you really feeling?"

"Okay, okay, fine. Then yes, I'm all of those, actually. I'm scared of dying and of not being good enough. I'm nervous about the Masquerade Ball, training, being the center of attention ... I'm discouraged by my own fears and lack of magical know-how. Abe ... there's just *so* much going on right now. Plus, Sonnet is here, and I have to keep an eye on her—make sure she's safe and hidden."

"You named her Sonnet?" Abe grinned.

"Huh? Oh, yeah, we did." I chuckled. "What do ya think? Good name?"

"That is a great name. I think it suits her very well. How's my makeshift splint holding up?"

"It's holding up great! She seems to have adapted to it already. How long do you think it should stay on?"

"Couple weeks, I think," he answered.

"Do you want to see her?"

"Can I?" Abe replied, both excited and uncertain. "Is that alright?"

"Of course!" I exclaimed. I rose to my feet and waited for him to do the same. Before Abe stood from the couch, Zoe flattened her pants and quietly walked over to the front door.

"I'm going down to get a mask for tonight. Gotta go down early and find the best one before the whole college buys them out!" She laughed before waving goodbye.

"Hey, Zoe, hang on a second! I got a question for ya," Abe hollered, rushing after her.

After he closed the door and ran after Zoe, I stood and watched for one of them to come back. Despite being in my own dorm, I felt weird in it. The feelings from the ceremony came surging back into my mind. The feeling of being on that stage, in front of the *entire* student body. The feeling of thousands of eyes on me at once ... Worst of all was seeing *Kiku Kaipan* scrawled in the snow. The ceremony had been going fine until that happened. It was the first time in a long time that I had felt an overwhelming sense of dread wash over me. I had performed in front of audiences before, but that moment was different. The only absolutely good thing about being selected for The Pit was that Abe would be there, too. Zoe and Abe were the only two people I trusted at this college, and thankfully, one of them knew what I was going through. Joan could help me all she wanted, but only Zoe and Abe can really make a difference.

A couple minutes had passed when Abe knocked.

"Sorry, I didn't mean to close it. Silly of me." He chuckled, nodding as I held the door open for him. "Just had a question to ask her, from Emilee. Beyond the field of thought for me."

"Okay," I replied, confused. "I'll show you where Sonnet is."

I closed the door and had him follow me to my room. "She's in here," I said, motioning for him to head in first.

"Wow. She looks really good! I love the nest you made her, too." Abe strolled right over to Sonnet's side and rubbed her injured wing. He carefully lifted it so he could see underneath. Peeking between her feathers, he carefully examined the area under her wing. The bleeding and pain had subsided, as Sonnet made no whimpers. She was calm as Abe inspected her injuries.

"Zoe made the bed, actually." I laughed.

"She did a super job! Seriously, Kiku, whatever you're doing, or whatever you and Zoe are doing, it's working. I'm dead serious!" Abe exclaimed, beaming his brown eyes at me like a warm fireplace.

"Please ... don't use the term ... 'dead.' It's just ... not the word I wanna hear right now. You know, with the ..." I stammered.

"Yes, yes, of course! I'm sorry. You're right, that was a poor choice of words. I apologize. All I meant to say is that you and Zoe are becoming very good adoptive caretakers." He chuckled slightly before suddenly howling with laughter. I was not sure why he was laughing, but I could use a good laugh today, so I joined him.

We laughed for a few moments while looking at each other. For this mere sliver of the day, I felt all my worries vanish. Being around Sonnet calmed me down, and Abe knew how to make me laugh, no matter how somber my emotions were.

"Where did the name come from?" he asked, checking for approval before sitting on the edge of my bed.

"When I was young, my mom used to sing me a lullaby to get me to sleep. Same one I sang to her in the woods the other day. Well, that lullaby is actually a sonnet. And funny enough, my mom always called me 'baby bird.' Not sure why, but she did. And when I said that name, Abe, Sonnet and I connected. She looked into my eyes, and I looked into hers, and we just ... connected."

"I knew you would." Abe grinned.

"There's no way ...!" I exclaimed happily.

"Yes way! I knew it. I knew that when you saw her in the stream and when you sang to her that you attached to her. And eventually, she would attach herself to you, too. It happened pretty quickly, sooner than I thought, but it happened all the same." The bliss on his face was so pure and genuine.

"Okay ... then you were right," I added, kneeling next to the bookshelf and softly stroking the back of her neck. Her black eyes blinked at me, and I saw my reflection in them. It was not sadness or pain. It was not fear or doubt. It was simple joy. She was happy to be safe and secure—to be with people who cared for her and who enjoyed her as much as she enjoyed them.

"I'm gonna take care of her, Abe. At all costs. I don't care what it takes," I said, staring into the midnight of Sonnet's eyes.

"I know that, too, Kiku. I trust you. I wouldn't have taken her back to the college and risked being caught if I didn't believe that you are the right person to do it. I'll check on her once in a while, but this is all up to you now. Feel free to ask me if you have any questions. I trust you'll make the right calls. That I have faith in, for certain."

Sonnet had sensed my touch and, with wings tucked tight against her body, she twirled her head around at the room. The sudden burst of awareness faded quickly as she curled her head back into place and closed her eyes again.

"Not a very lively bird, is she?" he remarked, glancing at random things around my bedroom. "You don't by chance know what kind of bird she is, do you? I've researched a little but haven't found anything helpful."

"No, I don't. I'll keep looking," I answered.

"Same here." He smiled. "Just think: The more we know about her species, the more effectively we can heal her. I'll ask Charlie at some point. You should ask Joan, too, or one of your other professors. One of us is bound to find out eventually."

I zoned out as I gingerly touched Sonnet's head.

Abe became quiet as he sat and watched the two of us enjoy each other's company. I could tell immediately that something else was on his mind.

"What is it?" I asked, removing my hand from Sonnet and moving back into the living room. Abe stopped to bid her goodbye, then followed.

"We need to talk about it," Abe replied somberly.

"Do you want something to drink or anything? Food? Anything at all?" I asked, getting up to grab a bottle of water.

"No, I'm good."

"Alright, let's talk about it, I guess." I sighed, sitting down next to him on the couch.

"What can I help with? What can I do to take some of the stress and anxiety off you?"

"Abe, there's nothing you can do. You talking to me is the best thing. Zoe helps a lot, too. But there's not a lot anyone can do. As soon as you leave, I'll be thinking about The Pit. Once I go to bed and Zoe's asleep, I'll be thinking about The Pit. When I go to class, when I eat, when I bathe, when I walk around the festival, when I go to the masquerade tonight, I'll be thinking about The Pit! Abe, to me, being selected for this tournament is a lose-lose in every scenario."

Abe looked kindly at me, but my own personal worries had already come to the surface.

"If by some chance I win, that means all of you are dead. That means *you're* dead, Abe. So, did I really win? No. But if I lose, that means *I'm* dead. So, did I win? No. It's a horrible and terrifying situation, regardless of the outcome. I want to do well and prove to myself and my fellow air mages that I can do this, but I don't know. I don't even know what to expect! It's so scary, Abe, not knowing what tomorrow will bring or what will happen tonight. After being selected this morning, I have come to the conclusion that life for me will *never* be the same. Don't you agree?"

"Yeah ... I kind of agree with you. But as long as you do your best and try your hardest, that's all anyone wants. That's all I want from you: just to ... try."

"And I will. I just wish I didn't think about it so much, you know? Like, I wish I could go back to earlier this semester, when the Pit Selection Ceremony was still weeks away. Wish I could go back to orientation day when I first arrived at the college and met Zoe. There are so many things here now," I stammered, covering my eyes and trying to hold back tears, "that I'll never be able to experience. Things I'll never do, and people I'll never meet, and places I'll never go, and magic I'll never see. It's not fair, Abe! It's not ..."

But I couldn't finish that thought; the tears had become too much to contain. My sleeves became damp, and tears fell on my sweatpants. I felt miserable, and while I knew it wasn't Abe's intention, The Pit was the absolute most depressing and tragic thing he could bring up.

Thankfully, he broke the somber tension in the room and slid over to my side. He wrapped his arms around my shoulders and pulled me in close. I had never been this close to him before, but I wasn't afraid. It was comforting to have someone understand the pressure and pain I was feeling right now. I needed him, like I needed Zoe.

"It's alright," he reassured delicately. He brushed away my tears with his sleeves and hugged me tighter. "It's going to be okay, Kiku. I don't know how, but I will protect you and help you in any way I can. I didn't mean to upset you like that. It's ... it's just that I always want to make sure you're doing okay. This is going to be a rough few months coming up. But I want you to keep in mind that I'm *always* here for you. And so is Zoe. I know I'm technically a competitor, but you and I are friends. So, that comes first. Remember those things, and everything else will fall into place."

My tears slowed down a little. Abe released me from his hug but stayed close by my side.

"It's the uncertainty and the mystery of it all. Not knowing or being able to see what's coming up or what to expect. Too many question marks after every thought I have about The Pit. How are you doing it? How are you not panicking for your life and collapsing into a ball of anxiety like I am? Teach me how to do it."

"Honestly, Kiku, I don't know. I wish there were a spell or trick I *could* teach you, but there isn't. If there was, trust me, I'd be using it right now. I have to stay strong for myself and for you, try to think positive about everything and keep my head held high. As long as I don't let The Pit control my emotions or thoughts, I'll be okay. And you will, too. I know it seems impossible and stupid but try and think of the positives. There aren't many, but they're there if you look for them."

His words were nice and soothing as I took a giant gulp from my water bottle.

"Speaking of positive things, why don't you tell me a story?" Abe said abruptly.

"A story?" I was puzzled, wiping my eyes one last time. "What kind of story?"

"Any story," he answered as my puffy red eyes stared back at his. "A story where things were stressful and the odds seemed unbeatable, yet, despite all that, you come out on top."

"Okay ..." I paused, glancing around the room for inspiration.

"Don't think *too* hard on it, now." He laughed, getting cozier on the couch as he slouched back and folded his arms across his chest, intrigued.

Taking a shorter sip of water, I thought back on a memory. "Okay, so, I was ten years old and a Noh performer. Noh is a type of Japanese theater where the actors wear masks, and it focuses on traditional folklore. My mother was a performer, too, when she was younger. Kind of runs in my family, I guess you could say." I paused shortly to see his reaction. Lounging and watching intently, Abe was listening closely.

I continued, "Anyway, at the time, I hadn't become a main performer yet, mostly because I was still too young and inexperienced. But I knew my craft and my routine perfectly—just hadn't done it on stage before. We were doing an abbreviated Noh program with two plays that day, with mine being the second one. The tale our group was doing was called *Hagoromo*, or 'The Feather Mantle.' In this play, a fisherman finds a feather mantle in a tree on his way home with his companions. It belongs to a female dancing spirit. She needs it back in order to go to heaven. The fisherman argues with her, but eventually promises to return it, though only if she will show him her dance. The dance is beautiful and symbolic; it portrays the phases of the moon. In the end, the spirit disappears in a cloud of mist."

Abe was still interested, but my expression now turned anxious.

"There were only two main actors on stage: the fisherman, who was always played by a male actor, and the dancing spirit, who was always a female. I was the understudy to the female spirit role and knew my entire routine, both the singing and the dancing. That day when I was ten years old, I was called upon to perform. The main actress was sick and couldn't do it, so I didn't have any choice but to agree. And that was less than twenty minutes before showtime! I hurried and got changed, makeup done and costume on, in the dressing room."

I sat upright on the couch, took another big sip of water, and stared at the wall ahead. "When I set foot on stage that night in my white mask and white dress, I immediately froze. I found my spot in the center in front of the other actor and just stared at him. He tried de-stressing me and paraphrasing tips and tricks for me to use, but it didn't work. I was so scared, Abe. Terrified. My mother had done many Noh performances in her life, and I just wanted to impress her. But even though I totally knew my lines and routine, like I said, I wasn't ready for the audience's attention—all those staring eyes eager for a mistake. Their collective focus was locked onto my every move, my every word! I had never felt so much pressure."

Then I turned to face Abe, looking right into his eyes. I let a little grin begin on my face. "It went great, though. I performed it perfectly! My lines were spot-on, and my singing was fantastic. When it was over, the crowd exploded in an uproar of applause. That day went from a living nightmare of stage fright to the happiest and most transformative moment of my life."

"That sounds incredible!" Abe said. "So, think about that when you start to worry about The Pit. Remind yourself of that day when you were ten, and you went from an understudy to a star actress in the blink of an eye."

"Thanks, Abe." I smiled.

"'Tis what I'm here for." He smiled kindly.

"Now it's your turn! You tell a story," I said.

We changed places as he leaned forward and I lay back to rest my head against the back of the sofa.

"My father, Roy, was an architect and a professor, as you know," he began. "I was homeschooled, so when I got to the college, it was my first experience with the school system. I was scared, too, but I already had the pressures of heavy workloads, classwork, and deadlines ... Anyway, I was graduating from homeschool, and the final project I needed to complete in order to do so was a scale model of a famous landmark. My father said it could be built with anything, but it had to be accurate. Now, coming from a professional architect himself, who teaches it on the regular, that was a seriously daunting task."

Abe turned to me with a solemn yet zealous expression.

"Imagine that your Noh dancing instructor, a master of artful movement, requested that you create a dance for her to judge. Or your voice coach asked you to write a song, and you had to sing it to her. Imagine Joan beginning a lesson using only your lesson plan. I'm sure you can imagine how it feels when the world is pushing down on your shoulders ..."

His face shone with intent as I took my final sip of water while never breaking eye contact.

"Yeah, I can," I replied softly.

"Can I see the gift box?" Abe asked.

"Huh?" I stammered, confused. "What?"

"The gift box? That one there," Abe clarified, pointing to it.

"Oh, this? Yeah, sure." I handed him the unwrapped white box.

Abe lifted the lid and brought out the mask, which was very beautiful and creative. He took out the invitation and read it to himself. Abe chuckled, placing it all back in the box and setting it back on the coffee table.

"Guess you'll find out tonight!" I said excitedly.

"Guess so."

He paused for a little and sat on the couch while I got up to throw away the empty bottle.

"I should be heading out, sadly," Abe said, standing at the same moment I came to sit back down. "Emilee's expecting me soon. Plus, with the masquerade tonight, I'd better be ready and dressed in time, or she'll have my head. Regardless, I'll see you tonight, Kiku. Hang in there."

"Wait!" I exclaimed. "You didn't finish your story. I finished mine; now you have to finish yours!"

Abe was already nearing the door. "Tonight, I will. Just remind me when you see me." He smiled as he reached for the doorknob.

"Alright," I sighed. "Promise?"

"Promise," he said, opening the door to the vacant hallway. Abe nodded to me and left the room. "You'll hear the end of my cliffhanger tonight. If nothing else, look forward to that ending. It'll be fun! Zoe will be there, and I'll be there, and Emilee will be there. A couple positive notes on an otherwise sour day."

I closed the door behind him and went back to my bedroom, where Sonnet was sleeping in her nest. Taking a seat on my bed, I looked at her as the sun's light brightened those dark gray feathers.

Adjusting myself on the bed, I stared at the ceiling while thinking again of everything that had happened today: the Pit Ceremony, being selected to compete in a death match, coming home to find a masquerade ball invitation, having to go to a party where I would be forced to be the center of attention, and now Abe, half completing a story that he claimed had a happy ending.

Why wouldn't he just finish it? Does it really have a happy ending? I wondered.

"One out of a thousand," I said to Sonnet. "There are literally thousands of students here, yet I was one of the five chosen. What are the odds? I hope Joan knows what she's doing, because this scared little girl is walking into her training room tomorrow. I do appreciate Abe's help, Sonnet. I really do! But as much as he helped, The Pit is too heavy a subject to think on."

I curled up in a position similar to Sonnet. Heavy thoughts and premonitions weighed on my mind. So, like my new companion sleeping on the bookshelf, I closed my eyes and attempted to do the same.

AARON IV

ONCE JAX FINISHED BACKSTAGE, he bid farewell to all of the Pit champions and their Mentors and left shortly after.

Five students walk in, and one walks out ... or limps out, most of the time.

I was having an out-of-body experience, floating somewhere above myself. Olivia had bolted out of this post-ceremony meeting instantly after Jax stopped talking, with Kira running after her. Then, the fire mage Kamaul and his Mentor, Nero, "snuck" out as loudly as they possibly could.

As I stood with the four remaining people backstage, I could only think of Luke's voice, teasing me with useless optimism that I would surely not be picked for The Pit. During a tutoring session, he had also made a point to remind me that when he was picked, he had made it out perfectly alive ... and mostly sane. Luke had made several attempts to remind me of the "incredibly low" likelihood of me being selected for the tournament. Yet here we are—and the one person I could count on to be at my side was not even present at the ceremony.

I've never seen Luke miss a class or call in a substitute teacher. Never seen him in a foul mood, or under any kind of duress. But now he fails simply to make a required appearance? Must have something to do with me, I thought, descending back into my real body.

I knew him as a professor, and it was clear around campus that Luke was the most liked of all the Mentors. Every student, every teacher, and nearly everyone who ever met him loved him. When Luke and the other Seeker had approached me and asked me to enroll in the school, I knew immediately that I needed to be placed in one of his classes. It was ironic: the professor everyone liked and thought fondly of, paired with the loser water mage who couldn't even swim. A match made in heaven, right? What were the odds that the most recognized Pit Mentor would be paired with someone nobody noticed?

I had to do something and find some answers, so I walked back down the tunnel. Turning the corner, I traveled straight through the open dirt area and out of The Trench. It opened into Market Square, a place I didn't think I'd ever been to.

I thought of all the questions I needed to ask Luke. I figured the best place to look for him was his classroom, so that's where I headed. The walk was not too far, and I pondered more questions as I went.

Where was he? Why didn't he come? What was so important that he had to bail on me?

A quick right turn, and I followed the sidewalk around the lake and the gazebo. While it was the most relaxing place on campus to me, the gazebo would have to wait, as Luke's absence made me increasingly more worried the longer I thought on it. What if he was dead? What if whatever emergency he needed to attend to required more than one day of his time? What if he dragged me into the mess he was dealing with?

"Why couldn't Luke just show up? It's not that hard!" I scoffed, nearing the water building.

Empty and quiet, the building was easy to navigate with only the dim glow of sunlight within its walls. Without the other students, the halls were eerie.

I arrived at Luke's classroom. The door was left open. I peeked inside to check it out.

Nobody was there—no students, no faculty, and no Luke.

"Maybe he'll return in a couple minutes if I hang out and wait," I told myself softly as I entered the room and left the door untouched.

Inching inside, I looked around at the minimal décor of Luke's Introduction to Magic classroom. At the head of the room, Luke's desk was clear of clutter and school papers; not even a speck of dust lay on its clean surface. However, the highlight of this room, and the aspect of it that everyone enjoyed the most, was the glass patio door that opened onto the elemental courtyard. It framed a large patch of perfectly manicured lawn outside. But much to the dismay of the more sensitive mages in his classes, Luke often left it wide open at all hours of the day and all seasons of the year.

The rear of the room was defined by a grand and elaborate tapestry that hung from brass hooks and depicted a black silhouette of Adarius in the center, surrounded by regions depicting the five elements: a green field for earth, an orange one for fire, yellow for air, blue for water, and gray for void. Each one portrayed how that element was formed and how its magic has changed over the ages.

Aside from the wall-sized tapestry and patio doors, Luke's classroom offered very little else to look at. Oh, sorry—I might have missed one tiny detail of the room. Behind Luke's desk was an ornate stained glass window depicting none other than himself, which beautifully caught the daily sun. In any class, a student might feel like they were getting lessons from two Lukes at the same time. One could say he was a bit egotistical.

"Always so subtle," I said jokingly to the stained glass window while hoping a little insanity would creep in and make it respond. "But you're not even here! The one place I suspected you'd be ... you're not."

Normally, if someone walked by and saw a student talking to this portrait of Luke, they'd report it and raise the alarm. Today though, not a soul walked these halls or entered these rooms, as the student body was partying at the Festival of the Elements.

"Wouldn't even be here if you had just showed up to the ceremony, like you were supposed to!" I shouted at nobody.

Discouraged, but not leaving yet, I took a seat in the front row of desks and waited.

I looked out the patio door across the grass. The wooden gazebo, peaceful and vacant above the frozen lake, was calling my name. I wanted to go and sit out there, but knowing my luck, that would be when Luke returned to his classroom. So, I stayed put and just stared at it.

Five minutes had gone by before I checked the door again. Of course, nothing.

Then I suddenly heard a creaking sound echoing down the halls, tearing my attention away from the empty campus outside. But it must've just been the building laughing at me for waiting on someone who was not going to show up.

Ten minutes passed.

Still no Luke.

Then fifteen.

No Luke.

My seat was becoming warm the longer I stupidly waited for him to arrive.

This is dumb, I concluded, rising to my feet and leaving the room. *Luke's not going to show up for me. He's made that clear today. I guess I have to go to him.* I sighed, frustrated, and slipped out the door without moving it.

Desperate now, I thought of the only other place he could be. I knew where it was, but it had felt too weird and definitely awkward to go there personally. But if there was even a slim chance that I would live through The Pit, it was in Luke's dorm, where hopefully he was too.

I hastily walked (or more like ran) to his private quarters in the faculty building nearby.

The realization came over me of how desperate I must look right now. I was chasing a teacher who was supposedly pivotal to my survival in the tournament. I had known Luke for months since coming to the college, yet I deeply craved his attention at this moment. I felt pathetic and weak.

"Luke," I began softly. "Please be in your room. That is my last resort. I swear, if you're not in there, I'll ... Well, I don't know what I'll do. So, please just be there."

Now I really sounded pathetic, like a lost son begging for his father to come back. But I couldn't help it; I needed Luke. There was no way I could survive longer than thirty seconds in the arena unless he was around to help me. Plus, anyone who saw me right now would have looked the other way, because I was a nobody ... and nobody cared about a nobody.

I opened the grand door to the faculty building and started scanning the hall signage for Luke's name. No luck on the first floor, so I tried the second, then the third. This was the top floor, and while the building was minuscule compared to the gigantic dormitory structure, having a room on the top level of any faculty building meant you were either highly regarded or knew your way with words to talk someone out of theirs.

Coming up the stairs, I spun left and headed towards the end of the hall. I had almost given up completely when I saw the last room. This one was his. But as with the classroom, this door stood open as well. It was as though someone had recently come in and forgotten to close it behind them. Despite feeling very awkward and scared to enter Luke's room uninvited, I had no choice and turned the knob to push my way in. I took a deep breath and closed my eyes for a second as I hoped not to see his dead body sprawled across the floor. Then I shut the door behind my feet after I walked inside.

"Luke?" I called, scanning the apartment. "Hello? Anyone here? Luke, if you're here, you left your door open, so I just ... uhhh ... let myself in. Hope you don't mind."

Of course he isn't here. Why would my luck be any different here than in his classroom?

Regardless of the discussion topic, Luke was perfect at everything. I swear! And his apartment was no different. Trophies lined several shelves of the living room. Everything was neat and orderly, aligned to the slightest degree, except a single empty space on the shelf, which stuck out like a sore thumb. Even his bed was perfect, with every blanket folded and the pillows all lined up properly. I had the awful urge to channel some anger and trash it simply because it looked so flawless.

Instead, I flopped back onto the leather sofa. I lay there for a minute or two and stared at the ceiling.

The words then slipped through my lips: "Why can't I be like you, Luke?"

Following this exhausted thought, a clanging sound rang out from the kitchen. Startled, I sprang upright on the couch and waited for someone to emerge.

I realized I was not alone. A tall man wandered in towards the coffee table.

"Who ... who are you?" I stammered, cautiously drawing back from the stranger.

"Hello, Aaron," he said politely. He had slicked-back black hair and a chiseled face, with structured cheekbones and an attractive smile. He was roughly Luke's height, and I noticed how similar they looked, almost as if this were an alternate version of him. This man's eyes were like little blue ponds of water. While his facial features were distinct, the rest of his body was hidden under a black cloak.

"How do you know who I am?" I rose from the sofa and stood frozen. "Who are you?"

"Sorry, where are my manners?" he exclaimed, reaching out for a handshake. "I'm one of Luke's friends. He has me staying here until he gets back, to make sure you weren't alone in his apartment."

"One of Luke's friends?" I muttered dubiously. I rejected his handshake.

"He probably never mentioned me," he said and laughed, as if reading my mind, before eating a few cashews from a bowl on the side table. "Always so private and secretive."

"Yeah ... I guess so," I said skeptically. "Do you know where he is then?"

"I might." He shrugged playfully.

"Can you tell me? Or show me?"

Something was suspicious about this man, but I figured he might be my only hope for finding my lost Mentor.

"No. I can do something far better than telling or showing you." He ran his hands over framed photos of Luke and the gleaming trophies. The strange man acted as if he lived here in Luke's place. "I can make you better than him. Make you stronger than him. More powerful than him! More successful than him! More liked than him. Do those things interest you, Aaron?"

"Very much so," I responded blindly.

"Do you know how I know Luke?" His voiced cracked slightly.

"No. Please tell me," I insisted.

"He and I are old friends. Worked together during his early years at this college. He was a troubled and struggling boy, like yourself. That's when I stepped in. I helped him blossom into the confident and strong man you see now. Ask him if you don't believe me! He'll tell you himself."

"Old friends, really? Wonder why he's never mentioned you ... But I do want to be like him! How did you do it? How did you help Luke become who he is?"

"So, you want to be like your Mentor, yes? My story intrigued you?" he inquired around tossing another handful of cashews into his mouth. The blue of his eyes darkened with intensity. "What if I told you that all you have to do is sign your name, and you'll be even better than him?"

"*Sign* something?" I paused, staring into his eyes. They were so intense that I was captivated by them.

"An agreement, Mr. Dirge," he said with another high-pitched voice crack and a smile.

"Between me and you?"

"Yup. Only me and you. It will be our secret agreement."

He snapped his fingers, and a scroll appeared, floating between us. However, I remained standing cautiously at Luke's bedroom doorway, and he at the foot of the coffee table. Shortly after, the cloaked man held out a quill made of small, pointy bones and gestured for me to take it.

"What's the catch?" I stammered, nearly reaching for the quill despite myself.

"No catch," he replied, in a dangerously different voice than before. This one wheezed out of him like a boiling tea kettle. "Think of it as a gift. You sign this contract, and I give you power beyond measure. It's very simple, you see? And when the time comes, you can repay the favor. Here, let me show you a sample of the magical power I can give you."

The man's hand glowed a dark purple as he closed his eyes and cast a lightning bolt spell at Luke's fireplace. With a flash of lightning, the fire ignited in a sizzling blaze.

I had read about this spell! It was one of my own—one of the storm magic spells. Stupidly, I had tried it before. All I had managed to do was give myself a headache for about a month, just from trying to concentrate hard enough to perform it.

Unfazed, the tall man continued to hold the quill out to me and stared into my eyes with conniving passion.

Frantically, I began thinking. *Is this my way out? Will signing this contract override Luke and make him useless? If he bails on me now, when I'm vulnerable and scared, what happens if he does this again? What if he's dead, and I'm good as dead, too? Maybe this is my chance to win ... or at least survive longer than a day.*

If I was going into The Pit alone with no one at my side, unlike the others, I figured a little extra help wouldn't hurt anything.

"You sure you're one of Luke's friends? You've helped him before ...?"

"One of his closest." He smiled sweetly, but his voice was shrill and ghastly.

My hands and arms were tingling.

"Think of the storm magic you'll be able to cast, with *one hundred percent* accuracy. Mr. Dirge, don't you want to be good at magic?" He paced the apartment and slowly made his way towards me as he spoke. "Don't you want to succeed your Mentor—be like him in every way? Make a name for yourself and solidify it on a gold trophy, like all of his? Well, if you want to be like him, then follow in his footsteps."

His feet stopped a few inches from mine, and he tilted the quill in his hand to examine its intricate bones.

"This is a blood quill. It will seal our deal. When you use it, it will prick your finger and infuse the ink with your blood."

I glanced down at his hands. Dark, sharp shapes appeared burned into them.

The man whisked the floating scroll over to his side and put it perfectly between us. He slid closer to me. The contract was extensive, yet I already knew I was not going to read it.

"Just sign and ... and that's it?" I asked uncertainly.

"Sign there by the X, and we are in business, my—"

The man choked off.

Looking up from the scroll, I saw a black spear of pure energy shoot through the man's chest. Without warning, his cloak caught fire and quickly burned to cinders. Before he disintegrated into a pile of ash, the man's face shriveled up into a bare skull; those blue pools in his eyes became sunken black holes. His cheeks were bone, and all his human features withered away. What I thought was a man was actually not a man at all, but a skeleton—a demon, no less. Then he disintegrated into a pile of ash.

I stared wide-eyed at the apartment door.

Luke was holding the shaft of a spectral weapon, and his entire body was covered in the same dark markings that I had noticed on the demon's hand—runes, I suddenly realized. The only differences I noticed were that Luke's did not go away instantly, and they seemed much older.

"Been searching for you," Luke said with his usual smile. "I see you met my old mentor. Kind of a drag, right? Pretty lifeless, if you ask me."

"Luke? Is it really you?" I stammered in disbelief. I scanned him up and down over and over again, just to be sure I was not being lied to.

"Sorry I missed your moment in the spotlight. Now, are you ready to learn a few new tricks?" Luke laughed as the runes burned into his skin started glowing.

"You're glowing ..." I managed, staring beyond his eyes.

"Why, thank you." He chuckled, then grabbed a broom to sweep up the man's ashes from his carpet. He gathered the pile in a dustpan and tossed it into the fire.

"What are those?" I asked, pointing at his hands and keeping my feet locked in place like they were stuck in concrete.

"A curse," he replied coolly.

"Where did that spear come from? Where did *you* come from?"

At the same moment, I wanted to hug him for saving my life—and strangle him for deserting me.

"Some powerful magic is what that spear was. It worked, didn't it? I was taking care of some business. Again, I am terribly sorry I missed the ceremony. How'd it go? Jax repeat himself, like always?"

Luke was much too nonchalant about the whole ordeal: his absence from the Pit Ceremony, his classroom left open and empty, his apartment left open and empty, and his convenient entrance at the perfect moment to kill a demon before it could make a deal with me? This whole situation seemed like too much to be just coincidence.

"WHAT JUST HAPPENED?!" I screamed.

"Nothing serious. Have a seat, Aaron."

Luke motioned for me to join him on the couch by the fireplace. Meanwhile, he escaped into the kitchen and came back with a small glass of brown liquor.

Feeling a freak-out coming on, I didn't try to stop it. "No. No. No. Luke, I can't do this." I fell back onto the recliner as he relaxed on the sofa. "Luke, I seriously can't do this! I'm panicking already, and we haven't even started the actual training yet!"

Luke took one gulp of the whiskey, and it was gone.

"Aaron, that was a demon. They're wickedly persuasive. I'm sure it promised you power or money, and that it would give it to you instantly. Demons can convince anyone to do anything. Know this, though, Aaron: Nothing worth having is easy. That's the first lesson I'm gonna teach you. Remember that for everything we'll do moving forward! There will be more tough times and more moments when you'd rather be dead. But it will get better! I'll help."

Uneasy and unsure of what to say, I anxiously watched the embers dance in the fireplace.

"Aaron, I had to take care of something. It was very important and took precedence over the ceremony. That was earlier—but this is now. I'm here now. I will protect you and guide you."

"I'm glad," I sighed. "But I think I need more guidance than I initially thought. Luke, I almost signed a deal with a demon! That *just* happened, in case you forgot!" Eyes on the floor, I sank into my chair before continuing. "I nearly signed my life away to an unnatural fiend! Am I that desperate and weak? Is my mind that easily corruptible? Am I that gullible, just to sign my name for the first person who offers aid? Am I—"

"No!" Luke interrupted. "You're not any of those things. You're just scared, and I should have been there for you when your name was called. I failed you, and for that, I am truly sorry, Aaron."

My emotions were all over the place, but I could tell he was sincere. "It's alright." Unexpectedly, I grinned.

"Good." He grinned in response. "So, how weird did it feel to be in my classroom alone? Enjoy being in the presence of my stained glass without me? Probably felt like I was there in spirit," he added, trying to ease the tension in the room.

"A bit, yeah," I responded, nervously grabbing a handful of nuts from the side table. "Did you actually know that thing, Luke? He claimed to have helped you in your life. Is that true?"

"It's too warm in here, wouldn't you agree?" Luke said abruptly, and I noticed the sweat on his forehead. The runes on his skin were finally starting to vanish. He snapped his fingers at the glow from the fire. I watched the blue flames change to orange, and they burned much cooler. In fact, the heat was gone completely, replaced with an icy December chill like that of an incoming blizzard. Little flurries of snow danced in the fireplace now rather than sparks.

"That is surprisingly better," I agreed, feeling more relaxed.

"There's a lot about my past that you don't know—some of which I will share, and some of which I hope you never find out. But my business is taken care of,

Aaron. It will not be an issue any longer. This I swear to you. You should get back to your dorm. It's still early. Try and get some rest. Maybe you'll feel more at ease with the whole day behind closed eyelids."

"Are you sure?" I asked.

"C'mon, Aaron, we can start for real tomorrow morning. You can ask all the questions you want then! Tonight, though, go out to the festival and have a good time. Take your mind off of me and The Pit and everything else. Think you could do that for me?"

"I can try," I answered, gazing at the blue flames.

"Good! Now, off you go!" Luke said, standing up and walking to the door. "Oh, and next time, Aaron, don't walk into my private quarters if the door's open. Nothing good is inside. My door should always be locked."

"Right," I answered, rising to my feet and making my way to exit.

"See you in the morning," he added.

I held out a hand and took Luke's in a firm grasp.

"Thank you, sir." I nodded.

"Ugh. No, Aaron; I'm just Luke to you, just like I am to everyone else. Or you can call me Mr. Demon Killer, if you prefer that." He beamed, showing perfect white teeth.

I laughed and started to pass through the doorway before pausing. "Thanks for saving my life. I fear you may have to get used to it," I sighed before checking the hallway for other wandering faculty.

"Don't be so hard on yourself. Demons are quite enticing. Like I said, they can fool anyone."

I nodded and started down the hall.

Luke threw one last line at me before I traveled back down the staircase. "At least make an effort to go. Tomorrow's training is going to be harsh, Aaron—you know that. So, please enjoy the night's festivities. If not for yourself, then do it for me."

KAMAUL IV

AFTER THE BACKSTAGE MEETING, the others bolted from Jax's office and snuck back to their miserable lives. I, however, stayed behind, alone in the arena while the workers and volunteers cleaned up around me. They hustled and bustled, hastily taking the stage apart piece by piece and schlepping it down the tunnels. With a crew of twenty, maybe thirty, the group of mages had the arena cleared of all ceremony remnants in mere minutes.

The scorching sun warmed the snow, and a little heat radiated from the ground. Sand was buried somewhere underneath the blanket of white fluff. It didn't bother me any, despite my sandals sinking into it. A couple students gave me weird looks, then smartly looked elsewhere when I gave them a "Watch ittttt!" kind of glare. Were my toes cold? Nah. Us Metjen brothers might have been born under the desert sun, but our blood was built for any climate. You think a little snow would be enough to subdue Kamaul Metjen, Penumbra? HA! Think again.

It was just me, the sun, and the silence. The distant sound of band music drifted into the stadium from the Festival Marketplace. The hum and buzz rumbling from afar failed to capture my full attention. That was reserved for her—the seductive mistress of bloodshed and competition. And what a temptation she was: Jett, Gladiator class, other classes with Nero ... They were never enough. My hunger only grew with each appetizer. But The Pit would be my main course—the comforting climax to satisfy my rage and adrenaline.

I glanced at the empty bleachers. My mind was busy planning and playing out scenarios, a healthy regimen of ... Well, I think it's best if we save my battle secrets for another time. I exhaled slowly and methodically, eyes closed, while soaking up the atmosphere. It was that ... that feeling from weekend mornings in Egypt. My father would wake up Kamuzu, Kasto, and me promptly at 5:00—no earlier, no later. "The early warrior swings the sword," he used to say. There were occasional times that I missed him. Truly, I did ... somewhere deep, deep down in my soul. But then I would think about getting up at 5:00 after a night of savage partying. Absolutely miserable. *I had a reputation to uphold, Dad!* I felt that work and pleasure should be equally balanced, but he never saw it that way. The constant admonitions to "Improve your craft, Kamaul!" and "You can sleep when you're dead, Kamaul!" played like a broken record in my brain most of those mornings. Ever wake up hungover, walk past your gardeners, trudge down the staircases, and sluggishly swing a longsword at the ass crack of dawn? No? Well, I'll fill you in: IT IS AS UNPLEASANT AS IT SOUNDS.

So, being alone in The Trench reawakened many memories, to say the least. But, I pushed those aside in order to take in the moment. The first Elemental Rite was one month away.

"I'm sorry, Adarius," I said boastfully to a nonexistent crowd while spinning around to see the entire stadium. "I'm sorry you're going to have to wait four weeks 'til you witness your second coming! I know, I know—bummer. But, I promise you, it'll be worth the wait. You'll see." I stopped, facing the tunnel. "They'll all see. Faculty, students, Adarius, the Seekers, Penumbra royalty ... They'll all see what a slag mage can do."

"I'm lookin' forward to it myself," answered a man's voice. It was not Nero's this time.

Despite being an echo mage like Renner, Sun Wu carried himself drastically differently from any other man or professor I'd met before. He was calm and collected, and his strategic understanding of warfare and life and politics was brilliant; he could finding silver linings in even the worst historical events. I'd never had a class with him, but in my three years at the college, Sun had taken me into his consideration on more than one instance. He was a short, bald Chinese man with a black goatee and a mustache. With a chubby face and stocky build, Sun Wu couldn't hold a candle to my or Nero's physique.

Wearing olive-green wizard robes, he held his hands behind his back as he approached me.

"Sun? What are you doing here? Did you see the ceremony today?!" I exclaimed.

"I did." He chuckled, coming towards me to shake my hand. He had the opposite mannerisms than Nero. He'd kill you, sure—but he'd probably bury you and give you a proper send-off afterwards. If Nero killed you, though ...? Yikes.

"I'm glad you were chosen, Kamaul," Sun continued. "You're more than capable. Magnus and the other Elders will be proud when the trials start in January. He who asks is a fool for five minutes, but he who does not ask remains a fool forever. So, should you decide to seek out opinions besides Nero's, knock on my door. You represent all of the fire community now, Kamaul—not just him, and not just yourself."

"Thanks, Sun. I'll keep that in mind." I nodded back to him.

Sun's optimism was alluring and penetrated my hard-shelled persona. Perhaps his help could actually be beneficial ... you know, if it were ever necessary, I suppose. He was a sweet guy. No need to dampen his positivity just yet.

"Well, I'll leave you then. Just wanted to stop by and—"

Sun was cut off by Nero, who emerged from the tunnel's shadow like a devil walking in the moonlight.

"Not so fast, Sun. Before you corrupt Kamaul's mind with your weak ideologies, allow me to counter your arguments. You preach about healthier tactics, yet you leech those lesson plans from my desk! If you want the lessons I throw out, all you have to do is ask. I'd be more than happy to give you my sloppy seconds. As for my 'aggressive teachings'? Grow up. Seriously, Sun. You're older and more experienced than I am, but here you are, trying to poach Kamaul for your own course-correcting pettiness. It's pathetic, and I'm not here to sell myself to you. My trophy from The Pit can do that on its own. Oh, wait ... have you ever competed in The Pit?"

Sun got in Nero's face as I backed away from the two of them, enamored by their stare-down. Sun Wu was the only professor to challenge Nero at his own game of chess, but Nero played that game really well.

"Still holding that over my head, Professor?" Sun snapped, flaring his nostrils. "Calling me pathetic ... Get a grip on reality, Nero. He who seeks revenge should remember to dig two graves. So, kindly back up, Nero, if you will."

At this moment, I thought I was going to be the sole witness to a murder. Even the sunlight's reflection in Nero's eyes was nothing in comparison to the fire in his soul. Though he clearly dwarfed Sun in height, he suddenly threw his hands up and retreated from the confrontation.

"I'll let you walk away on those stubby legs, Sun, if you leave now. Go ahead back to your classroom. Leave us, please. Kamaul doesn't need to witness your failures firsthand."

"Classic scare tactic. Look, Kamaul, if you need *real* help—or anything at all, for that matter—do not be afraid when the monkey sits on your shoulder ..." Sun darted his eyes from Nero's to mine. "I'm around. Teachers only open the door; you must walk through it yourself. Love to be of any help." Sun's gaze moved back to Nero's before the man vanished down the tunnel.

Abruptly, my reflection now appeared in Nero's fiery gaze.

"Why did you even talk to him? Why speak a word to that man about The Pit?! He's not involved. He's just trying to live out a pipe dream through you and me. Don't flatter that man with your attention, Kamaul. Keep your focus on the task at hand—winning!"

"Look, I was standing here after the backstage thing, and nobody else was around. He came over to talk to *me*! I was alone. How is this my fault? How was I supposed to know he was coming, or that you were gonna follow?"

"Level that tone, Kamaul," Nero demanded.

Eyes lowered, I blinked but nodded at the quiet arena.

"And don't let it happen again."

"I won't," I answered, gritting my teeth.

"We have a lot of work to do tomorrow. Party hard if you want to tonight. But come sunrise, I want you waiting in my classroom to start training. If you're late, I'll make you suffer. So, don't make me wait! I hate waiting!" His masculine tone raised another octave. "I will make your life hell if you want! It's not a problem at all."

I nodded reluctantly. "What do we have to work on, anyway? I'm great at combat. Clearly, best in my year!"

"First off, that ego of yours. It's gonna get you killed. Forget what's coming and worry about right now. And for now? You need to get back to your dorm, not do anything stupid tonight, and get to that training room before I do in the morning. Got it?"

"Yeah, I got it," I replied, a bit more sarcastically than I would have liked, but oh well.

"Good," Nero concluded before he, too, disappeared back into the tunnel.

As I cooled off a little from Nero's tirade, I thought earnestly about Sun Wu's offer. It was true: If I did utilize his knowledge, my Pit Mentor would never know. Yet that scenario would not end well for either of us. But it certainly was intriguing. Sun Wu was a brilliant professor, anxious to better any student who walked through his door. Even with those outside of our fire element, Sun Wu never turned a student away and lent a helping hand wherever possible, much to my dismay.

A pleasant quietness returned to the arena. I stood in it for a couple more moments while thinking about my experiences with my father and brothers and the inaugural Rite in January. One thing was on my mind at the moment: I could really use a drink. Not because I was stressed and needed to take the edge off—more like a celebratory one, a cheers to the future. Did I drink often? If you had asked my father, he would have said yes, but I would argue otherwise. Plus, he was dead, so ... I drank in social settings, no doubt. As I was part of a royal family, it came with the name and the magnitude of life in Egypt. Parties, galas, balls, festivals—everything had required the faces of the family to shine. It was no shocker that I loved myself, but the benefits of alcohol enhanced such sentiments in other people. Selling my own image was what I did best.

With drunken stories playing repeat in my brain, I exhaled a puff of chilled air and left under the arena bleachers.

I picked up the wine decanter and a ribbed glass. Uncapping it, I poured myself half a glass. I finished the drink in one gulp and returned for a second before placing the decanter back on the silver tray. Received as a gift, the wine was silky sweetness with a plum color and a pleasing strawberry-grape flavor.

Drinking a midday glass of wine triggered another flashback with my father. For a man I had loathed so much towards the end of his life, he sure was haunting me now. I stared into the liquid as I swirled the glass. In my reflection, I saw bits and pieces of my father's face.

As pharaoh, he had access to the most expensive and rarest syrahs and chardonnays in all of Africa. I had been too young to drink any of them, of course—but that did not mean I hadn't tried. At ages nine and twelve, I was caught red-handed, sneaking into his cabinets and having a sip of each wine for myself. The nausea and lingering stomach cramps were of no consequence to my father's anger. Being grounded in an Egyptian royal family was like being put in timeout for the world to watch. Every person under his reign had seen me as a screw-up at a young age. I supposed that had played a key role in the reckless partying of my teenage years.

I sipped a third glass of deep purple wine.

Stupid, Kamaul! Stop that. These drinks are a salute to my luck and good fortune! Never will I drink over sorrow and sadness. I shoved the lowly thoughts and memories out of mind and reminded myself only to drink to my achievements.

Sliding down to the floor, I looked up at the beige ceiling and raised my glass to toast to the three generations of myself. One for the child in me, lurking around my father's palace and getting into trouble wherever I could find it. I ran around it like a playground, imagining when it would be mine someday. Thinking of the illegal sips of pinots and cabernets I had snuck behind the guards' watch, I took a sip. Two for the teenager inside, partying and ransacking the palace like it was a live performance. As I drank and partied my way from fifteen to seventeen, my brothers hated the noise and ruckus I created. I laughed at their maturity and took another gulp of wine. Three for the man I was now, imagining the sounds of cheering students and prepping for a war between the elements. Throughout my life at the college, I focused on magic and battle, waiting for the right moment to strike. Then it came. When the world came knocking on Kamaul's door for The Pit Tournament, I smiled at the opportunity, because I was coming home with the trophy in my hands. And so, I took the final sip in my glass.

Placing the empty glass next to the elegant decanter, I stood by the front door and collected a good view of my themed dormitory. This place was my humble abode from the day I stepped on campus—a bestowed gift from Nero. He said my arrival at the college was shocking, but expected, so this dorm had been set up specifically for me.

I walked past the kitchen into my bedroom. The dishes in the sink had only been there for a few days, and platters of brownies and cookies from Gillian sat half-eaten on the counter. My kitchen was boring, eggshell white and bland, like the college intended. I spent the least amount of time there, usually getting food from the market or going to Dahir's dorm for dinner. Two magnificent Anubis statues stood opposite each other in the hallway.

Painted khaki, my bedroom was much smaller than I cared to admit. It was pretty classic: a bed, a pair of nightstands, a dresser, a wardrobe, and weapons and armor decorating the walls. Despite my alluring discussions with Jax to increase its size, he had declined every offer, saying it would "compromise other dorms in the building" and would trigger "complaints from other students about equality." Blah blah blah, if you asked me ... He just wanted me to earn it, which I respected. Thus, my crowning as champion of The Pit would clearly warrant an expanded bedroom, along with a flurry of other requests granted.

On the walls, my array of worldly weapons, held up by shoddy nail work, gleamed in the lamplight. I looked at pair of swords by my side tables. One was a short claymore sword from the Iberian Peninsula, with a studded hilt and a dent on the blade's tip. The other was a katana of sweet silver sharpness with a blue diamond handle, and my initials were carved on the *habaki*. Above my bed was a golden war scythe, a one-of-a-kind family heirloom from my grandfather, who had fought off the invading crusaders and became pharaoh of our city.

The first training day with Nero was officially less than twenty-four hours away. I kicked aside the piles of pants and socks and changed into a gold workout tank top and gathered sweatpants. Laundry had never been a priority of mine, as the servants and maids of the palace had handled it. None of that was here at the college, of course, but ... eh. I could always just buy more when the time came.

After changing and tidying up the bedroom, I shut the door and returned to the wine table. Lifting the beaker-shaped decanter, I poured the sweet strawberry nectar into a new glass and replaced it on the tray. I picked up the glass, swirled around the liquid inside, and took in the aromas of grape and plum. Just as the wine hit my lips, I heard a knock on the door.

"Who in the ...?" I groaned into the glass.

I raised the drink to attempt another sip, which was cut short again by another series of knocks.

"What do you want?!" I shouted.

"Open up, Kamaul. You know who it is. You get no other visitors! Who do you think it is?!" Nero's deep voice hollered back.

Slamming the glass down on the table, I made quick time to the front door and opened it.

Nero stood wearing pearl-white wizard robes with embroidered teal trim and tied with twine. Seeing my ruthless Mentor wearing something other than gladiator gear was frankly embarrassing. He was suddenly dressed like ... like one of them! Like one of the hundreds of other professors or faculty members in the college—another one of the lemmings. He looked weak and bleak, like a nobody trying to blend in with the crowd. It made me gag and feel sick to my stomach. A man poised with power and pride and prowess, stooping to their level? This wasn't Professor Nero—not the version I wanted to see or imagine.

Above his robes of eggshell, his usually stern, emotionless face wore an expression of delight and insight. What horrifying nightmare had I woken up in? Was that cabernet actually absinthe in disguise? I couldn't know for sure; I'd never tasted absinthe before. What world was I in? Was I drunk? It never took less than seven to do me in after a night of drinking. Had the college changed me that much—tamed my inner wolf?

No. There was no way. I wasn't drunk. My tan complexion in the living room mirror reflected the same physique as it always did: muscles bulging through the rips in the gold fabric. Not drunk, not hallucinating, and not under the influence of an echo mage, I simply stared at Nero in awe and tried to keep my eyes from drying out.

"Nero," I began, baffled and calmly irate. I yanked him into my dorm, checking outside to make sure it was clear of eavesdroppers, and slammed the door behind him.

An unfamiliar grin was spread across his face. It actually made me angrier to look at it, so I retrieved my wine glass and kept my attention on it instead. "What is this? Why are you here? And what are you wearing?"

"Are you done?" He glowered before letting a chuckle slip.

"No," I answered promptly. "What are those?" I pointed to his white robes. "What are you doing here? What are you carrying? What's so important that you had to arrive uninvited and unannounced at my dorm room?! I will see you in less than twenty-four hours. I literally *just* talked to you in the arena. So, what's so important that you had to see me in the middle of the day?!"

The volcanic anger began to boil in my blood as I stared unblinking at Nero and his stupid white robes dragging across my floor. He wandered around the room towards one of the Anubis statues and stood close to it, mimicking its stance, with one hand dropped to his side and the other holding an imaginary staff.

"I have gifts for you," he said, ignoring my questions.

"So, we're gonna ... gonna ignore everything I just said?" I muttered.

"I told you, Kamaul. I stopped by unannounced because I knew you'd say no if I asked. I need to speak with you before tomorrow's ... training lesson. Two gifts for you, my boy! C'mon! Live a little, Kamaul. Accept my gifts as a peace offering, and let's drink to our successes!" He threw his hands in the air and gyrated around near me.

"Are you drunk, sir?" I asked. "I mean that with all due respect, Nero. But seriously, are you drunk?"

"Drunk?" Nero laughed, inching closer to me. "Not at all." He patted my shoulder, placed his gift packages in the kitchen, and leaned against the counter. "I'm serious, Kamaul. I feel I've been too harsh on you. I really don't like people, and I have *no* problem showing that to them. I'm sure that also comes as no shock to you, being that you've been on the receiving end of that more times than anyone else. I won't apologize for Nero being Nero, but I oughta give you something for your troubles. Go 'head. Open it up. The one on the right's a bottle of syrah; that's obvious. It's the left one that'll catch your eye."

Nero's face blackened in the shadow of the room. His scowl matched Anubis's, and his snout bent towards the ground at those below him. Narrow pupils fixated on me, like the devil handing lollipops to a child.

There we go. That's more like the Nero I know.

"That's more like it." I smiled, reaching for the package.

"Open it." Nero threw his voice across the room while pouring himself a glass of my wine.

I tore open the wrapping to reveal a red velvet box. I pulled open its lid and brought out a small gold crown adorned with a cobra head and a single ruby encrusted in the snake's mouth. It was thin and lightweight as I examined it in full detail.

Not as lavish as I deserved, but it was a start.

"What's this for?" I asked, watching Nero finish his glass and set it near my empty one.

"It's for you," he scoffed. "Now let me tell you about this crown's secret!" Nero leapt towards me and snatched it from my hands. He held it to the ceiling, as if imagining the sun's bright light on it. Closing his right eye, he peered into the gemstone carefully, like it was a crystal ball full of churning clouds and mist.

"This crown ..." Nero continued, clearing his throat. "This crown can transport the wearer to a palace all their own. It's like a magical bubble, isolated, for a king to live as a king. The ruby was selected specifically for you, Kamaul. Only for you! This crown was forged in the fires of Magnus's hearth, and that gem was brought from the great city of Alexandria! Kamaul ... that crown was made for you to wear—made for you to place upon your head. This crown in my hand ..." He paused, knelt on the floor, and looked at me through the ruby's reflection. "... is yours. All you have to do is win The Pit."

"Really? From Alexandria, huh? That must've ..." I started, glancing over the crown again and seeing it differently.

"Must've been impossible to bring here?" Nero interjected. "Yeah. It was. But Kamaul, you are the prodigal son—the one who can carry fire into the promised land of victory and power! The Pit is the opportunity every element dreams of. It's the opportunity you've been dreaming of since you walked across the campus's threshold. I know that, Kamaul! I felt the same way when I first arrived. It's a chance to prove yourself—a way to etch your name into history. I want all of it *for* you! Starting with this crown right here."

Those words branded themselves on my chest like a blood pact. My face shone in the gem's red sparkle. The volcano bubbling in the pit of my stomach flattened out. Nero stood in front of me and held the crown in his hands, offering it to me. But before I could speak or reach my fingers out to touch it, he pulled it away again and softly spoke to the snake head.

"You place the crown on your head, and the magic begins. You and I will be teleported to the palace bubble. You will see what life lies beyond The Pit for you. Once you win, the palace and everything that comes with this crown will be yours—all yours, whenever you want it."

Nero handed me the crown. I took it in both hands and finally raised it towards my face. Images of my youth ran through my head. The frozen snake head glared at me with judgmental eyes, like my father any time I got in trouble. Faded memories of Thebes and Alexandria drifted to the surface as I looked into the red ruby, its glow somehow brilliant in my dimly lit living room. I had a lifetime of dreams where I had seen this exact moment play out—this exact feeling of a crown being placed atop my head, sometimes scripted like a play, sometimes a messy disaster, like one of Nero's Gladiator lessons. And sometimes it would be an empty black scene with only two golden images in sight: myself and the crown.

I placed the gold crown on my head and took in a long, deep inhale. Nothing happened immediately—no sparks erupting from my hair, no extravagant parade waltzing me down the street. But now, I felt a sense of completion, with the world at my fingertips. Everything racing through my mind was a pleasant thought. I felt like a king standing here in my humble dorm.

"King Kamaul," Nero said, sizing me up and grinning at the crown. "Has a nice ring to it, doesn't it? And it can be yours. All you have to do is win The Pit. Be the last student standing in that arena after the Duels ... and this crown is all yours. And you haven't even seen the palace yet! Care to find out for yourself? Dip your toe in that pond?" He strolled around my living room and kitchen.

I let the words sink in while staring forward to avoid Nero's eyes.

King Kamaul, I thought to myself. *Been waiting to hear those words my entire life. All I have to do is win this thing, huh, Nero? I can make that happen easily if it gets me this crown permanently.*

"Yeah," I answered softly, my voice calm and collected somehow. "I want to see it."

"Of course you do!" Nero exclaimed with a beaming smile. "Good. Now, let me show King Kamaul to his future palace."

His white ropes draped across my back as he placed a hand on my shoulder. The other hand gripped my neck tightly and slightly tilted my head downwards. He leaned toward my ear and whispered sternly. The words cut through my jolly spirit with devilish sweetness.

"If you should fail, however ... the crown and palace are destroyed. By my hands. They were built for you—and they can be destroyed because of you. DO NOT fail me, Kamaul. My wrath will be worse than death. My wrath will bring hellfire upon every ounce of your being if you do not win. Losing this palace will be the least of your concerns. Though I offer you all this tonight as a gift, it is not guaranteed. So, don't make me regret it."

He released his hand from my neck.

"Understood," I stammered, clearing my throat and looking into his eyes.

"Before we do that, I have something to confide in you, Kamaul. If you'll let me, that is," Nero began.

I nodded uncertainly.

"I know what happened between your father and you that night—the night the Seekers brought you here. I was not there to see it, but I know all the same. I know about the fire, about the collapse of the throne room, everything. As if I witnessed it with my own two eyes." He paused. "I can see it in your eyes. I can see it in the pain behind your smile and in your expressions. I understand what it's like to have rumors and wrongful accusations spread about your name for something you didn't do. I just want you to know that I have always held that silent connection between you and me very close. I know what those words can do to a person. And I also see on your face how the crown truly feels upon your head. It feels good—deserved. Because it is! Nothing was your fault that night, Kamaul. I believe you."

I watched and said nothing as Nero spoke. I appreciated him confiding in me, but I could not deduce the exact reason why. He was a very shallow and independent person who never shared anything personal with anyone at the college. It did prove his connection with me, however, to hear this now.

"I ... I feel nothing for that man. He was my father by birth, not by choice." I paused, lost in thought and anger. "You know ... I see those flames and the smoke billowing in the sky every now and then. I feel the heat and pressure of that collapsing temple ... The thick, choking smell of ash and dust, making it difficult to see even a foot in front of me ... The weight of stone and rubble and bricks on my bones ... Like you were saying! I feel all of those things, but nothing for my father. I think of him randomly from time to time ... but never any good memories or anything. Just frustration and resentment."

"I know what you mean. Felt the same way about my mother," Nero added solemnly.

Then a switch suddenly flipped in him. His tone changed. Nero's bitterness and emotionless face transformed back into the weird, celebratory, white-robe-wearing dreamer of peace who had first entered my dorm.

"Excellent! Let's get a-move on, then, shall we?" he said joyously. He shifted to face me again and let the long robe sleeves cover his hands and fingers. Sliding his arms across his chest, he nodded to the ruby and licked his lips. "Now that we've gotten that heartfelt crap off our chests ... do as I say. Touch your fingers to the ruby and repeat after me. You'll need to say the spell properly in order to teleport us to that palace."

"Yeah, I got ya," I replied, rising a finger to the red gem.

"Here we go, then," Nero said, placing a finger on it, too.

I locked eyes with him and repeated his words aloud: *"Duc me ad domus aurea."*

As I echoed the phrase, the ruby glowed like a brilliant solar flare. It blinded me, filling the room with a fierce white light that was intense even through my closed eyes. We kept a slight pressure on the crown's jewel while the faint sound of sands shifting loomed around us like we were caught in a giant hourglass. The ruby's glow grew even brighter, nearly unbearable, until everything beyond my eyelids turned to darkness.

A familiar dry heat greeted me the moment I opened my eyes. I was now standing in a desert courtyard inside a golden stone perimeter. Acacia trees of different shades sprouted from the corners, accented by low brush and tumbleweeds. A sandy path wove around through the scene, cutting past statues of soldiers, braziers, and fruitless olive trees. It was an unkempt courtyard, beautiful and lavish but clearly lacking any maintenance—not quite abandoned, but on pace for it.

"It's Roman?" I muttered, looking up perplexedly at the Parthenon-like palace.

"Well, of course it is, you fool!" Nero cackled, studying its architecture as if seeing it for the first time himself. "I designed it."

Wide steps led up to the palace's portico, where monstrous granite columns towered over us. The stone pediment was lined with golden shields, royal-blue paintings, and a Latin phrase across the front (though I hadn't a clue what it said). Nonetheless, the scale and magnitude of a palace that would possibly be mine drowned out those suspicions. Long red banners bore my family crest. This immense palace was easily twice the size of my father's in Egypt. But *this* place, the one now standing in my presence, was fit for my type of rule.

"Take me inside," I demanded as I walked up the steps and ran my hands down the ornate Corinthian columns.

"That's the spirit!" Nero exclaimed with his white robes billowing behind him.

Pushing open the bronze doors, Nero and I listened to their echo throughout the grand foyer. As we entered together, the heavy doors slammed shut behind us. White marble lined the palace floors, perfectly reflecting the sun's rays on their polished surface. A pair of ornate staircases flowed in a U shape towards the second floor.

"It's empty ...?" I mentioned irritably, having expected a lavish display to be awaiting my arrival.

Nero chuckled lightly and patted me on the back. "That's where you'll come in. Win this tournament, and this palace is yours. So, you can outfit it however you want."

"Awesome." I smiled, wandering across the marble.

Nero's unique vision of this palace included no ceilings, so when I looked up, expecting maybe a bright chandelier hanging above, my eyes were met with the sun's glare. The rooms would all be exposed to the elements.

"Well? What are you waiting for?" Nero continued, folding his arms across his chest. "Explore. Walk around! Have a look at the place. Let your imagination run wild."

Is Nero on drugs? I thought to myself, wondering about his obviously forced generosity. *If he is ... I want some.*

"Don't have to ask me twice," I answered, spinning around and heading off towards the left.

Massive groups of rooms ran into one another. In similar fashion to the lack of ceilings, the outer walls of these rooms were no walls at all, instead replaced by an open expanse of golden columns. Tucked away at the edges of each one were white drapes tied back with elegant rope. The sun mirrored my muscular self in the marble floor as the room and I basked in a relaxed heat.

I turned around to see Nero stalking me with a jarring gentle smile, as if he were a nosy shopkeeper impatiently chasing a sale. He followed me into the next few rooms like a shadow.

I wandered in and around the remaining rooms on the rest of the first floor. I pointed out a row of right-hand rooms that would make a great dining hall and kitchen combination. Despite that, however, nothing else on this level was really thrilling me or tickling my fancy. Without any decoration, every space looked the same—boring. So, I had Nero take the lead again as tour guide, and the two of us headed downstairs.

Once we were on the lower floor, three rooms finally lit up my eyes. Immediately upon exiting the hidden stairwell, I emerged behind Nero and spun to the right. A long hallway of auburn lighting led to the semi-indoor pool. With hieroglyphs painted in blue and gold on an accent wall, the pool's shimmering reflection lit up the room. A beautiful clear pool stretched far and wide, marble lining the bottom. I dipped my hand in the water, then moved back down the hallway.

"Soak it all in. Training for this to become yours begins in the morning," Nero interjected. The façade of kindness suddenly washed off his face and was replaced by a familiar emotionless stare.

"I am," I replied.

Abruptly, he stopped me in my tracks and placed both hands on my shoulders while standing behind me. As he leaned closer, his hands tightened their grip on my collarbone.

Ouch, I thought, grimacing to myself. *Well, the real him is back…*

I felt the burn of hatred in his voice again. "Enjoy the day today. Enjoy exploring my palace. Because while it could be yours, don't think I'll make it easy for you. I relish watching you squirm for success and redemption. I am rooting for you, Kamaul. Truly, I am. But I have more riding on this Pit Tournament than you do." Nero leaned in even more uncomfortably, to the point where his lips nearly touched my ear. "So, don't screw this up for us."

He paused to let the words sink in before releasing his grip on my shoulders.

"I gotcha," I answered bitterly, keeping my anger focused.

Nero had returned to his proper form. The gentle professor who had been walking with me was nothing but a smoke screen. Much like this palace, it was a fishing lure designed to entice my simpler desires. These lies hid the true intentions surrounding them.

Time was nearly up as we walked into a huge potential fitness center. My return to reality was approaching.

ABRAHAM IV

A MARVELOUS MAGE, CHARLIE carried himself as a diplomat and hobbled around with a mahogany cane. He wore a black frock suit and coat, like a typical man in those black-and-white photos who never smiles. Except for Charlie, that could not have been further from the truth. The bearded, bespectacled face of that six-ty-five-year-old man softly greeted everyone. As he was the Evolution professor, I'd had few interactions with him. Still, his reputation for friendliness and hospitality oozed through the halls. There wasn't a student who didn't gush over his lessons, or his creativity, or his lighthearted humor, or his charismatic conversations. In light of all this, it put a sudden pressure on me to impress him, not only as a hopeful student, but now as an assigned apprentice as well.

I approached the classroom door and tried to think of witty jokes or one-liners. I knocked gently with my wand, then tucked it back in my sock.

"Come ..." he answered in a surprised tone as he cleared his throat, "come in."

Pushing the door open, I was instantly grasped by the world of evolution. His classroom was manic and enthralling; the professor had created an environment like no other. It was the largest classroom on campus, and it swallowed me like a guppie in a school of fish. A pterodactyl skeleton hung from the ceiling on thin wires. The room's right wall was divided into a trio of wide windows, and the left wall housed glass cases filled with everything from a diagram of a falcooneek to the biological breakdown of a wyvern to the evolutionary changes in flightless birds. Not an inch of space was unused. This menagerie of a living classroom was wild to see for the first time; its reputation was as celebrated as the man teaching in it. It was one of those "you have to experience it for yourself" type of places. Despite being a fellow earth mage, I suddenly felt a little envious of evolution students.

I spun around to face the head of the room, and my eyes drifted to the professor's desk.

A black-and-gold cloud of smoke floated up to the ceiling, enveloping the pterodactyl wings. It filled the room with a sweet lavender aroma that swept underneath the panels of glass and between the other desks.

An odd man leaned back in Charlie's chair and displayed open-toed leather sandals propped up on the freshly polished desk. He was dressed in a faded green poncho and a wacky Peruvian hat, with its straps hanging below his shoulders. Like a passé hippie, the gentleman slouched down in the chair and puffed away on a rolled cigar held tight between two fingers.

"Uhhh ... 'Scuse me, sir," I interjected. "I'm looking for Professor Charlie? Have you seen him?"

Finally moving the sandals blocking his face, the man showed himself to me.

"Abraham!" Charlie coughed, forcing a smile to his face. Then he coughed again, raggedly, like someone trying to hide a pneumonia diagnosis. "Good to see you. Yes, sorry, seems I lost track of the time."

"Pr-professor?" I stammered, hastily looking him up and down. "Is that really you?"

"Who else would it be?" he replied, clearing his throat and extinguishing the cigar in a hidden ashtray. The smell of lavender lingered in the room as the smoke billowed in the air, its golden color more vibrant.

"Where's your ... suit and coat and loafers and cane? Surely this can't really be you."

"This is really me, Abe," Charlie answered with a chuckle. He coughed again before removing his woolen cap. "Very easy to trick the eye into seeing what you want it to."

"And, sir, you're smoking? With all due respect, an earth mage smoking cigars is pretty hypocritical. It's like a mage joining the church of Ha'thar."

"I know," Charlie sighed. "I hate it, too. Trust me. I've been trying to quit, but it's my escape from the world. At heart, Abe, I'm a simple man. Once you've taught evolution for years like I have, the incessant reruns of students clamoring for you to hear their newest theories or lend out your classroom space for their experiments just becomes exhausting. Living through The Pit was also ... exhausting. Smoking is my vice and my coping mechanism. It's a guilty pleasure—one I had hoped to quit by now. Don't tell anyone, would ya? Gotta keep my simple man schtick believable outside closed doors."

"Your addiction aside, this whole image of you is honestly a lot to take in, Professor. Poncho, sandals, hat, smoking a funky cigar ... It's very confusing. I've seen you around campus for years, and I always had this idea of you in my head. But, here you are in the comfort of your own classroom—nothing like that. If you're a hippie, you should be proud of that, sir."

"No, Abe, I am not a hippie." Charlie laughed, stepping out from behind his desk and reaching for the mahogany cane propped against it. "As I said, I am deep down a simple man who's coping with things how I need to cope with them. Showing a different side of myself to the public than in the privacy of this room isn't lying. It's more of a double life, and smoking a cigar to decompress is how Charlie functions as Charlie. Soon you will discover that the tribulations of The Pit can be unbearable. Earlier, being in The Trench, that ceremony, back in Jax's office ... Everything felt so real again, ya know? Like I was *there* again. Wearing the poncho and sandals allows me to reconnect with the old me before The Pit. This room is like my version of Superman's phone booth. When the frock coat old man hobbles back into the evolution classroom, students and professors are none the wiser. No one ever sees me in my wacky hat. Best to not show how much one event can alter the trajectory of your life."

"Wouldn't this ruse be more complicated? You're working an extra job when you don't have to."

"Quite the contrary. It's quite fun, actually. Takes my mind off of things for a little while. You're young and have many years to fight off the traumas of The Pit. Once you get into your sixties like me, Abe, many small problems seem larger than they really are. Lighting up a cigar of citumi and wearing flowy clothes distract me from everything else."

"What's citumi?"

"Citumi is the substance smoked in Penumbra's cigars. Earth has tobacco plants; we have citumi. It's grown and harvested like that, too. It mimics the smell of one's emotions; thus, everyone will note a unique aroma when smelling the same flower. Once the citumi plant is plucked and rolled into a cigar, my emotions burn through as I smoke. It produces a colored cloud to reflect that." Charlie solemnly looked up to the ceiling and observed the golden smoke. "What'd you smell, Abe? I'm tasting fields of strawberries right now. And that smoke? Yellow represents fear."

"I'm getting hints of lavender. But what are you afraid of, Professor?" I asked curiously, watching the cloud vaporize completely.

"I fear for you, Abe. The Pit changes you. It manipulates your mind and warps your perspective on life. You may not feel it take effect yet. The moment your name spilled out on the snow there, everything from this point forward will change."

"It's taken a toll on you, Professor. I'm sorry. I can see it. I understand why you hide your true self."

"You are smart and considerate, but don't be naïve. Don't feel sorry for me. I lived it! I fought in that tournament and survived. I had to make choices to keep myself alive and think selfishly to win the damn thing. Just ... all of that does take a toll on a person. That you are correct about."

I glanced at Charlie's unused cane. A weird atmosphere crept into the room. My brain was a jumbled mess now. Initially, I had known what to expect from visiting Charlie after the ceremony: I would see his classroom, see what all the hype was about, maybe chat about the tournament, and maybe showcase my magic. Even when knocking on the door, I had assumed certain things about what I would experience inside. But ever since I'd crossed its threshold, this room and its professor had been full of surprises. Gone were the frock suit and coat. Gone was his reliance on the walking cane. Gone were his covered feet. All of it had been replaced by a cigar-smoking, woolen-cap-wearing old man in a green poncho. Despite all of it, though, my fascination with Professor Charlie continued to grow like a newly planted garden.

"Fascinating," I said.

"You must be feeling overwhelmed," Charlie added, hiding the tray of cigars in a desk drawer before retrieving his walking stick. Suddenly, he dropped his cane and picked it back up with ease. As he retrieved it, the cane transformed into a black walnut wand. "Let's change the conversation from my own surprises to learning more about you, Mr. Morrison." Charlie leaned against his desk and adjusted his poncho. As he smoothed down nonexistent hair on his bald head, his smile was kind and charming.

"Yes, I am overwhelmed. Very much so. But okay. What would you like to know, Professor?"

"Please, Abe, call me Charlie. You've discovered my secret. No need for formalities."

"Well, Profess—err Sorry. Well, Charlie ... what would you like to know?"

"I already know plenty. Just need to confirm from my source whether the information I have on you is correct."

I nodded.

"Abraham Morrison. Fourth-year master germination mage. Top of his class in most subjects. Studying to become a professor—a respectable dream, if I do say so myself. Set to graduate next summer and finally bind with his elemental. Longs to be a Seeker. But despite your talking with them and pleading your case twice, they've turned you down twice." Charlie brushed lint off his poncho, casually studied his wand, then returned focus back to me. "How'd I do?"

"Yeah. Pretty spot-on. Even had to bring up those painful memories of being turned down for Seeker two times. So, thanks for that. But uh-huh—you summed it up pretty well. Missed a couple personal details, though ... Great girlfriend of over two-and-a-half years, Emilee. I can talk to plants as if it's a second piece of my brain. And ..." My voice trailed off as I looked at Charlie.

Don't. You cannot tell him about that. It needs to remain secret! No one must know about it!

"... And nearly finished with building my own house on campus," I concluded hastily.

"How excellent."

That raven idol secret belongs to me. Charlie may let his own private affairs slip, but I can't. The raven is possibly dangerous. No one can know about it.

"Professor, I appreciate your asking about me. But I frankly don't care to talk about myself at all. I wanna know more about you. I had this idea of you in my head, you see. But being here in your classroom has shown me not to trust first impressions. Fresh from the ceremony, what I really want to know about is The Pit. I want to know what to expect, what I'll see, what I'll face ..." I paused for a moment, then glanced at his cane. "Charlie ... I want to hear about your Pit experiences. The real stories—not the glossed-over, glorified versions of them that some other professors share. Not the rumor mill stories and hyperbolized crap. I want to hear *your* stories. From you."

Charlie graciously waved a hand for me to take a seat at a nearby desk, but I refused, preferring to wander along the walls and explore some of the diagrams.

"So, can you tell me about The Pit, Professor?" I asked.

"Charlie! Please, call me Charlie." He chuckled in response before transforming the walnut wand back into his wooden cane and folding his hands on its T-shaped handle. After a brief pause, he looked curiously at me and asked, "Abe, do you know why I fake having to use this cane?"

"If I've learned anything so far, Charlie, it's that I clearly don't know much about you," I replied.

"The 245th Pit Tournament was my summoning. Myers, Wilson, Arlyn, Tyson, and me. It was the final Rite, and there were only four of us left, after Myers was trampled in an Olerdolana stampede during the Earth Rite. Gruesome thing that was, too ... Anyway, the ... the final Rite was a race down this enormous mountain. Steep and dangerous and snowy, with blurred vision the entire time. Accidents waiting to happen at every turn. Frigid temperatures threatening hypothermia."

Charlie's face became sour and somber. As he put his full weight on the cane, his eyes flicked between me and the sounds of the festival resonating outside the windows.

"This Air Rite task seemed simple: Start at the top, and race to finish at the bottom. Of course, magic was allowed—and my magic was good, Abe. Like, *darn* good! Remarkable, even, according to my Mentor. The obvious struggle was the physical part—getting my two clumsy feet downhill. I was about as slow then as I am now. So, using a mutation spell, I conjured ostrich legs to replace my own. Those new legs propelled me down that mountain in no time! I was chugging along happily in first place! With the winds rushing against my face, I felt the triumph of victory at my fingertips. Adrenaline coursed through my veins, and I felt like a true champion already, as I could see the base of the mountain just up ahead. I heard other footsteps behind me, but they were further back. I was sailing steady."

Charlie laid his cane on the desk and slid his hands inside the poncho's sleeves.

"The memories are still fresh in my mind, as if they happened yesterday. I relive them all the time. Sneak up on you like a nightmare when you're sleeping. Any time I reminisce on those Pit experiences, they haunt me, as if I'm in the moment all over again. My body is thrown into years past, and I feel both the anxiety and the horror of them. What I'm getting at, Abe, is that The Pit is relentless. It does not care if you're great at magic or can barely cast it. It does not care if you're young or old, novice or master. It does not care if you're hungry for victory or just trying to stay alive. The Pit is a beast all its own. Treat it as such. Work *with* the arena, never against it. That's probably the most honest advice I'll ever give you."

The intensity in his voice remained as he returned to the mountain race memory.

"Anyway ... There I was on my ostrich legs, racing down a snow-covered moun-tain, when I heard a loud WHOOSH come past my head! It was the fire mage, Tyson. On dragon wings, he soared above me and landed between me and the finish line. Clearly now in first place, Tyson turned around and waved at the three of us trailing behind. Greedily, he blasted his wand at the hillside, sending chunks of rubble crumbling down the mountain. Right as my mutation spell was wearing off, one of the blasts hit next to my feet and flung me into the air. Soaring like a wounded duck, I whacked the snow with extreme force. The pain I felt was ..." His voice trailed off as he glanced down at the right side of his body, examining his shoulder and upper arm. "... incredible. It was a pain like no other. I wouldn't wish it on my worst enemy. It felt as though someone had removed my bones and put them back in the wrong order. After tumbling over the snow, I hastily retrieved my wand and cast aside the flying debris in my path. I tried to help Wilson and Arlyn, but I was more focused on crossing the finish line myself. Racing down the mountain with a possibly broken collarbone, I just sprinted, injured arm tucked against my hip. Abe, I crossed the finish line that day ... but I wished I hadn't."

Charlie paused again.

"As I turned around to check on my fellow competitors, I watched the mountain awaken. Tyson's blasts had caused an avalanche. More rocks and rubble cascaded down in a deadly mix of fog and snow. Tyson smirked at my side while I gripped my aching arm and searched for signs of Wilson and Arlyn. Then I spotted the water mage! She had made it out of the debris. But unfortunately for Wilson, he was still far up the mountain, and the avalanche overtook him. And so, I watched him disappear in the billowing white snow ..."

Charlie's voice drifted off, and the man lost himself in his words as they solemnly sunk into the floorboards. I felt horrible. Watching his reactions through this relived memory was eye-opening. It must have been dreadful for him. I came to Charlie's side and leaned against the long mahogany desk as he gazed blankly out the window.

"Seeing two people you've trained with for months die in the span of a few weeks is heartbreaking, Abe. But that's The Pit. It is a literal fight to the death. Either you win and see your name recorded in history, or you die and listen from above as the college mourns your loss. Abe ..." He turned to greet my eyes again. "I will help guide you and train you and teach you everything I can. However, there are many things about The Pit that I cannot teach you and that you will have to learn on your own. One thing that I can teach you right now ... is the internal strength to move on. Trust me, I wanted to end the tournament right then and hold a vigil for Wilson. But the Pit doesn't work like that. Once the last three people cross the finish line, that devious arena is already preparing for the next chapter." His eyes were vacant and distant as the radiant sun reflected in his glasses. I thought I saw a single tear fall down his cheek. "Do you understand this, Abe? Do you hear what I'm saying? I know what I describe to you may be hard to take in. But we must start somewhere and help you understand the deadly realism of this event. Do you know what I mean?"

"Yes ... I do, Charlie," I said, staring back at him apprehensively yet grateful.

"I hope so, because these memories are not shared happily, nor lightly. I need you to hear the words I say. Training will be intense. The entire event will overtake The College of Adarius and hold its audience captive. You will not be able to escape it. I will not be able to escape it. You follow me?"

"Yes, I do," I answered keenly.

He looked down at his aforementioned arm and held it out between us for me to examine.

"Once the pain of my broken bones subsided, I hunkered down and pushed on. I knew the nurses and medical mages would never be able to return my arm to its original functionality. So, I did it myself. Using *careful* evolution magic, I was successfully able to regrow and replace my right arm. The cane and the off-balance walking are designed to keep the illusion alive that I never healed properly. However, that is not true. While it's frowned upon to do experimental surgery on yourself, I could not risk losing the next event and dying because of it. I had to win. Not only for the element of earth, but to save my own life! I could have been the next Myers or Wilson, waiting from above to see which competitor joined me in death."

Charlie smiled briefly, then it withered away. He mindlessly laid out a row of textbooks and lesson plans while pondering his internal experience. It seemed as though no amount of happy thoughts or positive energy could brighten his mood. I appreciated his honesty, though.

"Thank you for sharing. I'm sorry to have brought back such troubled memories."

"It's alright." His tone shifted to a cheerful and pleasant one as he rose to his feet. With a wink, he continued, "You see, that's another thing I learned during The Pit: Never linger on the past, because the future is getting closer by the second."

I warmly smiled back, admiring how functional his arm was now.

"Now, if you'll excuse me for a moment, I need to finish up some things for my substitute to handle in my absence," Charlie said, returning to his work. "Ask questions and talk to me as much as you like. I am a talented multitasker."

"Very well," I replied. "Do you know who the substitute is going to be, sir?"

"No idea," he replied casually. "All I know is that this new professor will be handling my classes while we train together. Part of the duties of being a Pit Mentor. Impossible to split up your time."

I glanced at the ceiling and got a great view of the pterodactyl hanging above. With a wide wingspan and a thin neck, this dinosaur had once ruled the skies. Held by invisible wires, it loomed over the classroom like a hawk in flight stalking its prey. I imagined the tough skin and the dull, beautiful color of its body. I found myself lost in its impressive size; it was a large prehistoric beast suitable for the largest classroom.

"Were you scared, Charlie? You know, like ... when your name was called?" I asked.

It took a minute or so before he responded.

"Of course I was!" he exclaimed, shoving more things into his desk drawers than he was taking out of them. "The spotlight on me, thousands of eyes on me, my name spelled out in blood ... It was the scariest moment of my life, Abe! And if my early judgments are correct—which they normally are—you're scared as well. But yes, I know the feeling."

"Yeah, I am, actually. Never felt a fear like this before. A lot of emotions running through my head for the last twenty-four hours. Could give you a rundown of 'em, but ..." I joked, thinking what I said was an outrageous offer.

Charlie leapt at the idea. He immediately stopped working and stared at me. "Tomorrow, we will begin the official training process. But there's no time like the present to get a head start."

"Right. Yeah, okay. In that case ..." I began, pacing around the rows of desks. My eyes bounced from random spots on the floor to Charlie's eager gaze. "I feel ... fine. I'm confident enough in my skills to compete with any of 'em. First impressions can trick the eyes, right? Not after that ceremony! From the moment Kamaul opened his big mouth, I got agitated. I have no idea who he is, or who he *thinks* he is, but his smugness and ego are hard to miss. Kid's got a reputation, and not in a good way. With the rest of the competitors, it's really too soon to know my opinion. But it's here that I realized how much drive and hunger I have deep down to win. The last thing I want is to look down from the heavens and see an undeserving brute whooping and hollering as the champion. After the selection, the rest of the Pit Ceremony was honestly a blur. Jax was rambling on about training and festivals and managing classwork and challenges and ... It was just a lot. Now, though, after sitting with my emotions for a little, I think anticipation and anxiety are running the show."

"Information overload. Yeah, the ceremony can be a bit of a drag, too. Hard to process all of that and juggle your own emotions at the same time!" Charlie exclaimed, leaning against the front of his desk. "Yeah, five main challenges based around each element, known as the Elemental Rites. Training begins the day after the ceremony, which is tomorrow. Classwork, classwork ...? Hmmm. Oh, yeah! Pit competitors have the option either to split their time between classes and training or go full-time with training and catch up on those classes later."

"Oh. Okay. Understood more than I thought I did. Thanks."

A long pause swept through the room. The weight of the conversation to this point simmered around Charlie and me. Strolling over to the window, he gestured for me to follow. We stood at the glass and looked out across the ongoing extravaganza.

"Is this the festival Jax was talking about?"

"Yup. The Festival of the Elements. Every four years, when the tournament occurs, it transforms The College of Adarius into a vibrant experience. Market Square is reinvigorated with food booths, game booths, information booths ... Booths, booths, and more booths! It's a regular bazaar down there. Acting as the yin to The Pit's yang, the Festival of the Elements is a combination carnival, circus, and fiesta held within the normally empty field right next door. Most importantly, I might add, please try and experience all of it for yourself, won't you? I made the mistake of not doing it in my year. Missed out on many great memories. It's only for the six months of The Pit. Don't make the same mistake I did."

"Seems satirical and ironic to have those going on at the same time as the barbaric main event but ... alright. Yeah, it does look like fun. Emilee and I can go. Take all of my anxious thwarted excitement and channel it into the festival," I answered calmly.

"Splendid." Charlie chuckled, a soft twinkle in his eye as he watched a pair of small elves juggle flaming knives. "Might be a great distraction from everything else going on. Sure would've helped me. So, I can only insist you not follow in my footsteps on this one."

There was a small pause as my Mentor and I watched the Festival of the Elements from afar. Though I had been born a tree-hugging introvert, Emilee had a wonderfully eerie way of coercing me into public places. This could actually be fun.

"Thanks for sharing about your tournament experiences, Charlie. I could tell ... it brought up some unpleasant memories," I said, trying not to disturb the peace.

"Guess sometimes The Pit does more damage outside the arena than inside," he said gloomily as we each felt an invisible fog waft around us.

"I'll have to take your word for it," I added timidly.

"Take my word, then. It's ... uhhh ... very true," Charlie sighed, removing his glasses and wiping his eyes with the sleeve of his poncho. "It's a learning experience. You'll learn things about magic you never knew, and you'll learn even more about yourself that you never knew. I know we'll discover many new things together during our training. But that doesn't mean you should shut off your listening ears outside the classroom, too."

"'Listening ears,' Professor? Haven't heard that since fifth grade. And I was homeschooled!" I laughed, hoping to lighten the mood.

Charlie removed himself from the window and returned to his seat behind his desk. Yet this time, he requested my help. "What do ya say we shift focus from deep conversations for a bit? Assist me while we talk?"

"Sure," I answered, returning to his side.

In the rear corners of the room, Charlie had two newly finished display cases resting against the wall, ready to be added to the collection. One was a complete breakdown and history of animal tusks. The other showed creatures from the prehistoric era. It created a brilliant depiction of evolutionary changes from past to present. And I knew the moment I stole a glance at them that Charlie had solely created them himself, as they featured the same level of intricate detail as the others.

His dedication to his work wrapped me up in it, too. It was like the passion and pride I felt about building my house and listening to the flora of the world and their individual connections to it. And after making my way to the first glass case, I no longer heard the stifled murmur of the festival outside nor felt the invisible fog collecting in the room.

"Grab that end ... while I ... take this one ..." Charlie said, bending down to grab the case.

"Yup, got it."

We hoisted it into the air and carried it over to the wall opposite the windows. Placing it on the floor, Charlie and I removed the wyvern case and put up the prehistoric animal case in its place. Then we grabbed the old display case and brought it back over behind Charlie's desk before grabbing the next one. The flightless bird case was replaced with the animal tusks display, and the professor took a step back to size up the improved wall.

"Looks great!" he exclaimed.

"Hope you don't mind my asking ..." I started, watching him examine the setup of the display cases. "How old are you again, Professor?"

"Sixty-five," he answered immediately, without bothering to look in my direction.

"Sixty-five?" I gasped.

"Yes, Abe! Sixty-five. Why do you ask?"

"You lifted those cases more easily than I did. Hidden strength under that poncho, too?"

"No." Charlie laughed candidly. "Abe, I've been through some shit in my life! All of which has made me stronger, physically and mentally. Before the college. Training for the tournament. The Pit, and every moment after it. You got a first-person retelling of a Pit experience, and that was just *one* example. A mere ... a mere glimpse of what I saw in that ... event. You name it: I've either seen it or lived through it. So, to clarify my answer to your question ... I am a sixty-five-year-old hippie and aristocrat, leading a double life, and could easily take you in a one-on-one contest, if that's what you're asking. Do not judge a man by his age, Abe. That's not nice."

Charlie winked at me, then returned to his desk.

"You think so?" I joked, wandering over to a pair of enchanted glass boxes and pretending not to acknowledge his playful threat. One demonstrated a butterfly's life cycle in an animated projection; the other showed the evolution from neanderthal to modern man using magic clay.

"Oh, I know so!"

Charlie lifted his head up from underneath the desk drawers and grinned really wide at me, tempting me to take the bait and accept his challenge.

"Okay, Professor. Yes. Let's test that theory! So, what kinda contest are you thinkin'? Elemental mage duel? Friendly game of darts? Maybe a little magic trivia ...? Or something more classic, like poker or checkers or—"

"Chess."

"Yeah. Chess is an option, sure," I said, pausing in astonishment at such a cliché answer, before I noticed Charlie's stern face.

"No, Abe. The game I choose is chess. I have a set right here in my classroom."

"Right. Of course. Yeah." I nodded, watching Charlie retrieve a wooden chess set from a nearby cabinet. "The classic of all classics! That silly old game helped my father and I bond, you know. Being an orphan, I never had any true hobbies or interests. After Roy brought me home, I picked up some of his instead, including chess. He taught me how to play, the pawns and their uses, tricks of the trade—everything. He loved it as a kid and as an adult, and he certainly passed that on to me during my childhood."

"Funny you should mention that ..." Charlie grinned, taking two student desks in the front row and turning them to face one another. Their legs scraped lightly across the floor as the professor adjusted the chairs to match the new layout and created one long makeshift table. "It was a big part of my life, too."

Charlie unboxed the chess set on the desks before setting the pieces in their proper starting positions. The two sets were made of intricately-carved walnut and maple, representing the typical black and white pieces, respectively. Their beautiful yet simple craftsmanship caught my eye immediately.

"You will be playing the white pieces ... or maple pieces, in our case."

Gesturing for me to take the seat opposite him, the professor took his seat in the small student chair behind the walnut pieces and smiled intensely. I sat down and inspected the chess set. It made me envious, thinking of learning to play with a set as unique as this rather than my father's plastic set.

"When should we start?" I smirked, feeling confident in myself.

"You know the rules. Start whenever."

I let out a soothing exhale and eyed the pawns for my first move.

"White pawn to D4," I announced, resting my hands on the edges of the desk.

"What are you doing?" Charlie chuckled, folding his arms across his chest.

"We're in a magic school. This is a magic chess set. I say the move aloud, and the pieces move on their own, right?" I said, horrified.

Charlie's grin was judgmental and very amused. "Abe, yes, this is magic school. But *this* is a basic chess set—a gift from an old student of mine. Magic is not involved. Please physically move your pieces."

Feeling like a complete fool, I reached out and moved one of the maple pawns forward two spaces. After slouching back in my seat, I waited for the professor's serious game face to return as he reached out to make his first move.

"Well, that was embarrassing," I said. "Please don't ever bring it up again ..."

"Don't worry, Abe. Our secrets are safe here. Your mistake will stay in this room."

"Much appreciated." I nodded, eyeing the board for my next approach.

The expansive classroom felt truncated now, collapsed around our makeshift table. The walls of display cases closed in upon us like a small janitor's closet. The atmosphere was quiet. We traded moves for a while, seemingly matching each other's chess expertise. The moments between Charlie and me where we held our breath, waiting for the other's next move, reflected a similar suspense to when the names were revealed at the Pit Ceremony. Games of chess were often intense and exciting, and even this lighthearted challenge in Charlie's classroom evoked a tournament setting.

"So, you've shared your interest in chess with former students, then?" I asked softly, hyper-focused on Charlie's setup.

"I have, yes. A few select students know of it. But much like a lot of myself, I normally keep my hobbies hidden. I keep this wooden case for moments of boredom, really. I play every so often, even if it's just battling against myself."

"Why play with me, then, Professor?"

"Abe ... call me Charlie."

"Sorry, yes. It just feels so informal to be on a first-name basis after just meeting today, but you're right. So, why reveal your love for this game to me now?"

"Chess is a game of wits. You have to anticipate your opponent's actions and think like them to win—put your feet in their shoes to predict their next move. I feel like a broken record at this point, but The Pit is like a grandiose game of chess. You're playing the arena's game, like a pawn moved according to its desires. Your job in that tournament is to outsmart and outthink your opponents *and* the arena to win. The match we're playing right now gives me great insight into how your mind functions and what futures it sees."

"Your love for chess began much earlier than mine did, Charlie. I'm a novice compared to you, probably, though I like to think I can hold my own. Roy told me that chess reflects a lot about life: risking pieces to save yourself or sacrificing pawns to protect someone else. He said life is your enemy on a chessboard, and that it's up to you to play the right move at the right time."

"Abe, your father was an intelligent man. I know I've never met him, or even knew of him until today, but I know a smart man when I hear of one. He would be proud of you for keeping up his legacy and teachings. If you do decide to become a professor someday, I look forward to seeing how much of Roy you bring forth in your classroom."

"That is, if I'm still alive months from now," I answered solemnly, reminded of the nightmare death match starting tomorrow.

Our match was approaching its climax. The pieces were beginning to reach captivating places on the board, with our minds churning over how to win and the board itself acting as the canvas for our genius. The end was nearing, and both Charlie and I could sense it. He did not want to give a student half his age the satisfaction of beating him. And I, his younger and more brash opponent, did not want to prove the stereotype right that victory rewards the more experienced player.

"Age is but a number, Abraham," Charlie added, a daring smile traced across his lips. "Before The Pit, I carried the reputation of being a pacifist. I preferred to sharpen my mental wits in the classroom and fight my fights on a chessboard. Kept to my books and my studies. Other students on campus poked fun at all that and called me unfriendly names. Well, technically, the terms they used were 'coward' and 'wimp,' but I like to think 'quiet pacifist' is what they meant. I let the physically stronger guys handle the fighting. So, at my age, the number sixty-five is minuscule compared to my life experiences."

"Are you trying to distract me from the game, Professor?" I joked, inspecting my pieces on the board.

"I am merely spewing out autobiographical bullet points so you understand as much about me as I hope to understand about you. If that turns out to distract you from this riveting game ... then oops, I guess." Charlie shrugged a glint in his eyes.

He sat obnoxiously relaxed in his chair as I looked at the board and weighed my next options. I was without my knights or queen while Charlie had at least one of every piece. My king was protected by my remaining rook, and I had a clear path to capture his king. After a brief internal monologue, I discovered a move worthy of Roy's admiration and moved my rook to D8.

"Wow, Abe. I'm impressed. That's a bold move." Charlie nodded.

"I know," I sneered, slouching back in my seat, feeling pompous and proud of myself. "Don't sound so surprised, Professor! While you may have years on me, I have the gift of youth and boldness on my side. Expect the unexpected from me."

"A bold move, indeed," he repeated, leaning on the chessboard. "Roy certainly taught you a thing or two. I see you've made a play at my king—but that will ultimately leave yours unguarded ..." Charlie's pause was menacing as I suddenly realized my mistake. His eyes shifted from me to his queen, and he took the top of the walnut piece gracefully in his fingers. He reached across the board and knocked over my king. "Checkmate."

"What?" I muttered softly as my maple royalty toppled to the board.

"Rookie mistake." Charlie smiled, sliding back his chair and rising to his feet for a handshake. "Well played, though, Abe. I look forward to seeing how you improve at chess, and other things throughout our training."

I shook his hand and dropped my eyes to the finished game. My thoughts were anxiously thrust into the what-ifs and secondary moves and changes I could have made to beat Charlie. Too late now, but it still captivated my focus all the same. Looking disappointedly at the remaining pieces, I sighed and grinned faintly at the professor.

"I gotta ... I gotta get better at chess, I suppose. If The Pit is anything like it ... it will kill me. If I can't learn to make the correct moves at the correct time and balance the pace of the game, I'll be watching from the stars, wishing I had done things differently." Resentment and frustration washed over my face.

Charlie's smile was full of wisdom and heart. He spoke while replacing the pieces in his case and closing it up. "You'll get there, Abe. Don't worry. You and I will work on that together—both chess and The Pit." He laughed. "See? Maybe some time at the festival and the Masquerade Ball don't sound so bad now, do they?"

My energy dropped as my weary eyes looked at his. The serious tone of our earlier conversation returned, and a familiar fog wafted into the room.

"Charlie," I began, sitting upright in the desk chair, "how did it feel to ... to win The Pit? To be the *last* one standing? What was that like?"

"Honestly, Abe ... it is the wildest and most morally twisted feeling a mage can experience."

OLIVIA IV

"This place resembles a sleazy hole-in-the-wall tourist trap—one that we're about to fall prey to, Tarik. What kind of romantic beach getaway is this?"

"Hey," Tarik said, struggling to find the firmness in his voice. "You were complaining—*saying* how hungry you were a few minutes ago, so I found the best-looking spot I could. After all, it's rather difficult to spot a respectable restaurant at 10,000 feet, Olivia."

I scowled and stared straight ahead.

"Doesn't matter if you up and get us killed, 'cause I won't be the one dying," I added.

"Impossible ... but noted." Tarik laughed.

He tightened his grip on the reins and directed Chestnut's path towards an empty dirt lot next to the restaurant. I held onto Tarik's waist and tucked myself behind him as the wind picked up. The griffin stayed steady with Tarik's lead. I watched its feathers ripple in the breeze, lush brown fur fluffing in its downward trajectory. Chestnut leveled out once we approached the ground, and his front paws touched down in what I would have called an unpleasant landing.

"That was her first landing, bud. Little gentler next time," Tarik whispered in the griffin's ear. He rubbed the beast's mane while Chestnut sulked like a canine who has been caught jumping on the furniture.

"Not his fault," I corrected. "He didn't expect a detour either."

"Whaaaaat?! This is a cute little tavern! Perhaps an inn *and* tavern. Let's just check it out—see what it's about. What's the worst that could happen? Can't you trust me for once, Olivia? Please?"

"Fine," I replied reluctantly, peering at his puppy dog eyes. "But if they try and kill us with some poisoned ravioli, I will strangle you personally. Only difference between them and me is that I won't be using my hands at all."

I batted my eyes at him.

"Yes, ma'am," he said, pulling himself out of Chestnut's saddle before assisting me back to safety on the ground. I could tell he liked my awkward flirting by how white his smile became. It was a dashing smile, but I didn't know if I had the courage to say that to his face. Perhaps someday I would ... or I'd keep it bottled up deep down, like the creatures in Tartarus, and never let him know that I actually might like him! Yeah, I like option two better; let's go with that.

Looping Chestnut's reins through an arched wooden post, Tarik reached for the raw chunks of steak chilling in a mess of ice packs. He fed some to the satisfied griffin and returned his attention to me. But then Tarik began to chuckle. Nothing obnoxious or anything—just a slow, brooding giggle escaping his lips.

"What's so funny, Tarik? Care to share with the rest of the class?" I insisted, folding my arms over my chest.

"The restaurant's name! It's funny," he said. "The Pouncing Fish. Don't you get it?"

"It makes no sense," I added, turning away from Chestnut and Tarik. "Fish don't pounce."

"That's what makes it funny! It's an oxymoron."

"*You're* an oxymoron," I muttered under my breath before getting a full glance at the building myself. Tucked away off the beaten path, The Pouncing Fish tavern seemed to rely heavily on weary travelers and passersby for business. Meadows of dying grass lay to the right while the dirt roadway creepily rolled towards the horizon on the left. Fitting its surroundings, the inn and tavern was nothing spectacular. A sign hanging from an iron bar marked the entrance to the tavern. Many shuttered windows lined the building, and no light shone from within. The Pouncing Fish would have looked vacant and abandoned if not for the tavern doors propped wide open, inviting those eager enough to step inside.

"Sure ... about this place, Tarik?" I said, strolling and scanning the first floor of the tavern.

As he opened to respond, the flock of gray clouds suddenly steamrolled into the sky above us began to pour down rain. Loud and incessant, the raindrops soaked our clothes until we silently looked at each other in agreement that we had no alternative.

We entered The Pouncing Fish, now sopping wet from the freak thunderstorm.

"We'll stay here 'til we dry off, then head into town. It'll be quick and painless. Promise." He touched the tips of my fingers and nodded in reassurance.

"My creatures await you if this goes poorly," I answered coldly.

Tarik smiled carefully and announced our arrival, his weariness echoing across the empty bar and tables. A few drips from a leaking faucet answered the call, but no people or secondary voices.

Then I heard a light trot down the set of stairs tucked behind a pillar. Another set of footsteps followed quickly after. Turning the corner, an older couple whipped around a wooden beam and fully into view of Tarik and me.

The woman wore a faded yellow dress and had tufty white hair that resembled a cotton ball. A red scarf was wrapped around her neck. Her husband, while taller and leaner, was staying warm with a one-size-fits-all powder-blue sweater and a complementary brown-trousers-and-vest combination. He tipped his cuffed Hamburg hat to Tarik when the man's eyes met his. The pair smiled with grandparent-like generosity, which made my skin crawl, in a way that could only start with a candy-cane-and-gumdrop pathway and end in a giant, seemingly harmless gingerbread house. The couple definitely looked cute and harmless—but so did cobras, and I would never dream of waltzing into their den and asking for shelter. Nevertheless, I had to suppress my suspicions as a series of stomach growls encouraged the prospect of food.

"Why, hello, dearies! Welcome to The Pouncing Fish, a friendly restaurant for passing travelers!"

The heavyset woman grabbed a handful of cutlery wrapped in napkins and a pair of menus. The husband followed her lead, then vanished down a hallway. They seated us in their largest dining section near a well-maintained stone fireplace. If I were anyone else but me, I would have been crapping my pants amid the eeriness of the whole situation. But thankfully, since I was just me, I was quite enjoying this couple's murder mystery atmosphere.

"Wonderful. Thank you," Tarik said, assisting me to my seat before seating himself across the table.

I nodded shyly at the woman's pleasant demeanor.

"My name is Adelaide, loves. And my husband, wherever that string bean is off to, is Solomon. We run this place together, and you're our first customers for the day. So, if you need anything ... just holler!" Her voice rang under the tables and off the windows. Though I would never tell Tarik, of course, having the entire tavern to ourselves was a little charming—a *little* tiny bit.

"Thank you for your hospitality." Tarik smiled as Adelaide walked away.

Soon she brought over two glasses of water and asked for our orders. Honestly, I had not even looked at the menu; I had no clue what they served at all. My mind was preoccupied by the strange decor of The Pouncing Fish. Little wooden shelves lined with toy sailboats, seashells, ship's wheels, and nautical trinkets dotted the walls. The quirky restaurant perfectly matched the couple running it.

Bopping into the room from the kitchen, Solomon emerged with a dish rag thrown over his shoulder and held a pair of lavender bath towels in his right hand. "Here ya go! Dry off, kiddos. You look like you're freezing."

I accepted the gesture and took the towel to dry off my hair, clothes, and hands. Tarik did the same. We handed the damp towels back to Solomon, who slid happily out of sight into the kitchen.

"Ma'am," Tarik began, picking up his menu again, "what—"

"Call me Adelaide!"

"Adelaide," he began again, "what do you recommend we order? Any signature dishes or specials? Whatever you recommend is what we'll have."

"Well, we're offering a new meat pie dish. It's a new ... specialty Solomon and I have been working on. It's not ... perfect by any means, but we like it. You'll go with that, then?"

A smile, nearly bursting out of his ears, spread across Tarik's face.

"Yes, we'll take two of the meat pie specials. Please. Before my boyfriend here splits his head in half, either from hunger or excitement," I said as politely as I could.

"Splendid, dears! I'll tell Solomon to get started," Adelaide shrieked, frantically scribbling on her notepad and stuffing it into her apron. She hurried off through the traffic door.

"See?!" Tarik said after a few minutes of sitting in silence. "The Pouncing Fish isn't so bad. Quaint. Cute old couple—which could be us someday, if you play your cards right!"

"Please, Tarik," I snapped, peering deep into his innocent soul across the off-balance table. "Do not *ever* think of us as an old couple together in some cutesy, ooey-gooey, sappy love story kind of way ... or I swear on my devilish fiends and all their friends that you'll spend—"

"Your threats are adorable, Olivia. But I wasn't being serious. Okay? It was just a joke. Maybe not a funny joke, but a joke, nonetheless. And I'm sorry," Tarik cut in solemnly.

"That's ... that's alright," I stammered.

"You did, however, call me your 'boyfriend' a bit ago. You weren't joking about that. I could never miss those two words sewn together," Tarik replied, unraveling his fork and knife from his napkin.

"Pushing your luck, Tarik. And it was boy-*space*-friend. Two words, separated. Try not to get too rosy in the cheeks."

"Right." He nodded defensively.

Scanning the room, I could hear the clanging of pots and pans. Solomon emerged back into the dining room. Oddly enough, the old man carried a flying fish sculpture that looked homemade, complete with craftsmanship and a possible wandering-eye's look to detail. The fish itself was askew, the fins were wobbly at best, and the scales (if one could make them out) were flattened out like a textbook. All in all, it was a handcrafted smorgasbord of bronze and cheap metal.

"What kind of abomination do you have in your hands, there, sir?" I asked, folding my arms and glaring at the sculpture in shock.

"What she means is ..." Tarik began, eyeballing me. "What is that lovely piece of art?"

"Family heirloom. My grandparents before me crafted this fish to embody the never-ending spirit of flight through the waves of obstacles in our path. Sorry if that seems preachy, but it's engraved in the base, after all." He paused and ran his fingers down the fish's spine. "I just mean that we at The Pouncing Fish like to share a little bit of our family with yours. And we're happy to have customers like you supporting our family business again."

"That's wonderful. Thank you for your hospitality, your towels, and your food," Tarik replied, reaching out to shake the old man's hand.

"Ah! And speaking of food, my wonderful wife has it hot and ready for ya!" he exclaimed, holding the door open for her with the sculpture in hand.

Adelaide served two plates of meat pies. Bowls of golden crust and slightly burned edges sat steaming in front of us. The plates smelled excellent as the aroma of the meat pies swarmed our table. The ensemble looked delicious, and the pleasure on Adelaide's face while she set the meals down was enough to make my skin crawl.

"Looks great," I said, digging into the pot pie the moment the words left my mouth.

"Thank you, Adelaide. It'll be nice to have home-cooked food again," Tarik added gently.

While Tarik watched, I devoured one and a half of the woman's creations. It was a flaky pastry stuffed with ground meat, veggies, and a tasty gravy. I ate through nearly the entire meat pie before taking a long gulp of water to wash it down.

"Like a vacuum." Tarik chuckled as he nibbled on his like a chipmunk.

"Hush up, peanut gallery," I retorted, mouth still full.

Solomon and Adelaide fumbled out of the kitchen while arguing with one another. The chubby woman adjusted her apron and folded her hands before approaching our table. As she reached Tarik's side, my stomach began to knot and churn. I was slightly queasy, but comfortable.

"How's the food over here?" Her smile conveyed tenderness—and desperation.

I nodded at her after finishing my serving and looked for Tarik's response. He, however, quickly shoved an empty spoonful of nothing into his mouth and winked at Adelaide. He wasn't eating? Seemed peculiar for someone who would never turn down a plate of food.

As he laughed to himself, watching the white-haired woman walk out of view, I caught sight of Solomon watching us eat from the kitchen door. In the small window, it was incredibly obvious when two large eyes were peering at us from within. Yet I had no time to process or relay this information to Tarik. My body froze. My muscles tensed up, and I became paralyzed. I sat in the chair motionless for a second before slowly slouching into my plate. My nose pressed into the mushy remnants of meat and carrots and celery, and my forehead lay flat on the golden dough.

"What the—?!" Tarik exclaimed, jumping from his seat to my side. "Olivia? *Olivia?!* Hey! Can you hear me? Hey, Olivia?!"

"Tarik, I'm fine. What happened?"

That's what I tried to say, but between the bits of meat pie in my mouth, I doubt he heard anything.

As if perfectly timed, the couple burst into the room again and hovered at our table.

"Oh my goodness, sweetie!" the woman yelped, clutching her dirty apron and hands over her mouth. "Are you alright? What happened?"

"I should ask you the same thing!" Tarik shouted.

Meanwhile, I lay passed out in the remains of my meat pie, barely registering the sounds in the room. I was not quite unconscious, but in a comatose state, with no function in my limbs or muscles.

"Whatever do you mean, child?" Adelaide gasped.

"I think you tried to poison us! Inside those pies is ground meat infused with ... arsenic? Snake venom? No, no. Poison powder! I want to know why—and I want to know NOW!" Tarik shouted, pounding his fist on the table.

A kindling fire ignited in the fireplace.

"Poison?" I mumbled into the flaky dough.

"*Poison?* We would never! We wouldn't know—" Solomon began, before Tarik jumped back in.

"I know poison when I smell it! I don't care that you 'would never' or 'could never'—because you did! Tell me why I shouldn't turn you two in to the authorities right now!"

"Sweetie," Adelaide said feebly, "my husband and I are—"

"Adelaide, please!" Solomon paused for a moment to let the truth sink in before speaking again, this time in a slow and guilty manner. "There's no point in lying to the kid when his girlfriend is face down in a pile of our food."

Oh, for fuck's sake! my internal monologue sighed. *The word "girlfriend" is going to wind Tarik up like a toy race car and put enough spring in his step for him to out-jump a kangaroo! Plus, worst of all, I'll never* hear *the end of it, or* see *the end of it on his face ...*

"We poisoned the meat she ate, and that you were supposed to eat," Solomon admitted. "I can't think of why you chose not to eat, but it's a good thing. It won't kill her or harm her in any way. At least, I don't think it will ... To be frank, this is the first time we've ever had to do this. We had no idea if it was going to work or not."

I knew Tarik pulled out the wand tucked in his sock because I felt somebody stumble and nearly fall over—and I was certain it wasn't the boy wonder.

"Now, I'm not going to tell you how I figured it out. And no, I won't let you go off easily, because yes, this is a magic wand, and yes, I do know how to use it! As a poison mage, I am capable of doing many far worse things to you than lacing ground meat with a powder! Things that will make your skin boil before it literally peels from your body. But before I bring this girl back to consciousness, explain to me why I should restrain myself from poisoning you two right back!"

I listened to the couple stammer, cowering at the fate of Tarik's wand. They yelped and pleaded with him all at once. It was admittedly delightful, hearing him threaten a not-so-innocent team of restaurant owners. But it was a shame that I was not fully aware to witness it firsthand. Was it possible for me to feel jealousy and pride at the same time for someone other than myself?

"We ... we didn't ... We DID NOT intend to hurt anyone! Not your girlfriend, or anyone at all. We swear! We were only doing what we were told to keep her safe! I swear to you ... Please don't kill us! They forced our hand. We didn't have another option," they pleaded, no doubt hugging each other tightly at the possibility of Tarik's magic.

"She is my girlfriend, yes. Thank you for noticing. But who forced you? Why? And to keep who safe?" Tarik demanded, lightening his temper and probably dropping his threat.

My head sprung up from the table like a catapult as meat fell from my eye sockets, gravy poured down my cheeks, and carrots pebbled my face. It was so sudden and random, there was no way I could have done it myself. Tarik didn't notice.

"Honey, don't tell him. He doesn't need to know!" Adelaide whispered.

"And what's the point of hiding all that information now, Addy?" Solomon urged. "What good does it do us to keep this secret? We couldn't do it to the first customer, and we won't be able to do it to the next. So, we oughta just come clean." Solomon urged, releasing his wife and standing in front of her.

"Is she alright?" Adelaide asked cautiously.

"Who forced you, and why?" Tarik repeated more quietly, lowering the wand to his sock.

In a single deep breath, Solomon looked at the floor then disappointingly back to Tarik.

"Necromancers. Dozens of them swarmed Azuma Shores like bees to a hive. Poor little town ... Once the priest's protection went away, we never stood a chance; it became a playground for death and evil. The death of Saint Jonathon the Purifier created the perfect storm for them to fester here. He was the church head in Azuma. Well, when he died in a duel with Captain Arcelia, the necromancers waltzed in and took over the entire town. They quickly ripped through the townspeople and let the cemetery spirits loose. Then they had to branch out. That's when they came knocking on our doors. Notice how they're propped open? It's because two necromancers vaporized the hinges and left the doors simply leaning against the building."

"A priest and a captain held a duel that killed them both? Necromancers took over your beach town, then came to some rinky-dink tavern? C'mon, how naïve do you think I am?" Tarik said softly, lifting my head to look at my pupils. His expression never changed.

With the pair looking at us, he spun my chair around to face them directly. My head hung low near my chest. Tarik flung me upright in the seat and pointed his wand at my sternum. The crystal tip of his wand lit up in a vibrant red as it extracted the poison from my blood. How did I know it was being removed from me? I physically felt it flow backwards through my body. The black poison filled his wand's crystal, swirling around inside until the red color glowed bright, then disappeared without a trace.

"Witchcraft!" Adelaide shrieked. "You're no better than the necromancers! They probably sent you to test us—or worse, turn us in to them!"

"Easy with the accusations," I retorted, cracking my neck and coming back to life. "Yes, this is witchcraft. Elemental magic, to be exact. That white wand at his side can do a lot of damage a necromancer wouldn't dream of. I may have been comatose, but I still heard everything."

Tarik sighed, restraining me and glaring down at my hostility.

"Fine. Play the good cop *and* the bad cop. I never get to have any fun," I pouted.

"Nice to have you back in the land of the living. Now, heel, little demon," Tarik whispered in my ear before stepping up to resume center stage. He then addressed the couple again. "I don't believe you. But against my better judgement, continue on, please, Solomon. Tell me what's going on here that makes you feel that you need to poison your customers."

"As I was saying," Solomon began, "our daughter, Lily, and her son, Elliot, lived in The Pouncing Fish Inn connected to our tavern. They helped run the motel side of things while Adelaide and I ran the restaurant. Days ago, a nasty group of necromancers came to the four of us. They threatened to take their souls in exchange for our help! I love Lily and Elliot! I would never trade them for anything! Ever! I begged for them to let us live in peace. But ... that's ..."

He got choked up and held a fist to his mouth, quivering and closing his eyes.

Meanwhile, Adelaide cleared the table. She retreated into the kitchen to clean up while her husband spoke to us.

"When they kidnapped Lily and Elliot, they took 'em right from our feet—right from this very room!" Solomon wept through the sound of splashing water. "We waited a couple hours, then a day. Forty-eight hours later, the two necromancers returned. But this time, they stood in the parking lot with a third figure covered in black bed sheets while Adelaide and I watched from the Fish's entrance. They shoved the figure forward and removed the cover. It was our daughter! Or ... at least it somewhat resembled ... her ..."

His wife sobbed in the kitchen.

"She was a zombie—a wart-covered, disgusting, brain-hungry zombie." Solomon exhaled and looked directly at me. "Lily was in there, though. I know it. Beneath the soulless yellow eyes, I know my daughter was in there still! I could tell. I just knew it. Adelaide and I might have been afraid of that zombie, but we recognized our Lily when we saw her. We were so in love with the thought of having our daughter back that we didn't see the note hanging around her neck. It said that the necromancers would cut a deal with us. We poison innocent people and turn them over to the necros. In exchange, they will not harm our grandson, and they will make Lily human again. However, if we chose not to obey, they were going to gut the boy like a pouncing fish. So, we took their offer. What choice did we have? Days later, once the deal was done, after they handed Lily over, Adelaide and I agreed to keep her in the basement, away from the public eye. Her bare footprints are still fresh in our gravel parking lot. This deal was made on Friday. It's Saturday now. You're our first customers since they kidnapped Elliot and her."

"Let me get this straight," I cut in. "Necromancers threatened to kill your grandson and promised to make Lily human again, in exchange for you poisoning innocent people. Now you have a zombie daughter in your basement. And Tarik and I are your first victims?" I concluded, looking between Solomon and Tarik, gears turning hopefully in their heads.

"Yes," the lanky man answered, trying to shake the shame from his face. "That's correct."

"I get it. You'd do anything for your family and the ones you love," Tarik added, stepping to Solomon's side.

Then he hugged the man.

Wait ... what?!

Tarik, who just pointed his wand at this same man and made threats, was now hugging him?! I had not been unconscious long enough for something that crazy to occur. Solomon awkwardly hugged Tarik back before realizing how awkward it actually was.

"You like making deals? I got one for ya," I interjected.

Adelaide suddenly pushed into the room and rejoined her husband. They locked hands. She tucked herself close to his side. Solomon looked into her eyes with dread, then back into mine. "We're listening."

Speaking to both of them, I proposed my solution.

"Let us see the condition Lily is in. If we deem her savable, Tarik and I will personally return her humanity. If she's too far gone, I'll put her out of her misery and leave your restaurant. So ... you let me see the zombie, and I'll evaluate her myself and make the final call on her life. Otherwise, your daughter will die a rotting corpse, and we'll lead the necromancers right to your tavern door."

"How will you—"

"Deal," Adelaide cut in.

"Olivia," Tarik whispered the second the word left Adelaide's mouth, "I'm fairly certain we cannot bring that woman back from being a zombie. It will kill her, any way you slice it."

"And these two are dead if we don't try. Better for us to do it than the necromancers. They won't be as kind or as civil."

"You're saying you wish to help the couple who just tried to kill us?"

"Yes, I am," I whispered back.

"Well, well, well ..." Tarik said with a smirk. "Little Miss Shadow wants to help a desperate couple out of their predicament?"

"Maybe you're right. Maybe ... I should force-feed their meat pie to you, and let *you* fall into a coma. You and I both know you're the only one here who can cast the spell to remove it. See what happens to you then." I chuckled sarcastically. "Now cut the jokes and help me. This is your idea, after all."

"My idea?" he retorted.

"You hugged that guy out of nowhere! What kind of message does that send him?"

"Deal!" Tarik shouted, reaching out a hand to take Solomon's.

They shook and nodded to one another.

"Take us to the basement." I smiled.

Solomon and Adelaide held hands and led the way beyond the traffic doors. They were clearly distracted and upset. The man pointed out spots to buff out on their stove and ovens while the woman could only look at the pile of dishes lying in the sink's iridescent pool of water. Tarik and I followed them through the bulk of the kitchen. The four of us then came to an open storage room. Overstocked shelves of canned food, tubs of noodles and grains, unused pots and pans, and other dusty containers stuffed the walls, creating a perimeter around three sides. The other wall marked the entrance to the basement: a feeble wooden door with bloodstains splotched on the knob.

Despite reaching the threshold, Solomon and Adelaide stopped dead in their tracks. It felt as if there were an invisible barrier at the doorstep. I looked at them, though I already knew the answer to my question before I asked it.

"Something wrong?"

"We ... don't want to go down with you," Adelaide said. "You two go alone. You'll see her—it—down there. I don't need to stand witness. I know you'll do whatever you need to or you wouldn't have made that deal. So, do what you must, but I have no need to watch it myself. And I believe I speak for my husband, too," She stepped back towards the shelves and further from the door.

"That's true," Solomon added. "We trust you both to make the right call. Help our daughter if you can. Please."

Solomon reached out a hand to shake again. Tarik looked to me for advice, but I had none to give. The two shook hands and nodded at each other again in silent agreement.

"We will do what we have to. You have my word," Tarik said firmly.

The weary old man dug in his pocket, pulled out a ring with dozens of brass keys, and fumbled around for the right one. After inserting it into the lock, Solomon pulled the door all the way open, then stepped aside to be near his wife, who latched tightly back onto his arm.

"Like we said, we're on the sidelines for this part. Please do your best to save her!" Adelaide sobbed. "But if you can't ... we understand."

"Good. Thank you," I answered softly, forcing a pleasant smile with my mouth and eyes. I moved towards the doorframe and started down the stairs, where a homemade railing ran down the wall. Pulling a string above me, I illuminated the basement in a flickering light.

"Young man," Solomon said, grabbing Tarik by his shoulder as he approached the door. "I see the way you look at her. It's how I looked at Mrs. Leading when I was young, too. Be careful down there, son. That zombie may have hints of my daughter, but the rest is all zombie. If you're witches or wizards or whatever, work your magic. Do what you can. And be careful."

"Thank you, sir," Tarik said charmingly. "And we will. Olivia is a gifted witch, and there's no one in Penumbra I trust to do this job more than her. Your Lily is in good hands. Oh, and Solomon, don't lock that door behind us, because I'll know—and I won't be too happy."

I grinned to myself as I inched towards the foot of the staircase. Tarik scampered down the steps shortly after as the basement door closed us off from the old couple above.

"Quieter, will you?! This is a serious matter, not Christmas morning!"

"You're right, you're right. I'm sorry," he replied bashfully.

"Enough sappy shit, Tarik. We now have a job to do, and I'm quite looking forward to it," I responded.

Bland white walls surrounded us. Bent or broken boxes were stacked in the corners up to the ceiling. The entire room had been cleared out from one side to the other, splitting it between a cluttered cellar and a makeshift prison.

"Holy—"

"Don't finish that sentence," Tarik interposed, throwing up a finger to stop my words.

Tarik and I simultaneously laid eyes on the zombie, whose wrists and ankles were encircled by shackles bolted to the wall. These restraints allowed her just enough movement to live. Her skin was gray and rotted. Eyes bright white and mouth a blood-soaked black hole, the zombie snarled and growled and lashed at us as we got closer. Bones were exposed over her entire body, from the collarbone to the sternum to her feet. Nasty claw like fingernails scratched at the air. Dirt and blood were caked under her toenails, and her ragged black hair slowly fluttered off her scalp like thin, detached explosive wires. The final accent to Lily's ghastly appearance was a once lovely blue sundress that had since melded with her skin.

Like a scene from something I would create in my nightmares, the zombie jerked against her restraints and came very close to chomping off Tarik's ear. Saliva dripped from her teeth as it drooled out of her gaping mouth.

"Watch it!" Tarik exclaimed, recoiling from the attack.

I watched without laughing, which was difficult to do. After a second of gathering myself, I observed the zombie more closely. And in the span of a few minutes, I realized something I had feared before we came down those basement stairs.

"She's not in there anymore," I said flatly.

"That was quick," Tarik added, snooping through the restaurant's financials buried in cardboard boxes. "What makes you say that?"

"I say that because I don't see it anymore," I answered, kneeling down to inspect the backs of the zombie's ankles.

"See what?"

"The spark in her eyes, you buffoon! Souls can be seen through the pupils. If you look into the eyes of Lily, that zombie gnawing on her own chains, you'll see empty white sockets. Even in most undead creatures, there is usually *some* glimmer of life trapped inside. But with her," I said, pointing at Lily, "... I see no spark or soul in those eyes. Adelaide and Solomon's daughter is gone."

"Hey, I'm just a poison mage. If you say there's no soul in that thing, then I believe you," Tarik replied, watching the zombie cautiously from afar. Suddenly, it pivoted to face us, narrowed its eyes, and lunged at him. Like a kid who had poked the bear, Tarik nearly jumped out of his pants and hit the wall behind him. "Do what you need to, 'cause I don't like being around her! I mean it! Freaks me out. I'm not used to seeing the undead like you are, Olivia."

"How sweet," I added, batting my eyes at him again. "Heck of a date so far."

"Yeah. Not my intention, by the way."

"Now, I need you to use all your might to keep her restrained ... boyfriend."

"Did you ... Are you sure ... you want to use that word right now? 'Boyfriend.' I like the sound of it, too. Glad to hear you say it! And had you not included that little title in your request, I would've said no."

"And I would've laughed. Don't get a big head, okay? I can take it back at any point. That offer for you to join my nightmare realm still stands. They would love to meet a poisonous thing like you."

"Fine, fine. You've made your point—again," Tarik said, rising to his feet and pushing slowly off the wall.

"Can you keep her at bay? Or at bare minimum, away from my face?" I asked as he stepped forward.

"I can try, but no promises."

Tarik knelt in an odd stance, like he was trying to pacify a rodeo bull. His hands held steady in the air. He looked ridiculous, like a first-time stunt double in a horrible karate movie, arms flailing in a "threatening" manner.

"Good work over there," I said cynically.

"I'm ready. Do your worst," Tarik retorted.

I turned my focus to the zombie. Loud, eerie thoughts ricocheted inside my brain despite the relative silence in the basement.

"I'm going to help you, Lily," I told her, looking into her grim eyes. "You could be in there somewhere, and while I doubt that, it's my job to get you out if you are."

The zombie snapped and snarled at Tarik, though its focus was on me standing next to him. Bile splattered his palms. It turned and did the same to my face with a ghastly mixture of blood and slobber. I looked at Lily's zombified body. Unlike in Isaac's case, where I had watched two souls interweaving within, this time I noticed nothing—just a vacant black spot of nothing. This affirmed my realization earlier: There was no soul to suck out—no person inside to latch onto.

"What's the game plan here, chief?" Tarik demanded. "I'm sweatin' a little right now, and it doesn't look like you have one. So, enlighten me, please, before my brain becomes dessert!"

"Going to use my elemental extraction process and try to isolate the soul from its body. I've done it dozens of times. This time should be no different. I just need *silence*, and patience, Tarik," I instructed.

"Do we call this *thing* an 'it' or a 'her'?" Tarik added doubtfully.

I closed my eyes and waved my hands in smooth motions. The zombie gnawed on its wrist shackles. Channeling the nightmare magic within and not knowing what result my powers would produce, I pulled hopefully at the soul inside the slowly rotting corpse.

She cocked her head around like a tweaking addict suffering from withdrawals, rapidly flipping left and right. The zombie looked bleakly into my hazel eyes. Zombies had no functioning brain cells or emotions in their bodies. They felt nothing when they instinctively fed on living flesh or rotting corpses. Zombies were cold and heartless creatures that would do anything to survive. When the white eyes of Adelaide and Solomon's zombie looked into mine, I saw all of those things. It wanted to eat me, feast on my fresh skin. It wanted to rip my stomach open and pull out my intestines one by one, like a game of tug-of-war. Their daughter had zero say in what this zombie would think or do.

I pulled again, aiming at the head. My eyes shut tighter as my focus homed in on the finale. Draining my magic, I gently twisted my right hand. The zombie's head flicked rapidly like a convulsing animal as she thrashed around against her restraints. Contorting her body in horrifying ways, the possessed creature shrieked in terror and wailed at me. My arms continued moving methodically—until I watched the zombie explode in front of us.

"Olivia!" Tarik shrieked, staggering back to me. "What the hell was that?!"

The head popped open like a jack-in-the-box and landed on the floor. Blood and guts splattered the ceiling, dripping bile and other flesh. Limbs, fingers, bloody bones, and other remains littered the floor around Tarik and me.

"I tried to get Lily out is what that was, Tarik!" I replied harshly.

"By exploding the zombie from the inside? By spraying it all around us?!" he muttered, horrified.

"By doing what I had to!" I shouted in his face. "Your thing is poison and toxins. Mine is nightmares and the undead. So, that is exactly what I did: I tried to deal with it!"

Another feeling washed over me, an unfamiliar one: guilt.

"I failed, Tarik. I tried, using the only method I know ... rip the elemental from the body. But I shouldn't have done that. There were other ways to kill it. I was being overconfident."

"Olivia, are you saying you made a mistake?" Tarik stammered, staring at the darkened blood sluggishly pooling under the head in the corner.

"I'm ashamed of myself. What was I thinking?!" I shouted, annoyed at Tarik's nosiness and my own lack of judgment. "How could I pull a soul from a body where there was no soul?! That was stupid of me, Tarik. Do you not understand that?!

How did I not realize it beforehand? I ... I would like to leave now. Our job is done here, and so am I."

"Olivia," Tarik pleaded, placing a hand on my shoulder, "that could never work. They're not the same—"

"YOU THINK I DON'T FUCKING REALIZE THAT NOW?!" I screamed back at him. "Tarik, I know that now! I had no choice but to try ... and I failed."

He looked shocked and scared.

"There. The so-called 'most powerful nightmare mage' at the college, the best Marrick has ever seen, still has work to do. Maybe she is ... human after all? Happy now?"

"That's not what I said, Olivia," Tarik said timidly as I pushed his hand from my shoulder.

"But it is what you meant. Now, the job is done. You're pissing me off. And I'm ready to leave."

Raking the remains of the zombie off my clothes with bloody fingers, I stormed up the feeble wooden staircase, followed by Tarik, who moved as soft and cautious as a mouse. Turning the knob, I opened the basement door and reentered the storage area. Solomon sat on a milk crate with his face in his hands, and Adelaide was pacing back and forth.

"So? What happened?!" she begged, rushing to greet me at the door.

"I failed. Your daughter was not in that thing anymore. She was gone. It had taken her completely. So, I did what I needed to do."

"What does that mean?!" Solomon demanded.

Tarik looked shell-shocked.

"It means you're off the hook. And we're leaving. Thank you for sheltering us from the rainstorm," I concluded coldly, tugging on Tarik's sleeve before walking out of the kitchen. Reluctantly, he followed behind me through the swinging door. As the old couple scrambled down the basement stairs, we made our way out through the tavern's propped-open doors.

"Olivia, we need to talk about what just happened," Tarik said, leading the way over to Chestnut, who was quietly relaxing in the vacant lot.

"We'll talk when I'm ready to talk. Look, Tarik, we did nothing wrong there. We did what they asked us to do, and they knew the consequences going into it. That's all there is to it. Nothing more to discuss," I snapped.

"Okay, I'll drop it," he said wearily before unwrapping Chestnut's reins from the wooden post.

"Good. Now, let's continue our date," I said, grabbing his outstretched hand and hopping onto the griffin's back.

"Okay."

Tarik strapped himself to the saddle and held the reins tightly.

In a wild turn of events, the break intended get us out of the storm and fill our stomachs in a late lunch had become a near-death experience at the hands of an elderly couple compromising their own family business to appease a necromancer's demands. Tarik's face was awash with emotions, though I liked to think mine were more neutral. I could tell he was thoroughly processing seeing that final zombie detonation. He liked to socialize and conclude the conversation. I, on the other hand, did not want to see the couple's reaction to their daughter's severed head in the corner and the pieces of her everywhere.

"Tarik, I know you're recovering from what just happened," I started, holding tight to his waist as the griffin increased its sprint over the gravel. From a light trot to a full gallop, Chestnut sprang from his hind legs and flew into the air. With remarkable beauty, his brown feathers ruffled in the strong breeze as the road below us shrunk into a winding ribbon.

"I'm okay," he said uncertainly. "I'm more worried about you. That was so quick and sudden … It's a lot to take in right now. You're strong, and I know that. To me, it feels like a lot, so I wanted to make sure you're all good, too."

"Tarik." I smiled gently. "I'm fine. I've been through a lot harder and stranger situations than that back there."

I was lying. I had never made a lapsed judgment call like that. I had never made such a selfish decision, despite my better intentions. But I couldn't let him know any of those true feelings. That would show weakness, and I was not about to do that.

We leveled out amidst a thin layer of clouds, floating in and out of the mist. Like dewdrops on grass, small water droplets stuck to the goose bumps on my skin. I stayed leaning forward to steady my eyesight while allowing Tarik and Chestnut to block out the whipping wind.

"That place must be close now, huh?" I shouted through the fog.

"Yup," Tarik replied at once.

He tugged on the griffin's reins. The three of us unexpectedly dove towards the nothing beneath us. The clouds hid our surroundings, yet Chestnut tucked himself in tight and propelled us towards the ground.

As the mist cleared, a large beach town appeared. Azuma Shores slowly unfurled below like a scroll. Maroon rooftops cascaded down the rolling hills of the town.

Lingering, overcast clouds teased the sunshine as we approached our afternoon retreat. A jagged mountainside hid the landing spot from the fragments of bright light. The air was stagnant and clammy.

After a cold wind whisked at the two of us, I looked over Tarik's shoulder to get a better view of Azuma Shores.

"Town looks nearly abandoned. War-torn buildings and no people? Huh ..." I said as we came to a stop and Tarik leapt off Chestnut. "Seems like a fair place to go, I suppose."

"Oh ...?" Tarik began, like an annoying boyfriend who had finally won an argument. "Is Olivia, queen of the dark and dreary, beginning to find the idea of a daytime date cheery?"

"Did you just rhyme and use my name in the same sentence?" I snarked, verbally disgusted.

"I did, and I immediately regret it," Tarik answered more in line, like a foolish boyfriend admitting defeat. He nervously smiled and gathered steak pieces from the griffin's saddle bag.

"But to answer your question, no," I retorted. "Better than I expected, though. I'll give you that ..."

"And I'll take it." He chuckled in response, tossing two raw pieces of meat to Chestnut, who snagged them in midair. "Now that we're on the same page, let's make the most of this sunlight, and the beach, and the warm sand, and the peace and quiet, and—"

"I'm gonna stop you right there again, before I make like that zombie and microwave my own brain. While I might agree that the town looks quaint and peaceful, don't push your luck!" I smiled, pearly whites showing.

A golden glow broke through the shadow of the gray clouds, splitting them apart with its light. Feeling the subtle heat from the sun, I followed Tarik's lead down a winding sandy path. Chestnut stood proudly atop the plateau as we trekked towards the town. My boyfriend—no, sorry, that word still feels bizarre ... *Tarik* kicked aside overgrown bushes blocking our path.

Azuma Shores was nothing like Tarik had described, or as he was clearly hoping it would be; the dilapidated buildings proved that. Gray, unkempt storefronts greeted us at the first street. They looked weather-beaten from a freak hurricane, vandalized by looters who had broken in and robbed the shops clean, then abandoned by their shopkeepers, who left them to decay.

"This is ... uhhh ..." Tarik began, stumbling over his words.

"Wonderful!" I beamed, finishing his thought.

He swung around to face me. "I meant for this to be a quiet coastal getaway! Take your mind off The Pit before training starts, and ... But this place looks like a necromancer's paradise!"

"It is, I know!" I exclaimed, catching the eye of a beggar crouched behind a trash can.

"Coins! I need coins!" the beggar shouted, hearing our footsteps pass by her. "I need them. Anders and Alice won't stop asking me for coins. I have none to give them. Coins. Give me some!" She was speaking to an imaginary couple and yelling for our attention at the same time.

The cobblestone streets were discolored, faded browns and reds all molded into a single muddy shade. In glaring contrast to the properly kept buildings we were accustomed to back at the college, dirt and trash replaced the mortar holding the bricks together.

Making a left at the corner, we started down Rosewood Street and were greeted by a row of once elegant cafés and boutiques. Black iron tables had been thrown through the glass doors and windows. Ransacked from top to bottom, these buildings attested to a similar fate to the ones we'd seen thus far. In a pocket alley between Rosewood and Tamarack, walls of painted graffiti glowed in the dim light. The vibrant artwork decorated the surfaces as their rotting canvas, especially one depiction of a creepy crescent moon with big, droopy eyes forming a slanted smiley face. It was childish yet oddly maven.

"Beggars, graffiti, vandalism. Necromancers! This place has everything. I like it." I giggled.

"Greeeeat," Tarik added sarcastically.

As on the previous street, a shady figure stood barely in view. However, this one wore a long black robe covering their entire body. Hidden in the shadows of the clouds and the tall buildings, only their silhouette was visible as they leaned against a lamppost. Two white eyes looked towards mine when the figure suddenly flicked their robe and disappeared down an alley.

While I quite liked the whole ambience here, Tarik was feeling the eeriness and unease of being the only two visitors in town. We had seen a handful of shops and things—battered buildings and dirty streets. But aside from the homeless beggar, not a single other human was in sight.

"This is creepy, right?" Tarik said, scanning our surroundings.

We shifted to avoid bumping into a smashed hanging plant with dead flowers sprawled on the ground.

"A little bit, I suppose," I replied hesitantly. "But honestly, it's ..."

A faded poster hanging on a stone wall caught my eye. Instantly, I scanned over the details. Small red flame designs, branded onto the parchment like a wax seal, marked the top and bottom of the page. In the middle was a crude, poorly drawn image of a ghost.

"'WANTED. Removal of graveyard ghouls. Church of the Eternal Flame cemetery. Huge reward and donation in your name,'" I read aloud, with Tarik at my side and reading over my shoulder.

Before I could add anything else, he tore the slightly scorched poster down, crumpled it up, and threw it in the garbage. I spun to face him, irritated, like a toddler whose toy has been taken away.

"No!" he insisted, shaking his head and starting to walk towards the next street. "We are here for non-magical activities. Beach and sand and relaxation! That's it. You want to stay strangers here, right? How would that help keep our identities secret?"

We crossed under another archway and into a fruit market. However, this market was ... Well, you get the idea by now: bushels for apples ripped to shreds, empty wicker fruit baskets hanging from the canvas above, and rodent droppings lining the ground alongside peach pits and other debris.

"No! No ghoul hunting. This is not our town—not our problem."

"I know. But they need help. We can do it. It'll be fun!" I answered.

"You're in a very helpful mood, oddly, but we don't even know who *they* are! No, no, no. It'll only be fun for *you*. I just wanna have a nice day and enjoy ourselves, and—"

"No fun for Olivia. Fine. Let's just keep moving, then," I cut in, infuriated by his lack of flexibility.

"Okay," he sighed, stepping aside lightly to let me pass. "Moving along ..."

Cutting down Evergreen Street, Tarik and I silently walked by more abandoned dress shops, bookstores, craft stores, and flower boutiques, all vandalized and destroyed at the hands of scavengers and vagabonds, one of whom was unscrewing the brass doorknob from a shop when he caught sight of us. With a hiss, he leapt over the store shelves, ducked under the counter, and bolted from view.

Sycamore and Petunia Streets followed the trend of the once growing and proud destination of Azuma Shores, now a dirty and desolate town run by necromancers. A homeless couple offered us psychedelic drugs on Sycamore, which Tarik sternly turned down. So, as I said, no fun for Olivia.

A second wanted poster fell to the ground from its taped-up spot on a lamppost. I picked it up while Tarik walked on. I gingerly folded it up, and once I caught back up to him, snuck it into his palm. Tarik unconsciously squeezed his hand on it before noticing its existence. A sudden ocean breeze whirled down Lilac Street like it was a wind tunnel.

"Olivia," he began slowly, like a disappointed dad, "I already said no to the ghoul hunting—a firm no, at that."

"I have no idea what you're rambling on about," I answered coldly, pointing out a single candle lit in an apartment above Wilson's Wonderful Wax-Making candle shop. "You're going to have to elaborate, Tarik."

I twinkled my eyes at him, knowing exactly the game I was playing.

"Don't play dumb, because I know you're not. And I know you put this poster in my hand. And I also know the answer is still a flat no!"

"Bold accusation you're making. But here's a clue ..." I whispered in his ear. "I did put that in your hand. And I think deep down, you want to do it as badly as I do."

He halted in his tracks and pivoted to meet my eyes. Those curious emeralds looked back into mine with concern.

"What makes you say that, little demon?" He smiled.

"See!" I shrieked in joy. "Already on board. 'My little devil?' C'mon, Tarik, at least attempt to stay mad at me. I know it's impossible, but give it a better try next time, please. Your knees are buckling at my every whim, and faster each time. Do better." I winked and nudged him on the shoulder, breezing into a five-finger fork in the road ahead.

"Rubbing it in. A signature Olivia move."

Ignoring him, I approached the intersection and stopped. Tarik soon came to my side and waited for my signal. A sea breeze swept through the alleyways and streets, creating a calming yet intense feeling on my skin, with goose bumps nearly rising to the surface. I had never been to the ocean before. Well, I had never been *anywhere* before, for that matter. No family vacations to the beach or ski trips to the mountains or even dog-walking adventures in the local park. Nobody ever wanted to plan fun things with the girl "who creates chaos and destruction with every step she takes"—in the infamous words of one of my foster care workers.

But he'd had his fun for the day, right? It was my turn to captain this ship, and I say we go ghoul hunting!

"Poster says we need to go to ... the Church of the Eternal Flame. 'Eternal Flame.'" I chuckled. "Religious groups in Penumbra sure are subtle about their beliefs, aren't they? If I was a betting woman, and I am, it looks like we should take a right turn here. Can't believe followers of Ha'thar call *us* crazy."

"And you know all of that how?" Tarik puzzled, looking more dumbfounded than usual.

"Dude, the non-magical communities of Pen fucking hate magic and refute its existence entirely. Didn't you ever hear that? It's basically hardwired into our brains when we're babies. As for my directions to the church, maniacal intuition I guess," I retorted.

"And what happens when we get there?" Tarik asked.

"We talk to the priest. I scare the shit oughta him with my *MAAAGGGIICCCC*, we cut a deal, grab some cheap weapons, kick the ghouls out of the cemetery, and get a pretty payment when it's done."

"Wow, Olivia. Seem pretty confident about this before we even know what it really is we're doing."

"'Course I am! Do I have a reason not to be?" I added, my attention focused ahead on Lotus Street.

Lotus Street was lined with blackened lampposts with grim lights. Bits of sand littered the cracks in the cobblestone at our feet, and scattered patches of algae clung to the bottoms of the buildings. It looked as if the ocean was slowly reclaiming Azuma Shores from the hands of the vandals.

"So, you really never heard about the rift between magic users and Ha'thar's followers? Aren't you from Penumbra, Tarik?"

"Yeah. Just not from a religious area apparently," he replied.

We followed past more shops and cafés until we arrived at the garden courtyard of the church.

Like an old Victorian chapel, the Church of the Eternal Flame stood as the centerpiece of the town amidst the fallen statues, neglected rose bushes, and leafless trees. It was constructed of gray brick and stone with filthy windows, though the stained glass was still beautifully intact. (Must have been too high for deadbeat addicts to reach.) Patches of dead grass lined the dirt path. Like the opening scene of a horror novel, a light fog began to roll in just as Tarik and I reached the garden's iron gate.

"Eerie and spooky. Haunted garden. Alive with the dead and the undead. Throw in some creeps and beggars around street corners. Necromancers probably watching our every move. Tarik, this place has everything! Thank you so much for bringing me," I muttered while pulling open the gate.

"Oh, joy!" he said mockingly.

"Place looks abandoned. So, I'll go in first. They'll see the dark magic in my eyes and realize that I *am* the witchy devil their phoenix god tells them I am."

"How cute you are, Olivia. But also *incredibly* scary," he added.

We strolled beyond the smashed statues and up the stairs to the church's front. Grand doors, both with ornate etchings and a set of golden doorknobs, marked the Eternal Flame's chapel entrance. I knocked on it three times, then waited on the doorstep.

"Bethany! Hey, Bethany!" shouted a man's voice from deep inside. "Can you get the door, please? I am in the middle of my midday sermon practice. Would you get the door for me? Bethany!"

Tarik and I stood at the church's entrance.

A couple scoffs and disgruntled sighs on the other side inched closer. Then the knob twisted. One of the doors creaked open.

"Bethany, I know you're here to watch over me and all, but can you answer the door for our patrons? Be nice and greet them at the door when they arrive! No? Okay, wonderful. I'll do everything myself, then."

"*Beatriz*, Logan! My name is Beatriz, not Bethany. I'm here to help you. The least you could do is remember my name, huh?" muffled the woman's snappy response as her voice faded out in the distance.

I pushed the heavy opening door, and we let ourselves in. After closing it behind us, Tarik walked forward a bit and hollered to get the priest's attention. He called for him multiple times, and the man eventually turned around to reveal himself.

Standing at the podium was a man in his mid-thirties with the baby face of an immature eighteen-year-old boy. He had a nice complexion, rosy cheeks, and flowing black hair. His hazel eyes stared blankly at Tarik, then at me, and I saw nothing of value within. The man was barefoot with his hands folded at his waist. His maroon robes were clearly hand-me-downs and hung too big on his body. But the robes and the long white garments underneath were immaculate—a perfect representation of privilege and having others do your dirty work for you.

"*Wow*, Bethany. A little help would've been appreciated," the young man shouted aside before shoving a smile upon his face and approaching us. His voice screeched towards us from the back of the church like a wounded duck. "I'm terribly sorry, folks! Not very priestly of me, is it? Where are my manners? My name is Father Logan. It's so jovial to see friendly faces again in Azuma Shores. It's quite the literal ghost town out there," he joked, holding out his hands.

Though I didn't budge at the joke or his gesture, Tarik jumped at it and held out his hand to meet Logan's. He took Tarik's hand and clasped it between his own, soon nodding at me to follow suit.

"Tarik. This is Olivia. We're from out of town and wanted to stop by a peaceful beach retreat," Tarik said. "But it seems as though ... the, uhhhh ... *peaceful* part of Azuma Shores has been scared away."

The priest reached for my hand next. I quickly pulled away, and Logan returned his hands to his waist as if nothing had happened.

"Not a religious person myself," I added awkwardly, unsure of how to act around his arrogance. "Lovely chapel you have here."

"Oh, the Eternal Flame? Yeah, she's magnificent. A few blemishes, but nothing spoils her splendor, does it? Jonathon—er, my father—did most of the work around here to keep it as beautiful as you see it now. When I'm not on my hands and knees cleaning the pews, these ghouls and necromancers have stolen my attention with their skulking around the grounds like flies to a corpse." Logan chuckled, wiping a finger across the top of his podium. "I can't give you the whole backstory of our church and the Azuma Coast until we join the two of you under Ha'thar's glorious wings."

Has the poison not fully left my body or did I just hear Logan casually prompt an indoctrination?! I panicked.

Logan dipped his hands in a carved stoup filled with red clay. Tarik's naivety froze him in place as the priest covered his fingers in the substance, then slowly drew a long, wavy W-shape on his forehead. The clay hardened as it touched his skin. Again, the arrogant priest turned to paint on me after Tarik, but I gave that man-child a look that would petrify Medusa.

"I would prefer to keep my face as is without your clay drawings on it," I said.

"One of you is good enough for me. C'mon inside. I'll show you around."

"Yeah," Tarik answered nervously, "that would be great." However, the look on his face sold a different story.

A perfectly timed ray of sun shone through the stained glass window and illuminated the room in a colorful glow of oranges, yellows, pinks, and blues. Lined up in a dozen rows on either side of the aisle, wooden pews sat dusty and vacant. Like the golden gleam of a god shining down on its worshippers, Logan strolled to the front of the church and raised his hands, as if beginning a service.

"First off, welcome to the Azuma Coast. Usually, the only interesting thing about this town is the rising price of wine by the glass. It's bland and uninspiring. But, recently, the necromancers have added a lot of flavor." Logan's tone was lax and careless—difficult to believe from a passionate member of the church.

"Right ..." I nodded.

"Well, with the headquarters of the Eternal Flame south of Azuma Shores, our church is a staple in the community. It has been here for decades, enduring beyond changing priests any time one leaves for another division ... or passes away. Some people in town would've argued it crazy and authoritarian for a church to have this much power. Guess they'd think differently on that notion now, huh?" Logan's pearly whites twinkled in the sunlight. "Yeah, I took over about a week ago. These seven days have been a rigorous test on my willpower. Honestly, though, I'd say it's been smooth sailing for the most part."

Tarik opened his mouth to speak, but I leapt at the chance to respond before he got a word out. "Father Logan? Pastor Logan? Logi Bear? Nepo-baby? I'm not sure what to call you."

"Just call me one of Ha'thar's youngest and most loyal followers," Logan answered, tilting his head to the rafters and stretching his arms wide to show off their wingspan. He gestured to the giant phoenix statues near the altar—gargoyles watching over their subjects. I noted matching phoenix wing tattoos on either arm.

Douche-schnozzle. In my head, that's what I will call you, douche-schnozzle. But for the outside world, let's keep it PG and just stick with ...

"Logan it is then. Short and simple," I snickered curtly.

"First name basis already. We are off to a *swimming* start, my friends!" Logan nodded to the pews. "Now, I'm getting ahead of myself. Please sit! I insist we start the sermon with a light prayer. It's the least I can do for new travelers and new ears to the graces of Ha'thar. Come, have a seat in the first row. I won't bite, I promise. Savor in my brilliant glory."

"The thought of what you just said makes me wanna vomit my lunch. If we're to sit through a sermon, let's go back to the clay. Wipe it on my hands. I'd do that instead if you're gonna start preaching to us."

What a self-righteous dick.

"Harsh words, Olivia. Not a religious woman indeed. That's alright. We can start down a different avenue." The excitement of a potential gospel lesson still gleamed in his eyes.

I softly whacked Tarik on the arm to stand up, but his expression told me he didn't like being caught in this battle of egos.

"Hey, Logi," I started, feeling the judgment of those statues' eyes on me. "He and I are not here to join the church. Not in our particular wheelhouse. We're actually here about the wanted posters hung up across town. You've got ghouls in the graveyard? Well, we're your exterminators, and we've come to talk to you about 'em."

"Oh," Logan answered in surprise, dropping his hands to his side. The light in his eyes dimmed, the fire in his words faltered, and his oversized sleeves slipped to the tips of his fingers. "Yeah. What about it?"

"Oh? The passion has suddenly died out in you hasn't it, Logan?" I puzzled at the man cynically. "Talk of the church and Ha'thar perks you up, but the physical danger of ghouls in your cemetery rains on your parade? You'd think a supernatural danger like that would become the Eternal Flame's number one priority. So, yeah, I believe it is your turn to sit down. Tell us about why they're here and what they want," I demanded.

"Firstly," he began in a condescending tone, "I don't take demands from peasants! And secondly, you are in *my* church. My roof, my rules!"

"There we go ... The real priest has shown himself," I whispered to Tarik without breaking from Logan's glare.

"You're right. Our mistake," Tarik butted in.

"No. Not our mistake, Tarik," I interjected, darting a quick look to him before flipping back to Logan. "Time for you to start talking, and I don't mean about 'Ha'thar great gospel.'"

Logan sat on the ledge beneath his podium, matching the eye level of Tarik. He avoided my gaze. "It is your mistake, but I'll fill in the gaps for you. The Church of the Eternal Flame was the favorite child of my father, Jonathon—or The Purifier, as his devoted congregation called him. Unknown monsters threatened the sanctity of our town, so he set up a barrier against those spirits of the sea. I thought he was damn crazy, because Jonathon was required to stay in constant prayer to keep the barrier alive and strong."

"A barrier? To keep the spirits out of Azuma Shores, or to keep something else in?"

"Every couple years, the ocean tides change and bring in the Ghost Tide, a flurry of ancient water creatures, reanimated corpses lost in shipwrecks, and zombie pirates. A dead ship captain led the Ghost Tide. She ruled the Azuma Coast and assaulted its beaches with the undead. Jonathon's barrier was enough to keep her at bay. But, to end things once and for all, Jonathon and the captain clashed. In that duel, they slew each other, thereby banishing the Ghost Tide's lost sea souls back into the ocean and destroying my father's magical barrier, yada yada yada ... Anyway, this situation created the perfect playground for necros and other darker entities. They quickly swarmed Azuma Shores and wiped out the innocent bystanders. The surviving people fled as the town became an abandoned wasteland. Now, if you believe in divine magic, then sure, the barrier's destruction steered the flood of necromancers directly to us. But, I and the good people of Penumbra refute the existence of magic and know it to be a fabricated lie! Frankly, I don't think the barrier mattered at all, since it wasn't until Jonathon's death that the necromancers arrived. I think *he* was the real protector. Despite the fact he was a shitty father and treated the church like his only child, Jonathon was instrumental in this silly town's safety. Still, the idea of magic is simply asinine, and I won't hear otherwise."

"Well, I do believe in it, Logi Bear. Magic's fucking real. The necromancers are literally proof of that. Religion can be so thorough sometimes ... yet so dull others," I said bluntly. "So, with the barrier gone now and Saint Jonathon dead, you're in charge?"

"Exactly!" he exclaimed with euphoric jubilance, ignoring ninety percent of what I just said.

"The church HQ tasked you with bringing this spot back to power?" Tarik added.

"Who are you two, anyway? Travelers and tourists have all but removed Azuma Shores from their radar. Are you from the church? Are you working for Bethany? Did my father's goons from the Risen Wing or Undying Soul quadrant send you? Where does your allegiance lie?!"

"What? No. We don't even know who *Beatriz* is. We're from the east side of Penumbra and trying to get away from our stressful lives. We stopped nearby to grab a bite to eat and got much more than that at the Pouncing Fish. We saw the posters about slaying some ghosts and earning a reward for it. What sensible person would turn that opportunity down? How do we get to them?" Tarik answered.

"Cool. Well, I know they're in the cemetery, though by now I imagine the ghouls are haunting the streets, too. Coming clean here: I have no clue where that cemetery is and can't point you in its direction. I had some living church members pin up those posters and write whatever you read on them. They kept whining about 'their safety' and their 'well-being' and 'what about the children,' so I shooed them away to churn out the wanted ads."

Douche-schnozzle.

"You probably have no idea what we're talking about then?" I asked flatly.

"Oh, no, I do," Logan responded passive-aggressively as he retrieved a crumpled ball of paper from behind an altar. "I may not have physically written the words, but I instructed each one of them to be put on paper. So, Olivia, before you get all self-righteous with collecting spirits for Ha'thar's New World, let me humanize you a little ..."

My blood had reached a boiling point. Jonathon's son cared more about his own legacy than the church's security. He was simply going through the motions and playing a role to stay on that high horse of his. We've been here maybe ten minutes, and I already care more about this forsaken town than he ever could! Oooo, if I get close enough to him, I'll send him on a one-way ticket to ...

"I'll pay you when the job is done," Logan said, his twinkling eyes mastered in the art of not giving a shit. "If you are here to solve my ghoul problems, then great. Get to it! I have other more important things to attend to. I will keep my attention here while you two hired hands fix that pesky ghost issue for me. How's that sound, Tarik?" *It sounds like you need to see what dark magic can really do*, a voice growled in my head. I had an inkling Tarik was one handshake away from another unplanned deal today.

"Like we would ever make a deal without hearing our side of the bargain ..."

"Yup. Deal," he chimed in, shaking Logan's hand.

"Tarik! What's wrong with you? We don't even know what we get in return?"

"Excellent! I'll take care of sorting my needs here, and you take care of my real problems out there. Win-win scenario for both of us. Just don't come back for your payment until the deed is done."

"Wonderful," Tarik said. We left Logan and his pretentious phoenix tattoos to relish in the colorful rays of distorted stained glass. In the closing cracks of the church's giant wooden doors, the egotistical grin on his face and the scene around him looked like the cover of every self-help book on the market. Tarik yanked me out of the church and into the darkened streets outside.

"Finally we're out of that selfish twerp's church. Pompous, arrogant douche-schnozzle. I need to go blow off some steam. Thankfully, our mission is clear. I need to go to the nearest undamaged blacksmith and get some weapons. It's too bad Logan isn't a ghoul, because I'd start by taking him out of the picture first."

"Maybe it's our upbringings, but I don't understand why you were so hostile towards Logan in the church. Religion is a sketchy subject—I get that. It doesn't change its overwhelming presence in Penumbra."

"Logan's not a real priest. Wanna know how I know that?" I paused, waiting for Tarik's gullible, chirpy response, though I never intended to leave him enough time actually to speak. "Real priests are known as saints. When I asked Logan what to call him, he said only to refer to him by his first name. Err, wrong! More significantly, however, high ranking officials and saints of the church can smell magic and can sniff out magic users. If Logan was a real saint, he would've sniffed out our lies and the wretched odor of elemental magic on us. But, he didn't. He's not a saint or a high-ranking official. He's barely a devotee of the church! He only watches over this church 'cause it was handed to him by HQ—a gift presented at his feet by his father's achievements. I don't care to insult *Father* Logan or hurt his feelings because he is not a real member of the church he watches over!"

"Damn. I never ... picked up on any of that. I grew up respecting the church, and, while I personally didn't follow it, I never disparaged anybody who honored Ha'thar. Things like that would be a death sentence in most cities in Penumbra." Tarik's voice was humbling, and he softened the tension in his bones. "Alright, Olivia. I won't stop you in killing Logan if it comes to that. But it's a huge *if*. Now, c'mon, let's find the blacksmith. Something tells me you already—"

"Yup!" I shouted happily. "Noticed it when we came to that fork in the road. It was down Dahlia Street."

"Remarkable you are sometimes," Tarik laughed. "Unpredictable and unhinged, but brilliant and remarkable nonetheless."

The returned glimmer of his eyes reminded me that today was supposed to be a date. Zombies in the basement of a mom-and-pop shop. Necromancers around town like hyenas hunting in a pack. A nepo-baby church man in oversized robes playing the role of leader in a town in dire need of his help. These may not be Tarik's idea of a fun date, but I sure am enjoying it.

"This is still a great day, Tarik," I admitted softly. "Rather entertaining, if I do say so myself."

"Glad you think so, 'cause in my eyes, it has gone the opposite of great," he joked.

From the statue garden, we turned down Dahlia Street. Passing by a handful of boutiques, Tarik and I soon came to the outdoor blacksmith.

Intensely sharpening a dagger on her grindstone, the blacksmith pressed her blade against the spinning wheel. She wore a brown wool tunic and a leather apron. Her hair bobbed as she ran the sword back and forth. Sweat was dripping down her cheeks, and dirt was smeared on her lap.

"Couple o' brave souls to enter Azuma Shores of your own accord," she shouted over the loud grinding wheel. Her boot, which was tapping the foot pedal, slowed to a stop. She spun on her seat and tossed the dagger onto the workbench. Through sun-kissed auburn hair, the blacksmith's welcoming face nodded at us.

"Wow," she said, wiping her hands with a dirty rag. "What's a cute young couple like you doing in a nasty town like this? Y'all lost? Take a bad road? Wrong turn?"

"No, no." Tarik laughed cautiously. "Funny enough, we came to your shop on purpose to do business."

"Buying weapons, huh? You've come to the right place, then! Name's Heather, and I run The Broken Nail, your one-stop shop for anything that can hit, whack, mangle, strangle, or destroy! Came up with the name myself. Clever, huh?" As she walked and talked, Heather indicated two iron racks of swords, daggers, and axes. "Little bit o' everything. Whatcha looking for?"

"Great selection," Tarik observed, ogling her unsmeared cherry-red lipstick.

"And you're a handsome young man to be needing my expertise. Wouldn't wanna damage that pretty face of yours," Heather remarked, smiling to show a little teeth.

"Tarik, can we just get to it, huh?" I requested.

"Pretty and protective, aren't you?" Heather winked. "I don't blame you. He's cute. Wouldn't last long in the dating field if he were single."

"Please," I scoffed, glaring at him with unspoken rage.

"Hey, what do you two need with my weapons, anyway? You're either dating, or just, like, *really* good friends. Which is it? Both way too young and pretty to be needing any of my help," she said, waving around iron rods like a butcher showcasing slabs of meat.

"Look, lady, we are here to buy some sharp things, not talk about our personal lives," I interjected, shooting both Tarik and Heather a grimy look. "So, do you have anything to sell, or not?"

"Ooooh, a woman who knows what she wants and doesn't like unnecessary chit-chat! Yeah, I got some weapons for ya," she answered, looking at me directly as she spoke. "In all seriousness, though, are you guys dating, or just good friends?"

"Dating," Tarik and I answered, shockingly in unison.

We looked at each other.

"Weird, 'cause there's no hand-holding, no kissing, no touching—not even standing that close to one another. You sure?" Heather asked, peering at each of us and setting the weapon racks on workbenches.

"It's our own relationship, thank you," I scoffed.

"Sassy and respectful. I like that. Good combo. Love the hair, by the way. I'm a sucker for luscious black locks like yours, what can I say?"

"Yeah. A monster cut it for me."

"That so? Yeah, yeah, yeah ... a 'monster' cut mine, too!" Heather chuckled, bringing forth more axes and swords and bows from her storage.

"You laugh, but I was being serious," I muttered softly, enamored with the sharpened plethora of The Broken Nail's finest wares.

"I'm sure you were," Heather answered, trailing Tarik and I while we made our selection. "You've got a great energy about you, miss. I dig—"

"The longsword and spear. How much?" I interrupted.

She pushed the auburn hair out of her face, rubbed her hands on her leather apron, and picked up the pair of weapons. "These two?"

The black spear with its sharp, shiny arrowhead blade at the top was for me; the longsword with its silver-crusted grip and hilt encased in a thick leather scabbard was for Tarik. Heather held them at her sides and approached to hand them to each of us. Tarik excitedly pulled the sword from its scabbard and inspected every inch of it. I, on the other hand, took the spear in two hands and made fake jabbing motions towards Heather.

"Easy there, tiger." The blacksmith beamed at me. "It's three thousand. Each."

"Whoa ..." I stammered, shoving the spear against the rack. "That's outrageous! We're not paying that! No wonder you have so little business!"

"Yeah, sorry. The necromancers have killed every inch of my business. All I do is hammer away on an anvil, sharpen blades until my hands go numb, and stare at my own reflection through the flames of a furnace. You two are the first people to come into my shop in weeks. I have to charge what I have to charge. So ... that'll be six thousand gold."

"Steep price," Tarik replied, digging into his pockets. "But weapons are what we need, so ..."

"You brought six thousand gold with you and never said anything?!" I yelled, whacking him in the ribs.

"Yeah, hid it in Chestnut's saddlebags, so you'd never see."

Tarik began counting out the coins on Heather's workbench.

"That's stupid, Tarik. Way too much money to bring!" I hollered.

He looked at me, those stupid hazel eyes peering deeper into my soul. "I wanted to go all out for today's date, okay? With The Pit coming up, I had no idea what was going to happen to us next. I still have no idea, frankly! I needed to do everything and anything in my power to have a nice, relaxing date—a calm before the storm ... so I brought most of my gold. We need the weapons to kill the ghouls. PLUS ... the reward is probably gold anyway. So, I'll get some of it back when the deed is done. I ... I just wanted today to go well."

"Adorable, you are," Heather broke in. "You two do make a cute couple. Don't do anything foolish to each other and screw it up! Thanks for the payment ... Although, if you do end up in Azuma Shores again, come back to The Broken Nail anytime you'd like. These are six thousand, but the next batch of killin' tools are on the house."

She gave each of us a flirty shoulder flick. Gathering the gold and recounting it into her apron pouch, Heather vanished into her shop and rekindled the furnace's fiery glow.

"Ready to slaughter?" Tarik asked, carrying the sword on his shoulder.

"Thought you'd never ask," I answered, tucking the spear under my armpit.

Like a murderous couple ready for a rampage, we walked coolly out of The Broken Nail and back onto Dahlia Street.

This is a fun day, I thought maniacally, looking at Tarik's distraught-yet-gleeful expression as he held the sword.

"Now," he wondered, "any idea where the cemetery is?"

"Gotta be near the church, right?" I said, taking the lead.

The Eternal Flame chapel beamed over us again, its ominous silhouette illumined by sunlight. I felt Logan's presence differently this time as we neared the church. Perhaps it was the sharp spear hanging under my arm, or the beautiful longsword in Tarik's hands, but I knew his high horse wouldn't feel so high or regal if we walked in like this right now.

Olivia, that little rug rat can wait. One thing at a time!

"Yikes. It's chilly over here now," Tarik said.

We walked around the side of the church opposite the garden and arrived at a tree line of waving palms and oaks. Thick leaves with moss draped along them hung towards the ground blockade of shaded green, the church's tree line thoroughly obscured any view of the other side, that lent mystery and privacy to the property.

"This way," I gestured, ushering warrior-wonder-boy in the same direction.

"If you say so." Tarik snickered, aimlessly darting his eyes around, when I shot him a look.

"You flirted with that blacksmith back there. Clear as day, too! I saw it. You saw it. Don't deny it," I said, walking strategically around the sand and grass. I watched Tarik's reflection in the spear's blade. His eyes followed my movement though his head was bent the ground.

"Okay, well, you did, too, letting her touch your hair and complimenting you and all. You're not innocent in this either, Olivia."

"I did it in retaliation for when you did it! All's fair in love and war, honey. Interesting to see that it got under your skin."

"Of course it does, Olivia, because I like you," Tarik said earnestly. "I keep trying to show you that, tell you that, make sure you see that. I'm not hiding it or keeping it secret from you. If you don't like me in that way, fine. But you ought to know where I stand, at least. Today's date. Lunch at The Pouncing Fish. Walking around Azuma Shores ... All with good intentions, to showcase my feelings for you! Be snarky and crabby if you want, but it's all for you, Olivia. I mean, look at what we're carrying and where we're going! You think this was in my original game plan? No. But I do it, because it makes you happy. I will always change any plans of mine to accommodate you."

I took a humbled deep breath and wove around a couple palm trees. "I like you, too, Tarik. You certainly try harder to keep my attention than anyone I've ever met, often even more than Marrick ... and that's saying something!" I chuckled lightly, keeping my eyes on the distorted path ahead. "I appreciate your willingness to change for me, and I enjoy that about you. Today hasn't gone great in your eyes, maybe. But in mine, it's been a lot of fun, and way more effort than anyone has *ever* put in for me. Ever! I'm not kidding. Like I've said probably a dozen times, most kids at the college don't give me a second glance. You do, and I see that. So ... thank you."

"You're welcome. And thank you also. Give me time, little demon. I'll grow on you."

"You're definitely somethin', alright, that's for sure." I snickered faintly.

What's happening to me? Did Tarik break through my feelings fortress? Has he broken me out of my shell? Many have tried, and all have failed. Why do I feel okay with it, though? I was petrified for years of letting anyone get close to me. For their safety. Tarik's not like the people before him. It was a scary revelation for the baddest witch in Penumbra.

"Meant every word, Olivia," Tarik muttered, shuffling his shoes through the sand.

"Ya know, for towering trees, these oaks and palms sure provide great protection. No one would've guessed that church's little tree line would be such a dense forest!"

Admirable topic change, Olivia. It was almost as good a transition as the time you used glacial akinak scales instead of radioactive akinak scales to make an asphyxiation potion. Not quite, though, because that was a stroke of pure brilliance! I laughed at my inner voice. *Wait ... Everyone talks to themselves in third person, right? People who don't are insane. And after all, I am the most sane person I know.*

"Yeah," he replied awkwardly as we broke through the trees.

The cemetery's cold coastal atmosphere entrapped us immediately. Gravestones were hidden by stacked corpses, flies swarming all around them. The mausoleums and tombs appeared full of dead townsfolk. The ghouls and necromancers had killed enough of the town that the living had to "bury" the dead aboveground. The scene reminded me of what I'd read about the Black Plague, where people died quicker than graves could be dug for the bodies.

But the most prevalent aspect of the cemetery was the twenty, maybe thirty ghouls scavenging in the grass. I saw one of them wandering aimlessly while munching on a bloody limb like it was a turkey leg. Tarik pointed out more ghouls kneeling down, eating the intestines of a fresh corpse like spaghetti, slopping flesh and crimson blood on the grass. They were an ugly greenish-gray, with thin strands of hair sprouting from their heads. Textured like human muscle, their thick skin looked smooth yet rugged at the same time and offset the jagged black nails on their hands. Some had a pair of bulging white eyes while others had only a single eye. Nearly five feet tall, the ghouls appeared stitched together, as if each limb were sewn onto the next.

"Found the cemetery, and ... found the ghouls," Tarik noted, stepping to my side at the white slab wall perimeter.

"Yeah. Thanks for that, Tarik," I said, shaking my head.

"Wanna have a little fun with this?"

"More than I'm already going to have? Sure."

"They're ghouls. Removing them should be a piece of cake. Make it more interesting with a friendly competition?"

"Love to! What's in it for me?" I wondered, rubbing my fingers on the spear's blade to prepare it for work.

"Bragging rights. The feeling of always being better than me. Holding this loss over my head for eternity. The—"

"Stop. Yup, I'm in! The person with the most ghoul kills wins. Keep count of your own."

"But before we start," he said, pivoting to look at me and placing his hands on my shoulders, "*NO MAGIC*! Got it? We still want to keep a low profile, and for our identities to remain a secret. Magic blows our cover. So, don't use it! Understand? I'm serious, Olivia—we cannot use it!"

"Yes, *Marrick*. I understand. Magical college students shouldn't use magic outside of the college campus. I know the rules, Tarik. Broke 'em already earlier. So, when do we start, then?"

"How about ... now!" Tarik shouted, leaping over the wall and zooming towards an unsuspecting ghoul. The ghoul swung around and aimlessly slashed at the air as Tarik neared it. He dodged and swung the longsword down swiftly with both hands into its neck, slicing the head clean off. Black goo splattered his collar. The ghoul's lower half hit the ground with a loud thud, and Tarik spun around to see me still standing outside of the cemetery.

"Uh oh ..." He giggled wildly. "It's already Tarik one, Olivia zero. Better get going before I steal all the fun!"

I hopped the white wall and caught Tarik's eyes again, this time as his sword plunged through the chest of a second ghoul. As he pulled it out, the lifeless creature fell on a miniature gravestone and toppled it to the ground.

"Two to zero!" he shouted, racing off to the right. His jacket was torn slightly along the sleeve, and ghoul's blood had made it onto his back somehow.

I turned my eyes from him to the grisly scene before me. A ghoul rose up in front of me from feasting on a corpse's insides, groaning and growling, an elbow sticking out of its mouth. It snarled at me, jawline splitting down the cheeks, showing the inner workings. Chomping its teeth at me, it suddenly revealed another set of arms. The four-armed, one-eyed, straggly-haired ghoul targeted me as its next meal. I wielded the spear and snarled back at it.

It charged me, and in the split second that I reacted to its movement, one of the ghoul's friends appeared from behind a mausoleum and focused on me as live prey. The first ghoul raced towards me; I steadied the spear at its chest and waited to pierce it like a jousting horseman. A loud growl bounced from the nearby gravestones before the other ghoul ran towards me, too.

My spear shot through the ghoul's side, and greenish fluids spilled from its tip. But before I could bask in glory, another one rushed in from the left. It knocked me into a pile of smelly rotting bodies. In a flare of rage and disgust, I javelined the shaken ghoul right through the head. Covered in the same black goo as Tarik's jacket, my spear wedged itself in the dirt near a gravestone. I quickly sprung to my feet, dodging another ghoul, which sped into the pile of corpses. As it regathered itself and charged again, I grabbed the spear and poised it irritably at its flesh-encased mouth. Yelling like a cavewoman, I raced towards it.

"Already up to six!" Tarik shouted across the cemetery. His voice burned into my skin like an infection.

"Of course he is," I muttered, anticipating the death of this ghoul.

The spear easily pierced through its thick, gray skin—but the ghoul didn't drop. Instead, it smirked at the intruding blade and whacked me with its claws out. The warm sensation of blood on my cheek distracted my mind until I was flung into a sturdy gravestone and cracked it on impact. I groaned and grimaced, dabbing my cheek with my fingers to inspect the damage.

"SEVEN!" the annoying void boy hollered.

I'd barely killed one!

"Tarik's no-magic rule is stupid and pointless. What kind of magical college student doesn't use magic? Makes no sense, and neither does he. I'm winning this game, no matter the cost, Tarik! Forget your rule, 'cause I'm not letting you hold this thing over me forever, and I'm not giving you the satisfaction of being the winner!"

I blasted the ghoul who injured me with a madness spell. As I rose to my feet and wiped the dripping blood off my cheek, a satisfied smile shone on my face. I watched as the ghoul's eyes rolled back in its head and imploded in a righteous detonation of guts and goo. Some landed on my pants and shoes, but most of the poor creature splattered across the grass.

Thoroughly enjoying cheating at Tarik's game, I silently cast another madness spell on a feeding ghoul. Its mind collapsed under hallucinations and nonsense until it exploded in another blast of flesh and goo. What a glorious sight it was, too!

Suddenly, Tarik came into view, chased by three ghouls, the scraggly hairs on their heads blowing in the breeze, their grayish color blending into the scene around them. But beyond the mist and piles of bodies, a new ghoul emerged. This one had smooth, pale white skin and was almost double their size at eight feet tall. Its feet and facial features were humanoid, but the prehensile tongue and extreme claws stood out. Its arms stretched to the ground. Completing the image of ghostly white skin and long pink tongue were the small pieces of brown fabric clinging to its body.

"Help! Olivia, help, please!" Tarik shouted, coming to my side and breathing heavily. His maroon jacket had darkened to black, and I was horrified to notice the amount of ghoul goo encasing it in a horrid shell. Meanwhile, he looked me up and down, clearly noticing that I had taken some battle scars myself.

"How you doin'?" I asked.

"Great, yeah. You?" Tarik answered, catching his breath.

"Terrific, yeah."

"Cut on your face? That's new. You alright, though?"

"Terrific, yup. New jacket?"

"Bits of goo and plasma, but ... Yeah, I like that version better."

This entire conversation only took place over the course of one minute. Tarik and I never met each other's eyes, entirely focused on the ghast and the feeding-frenzied other ghouls that were rapidly approaching. He wielded the longsword in his sweaty hands, and I drew back the spear in anticipation. With no real time to think, we stood back-to-back as our group of enemies advanced. Many more ghouls suddenly showed up to the party, now placing Tarik and me between the last seven ghouls, with one ghast to deal with.

"Score is, like, eight to three, I think. I stopped keeping score," he whispered, leaning his lips towards my ear.

"I have, like, four—and easily handled mine without any help. Unlike ... *ahem* ... you!" I retorted playfully. He didn't need to know about my magic usage. Better for him not to, anyway.

"Easy now, little demon. Time to finish the job ... together."

"Yup," I answered before screeching like a banshee at the ghouls waiting around us.

Then, in the innocent beach cemetery of Azuma Shores, all hell broke loose.

A ghoul rushed me, but I speared it through the chest and tossed it to the side. Behind me, Tarik hacked off another's arms and kicked it to the ground. In that moment, I tugged on his jacket sleeve as an incoming ghoul targeted me. I was trying to retrieve my spear from my previous victim when I nudged for his help.

"DUCK!" he yelled in my direction.

Immediately, he swung around, longsword outstretched in his tight grip. I dropped to the ground, and Tarik sliced the ghoul clean in half. Once he returned to my side, I stood upright again and pushed its lower torso into the dirt.

"Disgusting," I muttered as I kicked plasma off my shoes and jeans. No time to waste on that ghoul, as the next one was nearing. I tucked the spear under my armpit once again and snarled at it through clenched teeth.

"I'm kind of sweating over here. How you doin', Olivia?" Tarik asked.

"Barely broke a sweat! HA!" I shouted—lying through my teeth.

Tarik stabbed a ghoul through the chest and bulldozed it into a gravestone, leaving a large indent in the slab. The life force inside it vanished on impact as Tarik pulled the sword out of its stomach.

I was then blindsided by the last few ghouls, who charged at me and pinned my arms to the ground. One of them stood on top of me like a jaguar tormenting its prey, slobbering drool and blood on my chest and face. Its breath smelled like garbage, decaying flesh, and maggots. Trying to wiggle free, I squirmed under the ghoul's sharp claws. Twisting and tossing my head to avoid its teeth, I screamed for Tarik, who tossed his longsword aside and pulled the ghoul off my body. It thrashed at him, slashing across his elbows, and blood blossomed through his ripped sleeve. My attention then flicked to the longsword, and I grabbed ahold of it. In the meantime, Tarik was now pinning that same ghoul to the ground. I leapt to my feet, dusted the sand off my clothes, and drove the sword's sharp blade into its forehead. I let go of Tarik's weapon and fell to the ground; he jumped to his feet and helped me back to mine. Exhausted and covered in plasma, he and I finally turned to address the ghost, which had hung back like a king directing his minions to their deaths.

Tongue dangling from its the mouth, the tall creature roared. Sharp nails shot out from its hand like eagle talons, and vampire teeth flashed at us in its blind rage. The sound was enough to alert the entire town. Saliva slowly dripped from its fangs and landed between blades of grass.

Roaring a second time, the ghost raced at us while Tarik and I readied our weapons for it to pounce. It ran like a human, stomping on huge feet. Like a rotten-egg-and-dead-meat smoothie, the smell of it gagged me and almost made Tarik's face turn pale green.

I angled back the spear and threw it at the ghost's right leg, hoping to topple it over by spearing the kneecap. That idea was incredible in concept but played out horribly in reality; the giant white creature shrugged off my spear and swiped me off my feet. It tossed me several feet before I rolled across the grass into a stack of corpses. Blood seeped from the ghost's claw marks on my cheek. I wiped them clean with my sleeve and slowly rose to my feet.

Looking across the scene to Tarik, I saw that he shared a similar fat: He was smashed into a broken mausoleum as pieces of stone and rubble collapsed around him. He moaned and groaned before gingerly getting back up again while gripping his ribs tightly. As he winced in pain, the ghost walked over to the crumbling tomb, with Tarik weak and trapped inside.

I ran forward, screaming and waving my arms around to recapture its attention, but to no avail. The ghost had its sunken black eyes locked onto Tarik to deliver a final blow. I threw a handful of rocks at its back. Still nothing as it mounted the rubble.

"Hey! Over here!" I hollered. "You big idiot, look! Right here! Fresh meat begging to be eaten!"

The ghost never budged its focus from casting aside large pieces of stone above Tarik's head.

"Olivia!" he shouted through the cracks. He flinched and grimaced before speaking again, still clutching his ribs. "Use magic! I'm allowing you to use magic! Just kill this thing! Do it—now!"

If you say so ... I gleamed at my greedy inner voice.

"That's cheating, Tarik! I'm not breaking the rules!" I yelled facetiously.

"WHAT?!" he screeched, darting his eyes at me under the ghost. "Are you kidding me?! We've broken the no-magic rule already today! We flew here on a supposedly mythical creature and exploded a zombie from the inside like a rotten grape. And

Olivia, you break rules all the time! I'm asking you to do it again. Use magic, Olivia! Screw my rules!"

"ALRIGHT!" I shouted, coy yet bursting with excitement.

The ghast then lunged an arm through the debris at Tarik, who shifted to the left just in time to avoid its talons.

I closed my eyes briefly and centered my attention on my magic. Placing myself in the most soothing mindset I could muster, I channeled the nightmares. A world of shadows and darkness circulated through my body, at my fingertips. I aimed for the ghast's bald head and cast a crueler madness spell. It felt that instantly, recoiling and retreating from the mausoleum. Scratching at its head, the ghast wobbled away and was nearly tripped by its own dead ghouls strewn on the ground.

"Thanks for that," Tarik muttered, wiggling out of the collapsed rubble.

"Don't mention it," I answered, watching the vampire-like ghast literally claw at its own brain, trying to use those horrible nails to dig through that thick skull and stop my spell from spreading. Tarik and I silently nodded to one another and came to the perfect unspoken solution: Time to knock it to the ground.

We charged weaponless at the staggering creature. Together, our brute force pushed it back against the gravestones and unburied bodies, and it fell to the ground in a massive thud that shook the earth beneath our feet.

"Care to do the honors?" Tarik smiled cutely, retrieving his longsword for me.

"It would be my pleasure." I grinned.

I took the sword from his outstretched hands, and he used his jacket sleeve to clear the warm, moist blood from my cheeks. I had completely forgotten it was there in the first place until a few drops splashed onto the sword hilt.

"Have at it. He's got a lot on his mind at the moment. Best put him out of his misery."

Tarik grinned a cute, sadistic grin that looked too genuine to be fake, but he continued to wince at his chest injuries.

With pep in my step, I climbed atop the ghast, standing on its belly, and held the longsword high in both hands. In a single smooth motion, I drove the blade into its heart.

Its legs went limp. Its arms dropped to the dirt. And its eyes closed as it met the same fate as the other ghouls. I jumped off and rejoined Tarik at the ghast's feet. We looked at each other, but we didn't say anything right away.

Glancing over the black goo and plasma splashed across his shirt, I leaned up to Tarik and kissed him on the lips.

Say something, Olivia. You kissed him out of nowhere, and now you're just staring at him, flabbergasted by what happened. Say something—anything!

"I ... I am so ... sorry. I ... I don't ... I don't know what came over ... came over me, honestly. I'm really sorry," I finally said.

Tarik laughed, still gazing into my eyes. "Don't be sorry, little demon! I really do care for you. And ... happy one month anniversary," he said with a sappy smile. His warm, dirty hands gently grabbed my cheeks and rubbed away the remaining dried blood. He pulled me in to kiss me again on the lips, for longer than the small peck I gave him.

Tarik, you are breaking my emotionless, heartless persona! Why did I just kiss you? What made me do it? Am I possessed, or having an out-of-body experience? No idea! But as awful and wretched as it sounds, I didn't hate it. Oh no ... What's wrong with me? I actually enjoyed our date today—us hanging out together! On second thought, the kiss probably told him that already. It was ... perfectly imperfect, just like me. Maybe that's why I did it? Maybe that's why I like you so much? I threaten you, but you just laugh it off and say, "That's Olivia for ya!" I yell at you for saying something objectively stupid; you apologize and correct it next time. You are the first person in a long time who doesn't fear me—who doesn't run for the hills when I get close. You make me feel comfortable to be myself, to be in my own skin. No one has made me feel this way before.

"Now we go back to the college and get ready for the ball. What do ya say? Ready to head back?" he asked, flashing the widest smile I had ever seen on any man.

All of that terrifies me more than The Pit ever will: the idea of knocking down my walls and letting someone in. Letting my guard down for someone else. Allowing someone to get close and personal with me. I've been afraid to do it for anyone. But, Tarik ... for you? I might be willing to do that. Fuck me.

Like soldiers recovering from battle, I clung tightly to his waist and helped him walk. Warily, he held onto mine; both of us were damaged in more ways than one.

"Pampered at the ball like a suckling pig? Yeah, no. By all means, please piss me off when you've *just* redeemed our date," I retaliated, smirking devilishly at him as my eyes shot daggers at his. "Let's be sure to get paid first before we leave. The college may work me for free, but the churches of Ha'thar won't."

KIKU V

"Kiku?" Zoe hollered through the wall between our rooms. "Hey ... you ready yet?"

"Yes. Wait ... No! Maybe?" I stammered, tying a black *obijime* snugly around my waist. "I mean, I'm dressed, but I don't think people are gonna like it. I ... I'm not sure if I like it, honestly ..."

"Aww, c'mon. You're being too hard on yourself! I'm sure you look great. Lemme see!" she shouted encouragingly.

I stood in front of my mirror in a traditional white kimono. Black lotus flowers were embroidered along the bottom—a small touch of nature added by my mother. While she would be proud to see our heritage represented in my outfit, I'm not sure the rest of the college is going to see that. Would it stand out too much to be suitable for the masquerade? Would it be too different from the other mages' fancy gowns and dresses? What would Zoe think? What would Abe think? Would it just attract more unwanted attention?

Adjusting my kimono in the mirror, a bleached blonde head peeked through my bedroom doorway. Zoe's eyes bobbed in and out of view. Despite my hesitation, I nodded to her and continued to judge my outfit in the mirror.

"You can come in, but don't make a big deal of it, please!" I announced, pointing a finger at her over my shoulder.

Zoe flung herself into the room. I watched her royal-blue nails twinkle as her hands immediately rose up to cover her nose and mouth. Her eyes lit up big and wide once they met mine in the standing mirror's reflection.

"Kiku ..." she began.

I spun around and interjected, "Ah, ah, ah! No! Zoe, no. Don't say anything. I asked you not to make a big deal of it, so please don't. I'm not sure how I feel about it yet ..."

Meanwhile, my Australian roommate looked regal in a dazzling blue dress, its frilly hem draped along our carpeted floor. Embroidered designs adorned the sides like it was a Victorian ballgown. Offsetting her white-blonde hair, the A-line dress fit her figure perfectly and looked gorgeous on her, which only heightened my trepidation over my own choice of outfit.

"Kiku ..." she started again.

"Okay, fine. What do you think? Is it too much? Not enough?" I sighed, facing the mirror again and twirling around to find a good angle.

"You look beautiful. Like, stunning. And no, not too much, or too little. It's perfect."

"Really?" I grinned, fixing the sleeves and collar. "You think so?"

"Absolutely! ... Oh my! I mean, even Sonnet's alert for this moment," Zoe added, gesturing to our adopted pet bird in her nest. It was true: Impossibly, Sonnet appeared to smile in the mirror's reflection., an approving glint shimmering in her eyes.

"But compared to you, I look—"

"Stop! Don't compare yourself to mine or me or anyone else! We are not you, and we are not rockin' that white kimono like you are!" Zoe said, clapping as she spoke.

In our masquerade outfits of white and blue, Zoe and I posed side by side in my mirror while she encouraged me to model for her. She put a genuine smile on my face as she spun me around like her imaginary dance partner. Laughter overtook the angsty tension in my bedroom—a welcome change of pace often granted by Zoe's bubbly presence.

"Hey, Zo ..." I started, breaking away from the song and dance to pet Sonnet's head. Then I stepped back to Zoe's side—and somehow felt inferior again. A short Japanese girl in a kimono, standing next to a tall fairy tale princess? No matter how many times Zoe might say it, I still didn't feel like the star of the show. Now that I'd been selected for The Pit, I felt a horrifying urge to go against my senses and absorb the spotlight in any instance. "I'm still shaken up from the ceremony," I admitted.

"I know you are," Zoe replied consolingly. Her eyes were tender when they locked onto mine. "I know. But it'll be okay. I'll be here the entire time. You won't have to tackle it alone."

She smiled at me and Sonnet.

"Thank goodness! I'm still panicking and feeling my stomach doing somersaults, but thank you. Your kind words do help."

We both glanced at the clock: 19:48.

"Okay. Yes! Now, Keeks, you ready to go to the masquerade?" Zoe asked, her tone a mixture of restraint and optimism.

"As I'll ever be," I said shyly, breathing out a long exhale. My foot tapped on the carpet, and my heartbeat kicked up like a drumroll.

"You'll be alright, Kiku, I promise. Never an awkward situation for me, because I thrive in awkward situations. That's my comfort zone!" She chuckled. "I'll be your sidekick—your navigator for the entire night."

My feelings didn't change immediately, like Zoe was hoping, but my foot tapping on the carpet and the pitter-patter of my heart remained steady.

"Look, I'm nervous about tonight, too," she added lightly. "I've never been to a masquerade ball; I barely even have any idea what it is! I imagine it's like a huge school dance—but I've never been to one of those either. So, it'll be scary territory for both of us."

"Well, that makes me feel better ... and worse," I sighed, following Zoe into the living room. "But yeah, you're right. Let's just go and get this over with."

"That's the spirit ...?" my roommate replied uncertainly.

Zoe and I paused at the coffee table on our way out and grabbed our masquerade masks. Gifted from Joan, mine was the golden one with music notes painted on it. Zoe's, however, I had yet to see until now. Her mask only covered one side of her face, elegantly concealing a single eye, like she was the phantom of the opera. Intricate designs of thin, gold metal wove through one another for added affect.

"Wow ..." I stammered. "That's yours?"

"Yeah!" Zoe exclaimed, nearly choking on sips of water. "Yup, it's mine. I went for a similar look to yours. Not as on the nose as yours, but still gorgeous."

"It's lovely." I grinned.

"Should we wear them on the way over?" Zoe asked, holding hers up to her face.

I didn't answer right away. Instead, I simply stared at my mask on the table and wondered. Thoughts raced inside my head at a mile a minute as the black music notes seemed to sing to me. Their music mocked me while I zoned out. The masks were beautiful, don't get me wrong! It was just that they couldn't cover up everything. I'd still be on everyone's radar because of The Pit. From the professors to the students to Jax, all of those people would only have eyes for five people tonight, and I was one of them. It was a little hard to conceal your entire existence behind a mask or a dress.

Despite all that, the mask might help with my anxiety.

"Yeah, we should," I replied, confident enough to speak it aloud.

Zoe helped lace up my mask before putting on her own. With both of us dressed to the nines and masks wrapped on as the finishing touch, we were ready for the Masquerade Ball. It was nearly eight o'clock, but she cutely reassured me that it was "quite typical for the kings and queens to arrive late to their own parties." A tortuous gift from my mother, my need to be present for important things was paramount in my life. And while I love my roommate's carefree attitude, I did not relish being late.

"Don't worry, Keeks. We'll be properly on time. Plus, they're already waiting for your arrival anyway, right? Soooooo, why not widen their peepers and make them tuck in their tails a little?" Zoe chuckled, throwing her voice from her bedroom as she had left my side briefly to double-check her ball outfit one last time.

Meanwhile, I opened the front door and nervously called for her to rejoin me. "C'mon, Zo. I just wanna get going at this point. The quicker we get there, the quicker I can escape the spotlight. Let's go and get this over with."

"I'm here," she said, smiling and closing the door behind us.

We began our walk to the Festival of the Elements.

Wearing a white kimono and a gold music mask, I felt hidden in a way, like I was a total stranger. I couldn't tell if this weird feeling was a good one or a bad one. Then there was Zoe, who could have been the cover model for a modern fairy tale novel in her dazzling blue gown and opera-ready mask. Unlike me, she dressed and acted like the limelight was made for her. Her encouraging words were a relief and a blessing, but honestly, I couldn't help but think how much better equipped she was for the tournament than me.

"Hey, Zo," I said to break the silence while rubbing my arms nervously, "thank you. For helping me through this so far, and boosting my spirits about my outfit."

"No problem. It's my pleasure." Zoe laughed affectionately.

Our heels clacking on the cement sidewalks around the gazebo, the two of us left the air dorm area and headed for the festival. The evening was perfect, with clear skies and the glimmering pink glow of the fading sunset. The calm water of the lake reflected the setting sun in a picturesque moment as the orange haze greeted it on the horizon, embracing the gazebo in a striking silhouette. This scene could have been an oil painting hung in a museum. With the music getting louder and the cheering of students growing as we continued, Zoe and I nodded to each other. Tonight would be an evening neither of us would forget. My heart nearly beat out of my chest as the momentum built up to the grand reveal.

Whew ... Just take deep breaths, Kiku. You'll be alright. You have Zoe! She won't let anything embarrassing or ridiculous happen to you, I reassured myself. *Plus, you've been in the spotlight before with kabuki performances, so this is no different. You won't be alone! Keep that in mind.*

At the fork in the road, we made a right and kept on towards the festival. The flashing lights, the loud sounds of the crowd, and the orchestra playing in the backdrop only escalated my fluttering stomach. I took a big gulp and readjusted my mask to fit snug on my face. Looking to Zoe in a mix of desperation and tension, I grabbed ahold of her hand as we left the quiet college campus.

"Wait ... the masquerade is *inside* the festival?" I asked Zoe, gripping her hand tightly as I raised my voice over the commotion.

"Yup! Gotta go through the festival to get to the ball! But don't fret, my pet! Maybe we'll see a couple circus acts or somethin'. I don't know, but I'll help you stay on track," Zoe whispered quickly. She chuckled and yanked my arm a little as her excitement kicked in, edging us forward.

Disguised in a flurry of vibrant colors, the Festival of the Elements engulfed us the moment we stepped underneath its grand illuminated marquee. The grounds were enormous, alive with hundreds of gown-wearing girls and tuxedo-wearing boys dancing throughout. Little flags bearing the elemental symbols waved in the breeze like it was a street fiesta. The atmosphere was admittedly incredible. This immediate reveal of masked mages swaying to the ambient music and playing ring toss and beanbag games and the event performers showcasing their skills in various corners of the festival was a lot to take in. "A party for the ages," as many had called it over the past week or so. Although seeing it all in person was too intense to absorb all at once: Every direction looked like a new challenge for me to conquer.

"I know it's a lot," Zoe whispered. "Just remember to take it one step at a time."

"It's like you're reading my mind ..." I stammered, anxiously ushering Zoe deeper into the festival amidst masks staring in my direction.

"Ahh, yes! The correct term is Telepathic Roommate Symbiosis, where two charming and endearing roommates seem to combine into one person due to their close friendship. It's a hidden phenomenon that acts as an unspoken connection between the pair." Zoe laughed, watching for my reaction to her nonsense.

"You made that up." I chuckled back while dodging skeptical looks from Mason and Wolf, a germination mage who preferred the company of animals.

"Not important. What is important is that you trust me and just enjoy yourself a little." She laughed back, smiling and waving at Caroline, who was walking with a cupcake in her hand towards Heather. Zoe waved to her, too, like a queen greeting a fellow queen. "Please. For me?"

"Hey, ladies!" interjected Kamaul, who had ditched his mask, before whisking the two mages from Zoe's side. They giggled and flirted as he escorted them away. Thankfully, I didn't think he recognized Zoe or me.

"Hey," Zoe added, "let's check out the sword swallower!"

"Sword swallower?" I nodded.

"Yup. It'll be fun."

Gotta get better at being in the public eye, Kiku, I reminded myself. *You've done it before. Use Zoe as a crutch if you need to; she's a great sidekick who can handle any craziness thrown your direction.*

"Actually, yeah. Maybe a distraction would be good right now," I said.

"That's the spirit, Keeks!" Zoe said, tugging my arm nearly out of its socket.

The other girls in heels made it look so easy, like they had been classically trained in this fine art as toddlers or something. They made it look so effortless as they trekked through the dirt and grass. How did they do it? I was only sixteen, but I felt juvenile when it came to this. It seemed like the only thing I was good at now was pretending to be a good bookworm and a good student. Meanwhile, as a child, I had been proficient in plays and kabuki theater and memorized the lead's performances as her understudy. But how did any of that help me now in this strange new world? Apparently, those lost arts had been forgotten the minute I set foot on this foreign campus.

Gathered within a large huddle of masqueraders stood a tall red-haired man, who leapt around wildly within the circle. His energy was infectious, smoothly elevating the crowd's excitement and hysteria. While he hopped around, two elves stood juggling flaming knives on either side of him. Draped behind the trio was a canvas banner reading: Ivan Ives, Sword Swallowing Connoisseur.

"Ivan! Ivan! Ivan! Ivan!" the crowd chanted.

"You wanna see more? Another dagger? How 'bout a longsword this time, huh?"

Zoe and I silently squeezed into the circle.

"Ivan! Ivan!"

Cute boys in black suits. Purple ball gowns. Blue dresses. Orange ones, white ones, green ones, black ones ... It was a collage of beauty and elegance in each direction. They stood next to us among the sword swallower's audience. It was either a classically dressed princess starring in her own fairy tale or Prince Charming hoping to sweep her off her feet. No one else was wearing a kimono. Each student looked modern but unconventional, sleek and stylish. I felt so out of place in my chosen ball outfit. Sure, it was true to me, but at what cost? To stand out like a sore thumb? To bring more attention to me than the Pit Ceremony already had? Maybe my initial worries were right; maybe it was the wrong choice ...

"Who's ready for a show?!" Ivan Ives exclaimed, whirling up his crowd.

Zoe began clapping, too.

"YEAH!" everyone screamed.

The sword swallower clamored for more applause and waved his hands for the jugglers to assist. One of the elves brought over a sleek black wand and handed it to Ivan. The other dwarf ran to retrieve a steel flamberge longsword from his sack.

"Then a show I will give!" he yelled.

He tapped the wand to his stomach and illuminated the tip against his chest. Ivan's bare chest became transparent, revealing the organs and ribcage inside. They were just on display right there, as in some type of morbid X-ray on himself. Somehow, I could not look away, like it was a catastrophic accident.

"Eww," I muttered.

"Cool," Zoe said simultaneously.

How? How ... is that possible? I asked myself, completely ignoring the longsword pointing down towards Ivan's open mouth. *Magic? Has to be. But what kind?*

The elves called for more cheering and clapping. Ivan spread his feet apart and lifted his neck back. With the wavy tip of the blade nearing his teeth, he stuck his tongue out and ushered the sword down his gullet. I watched intently, as did Zoe and the rest of the crowd. It was odd to watch a tattooed performer swallowing steel blades while people in ball gowns and painted masks watched with eager eyes.

Ivan slid the longsword down his throat until the hilt caught the edges of his mouth. He held his arms out to catch the applause, and our awestruck group obliged. He spun around to show everyone, barely flinching at the sharp blade inches away from his organs. Speaking of which, the enchantment on his stomach and chest enabled us to witness the entire act from an ... interesting point of view. The sword fit perfectly through his visible ribs, dipping down past his liver.

I had heard and watched sword swallowers before as a kid, in theatrical performances and stuff back home. But for clear reasons, this time was different. It was morbidly fascinating to see the sword ACTUALLY pass through the body. The act of sword swallowing always evoked mystery and mystique, for once the blade vanished inside the person's mouth, you never saw the full thing again until the performance was over. Ivan, however, using magic (I'm assuming), had removed that prenotion and lifted the curtain on what was usually a secret. It was kinda gross, but I had to hand it to him: He knew how to grab an audience's attention.

One dwarf grabbed a second longsword and carefully handed it off to Ivan, whose focus never left the blade currently plunged inside him. He took this new sword and slid it down his throat, too. With two wavy-bladed longswords inside him, Ivan remained cool as a cucumber. The crowd cheered to new heights, and the dwarf left to gather a third and fourth blade. These were daggers, however, short and sharp.

Then, Zoe and I shared an unspoken look, a silent cue in both our minds, and we decided now was a good time to slip away from the crowd and find the next festival act.

"That was ... uhhh ... interesting, huh?" I muttered to her.

"Oh, yes. 'Interesting' is the perfect word." Zoe giggled.

"Where to next?" I asked, feeling every nearby student dart their eyes at me. Even masked, I was like a beacon for everyone's attention, like all the shows had ceased and the games had ended. Their chatter went silent as we passed. Could they tell it was Kiku Kaipan underneath the gold music mask? Who knows ... but one thing I did know for certain was the panic settling in inside me. So were fear, and embarrassment, and hyperventilation, and—

"Kiku? Hey, you alright? You look like you just saw a ghost!" Zoe questioned, pausing for a moment to look carefully into my eyes.

"Yeah ... Yeah," I said, calming my heart rate down and lowering my head to examine the dirt. "Just a lot of eyes on me. It's like they know it's me, even under the mask, which I told you would—"

"Keeks, stop. It's alright. They don't know who you are. They just saw us walk by and were curious. It's alright, I promise. Okay?"

"Sure." I nodded, slowly raising my head to level with the others. "It's everyone, though, not just this group or that one. It feels like every pair of eyes knows where I am and who's underneath this mask."

Walking between ring toss, balloon popping, and bottle knockdown games, Zoe and I moved deeper into the festival. Hooting and hollering from the sword swallower's area permeated my ears, mixing with the oohs and ahhs of the victorious carnival winners. Tiny banners bearing flames, snowflakes, trees, shadows, or wings swayed in the light breeze. Bright orbs drifted high into the sky like Chinese lanterns, illuminating the outdoor festival in a creative yellow glow.

Despite the admittedly exciting and impressive layout, I still could not shake my nerves. The dresses and the skirts and the ballgowns ... the suits and the tuxedos and the fancy vests ... Like the high school dances that Zoe had mentioned, I imagined this to be what that environment felt like. I hadn't even attended high school on Earth, and somehow the prospect of walking through those doors already terrified me. But those emotions were for another day—that is, if I was still alive by that time.

No, Kiku! Happy thoughts! I yelled to my inner self. *If Zoe could read your mind or see inside it, she would slap the negativity right out of it.*

"I hear there's a puppet show. That's gotta be ... pretty fascinating, too, huh?" I said, spontaneously feeling the sudden urge to start leading Zoe around.

"Yeah!" she replied, pleasantly surprised that I was taking charge.

I pulled us into another watchful crowd.

With a tacky yet grand stage, the puppet show featured unnamed and unseen mages working wooden puppets. I quickly realized that it was mid-performance, and we had no idea what the story was. All that I could see was the puppets on the giant stage surrounded by velvet maroon drapes that hid the backstage elements.

The audience was silent.

"What's it about?" I asked Zoe, unable to take my eyes off the ongoing show. I nudged my small figure in front of two guys and tried to get a better look.

"Don't know," she whispered.

A trio of male voices were bickering with one another. Each one was operating his own carved marionette. They wore black, grim-reaper-like cloaks, with hoods over their wooden faces. It was hard to tell what or whom the puppets represented.

"You think we're all doomed?!" exclaimed a girl puppet.

"Of course! We were condemned to death the moment we walked on stage!" replied another.

"Wait ..." the girl answered as her puppet spun to face the other. "You *walked* on stage? I just, like, floated over here somehow."

Laughter cackled from some viewers in the crowd. I did not, however, as I was still trying to figure out what was going on.

"Ye are doomed!" shouted a booming voice from a male hooded puppet. The three original ones at center stage looked identical, though this one had a much deeper, creepier tone.

Two more puppets matching the appearance of the rest arrived from underneath.

"How can we be doomed already?" screeched a shrill voice. "The night has just started! I haven't even had the chance to try the muffins, or play a game, or have an awkward first dance!"

Some girls let out a couple of pity chuckles next to me.

"Doomed, I say!" yelled the booming voice.

"Wait ... You're one of us? Why are you saying we're doomed?"

"Oh, I don't know. I just have a great feeling about today, you know?" he answered sarcastically, reeling the octave down to a normal speaking tone. "That ceremony really did a number on my confidence."

"Maybe we're already in purgatory. I hear it's lovely there!"

More laughter ensued.

Zoe reached for my arm, nearly scaring me half to death.

"Hey! What the—"

"Let's leave. There are better shows than this one. C'mon," Zoe muttered.

"No, I wanna see what this one's about."

Zoe tugged again and gave me an *"I'm ready to leave"* look.

"What's the show about, then? I wanna know. Do you know?"

"Hey! Zip it, would ya?" Gabby shushed me, holding a finger up to her mouth under a Venetian-style mask.

"Sorry," I whispered back, retreating slightly into Zoe.

"Oh, Kamaul. We know nothing is gonna shake that ego of yours. Only person I'd actually believe that from is Kiku—who's already in the corner and rocking back and forth in the fetal position!" cackled one of the puppets.

"You're right, Your Highness. Where are my manners? Terrify the girl before she dies. That'll spice up her flavor for the devil!" The other puppet laughed.

"They're making fun of me ..." I frowned, feeling my lip quiver.

"Yeah. Let's go," Zoe said, concerned, yanking me away from the crowd as my eyes locked onto the puppet that was supposed to be me.

"They're making fun of us, Zoe! Of me! Mocking me and ... and the ceremony, like ... like it's some kind of joke!" I cried, letting a tear fall down my cheek.

"I know," she sighed, looking at the ground, then at me. "You agree, then, that maybe now is a good time to leave?"

"Yes, Zoe," I snapped passive-aggressively. My emotions were scattered like a bowl of alphabet soup, and I could not get a fix on any of them. "I agree, it's time to leave. But ... where do we go? Another show ...?" My voice breaking between the words.

"I ... I don't know. Are you hungry? Wanna take a break from the performances and get somethin' to eat? Or a drink, if you're thirsty?" Zoe pleaded.

"Yeah," I sniffled, lifting up my mask to wipe my eyes with my sleeve. "Yeah, I am a little hungry."

I smiled bleakly and narrowed my focus to Zoe. I knew she could sense the sadness in my eyes, but I had most of it hidden under the rest of the mask. I couldn't let anyone else see how the "feeble, terrified girl" really felt about the tournament.

"Let's grab a bite. Take your mind off that puppet show."

"I've gotta hand it to you, Zo. I appreciate your trying to help boost my spirits. I don't have to like all of it, but I do have to go along with it. So, thank you ... Thanks for your help."

"That's my girl." Zoe winked.

Ignoring the watchful beady eyes, she and I shared a nice hug. We smiled at each other and stepped back into the festival. Perhaps there was some truth to that made-up Telepathic Roommate Symbiosis after all. Releasing me, Zoe left my side to find food, and I made a slight turn towards—

"Oh my! I'm so sorry," I stammered, stumbling and reaching out a hand to help.

"It's no worry, my dear," answered a woman's fragile voice. With a wrinkled grin, she smiled kindly at me as she gripped the top of her cane. She wore heavy, quilted beggar's clothes, where snags and little holes showed their age. Their maroon color offset her pale face and simple eyes tucked underneath more wrinkles. A kind and weary woman, she looked old and out of sorts at the festival.

"You alright, ma'am?" I asked tenderly, keeping a hand out in case she needed support.

She properly regained her footing and looked at me. "Yes, of course. Just stumbled a bit." The smile never faded from her face.

"Do you need something?"

"How sweet you are, dear." She giggled cautiously, then winced as if in slight stomach pain.

"Thanks," I answered nervously.

"Actually," the woman added, "spare change would be nice, if you could. Haven't eaten in a few days. If not, I understand. It's just that—"

"Oh. Yes, of course. I have some to spare," I said, reaching for imaginary pockets.

"Thank you," she answered, glancing around at the distressed onlookers passing by us.

"I'm sorry, miss. I don't have much to offer. But ... here ..."

I managed to find some gold and handed it to her. I also found the granola bar I had snuck in under my kimono (in case I had "the panic hungers") and gave that to her as well.

Suddenly, Zoe returned and didn't seem to take too kindly to the older woman.

"Hey, Kiku, what are you doing? Do you know her? Who are you?" she demanded.

"I'm sorry," the woman answered. The fragility in her voice could have broken a vase. Her face was still directed at me. "I was just getting my things in order."

"Zo, it's fine. She was just hungry. I gave her some coins and—"

"Kiku, we don't talk to strangers! No matter how nice they seem. You're a ... popular person now. A target. An instant sensation. You never know someone else's agenda. Gotta be extra careful. Okay?" Zoe instructed me, her eyes stern and unwavering.

"Yeah, yeah, I know. I'm sorry. Guess I didn't think about all that."

"She's right, dear," the woman added. "You should be cautious. But Ha'thar and I are grateful for your kindness. Truly. I will be able to eat now because of you. You're a good person."

"Thanks." I grinned timidly. "Are you lost?"

"Not anymore, dear." She smiled.

Then as quickly as she had appeared, she seemed to vanish.

Out of nowhere, I saw a man stomping through the crowds and parting huddled teens before snaking his arm around the woman's and dragging her away. Strong but strange, the man wasn't ... whole. I knew that didn't make any sense, but he wasn't all ... *there*. It was like he was partially invisible or something; I could only make out parts of him. The bandages wrapping his face twitched and shriveled with his tone. He just came over, whisked her away from Zoe and me, and retreated with her behind the busy game booths.

"What was that? *Who* was that?" Zoe asked, clearly disturbed. She looked out of sorts, too.

"I ... I don't know. She was here, then ... she was gone. Someone ... like ... took her away. I'm not sure myself what just happened."

"C'mon, Keeks, this little corner of the festival is givin' me the creeps. Let's roll over to another show or something. We can eat these over there," Zoe said, her focus never leaving the same direction I was locked onto. We both probably looked insane as we stared at the darkness between the colorful, striped pop-up booths.

"Yeah ..." I started as my feet propelled me after the woman and her captor. "You know what? I'll catch up with you in a sec. I just wanna make sure she's okay, you know? I'll be quick, don't worry."

I was sinking into tunnel vision. I completely forgot Zoe was behind me now, and forgot everyone else existed, too. I was chasing after the old beggar, careful and cautious, so as not to be heard by the man with her. The music, the games, the performers—I tuned all of it out. I just zeroed in on following and listening for where they went and what happened to her.

As I split between the booths, I heard soft but frantic calls from Zoe, who was rightfully concerned but didn't want to cause a scene.

"What were you doing back there, huh?" shouted the half-man thing.

I could tell that he was upset by the tone of his voice. It was shrill and angry, like a ghost or demon.

"I was just observing," the old woman answered. Her tone was cool and calm in rebuttal.

"'Observing'? We should not be interfering in our competitor's lives! Can't be seen by the public. The only one I will accept that from is Kai, who has a reputation to uphold for his element. But you and me? We can't be seen! Now that you have been ... you need to leave. *We* need to leave. Now!"

"Fine. But I will hear none of this hypocrisy from you! You are guilty of spying on them, just as I am. Don't act all noble on me. But I agree; I may have overstayed my welcome. That comment, however, I came to on my own accord—not thanks to your spontaneous outburst!"

"Then it's settled," the nearly invisible figure replied as his face looked to the darkened sky.

The old woman dropped her cane and looked at the man, then to the sky herself.

What I saw next only had one true explanation that I could fathom: Magic was wild and impressive—and unpredictable.

Both figures started to fade away, evaporating right in front of me. I was out of sight from them, of course, but I saw the whole thing. Their bodies transformed from flesh and bone into a swarm of particles. Like sand, the old woman's dispersed form and floated up into the sky, while the shadowy male figure became wispy black smoke and followed after. The pair's new forms rose high towards the night skies above and completely disappeared from view, gone with the wind like dandelion fuzz.

I watched for a few seconds to get my own story straight. But let's be honest here: When I told Zoe, she wouldn't believe me anyway. I wouldn't if I were her.

Then again, I wondered, *why tell her? She won't believe you anyway, so what's the point? What I keep to myself won't hurt her or anyone else. Yeah, I'll keep this little moment to myself. It makes it more special to have seen it alone, firsthand.*

Dusting light debris off of my white kimono, I turned to face Zoe and walked back to her, arriving at her side.

"Okay, what was that?" she said immediately.

"Nothing, really. Must've been friends, 'cause they sat behind a booth and shared the granola bar. When they saw me, they got scared and ran off," I lied.

"Oh? Okay. Scared me for a second," Zoe added, handing me an edible pink rose on a stem.

"Yeah." I chuckled, cautious not to show the truth on my face. "Me too. Like, that was weird, right?"

I never lied, so I had to try and make it believable.

"Right!" Zoe shrieked with a smile. "Told you, didn't I? This corner of the festival is ... weird. Let's roll on back to the circus shows and stuff. Try and fit in a bit."

"Deal." I smiled at her.

We finished our surprisingly delectable roses and walked side by side to the ongoing festival performances.

While Zoe talked about how she ran into Iris and Atlas over by the food, I spun around to look back at that alley between those colorful striped booths. It was a moment I would never forget. I was still processing what exactly had happened. But I had to believe what I had seen. What choice did I have? I had witnessed it—saw it with my own two eyes!

"So, uhhh ..." I started, squeezing myself back into the conversation. "Where are we off to, exactly?"

Zoe sprang her arms out in front of her and waved them across the air like she was making some kind of grand reveal. "Maggie and Malice, the Dynamic Dragon Duo!" she announced like an emcee.

"The who and the who are doing what now?" I giggled at her ridiculousness.

"You heard me, sister. I'm just reading what's on their banner."

Zoe pointed ahead to a brightly lit banner floating above a massive crowd of people: *Maggie and Malice, the Dynamic Dragon Duo*. It was written in calligraphy, and I could tell this show was more impressive and elaborate than the prior others.

"Well, okay, then."

Maggie, whose presence was like Ivan the sword swallower, but more classy in the approach, stood atop a big brown boulder and commanded the crowd. Her Viking attire matched the thick saddle on the dragon's back. With fur-lined boots, winter robes, and hair as white as snow, she was like a character from Norse mythology. With her strong voice and the confident manner to fit it, Maggie caught my attention instantly and pulled me into the crowd among the others.

That is when I realized that the "stage" Maggie had created for her and the dragon was actually a sunken crater in the middle of the festival, like something a small meteor would leave behind. While we watched from above, Maggie gave a breakdown of her show and allowed us to enter her domain.

"What a strong, brilliant woman," I whispered to myself, shockingly louder than I liked.

"Agreed," Zoe muttered, awestruck as well.

"Welcome, friends, to the DRAGON DOME!" she shouted, using her wand to elevate the boom in her voice, like Jax had for the Pit Ceremony.

Cheering ensued, with clapping and hollering throughout the crowd of eager students. There must have been two or three hundred gathered here now.

Vacant white eyes sat deep within the dragon's thorny skull. Jagged scales ran down its back like little mountain peaks that gave Malice his terrifying appearance. His snout was long and sharp, and dirty teeth poked out the sides of his jaw line. Moss green in color, Malice darted his head around at the crowd, sneering and snarling with flared nostrils. I thought I heard him laugh as Maggie introduced the show.

Digging his sharp talons into the stone, Malice then climbed to the top of the boulder. Pieces of debris fell as it methodically reached the small summit next to Maggie. The green dragon tilted its head to the sky and held his mouth open. She began clapping, slow and rhythmic, while directing the crowd to follow her pattern. The vigilant mages listened and joined her.

"I don't think they're excited, Malice!" she yelled, whispering her words into the dragon's narrow ear. "I can hardly hear you! Louder! Malice demands more enthusiasm!"

An enormous roar erupted from the crowd as we gathered tightly on the rim above their crater arena. Maggie's words sparked audible pandemonium.

"THAT'S BETTER! YEAH!" she shouted hoarsely.

Malice agreed and rewarded our excitement. With timed releases, he let out quick bursts of fire for each rhythmic clap. I was enthralled by their partnership: an unfazed tamer standing next to a fire-breathing dragon who was launching a scorching blaze just inches from her hair.

Though harder to hear, Maggie officially started the show and waved Malice down so she could ride atop his back.

"Time to start, buddy! Let's give these lovely people a show that'll stay with them forever. What do ya think?"

The dragon grunted and bowed his head to the crowd.

Then ... they took off!

Malice launched the duo off his perch. As his wings flapped with palpable gusts of wind, they took to the skies and soared above the viewers just high enough where Malice's claws nearly scraped across people's heads. Zoe and I fell silent, locked onto his gaze. I watched Maggie stand fully upright on his back while they flew.

After several minutes of diving to the ground, narrowly missing their deaths, along with graceful gliding above the arena and tight twists in the night sky, Maggie and Malice settled themselves back on the boulder. Nimble like a butterfly, the dragon gripped the stone with his talons and eased his chest down to let Maggie out of the saddle. She petted him on his jagged skull, tossed a full steak to him from her waist pouch, and pulled out her wand.

Through labored breathing and sweat, she addressed the crowd. "Alright! What did we think of that?" Faint laughter and long exhales slipped into her amplified wand.

Another huge uproar answered her question. Zoe and me included.

"Excellent, excellent! Now for the next part of the show. Malice and I are going to perform some tricks for you all. We hope you like it!"

Maggie clapped to herself before running out of sight, deeper into the crater.

"Pretty impressive," I murmured to Zoe.

"Yeah! All of it!" she replied absentmindedly.

"I mean that she's a mage but doesn't use magic for the actual act. That's cool! Well ... it's cool to me, at least."

Sadly, I could tell that Zoe was barely listening to me as she shifted her head around to catch a glimpse of Maggie's next move. Only a couple seconds passed before we saw her again. Nothing had changed, because she simply grabbed more meat for Malice.

Once she came fully into view, Maggie called to her dragon and pointed for him to stand on the highest boulder. She, meanwhile, walked around in a circle as she spoke.

"Okay, bud, show off your features for the people!" Maggie announced, waving a hand as the dragon lifted up on his hind legs. "Now, who here has ever seen a dragon in real life? Raise your hand!"

A few arms shot into the air. Not many, though.

"Okay, just a few." Maggie chuckled casually. She pointed to different aspects of Malice's body as she talked, giving her audience a full breakdown of these stunning creatures.

"His feet are fitted with four toes and dangerously sharp talons. One slice from these bad boys could land you an unscheduled appointment in your school's infirmary. Not a fun time."

Her attention moved to the tail. "Thick and sturdy like a rhinoceros, Malice's tail is strong enough to destroy one of those dorm buildings with a single flick. He won't do it—but he could. Finally get Jax to upgrade those cheap rooms, am I right?"

Small chuckles came from the loosened-up crowd.

"His wings!" Maggie shouted, spinning around the dragon and instructing him to outstretch his wings like a stork. "Beautiful and scaly, just like the rest of his body. Their color and texture help to camouflage him once he's tucked inside. He moves through the skies with ease like a hot knife through butter. His wings can create gusts with the strength of forty elephants!"

"Wow!" exclaimed some unfamiliar voices nearby.

"Finally ... Malice is equipped with a dangerous jaw, packing razor-sharp teeth inside. Trust me: You do not want to be on the receiving end of these things during a food scarce."

Maggie tilted Malice's head down toward the ground and lifted up the dragon's lips to show the crowd. Oohs and ahhs escalated in a chorus of awe.

"Thank you, buddy," she said, releasing his mouth and tossing two steaks down his throat.

"Now ..." she began, more stiff and serious than before. "I have worked with Malice for nearly fifteen years. Known him since he was just an egg." Malice stood proud, glaring around at the crowd at eye level. Then, our eyes met. "Now, even though I have been with this dragon for a long time, things can happen. He is, after all, a wild animal at heart. So, expect the unexpected. And above all else ... please be careful and stay away from the edge."

Malice left the stone by Maggie. Below our feet, the dragon slowly began to trace the perimeter of the crater arena. He was careful with each step, allowing the dirt to crunch subtly under his talons. The part that gave me goose bumps was Malice's expression, which was cold and focused as he paced in slow motion.

"Dragons are beautiful and resilient creatures. Malice is a dragon in every department, from hunting prey like a jaguar to traversing the skies like a falcon. So, I must be careful and methodical with everything I do. One small slip, and I'm his next meal."

The crowd let out a collective gasp.

"It's no problem, though. Not that often, at least. BECAUSE ... Malice and I have worked together for many years. We have full faith in each other. We've done this show a trillion times."

Malice stopped dead in his tracks. He was directly beneath me, but his attention was narrowed on something else.

"For our next act, my dragon and I ... will ..."

Maggie quieted instantly when she recognized the dragon's intent. The viewers and I fell silent, too, mutually catching our breath. Malice moved stealthily to the center of the sunken arena.

Directly across from me was a brutish boy wearing a tight purple suit with his mask strapped on backwards. Talking to the other guys near him, he was clearly not paying the slightest attention to the dragon or the show. Rolling his eyes, they finally locked onto Malice, who climbed gently to the highest rock.

"Young man ..." Maggie instructed. She followed close to the left of the dragon. "Stay very still. Everything is going to be fine."

The air went still. Snow flurries started to fall.

"Do not move. I will handle this. I know how to deal with situations like this."

Malice inched closer to the boy. Maggie inched closer to Malice.

The boy's smug face vanished, and he appeared frozen and startled, filled with fear and panic.

"Don't ... move ..." Maggie said, stepping near Malice's left wing without him realizing it.

Malice's front claw clenched onto the wall of the crater arena, and his snout pushed towards the audience. Maggie came to the same rock as the dragon and raised her hand to his back.

Suddenly, Malice opened his jagged jaws and lunged at the boy. Maggie leapt off with a single foot and flung herself into the dragon's open jaws. With her feet on Malice's tongue and her hands pressed to the roof of its mouth, the veins in her muscles popped out. The pressure of Malice pushed down on Maggie as she tried to keep his mouth open. Any slight slip would kill her. No one made a sound.

The dragon forced its jaws closed. She winced and attempted to pry them back open. Trapped in a horrifying tug-of-war, one of the two was bound to give. But who? We watched intensely, wishing we could assist her.

Struggling, the dragon tamer finally managed to push Malice's forceful jaws and jump out of their grasp. Breathing heavily, Maggie spun to face her dragon and yelled for his attention.

"MALICE! MALICE!" she cried. "Settle yourself! Come down from there! Now!"

The dragon didn't budge. It's cold white eyes stayed on the purple-suited boy, whose chest pulsed up and down rapidly in dread.

We all feared for him, too.

"Malice! This is Maggie. You know me. Do not do this. Come down from there!"

Begrudgingly, he did. He pulled his talons out from the wall and retreated from the boulder as rubble tumbled deep into the crater. Malice looked cold and unafraid. He listened to Maggie, but it was clear that he still felt the strength in his chest to finish the job. Was Maggie now on the menu? She held out her hand and moved towards him again, stone crunching under her boots. Malice flared his nostrils.

"Listen to me, Malice. You don't want to do this. It's me. It's Maggie."

The dragon tucked its wings back and angrily lowered its head to the ground, though his eyes, undaunted and unblinking, stayed upon Maggie. Keeping her eyes on him, too, Maggie reached for a steak in her leather pouch and brought it out with her other hand. Edging it towards Malice's mouth, from which she'd just barely escaped, she moved closer to the massive green beast. He took the meat with a quick snap of his jaws and pulled away from her attention to eat it.

The audience and Maggie let out a joint sigh of relief as she faked a smile and looked up to address us. She was visibly scared. This had not been part of an act.

"Everything's fine. Is everyone alright?" she asked, sure to greet everyone's anxious eyes. Then she turned to the boy who had nearly been Malice's dinner. "You alright, son?"

He nodded, but did not speak. His focus was on the dragon devouring its steak.

"Good. Now …" Maggie started once more, attempting to calm herself and the crowd. "Like I said, expect the unexpected. While Malice and I have worked together for years, anything can happen. You do need to be quick on your feet … but patient. These dragons are passionate and determined creatures. One can only subdue so much of them before natural instinct takes over."

No one clapped or moved. We watched, frozen, as the flurries drifted onto the brown stone of her arena. White flakes dusted the campus behind it.

"I think that'll do it for this performance. I truly am sorry for the scare, but everything is fine—I promise. I do hope you enjoyed the rest of our show, however, and will take that part away from all this. So, thank you, and be safe. Have fun tonight, everyone."

Timid, staggered clapping came from the uneasy audience. Zoe and I clapped out of awkwardness, I think.

The masses of people dispersed in various directions away from the arena.

Zoe fixed her dress while we stayed behind, listening to the groups of gossiping mages. Most were clearly upset and confused by the whole event. They were harsh in their review of Maggie and Malice's show. I felt bad for the tamer and her dragon. An unforeseen ending to the show had tarnished the rest of its beauty and splendor.

"That moment with Malice at the end ... Makes you kinda worry and wonder about Sonnet, doesn't it?" Zoe asked, zoning out at the dragon settling back into its previous demeanor.

"For sure," I replied in blind agreement while still watching them, too.

Holy crap! I thought to myself. *That could have gone horribly wrong. Almost murder! That poor boy was almost a delicious snack for a dragon! Like ... what?! Holy crap. Holy crap ...*

Only Zoe and I remained now. I didn't want to leave, because a part of me wanted to be Maggie so badly. Fearless and powerful, she captivated the audience and kept the dragon at bay at the same time. One wrong move, and she was dead. But she knew that and jumped into Malice's jaws at full strength anyway.

Now, since the show had ended and the audience had disappeared, Maggie calmed down her dragon and sat coolly next to him like an owner with their dog. They clearly had a mutual respect and understanding for one another, despite their instincts. That right there was what I wanted for Sonnet and me: the powerful, unbreakable bond between girl and beast.

"Time to head to the ball, I think. Gotta be getting close," Zoe said, tearing her gaze away and turning to face the festival behind us. She nodded and ushered for me to follow. "Shall we?"

"Yeah ... I guess so." I gulped.

Zoe started walking before I fully committed to joining her. While my feet propelled me forward, my mind was completely elsewhere. It bounced from the random pair vaporizing behind the game booths to the bloodbath we had almost witnessed to my anxiety over the approaching masquerade. I started to walk slower without realizing it and soon fell behind Zoe, who trudged on as the orchestra's music grew loud and clear.

I sped to catch up to her, but someone bumped into me.

"Sorry, sorry ... I should really watch where I'm going ..." I stammered.

Similar to the old woman, I was embarrassed to be so clumsy. But, as if I were remembering a smell from my childhood, the stranger's energy impacted me. I had no idea why, but I was not afraid of her. The woman did not feel like a stranger, and it didn't feel like we'd bumped into each other on accident. She was tall, probably

5'10" or 5'11". She wore a flattering royal-blue halter dress, slightly darker than Zoe's gown. The bottom was decorated with silver astral illustrations of moons, suns, and stars. A mesh veil came off the shoulders and flowed to the ground, revealing her elegant, heeled gladiator sandals. I couldn't make out much of her face behind a brilliant sun-and-moon mask of alternating blues and golds.

"Hello, stranger." The voice was delicate but deliberate.

"Hello ...," I answered cautiously, fixing my dress.

"It's me, Kiku. It's Niko."

"No, no, no. No! This isn't real. It ... it can't be. You left ... This is not ..." I pushed the words out, but my emotions couldn't piece any of them together. If it was truly Niko, it had been seven years since we last saw each other! That is simply impossible. No way. What logical, believable reason would my older sister have for being at the College of Adarius? Her bumping into me during a masquerade ball at a magical school in a foreign place is one of the most insane things to happen in my life. It currently ranks at the top of that list.

"It's Niko. I know you haven't seen me in years, but it's really me. I promise." Niko walked towards me and stopped by my side. She softly rested her hand on my shoulder and whispered. I gazed up at her kind eyes peeking through the cosmic mask. "I've missed you, Kiku, and I want to talk to you. We have lots to catch up on."

Then, as quickly as my estranged sister strode into my life, Niko walked away into the crowd and left me flabbergasted like someone who had sworn they just saw a ghost.

KAMAUL V

"You look like the reincarnation of Ra. A young Adonis!" I yelled, flexing at my reflection enough to stretch the seams of my undershirt slightly. "You are strong! Sexy! Handsome! And you're killin' it in that cherry-red suit with the matte black shirt and tie. Black handkerchief, too. C'mon, dude! You look fuckin' incredible!"

Dipping my hands under the running water, I splashed some on my face and tried to scrub the wine stains off my lips. I reached for my mask and slipped the band around my wrist. It was a bronze *bauta* mask depicting Pegasus, with golden accenting the edges. But trust me, it looked much more manly than I'm making it out to be. It was a gift from Nero—so if I got any weird looks, they were *his* fault.

"Every girl wants you, and every guy wants to be you, man. You're the star of The Pit. Now get back out there!" I announced to the empty bathroom, where my voice echoed like it was an empty throne room. Fixing my cuffs, I slapped the pity from my face.

"Here, man," Dahir added quietly, handing me a stack of paper towels. Admittedly, I had forgotten he was in here with me. I held my hands straight out and waited for him to dry them, which he did with a happy scowl.

"Have I had too much to drink?" I asked as he threw away the dampened rags.

"Haven't we all?" He laughed awkwardly, eyes wide with surprise.

"No, really! Must've been a lot, 'cause I never give myself a pep talk. Ever! I crush it. Like, every ... single ... day. But seriously, have I had a lot? Be honest," I demanded, admiring my jawline in the mirror.

"No more than I have!" Dahir shouted, raising his hand for a high five.

"That's the spirit! Time to rejoin the party!"

"Nailed it!" he exclaimed, smacking his own hand.

Nearly ripping the metal handle off the door, I swung out of the bathroom and embraced the outside world—and it smelled worse than a sweaty men's sauna. I suddenly missed the inviting aroma of teakwood and vanilla from the void-themed lavatory.

You're losin' it, Kamaul! I yelled at my inner consciousness. *You're talking to yourself like a pansy, and ... really? Hung up on the smells of a restroom? Seriously? Get a hold of yourself, dude!*

"So, that puppet show, huh?" Dahir huffed, putting his arm around my shoulder.

"What?" I muttered before realizing what he was talking about and laughing about it. "I mean, yeah, it was pretty cool—and I personally thought it was funny. Figures that they'd mock it, being that they aren't in it!"

"Yeah, totally," he agreed.

"Hey, Kamaul!" shouted Bosamma, racing towards us. "We're roo—rooting for you, man! You're gonna ... *hic* ... you're gonna win this thing ... *hic* ... EASY!" His wobbly hand shot into the air to whack mine before it fell down to hold his crotch. Belching and blinking blearily, he pushed through the door and disappeared inside.

"Thought he hated you?" Dahir interjected as we squeezed between a group of students.

"Hey, what can I say?" I tossed back with a bombastic smile. "The Pit changes people, man. Maybe he's realizing I'm our element's best chance at winning the thing. And let's face it ..." I wrapped my arms around him and massaged his shoulders while hollering like a barbarian over his head. "HE'S RIIIIIIGHT!"

Soon, we reentered the Festival of the Elements. From the dancing girls in colorful dresses to the wild performances echoing beyond the crowds, it was exactly my type of event. The atmosphere was alive! The smells weren't ideal, but the rest of it was perfect. From the middle of this scene, I was witnessing a different side of the college—the exact "party for the ages" that I'd been preaching about.

"You heard anything about that siren show yet?" I asked Dahir while distracted by a gorgeous girl wearing a white pencil skirt.

"Absolutely!" He chuckled, acting like a really bad hypnotist. "Heard it messes with your mind! Like, seeing and hearing things. Wild stuff, man. Why? You wanna go?"

"Why would I bring it up if I didn't?" I answered, catching the eye of Heather and Caroline.

We started towards two girls, who were casually walking with cupcakes in hand. Heather was a cute poison mage who had seen plenty of my face in the infirmary over the last few days. Clearly, I needed to scrub the bruised-and-battered image of me out of her mind. Caroline, on the other hand, I knew very little about, other than that she had a bubbly personality and worked as Phoebe's sidekick for new recruits to the college.

"Just hush and let me handle this, okay?" I insisted to Dahir, seeing the timid fear he got in his eyes whenever pretty girls were near.

"Hey, ladies!" I exclaimed, announcing our presence and holding my hands out for applause. They did not oblige. They did, however, laugh and giggle as I flung one arm around each girl and escorted them towards the siren show with Dahir and me.

"Cupcake, huh? Looks delicious," I said to Caroline.

"Oh, it is!" She smiled at me and took a small bite. "You want a bite?"

"Of course!" I answered, biting a piece next to hers and winking as she watched.

"So, where are you taking us, Kamaul?" Heather laughed nervously.

"Well, Nurse Heather, I am hoping you lovely ladies will accompany my friend and me to the siren show."

"Sure!" Caroline interjected before Heather could answer.

"Great." I smiled, looking between the two girls and nudging Dahir.

"Hey, Dahir," Heather said, realizing Dahir was walking next to her.

"Hi," he said quickly. His eyes never met hers; instead, they darted across the festival at anything else.

The four of us strolled past the dragon show and carnival games.

"*Pssst*, Kamaul," Dahir whispered behind the girls. "Thought you wanted to go back to the party?"

"I do! But ... I need to take a break from the drinking and get some fresh air. Too much wine for me, and ... well ... you know how I get when I'm drunk," I answered, conveying my emotions with sharp eyes and gritted teeth.

"Riiiiiight ..." Dahir nodded, turning to face forward.

"Focus, Dahir!" I grunted. "Now ... please get us two waters."

"Yes, of course. No problem," Dahir replied, nodding vigorously.

"Thanks," I sighed, pointing him in the correct direction.

Before he left, he snuck over to my side and whispered quietly in my left ear. "Hey ... uhhh... Hey, man, I hate doing this, I feel so awkward asking this, but—"

"Dahir! Ask me, already!" I grunted, freaking out the girls next to us.

"Can I have some gold for the water?" he said, way above the appropriate whispered tone.

"Whoa, man," I grumbled. "But yeah. Yeah, here, have some."

I reached into my pocket, plopped seven coins in his hands, and sent him off towards the food booths. I heard a muffled "Thanks, Kamaul" before he stumbled on the dirt.

Along with Caroline and Heather, I slowly came closer to the siren's crowd. Scattered students (mostly men) were gazing intently at a giant tank of water ahead. In it, I saw a pair of splashing and diving beautiful women in bikini tops; one had black hair and the other blonde. They captivated the crowd with their movements. With eyes nearly bugging out of their skulls, every guy had their gaze locked on these broads as if nothing else existed. The sides of the glass box were so cloudy, though, that nothing below the girls' waists was visible.

As I blindly continued towards the tank, I heard the most exquisite sound. The two women were humming the sweetest tune. The closer I moved to them, the clearer and more intense it became. I was ... lost. Beside myself. My legs moved, but my mind wasn't telling them to. Shoving past other guys, I inched close enough to smell the aroma of dirty sea water.

"'Sup, Kamaul," Duke said, nudging me with his elbow, despite never engaging me with his eyes.

"What's up, Duke?" I answered, trying to punch him in the arm and missing horribly.

"Wanted to wish you luck, man. Aaron will be ... such an easy ... uhhh ... You know, these women have such beautiful voices. It's like the angels are speaking only to me ..."

Duke's eyes were bulging out of their sockets and appeared drier than the Sahara. He was whining about back pains and neck itches. Luckily, I felt none of those things, so I smiled on and listened to every word they sang.

"I have had many beers tonight ... but I now know true beauty. These women are stunning and ... have the voices to match." Duke laughed, forcing him and me closer to the sirens.

"They really do! I've had a questionable amount of wine—Dahir won't tell me how much—and even I know they sing beautifully. Like ... wow."

"Hey, Kamaul. Got those waters ... for ya," Dahir interjected, tapping me on the shoulder with a bottle.

"Yeah. Thanks, man," I answered, making kissy faces at the black-haired woman.

"Seems ..." Dahir started uncertainly. "Seems funny to drink water next to a huge tank of it, but ..."

"Yeah, I ... guess it does ..." I muttered thoughtlessly.

"Wow, these women, man! They're ... they're somethin' else, huh?" Duke added.

"Yes, they are," Dahir and I responded in unison.

I felt my eyes growing in size now, too. Veins in my body started to pound, like a painful poison was cruising through my bloodstream. My muscles ached. My bones felt sore. Unexpectedly, I felt the same sensation of agonizing discomfort that Duke had mentioned. I felt it all—but I didn't care. I was so laser-focused on the women swimming in the tank that I honestly did not care. I also did not care anymore about how much wine I may or may not have had up to this point.

Along with dozens of other wide-eyed men, Duke, Dahir, and I came within splashing distance of the tank. In fact, at this point, there were no girls nearby—not a single one.

"Caroline and Heather still here?" I muttered with a smile at Dahir.

"Nope," he answered bluntly. "Said something about terrible music and not getting it? I don't know. They're gone, man. Don't worry. We have much prettier ladies in our presence."

"Right, right. Well, that's fine ..." I mumbled.

"Hello, boys," the two women said seductively, ushering the three of us closer to their tank. Their speaking voices were just as beautiful as their singing was. It was intoxicating.

"Hi there ... Hey. How's it goin'?" I asked, flexing my eyebrows, then my calves, then my biceps.

"Hello, ladies!" Dahir shouted uncertainly.

"Don't blow this!" I hissed at him through gritted teeth.

"You like what you see?" the black-haired women asked, winking at Duke.

"Ye—yes! Yeah! You b-bet I do," he stammered, breaking character with a voice reminiscent of a nerdy prepubescent boy.

"Then come closer, boys. What are you afraid of?" the pair of women whispered gently. "We don't bite."

"Okay," we all said simultaneously.

Our noses were pressed against the glass as we peered up eagerly at the girls. Their lovely hair cascaded down the sides of the glass. The blonde woman leaned on the rim and held her face with soft, delicate hands. She was looking at me, too—but only at me! Dahir and Duke thought it was at them, but I knew who her sweet pupils were laying into.

"We're at a school of magic, aren't we? Wanna see a magic trick?" said one of them.

Both girls giggled.

"Sure." Duke nodded.

"Okay. Watch the water, boys. Keep your eyes under the surface."

"Yeah, you got it, ladies," I added, bobbing my head up and down mindlessly.

"Great. Hang tight." The blonde girl winked at me.

"She winked at me, man!" Dahir exclaimed, hitting me in the arm.

"Not to you! That one was for *me*." I smiled, winking back at her as she disappeared under the water.

"Doubt it. That one was directed at me, fellas," Duke interjected, pointing finger guns at us.

We waited, staring keenly at the cloudy tank. I still could not see anything. The smell of ocean water was very strong, like a sunken ship desecrated by barnacles and algae. But then, just as the hum of their song was dying out above us, webbed fingers wiped away the grime. Fully able to see the water now, I saw that it was deep teal and somehow lit from underneath, like a reverse sunset.

"Where ... where they'd go?!" Dahir stammered, voice in a panic.

"I don't know!" Duke screamed, immediately pressing his face back against the glass.

But it was at this moment that we found out the hard way what sirens were.

The pair of lovely singing voices became nothing but loud, inaudible noise. Their wavy hair vanished, replaced by sharp tentacles sticking out from their heads. Their gorgeous, fit figures in colorful swimsuit tops transformed into ugly, barracuda-like creatures. They were swimming towards us, *very* fast. Gross blackish scales lined their bodies. Disgusting jagged teeth jutted above their underbites.

"AAAH! What the—?!" Dahir and I screamed, staggering backwards and nearly falling over.

"Uhhh, Kamaul!" Dahir shouted. "We gotta go! I suddenly have the urge to guzzle wine straight from the bottle!"

"No, no, no, no, no!" Duke hollered, violently rubbing the sight from his eyes. He spun around and dashed away, toppling over two other guys.

"Yup. Couldn't agree more! Duke, it was great seeing you. But I have a date with alcohol that I am terribly late for. Later, man!" I shouted over my shoulder, not bothering to face him as I spoke.

Dahir and I sprinted away from the siren tank while watching the other foolish, hopeful men waltz closer to it.

"They are so doomed." I laughed in Dahir's ear and propelled my body away from the scene.

"Should we tell 'em, then?" he answered between breaths.

"NO!" I cackled like a hyena. "*So* much more fun if we don't. Let 'em find out for themselves. We'll laugh about this later. Trust me."

"If you say so." He giggled.

We arrived at the ballroom and wiped the horrified looks off our faces. Dahir slapped me in the face, and I slapped him back. Shaking the pain away, we laughed at the wild moment and acted completely casual. As the music carried us inside, Dahir and I fixed each other's suits and raced to see who could drink their bottle of water faster, which was obviously me.

"Kamaul! The mask, please. Put it on!" Jax demanded from a dark corner.

"Yes, sir. Right away, sir," I mocked, holding the mask to my face, but not lacing it around my head.

"I mean it, Kamaul!" Jax shouted again, louder the second time.

"Yeah, yeah, yeah," I muttered, flinging my hands in the air.

"Drink number five, Kamaul!" Atlas exclaimed, appearing out of nowhere with a lovely glass of red wine.

"Number five!" Dahir and I shouted in unison, sharing a eureka moment that Atlas clearly did not understand.

"Yeah. Now, c'mon. Your royal subjects are awaiting your return, my king."

"Splendid, Atlas." I nodded, finishing the glass in a single swig before shipping the evolution mage to fetch another.

I wrapped my arm around Dahir and walked around the edge of the dance floor. Every guy and girl looked silly with their obnoxious masks covering their faces. Slow dancers, way-too-fast dancers, and bad dancers swayed and bounced under the hanging golden lights. Marble columns that matched the solid white floors underneath the flowing gowns rose to the ceiling. Black drapes hung from the balcony between the pillars, hiding the tabled sections from the Masquerade Ball. The event was grand and elegant, with orchestra music softly playing in the background. A gold-painted ceiling, candelabras, and ornate railings accented the features of the huge ballroom wonderfully. And ...

Wait—what am I saying?

Yeah, in all honesty, I really didn't care about how the ballroom looked, but there it was. It looked great. Very gold, though.

The *unique* orchestra members, however, were the actual sight to see. The only bronze thing in the entire room, the ten statues were playing classical tunes. These statues, animated by magic or something, swayed on stage with their instruments, many of which I had never seen or heard of. The music was charming, but admittedly not my style. So, while the hundreds of students strolled hand in hand with one another, I ignored their nauseating closeness and headed for *my* table of thirsty patrons.

"The slow dancing is forcing the wine back up my throat—and I don't even have to vomit. Get me to my people, please," I passive-aggressively whispered in Dahir's ear.

"Right away, Your Highness," he said, forcing me in the direction I was already going. Dahir and I are friends and all, but, believe me, I smacked his hand quickly away from my waist.

We rejoined my party in the corner. It was a pretty interesting cast of characters, too. There was Moose, a strange boy from Canada, sipping glasses of mead like it was water while draping his arms over our black velvet sofa. Reagan, whom I'd just met today, helped herself to a decanter of cheap chardonnay. After leaving my side, Dahir immediately pressed himself against Mina and began chatting her ear off. Once we're around her, he is totally useless.

Atlas swung in and handed me a glass of plum wine on his way over to Bosamma.

"Thanks, man," I said, winking past him at Caroline, who was approaching out of the blue.

"We got the ... see-rah? Sierra? The Sri Lanka? I don't know, Kamaul, but we got you the fancy Egyptian wine, like you asked!" Samara and Gillian shouted together.

"Wonderful, ladies. Add it to the table," I answered, shooing them in that direction.

"You got it." Samara giggled, heading over to gossip with Kyang and Reagan.

Taking a sip from my glass, I welcomed Caroline to my group of supporters and waved my hands to get their attention. Soon, I had all eyes on me. I needed her to see the proper kingly side of Kamaul Metjen. After all, it was my better half.

"Who's gonna win The Pit this year, folks?!" I yelled to the group of nearly ten people.

"Kamaul!"

"You're the man!"

"Kamaul, king of the fire element!"

Various glorious answers rang in my ears.

"Wow, Kamaul, I'm impressed." Caroline smiled.

"Please, guys. All this commotion ... is not necessary," I groaned, secretly gesturing behind my back to encourage them.

"Very funny. I already know you're gonna win." She winked, ignoring the group and focusing on me. "I'm here, aren't I?"

I smiled at her with my pearly whites and finished my glass of wine.

What drink number was that, Kamaul? Are you keeping track? Dahir won't, if he's got googly eyes for Mina all night.

"You hear that?" I stammered, randomly reaching for her shoulder in a quick panic.

"Kamaul? I heard nothing. Maybe it was the music? I wish the orchestra would actually move onto something other than slow jams!" Caroline said, darting her eyes between my face and the strutting bronze statues.

"Yeah. Never mind then."

"So, are you worried about The Pit at all?" she asked sweetly before leaning on the velvet sofa.

"Not ... *hic* ... not even slightly. The Pit should be the one worried about *me*!" I shouted ineptly, not loving any of the words or sounds that emitted from my mouth.

Uh-oh, I thought. *Well, no worries—that was only drink number five. Keep it together.*

"How's working with Phoebe going? She can be a ... a real handful, I would imagine? Lotta work with those novice mages, huh?" I asked, gently combing her bleach blonde hair with my hand.

With a girly giggle, Caroline replied, "She can be a lot to deal with sometimes. But I love her. And the new recruits? Yeah, they can be a challenge, too. It's alright, though. Teamwork makes the dream work!"

"Is it hot in here, or is it just me?" I said, wafting air at my face.

"It is a little warm, yeah," Caroline answered. She was trying (yet failing) not to admire my arm muscles.

Dipping my shoulder, I started sliding off my scarlet sport coat but pretended to struggle.

"Can you ... uh ... gimme a hand?" I chuckled.

"Absolutely."

Caroline helped with my left sleeve, hugging tight to my back and holding the jacket as it came fully off.

"Thanks," I said.

As I laid my suit jacket on the sofa, she instantly popped up. Our faces nearly touched, her soft hands accidentally brushing my chin as she helped unwrap the tie around my neck. I flexed my biceps when she insisted that I remove the black vest next. I didn't care, because the humidity in the ballroom was insisting that I do that anyway. With just the matte black undershirt left, I loosened the two topmost buttons.

"Care to ... get 'nother drink with me?" I asked, tilting my head at the bar.

"I would love to." Caroline smiled.

"Dahir? Hey, you're in charge of my table while I'm gone. Take care of it, and make sure no one overstays their welcome!" I shouted to him, waving my hand to get his attention and realizing that he was not hearing a word I said.

Useless. Exactly what I feared.

Caroline and I walked past the dance floor and soon came to a pair of enormous double doors. Standing on either side were two equally brutish men. They lifted their wands to each of us and asked for our index fingers. After scanning our fingerprints, the men nodded to Caroline and me and allowed us in.

Approaching the concealed bar area, I pulled out a stool for her and slid it back in place after she sat down. A stranger tried to squeeze in behind me before I grabbed him by his collar and demanded that he do the same for my seat.

"Thank you, kind citizen," I grunted, with discouraged eyes and flared nostrils. Once Caroline was distracted by the bartender, I yanked him close to me and whisper-shouted in his ear. "You should have pulled back my seat out of pure decency. Instead, I had to force your hand because your moronic brain didn't realize it was in the presence of a king. When I win The Pit, they'll engrave my name in stone and in history. No one will remember yours until it's on a gravestone. Now get lost."

The frightened teen's legs barely kept him upright as he scampered out of sight.

I returned to the cute astral mage and took a seat next to her. The bartender slung tiny napkins in front of us and brought out a tall hourglass-shaped bottle.

"Here you are, miss," he said firmly. "The Glauser, as requested."

"Glauser? What ... what's that?"

"It's a fancy liquor from Switzerland. It's strong and has a lemony flavor. Super good. I got us two shot glasses to try it."

"Switzerland, huh? Are you from there?"

"I am, yeah." She giggled, twirling the napkin in a circle. "What? Did the bleach-blonde hair, pale skin, and blue eyes not give it away?"

"Honestly, I know nothing about Switzerland ... or the ... *hic* ... or Swiss women."

"Lucky for you, I can tell you anything you wanna know," Caroline said, pouring the Glauser into the two shot glasses.

"What's this stuff again?"

"Don't worry about it. Cheers!" Caroline said as we raised our glasses, interlocked our arms, and downed the lemon-flavored bitterness.

Wow. That was putrid.

"Wow. That was delicious! Yeah! Just phenomenal ... err ... tremendous. I want ..." I felt my stomach churning beneath the lies. "I want another ...?"

"Oh, yeah?" Caroline laughed, seeing right through my lies. "Another one?"

She reached for the bottle again. I shot my hand out to stop her, touching her fingers.

"Yeah, no. Actually ..." I started before being distracted by a black-haired woman sitting at the far end of the bar. We never made eye contact, as her gaze was focused on the mead swirling in her glass. "Actually ... uhhh ... I'm good. That was *so* good that I want to save it for laterrrrrr ..."

"Unconvincing and distracted." Caroline chuckled lightly. "Key symptoms of Glauser. So, a break between shots is probably a great idea."

"Right. Yes, thanks."

I felt flustered and anxious suddenly. I looked at Caroline's face, sweet and kind. I was trying to keep my eyes focused on her, but they flickered between her and the other girl. Why, though? I had no idea. She looked pretty, sporting a purple silk dress and a shiny female version of my *bauta* mask. Barely able to see the rest of her face, I was entranced, like I was back at the siren tank. Was she a siren? Was this siren disguised as a student at the college?

Then, sadness.

Yup. My eyes became droopy, and my cheeks felt puffy, like I was going to cry. Not about anything in particular, but something came over me and faded the glory from my eyes. I looked firmly now at Caroline, whose reflection conveyed a lot of concern.

"Kamaul? Everything alright?" she asked, placing a hand kindly on my shoulder.

"Me? Yeah ... yeah. Totally fine! Yes!" I yelled weakly, trying to shake the look from my face.

"You sure?" she whispered. "You look pale."

"I do? Really? Wow, that's not like me. I ... uhhh ... I'm from Egypt! So, my skin should be the opposite of pale."

"Let's get you some water, okay? Hey, bartender, can I get two waters here? Thank you," Caroline called, holding up a finger to get the attention of the man in suspenders.

My gaze was narrowed on the other girl until Caroline ordered the water. Once my eyes fell back to her, I felt dizzy. Only slightly, though ... I thought? I wasn't a hundred percent sure.

"Thank you. Yes, water would be great." I smiled, feeling my eyelids begin to sag.

When my focus returned to the *bauta* mask girl, she was gone—vanished. The seat was empty. Caroline and I remained the only ones at the bar.

"Did you see that girl over there?" I asked, spinning her around to face the other end of the bar.

"What girl? Kamaul, who are you talking about?" Caroline asked, shaking her head.

"*Bauta* mask! Purple dress. Black hair! You didn't see her? Really?!" I exclaimed, probably gripping too tightly to her waist.

"Kamaul, you're scaring me. I saw nobody, I swear."

The bartender slid the glasses of water perfectly into our hands. Caroline took a few sips of hers and helped me do the same.

"I need to use the little girls' room. You gonna be alright here? Just for, like, a couple minutes?"

"Huh?!" I said, jumping in my seat after staring into the rippling water.

"Earth to Kamaul! You gonna be alright here by yourself for a couple minutes? I'll be back soon."

"Yes. Yeah. I'll be fine." I tried to sound encouraging.

Caroline kissed my cheek and stepped away towards the bathroom. I smiled at her as she walked off down the hallway. Once she was out of sight, I poured myself a second shot of Glauser and downed it immediately. No clue why I did it, because the horrific taste of lemons and apricots clotted my throat and sank unsettlingly into my stomach. Staring at the oddly shaped bottle, I took a huge gulp of water and tried to wash the taste off my tongue.

Why, Kamaul? Why would you do that? Glutton for punishment, suddenly? Yikes, I have had many a drink tonight. And ... we know what that leads to ...

Dipping my fingers in my water, I splashed my face, stretched my jaw, and shook the visible insanity from my current expression. I knew it probably did not work, but I had to try.

"Hey, barkeep," I hollered to the man pouring white wine into three chalices.

He ignored me and smiled to the girl who carried the drinks away.

"Barman!" I yelled again.

Nope. Still ignoring me.

"HEY! Suspenders! Wanna help an *important* patron, for a change?" I demand-ed, slamming my fist down on the counter.

"Easy, pal," the man grumbled, wiping his hands on a nasty rag. "I have customers other than you."

"See, that's where you're wrong. Their business doesn't matter. Mine does!"

"Oh, yeah? That true?" he added, walking towards me reluctantly. "What do you want?"

Not taking kindly to his tone, I kept my hand in a fist on the bar and answered sternly, "Do you know who I am ... Eugene?" My gaze dropped to his name tag and returned to his cold brown eyes.

"Yeah. Who cares?"

A blunt feeling of anger and paranoia tinkered inside my chest, like a jammed cog in the machine.

"If I were you, I would pick my alliances very carefully, pal," I growled.

"Got it." He nodded carelessly. "Now order something or leave my bar."

A peasant, Kamaul. Not worth your time.

"I need a glass of Shedeh. And for your tiny brain, that is an ancient Egyptian staple. Smells like pomegranates, but it isn't. More grape-flavored. A little salty. I can draw a picture for you, if that's any easier."

"I'll see what I have."

Suspenders left and checked his circular bar, looking for my wine. I doubt he really knew what I was talking about. A picture would probably have been helpful.

"Here," he said, sliding into view and setting a half-full glass in front of me.

"Thank you for your troubles, Eugene. You are such a wonderful, useful human being—the mortal all mortals should strive to be," I added sarcastically with a sinister grin.

"I liked the girl better," he mumbled, walking over to the sink to clean some dirty glasses.

"Don't care." I shrugged between sips of wine.

Then I heard someone sit down to my right.

"Feel better? Feel more relieved?" I laughed, excited to see Caroline's face.

After another gulp of the delicious liquid, I turned to face her.

"Not relieved at all, actually, Kamaul," replied a deep, haunting voice.

My body felt glued to the seat. My brain went dead, and my heart stood still. This was not Caroline. It was ... someone I hadn't seen in years. Someone who sounded like ...

No, Kamaul. Stop it! That's impossible. That person is dead ...

"You're not even going to address your own father, son?"

"Y-yes. Hi. Hello, Pharaoh," I stammered, trying to rub the boozy expression from my eyes and forcing a fake cordial smile.

I took a long inhale and finished my Shedeh before spinning on the stool to face him. My eyes saw it, but my brain couldn't believe it. The man who had made my life an endless routine of violence for years was now sitting at this bar, at The College of Adarius, no less—a place I knew he hadn't the slightest idea about. But you know what? None of this was real, so none of that mattered!

"You look different, son, and not for the better. Stressed. A little panicked. Maybe gained a little weight, too."

"How are you here? At my school? You should be ..." I cleared my throat.

"Dead? Is that right?" His voice sounded cautious yet stern, but his face was the exact depiction of disappointment.

I stiffened up, fixed my shirt by buttoning the two undone buttons, and drove the fear out of my eyes.

"You 'member the last time we saw each other?" I asked coldly.

The muscles in his face contorted, and he answered my question with contempt. "No. Refresh my memory, son. That day is a bit foggy for me."

With similar feelings in the pit of my stomach like I had that fateful day, my anger simmered as I spoke directly to him ... or to his ghost; I was honestly not quite sure.

Kamaul, this is why you stop at six drinks. SIX! Any more beyond that, and paranoia mixes your past and present to create living nightmares! You'll lose your mind!

"You called me into your throne room for a 'family meeting.' Remember that? You summoned me ... into that room ... to tell me that I was too hotheaded and ill-tempered to man the throne. 'Unqualified' was the word you used, I believe."

"Oh, those words I remember. Go on. I'm sure you could reiterate that day moment by moment, being that you are the lone survivor of it."

I fell silent. It felt like I was trapped in a memory, frozen and unable to move. It was like being trapped in my own mind. Was any of this real? No, that was impossible. I knew that! So, why was I even acknowledging his existence? This was stupid ...

"No. You know what? I hated you, Father—hated you as much as you disapproved of me becoming the pharaoh of Egypt. The throne room became a blazing inferno and trapped you inside. I'm *glad* you died in that room. Was making me fight my brothers just a demented game for your amusement? Is that it? Wow, because that ... is so ... funny!" I laughed passive-aggressively, clapping ironically for effect. "Well, we gave you quite a show, the three of us! But I am your eldest son, Father! The eldest! When you croaked, that throne of yours was mine. And you decided to take my birthright from me!"

"See that? See the vein popping out in your neck, and the one protruding from your forehead? That's your problem, Kamaul: your uncontrollable anger! About everything! Even all these years later, whether I'm in your life or not, you still cannot control it. You can't contain it. And you know it's the reason I'm dead."

My head flung around to see if anyone else was nearby.

"I am not the reason you're dead, Father! Get over it!" I shouted. "Your death was just as fair and equal as your sadistic games were. You knew who was going to assume your throne when you died, had it all planned out. I'm not dumb, Pharaoh! You took something from me and—and the gods took something from you. How's that for justice?"

His ghost-pale forehead now showed the same popping vein as mine. "You couldn't handle the pressure. Never could, and never will. You need to get over that. Lose the fake king persona and become your own person, not just an inferior copy of me."

"I feel bad for you, old man." I snickered. "I really do. You won't ... *hic* ... be alive to see me win The Pit. How does that feel, huh? Your highest regarded son, your pride and joy, your crown jewel! Whether you're a ghost or in true physical form ... you will not be alive to witness ... *hic* ... your eldest son's true glory... I don't need your pathetic kingdom or your throne room. I will take the leader role over this school and rebuild it in my own image, without anyone else's help!"

I smiled. With a droopy face and fading words, I glared at my father's vacant eyes.

Without warning, he launched from his barstool and wrapped his thick hands around my throat. Dropping us both to the floor, my father violently pinned me to the ground. His weight and pressure were choking me. It was becoming incredibly hard to breathe. Whether a very lucid dream or a haunting nightmare, my dead dad's hands were around my neck, cutting off my circulation, and cutting off ... logic ... anything ...

I was losing consciousness. While the wine and Glauser did not matter right now, they weren't helping either. This suddenly felt very scary ... and very real at the same time. Ooooh ... Yup. My father was trying to kill me.

"Kamaul."

The voice was foggy and dying after it slipped into my ears.

"Kamaul! Hey, man, it's alright!"

Was that my father? No, no, no way; this voice was too weak and feeble to be his. My father's voice usually echoed through a room like it was an empty cave and burrowed into your brain like a termite.

Then somebody slapped me!

I immediately came out of the trance and returned to reality. Still lying on the revolting floor, I wiped my eyes.

"Kamaul? Can you hear me, man? It's alright. It's Ankhor. It's Dahir," Dahir shouted, waving his hands over my face.

"Yes. Yeah. I'm fine. I just saw my ... Wait—who I was just talking to?"

"It's been me the whole time, Kamaul," Dahir said, equal parts curious and concerned. "You have been talking to me. Mina left to go to the bathroom and ran into Caroline, who told her that you didn't look so good when she left. Once Mina came back and told me, I ran over and sat next to you. We've been chatting about your past, and your—"

"Shut your mouth! I never talk about my past. That's how I know you're lyin'! What did I say?" I demanded, pushing myself back to my feet, dusting off the matte black shirt, and sitting on the stool. "Tell me what I said about my past, Dahir!"

I snapped my fingers to get the bartender's attention. I pointed to my glass and instructed that he get me another Shedeh. He groaned and gave me a dirty look.

"Nothing, man! Nothing! I swear," he said, innocently flinging his hands up. "You never say anything about it, so I try not to ask."

"Good. And you'd better be telling the truth. I'll know if you aren't."

"I am. I am, man! Don't worry! You were flailing on the floor and screaming in pain with your hands at your neck, like someone was strangling you."

"Never speak of this, or I will ruin your chances with Mina—I swear to you on that." I took a satisfying sip of Shedeh and sighed. "This conversation does not leave this bar. And ... and ... uh ..." I felt the sudden urge to puke, took a moment to stare at the mahogany-colored wine, and paused before I spoke again. "Nope. Vomit's gone. Nothing spewing out of this hole."

Dahir looked relieved, but he was pushing my wine away from me. He tried to keep my attention, clearly hoping the distraction of his laughter was working.

Hate to break it to ya, pal, but it isn't.

"Gimme my wine back, Dahir."

"Can't do that. You've hit your limit. You 'get paranoia and nightmares' after drink nine. Clearly, too, 'cause you were screaming like someone was strangling you! So, you, my king, are cut off. Hate to do it, but I have to. Your rules, not mine."

"My wine. Give it back."

"Nope."

"Gimme!"

"No, sir."

"Fine! But if you're just yelling at me because you wanna finish it yourself, you'd better do it with a smile! Shedeh is a very expensive and delicate wine! Don't guzzle it like a caveman! Do it with dignity. And don't embarrass me. I ... *hic* ... I'm gonna get some fresh air."

"Kamaul, you're drunk. Let's head back to the sofas and sober up with some water. Let me take care of you, Your Highness."

"You're being ... ridicu-lush... 'm not that drunk ... You can barely tell," I mumbled as I motioned to stand up on my own.

"Please, Kamaul, I'm serious. Water, then rest, 'cause you've got that First Dance thing in, like, twenty minutes. It's 20:40. All the contestants have to be there. I know you're gonna hate it. I'm gonna hate it, too. But you gotta be there, man. Sobering you up is the goal now."

"I can ... hander my own situation. Thank you very mush. Let me get some fresh hair, and then I'll drink water. Finish my wine. I'll be back really quick. You'll barely even notice I'm gone."

"Can't let you do that," Dahir said, shaking his head and reaching out an arm to help stabilize me. I did manage to stand up on my own, though his hand was admittedly helpful. Or maybe he did my standing for me? I didn't know.

"Gotta get some hair, man. Please. I don't want any more chardonnay or see-rah or anything. Just the cold winner's air. Promise." I tried to twist my face into a believable look, then let out a deep, hopeful groan.

"Fine. Fine!" he snapped. "I'm a bad friend for doing this, Kamaul. But fine. You get five minutes outside, then I'm comin' out there like a search-and-rescue team to find your sorry ass! Got it?"

"Yes, Mother." I snickered, blowing raspberries at him.

"This is bad for your image, my king!" he shouted from the bar while I slowly walked past the bathroom hallway and out a hidden door at the back of the ballroom.

As I blasted the wooden door open, the outside world hit me like a frightened horse kicking. Brisk, frigid air hit my face. The heat and sweat of my body vanished as goose bumps ran over my skin. My hairs stood up, and my eyes squinted in the whispering breeze. Still, it was nice to be outside. A lot colder than I'd imagined it would be, but nice—the exact fresh air I needed.

Man, Egyptians are not made for these dumb December winters, I thought, shoving my hands in the tight pockets of my slacks.

As I glanced at my surroundings, it was quiet. I must have been behind the ballroom tent, away from the classical music and the outrageous sounds of the festival. I felt like I had escaped from the whole night and was alone on the campus.

I wasn't alone, however; I saw the girl from the bar earlier in the distance. She was walking towards the gazebo with her lush black hair flowing down her back. Her purple dress sparkled in the light of the nearby festival lanterns. Blindly, I started following her. Did she know I was there? Was this another twisted dream of paranoia? Was this my father in disguise, or another siren trick ...?

A spontaneous urge to puke came over me, forcing me to hunch over and face the barren dirt. I tried getting something to come up, yet nothing did. Frustrated, I stood up tall and carefully strolled along, following her high heel tracks. It was tough to keep my eye on both them and her.

"Hey! Wait!" I called.

No response—only the light sound of high heels swishing through the grass. I stayed nimble and kept pace as she continued onto the sidewalk towards the gazebo.

The college has a gazebo? Huh. Neat.

I did the same, my now dirty loafers touching smooth on the vacant pavement. She still did not acknowledge me behind her. It was only the two of us in this area of the campus.

"Eliza! Caroline!" I shouted, hearing my voice echo in the emptiness. "Irina!" I called, my lip beginning to quiver randomly. "Selena? Serena? Samara ...? Is that you?"

While it was obvious that none of those names were hers, I still chased after. Then, just as I felt the urge to puke coming up again, the girl turned around. She stopped in the gazebo, with its cheerful floating lanterns displayed in the lake's icy reflection. As she turned to face me, the look in her eyes was not one of *"No, no, no, stop, you crazy stalker!"* To my relief, it was pleasant and relieved.

"Kamaul," she began, her voice so soft and tender—the total opposite of my father's. "It's so good to see you again."

"Do ... do I know you?" I muttered, confused that she somehow recognized me. "I l—love the purple dress you're wearing, by the way. But I don't know you. I'm sorry."

She giggled. "First off, my dress is black. Secondly, Kamaul, yes you do. It's Talia. Believe me, you know me," she insisted, removing her mask to reveal fierce hazel eyes and pastel-pink lips.

"Oh, it's black? Huh ... Wonder what else I've miscolo—*hic*—misperceived tonight." I paused, glancing numbly at the stars. "Doesn't matter! Did you say Talia? As in, Talia from my arranged marriage? You ... you're here? At my college? Why? How did you ... how'd you find me? How'd you ... get here?" I hesitated, mind spinning, and not just from the drinks.

Talia was tall and stunning with flowing black hair. With her flawless tan complexion and the strangest twinkle in her eyes, this Talia looked completely incomparable to the last time I'd seen her—which, funny enough, was the same day as my father's death. Yup. How 'bout that? It was a very troubling yet momentous day in Kamaul's life.

"I found you." She chuckled gently. "Funny as it may sound. Sorry, not funny; more like creepy. I'm sure you must think of me as a crazy stalker ..."

Oh my ... She is now a mage and apparently a mind reader. AAAAH! Dangerous combo!

"But I'm not. I needed to talk to you and ... figure things out. You left out of nowhere. The rest of the kingdom assumed you were dead. I didn't believe it, though. I believed you were still out there somewhere, maybe in hiding, or conquering another town. And look what I found."

Talia strolled over to the gazebo railing and leaned against it, with her gladiator heels crossed at the ankles. Even now, she was taller than me—a hateful detail about this woman that I ignored.

"Look what you found!" I exclaimed, shocked but pleased. "You found me. Don't know how, and don't wanna know. But you ... err ... you found me. Someone who maybe didn't want to be found."

"It's been three years since I've seen you, you know. Three years—you believe that? I last saw you as an eighteen-year-old ticking time bomb. Cute, but too high-tempered for my taste. We were set to marry, in case you forgot. Your family and my family set it up, like fate had woven our lives together. But then you ran away after your father's death and never spoke to me again. We're both twenty-one now and still in love. So ... I just want some answers."

"I don't even know if you're real! A lot of wine plus the last ten minutes of what I've seen are not helping your case," I exclaimed, pointing at the ballroom behind us. "So, how do I even know you're real? If he wasn't, I doubt you are."

"I assure you, Kamaul, I am real. As real as you abandoning me. You abandoned your whole kingdom, Kamaul! Whether you were the rightful ruler or not, you left us to fend for ourselves from that day forward. Your brother took over the throne, and he did a fine job. But the citizens of our town know it was supposed to be you. Where were you, though? Nowhere to be seen. Meanwhile, I matured, moved on from your father's death, and lived my own life. And where was Kamaul Metjen? Hiding away at some college of wizards? Are you actually magical? Like, real, physical magic? 'Cause honestly, it's not something you seem capable of."

Her words were probably truthful, but I was in no state to clarify anything.

"Talia, I'm sorry, but I can't apologize for anything that day. I did what I did and do not regret any of it. The pharaoh was a greedy, stupid man and was going to die from old age anyway. Death was coming for him eventually; I simply sped up the process. Talia, if you know me and love me so much, even today, how did you not see that coming? Oh, and about my magic? That is very real, and very cool, and dangerous, and powerful, and all mine! Here, I'll prove it!"

I clumsily launched a slag ball across the icy lake. It flew over the sidewalks and hit a tree at the edge of the woods. Maybe it caught on fire; maybe it didn't. I watched the whole thing and only absorbed about twenty-five percent of it.

"Fine. Magic is *real*." she laughed sincerely. "Kinda lame, but whatever. So, why'd you leave me? Didn't you love me? Didn't you feel what I felt?"

"I don't love anyone except myself. The only person I smile at is myself, in every mirror I come across. Bathroom mirrors, bedroom mirrors, girls' eyes, reflections in the water ... No, I didn't love you. I *don't* love you. Talia, I hate to break it to you ... *hic* ... but our proposed marriage was merely a setup by my family and yours. Your mother and my father put us together to be a cordial couple. Was it ever going to work? Who knows? But I do know that it would probably have failed. I dunno if it would've worked—and frankly, I don't care. I'm at this college now; I've moved on to bigger and better kingdoms."

Odd as it sounds, I suddenly noticed a pair of cat whiskers sticking out above her pink lips.

"How dare you insult the sacred oath of marriage, Kamaul? How dare you insult my family and my mother's intuition!? Sure, adding a person like you to my family would've been like adding fuel to a wild fire. *But*, it would've also been a tango of bold personalities and beauty. A loving game of cat and mouse. I, obviously, would have been the cat. You hide the cowardness in your heart behind a façade of fury."

"Now you're speaking my language, Talia! That's what I'm sayin'! We would not have worked out. Thank you for seeing it as it really was." I breathed a sigh of relief and leaned next to her on the railing. The ice sparkled underneath the wooden boards. "Wait ... did you just call me a coward? A *coward*? Really?!" I squealed, letting the first ever tear in my twenty-one years of life fall down my cheek.

She laughed. "And now the man with the frozen heart wants to cry. What kind of *man* are you?"

Is this night going to be an endless assault on my mind and feelings? Feelings I didn't know were real, or that I was weak enough to have!

"I am my own man, dealing with my own stuff my own way!"

"Barely, from what I can see." Talia snickered, her voice dropping an octave. She eyed me up and down. "Drunk. Slurring your words. Calling out random girls' names. Yeah ... Sounds like you're killing it in the coping department, not crumbling under the pressure of The Pit at all."

"My father did not appear to me out of guilt! His death was his own fault. The gods playing gods took him when they decided to take him! I had NOTH-ING to do with it! And crumbling? No. I am ... thribing! This is my best shelf! The best I have ever looked!" I shouted irritably, waving my arms from head to toe to display my seriousness.

How 'bout that magic, huh? Oh, it's a wild thing—and there was more to come. I watched in horror as Talia's tan, pretty-in-a-scary-way face shifted to that of a cat. Her nose stretched into the snout of a ferocious lioness. Glowing yellow eyes replaced her hazel ones, which narrowed at me from a few inches away. Her purple dress transformed into the royal robes of Sekhmet, the Egyptian cat goddess. (See what I did there with "wild"?! Hee hee! "Wild," 'cause she was a jungle cat, and her magical transformation was genuinely terrifying.)

Stumbling away from her, I tripped over my own feet and fell to the cold gazebo floor.

"How did you do that?" I stammered. "Where did Talia go? Not that I really *want* to see her again, but where did she go? Are you her? Is she you?" I felt my incredulous stare border on cross-eyed.

Standing over my body with her paws near my loafers, the severity and re-sentment in her expression towered above me. She pointed her hooked scepter at my chest. "The gods are coming to judge you, Kamaul Metjen. We will determine your worthiness. I will be back to judge you myself. Clean up your act, *my king*, because I will not be so kind next time!"

Then she slammed the bottom of her scepter on the ground and vanished in a cloud of dirty smoke.

Frightened like a teenage version of myself, I clumsily rose to my feet and dusted my shirt off. It was completely clean and untouched, but I was so freaked out that I did it without thinking.

"Kamaul!" I shouted at nobody, hearing the ugly chime of my own voice. "Never hit the ten-drink limit again! You'll hallucinate fucking ... dead people who've returned to haunt you! DON'T DO IT AGAIN!"

"There you are!" Dahir's voice shouted from afar. "Been looking for you, man!"

"Who ... who are you?" I stammered, feeling my brain turning to goo inside my head.

"Kamaul, it's me, Ankhor. I told you that, after five minutes, I was coming to find you. This gazebo is an interesting place. I didn't think you knew ... it existed. Doesn't matter ... We gotta get you back to the ballroom. The First Dance is starting in, like, ten minutes, and you're required to attend it!"

Seeing my distress, he raced to my side and wrapped his arm around me like I had broken my ankle on the playground. I used him for unnecessary support and whispered something belligerent in his ear, and we walked down the sidewalk as single unit.

"Dude, you gotta stop me at eight drinks. Ten is way too many. I just saw two fucking ghosts!"

"Yeah. Yeah, I know, Your Highness. We need to get you some water, ASAP! Eight drinks is definitely the limit. Now, c'mon. Your people are waiting," Dahir grumbled.

"They're fucking coming for me, Dahir!" I screamed, wailing like a baby seal in his ear. "The gods of Egypt are coming to judge me!"

ABRAHAM V

THE SLOW MUSIC OF the orchestra swelled in the ballroom as Emilee and I made our way to the dance floor. Our mere existence attracted an influx of curious and skeptical looks from a variety of dancing mages. The selections for the Pit Ceremony had only been made about twelve hours ago, so it was very fresh in people's minds. Their gears must have been spinning in overdrive while the freak who could speak with plants and the insect girl wearing a beetle broach split the crowds and entered the center of the marble floor. We were the unlikeliest of popular people, but The Pit changed perceptions in an instant.

But none of that mattered, because my girlfriend looked absolutely amazing tonight. She was wearing a stunning salmon-pink dress with a floral lace-up back. The bottom of her gown was embroidered with vibrant flowers that extended to the train trailing majestically behind her. Enchanting green eyes beamed at me above lips of sparkly coral. Perched at the top of her dress, Emilee's beetle broach symbolized the oddity and uniqueness of her all in one place.

As we took our places, the dimples in her smile ignited a smile of my own, and I flashed pearly whites proudly back at her. I looked into those green eyes and watched everything around me vanish. She was stunning, as always, but something about this moment was special. Her mask was of her own creation, fashioned after Columbina from the old *commedia dell'arte* shows and brown with small butterfly antenna sticking out from the top and yellow trim around the eyeholes. Even in the public eye, Emilee was true to her own style.

Animated bronze statues bearing violins, clarinets, saxophones, and trumpets sauntered on stage. Their soft classical sound only enhanced the masquerade. Emilee and I circled each other like some kind of weird ritualistic dance. We bowed to one another, then I placed a hand on her back as she placed hers on my shoulder while our free hands clasped together. The moment was perfect as we looked into each other's eyes and ignored the darting glances surrounding us. Then ... we danced.

But like a flawed harmony, Emilee was clearly distracted by something else. "Abe," she whispered, her voice tender in my ear. "Everybody is looking at us."

The orchestra's song picked up, yet I felt relaxed, even while being careful not to step on her dress. Our bodies moved in sync with the melody and rhythm of the music.

"Guess I didn't notice." I chuckled softly.

I guided us across the dance floor. The gleam in her eye was fading, so I pulled her closer. Our heartbeats aligned when my chest touched hers. It was like a dream where only Emilee and I existed, and the music was made for just the two of us. We were alone. The warmth between us grew more powerful with each passing moment.

"Just a lot for me to take in, Abe," she sighed, shrugging. "I'm not in the tournament like you are. Like, how ... how are you so calm?"

"Hun, I don't know. I ... I just am. Being chosen for The Pit is out of anyone's control, right? I figure I might as well make the most of it. I never wanted or asked to be in it, but here we are. We just have to take it day by day and roll with the punches. What choice do I have?" I whispered, holding tightly to her hand.

"I'm ... worried about you now. More than usual," she stammered, hopeful eyes looking up at me.

"I know. I'm worried, too. Just ... about other things besides myself."

"Oh? Such as ...?" Emilee smiled, anxiously awaiting my answer.

"Kiku, for starters. Poor girl is traumatized by the whole day, I bet. New to the school, new to magic, new to the idea of The Pit—and now competing in it? Yikes. That's a lot to take in."

Clearly that was not quite the answer she had hoped to hear, as her eyes fell to the floor in disappointment. When they returned to mine, her scowl turned my face sour.

"Kiku?" Emilee muttered, confused and concerned. "Why are you so worried about Kiku? Shouldn't you be worried about yourself?"

"Because, Emilee," I started, carefully bringing her close, "she's just a kid. This tournament ... is not for the faint of heart. It's a brutal bloodbath, where four of us are going to die. I don't wanna have to go to her funeral, Emilee. This whole thing ... isn't fair to anyone. And the Elders know that, but they don't care. So, someone has to, right?"

"I guess so, Abe? But you need to think about yourself, too! She's not your concern anymore. I'm sorry to be harsh, but she isn't; she is Joan's concern. As much as her life is at risk, so is yours! I only ask that you be careful. You can protect yourself and still keep an eye on Kiku. Don't get upset with me because I am the one looking out for you. I care about you, Abe! I love you. If you won't worry about yourself, then I will." Her voice was fragile and afraid and astonishingly hushed, given the circumstances.

"I am worried, Emilee. And I love you, too! I ... I'm sorry I get so caught up in worrying about others. I can't help it. I wanna try and protect other people if I can. It's just who I am."

Holding onto one another, Emilee and I went quiet soon after. We swayed to the descending music as the statues seemed to move in slow motion. Even Kamaul's obnoxious group of arrogant and devoted followers in the corner could not divert me from this moment. I leaned in and kissed Emilee on the cheek.

"I appreciate your looking after me. I will be fine, though, okay? I promise."

"I know. It's just ..." Emilee dropped her head to my shoulder, and the edge of her mask brushed against my white shirt. "I can't help it either."

"And I know that, too," I said shyly.

I held snug to her waist while her hand held firmly on my shoulder.

My gold-and-green-stitched vest and I embraced being the center of attention inside the Masquerade Ball. While salmon pink and pine green weren't an ideal color palette match, I liked to think Emilee and I pulled it off. And as for the eagle-eyed onlookers, they could all have simply been staring at my aggressively impressive mask. With curved horns on top and tiny branches sticking out like deer ears, my heavy mask was a bit terrifying. It bore the head of a bird head minus the beak, and live moss grew on it. Emilee had made this mask, too. Much like with Charlie's cane, she hoped it would show that there was more to the Pit's earth mage than meets the eye.

As the orchestra took a moment between songs, I let my eyes wander. All the students who normally wore a simple hoodie and jeans had seemingly arrived at the Festival of the Elements with new personas on display. It was like classes, professors, syllabuses, homework, and school projects were thrown out the window for one night.

I noticed Kamaul leaving his gang of groupies and vanishing into the bar area. I think Caroline was with him. And in typical Kamaul fashion, the arrogant slag mage had his mask slung over his wrist. No regard for Jax's wishes, and no common courtesy—he just did whatever he wanted.

Why am I focused on Kamaul's antics and not ...?

"Hey," I whispered to Emilee, turning back to face her.

"Yeah?" she giggled.

A sad-sounding cello and harp ballad began from the stage behind us. I slowed our dance to a stop. Cutting through the crowd, I took Emilee's hand and wove us off the dance floor. We found a marble column and both leaned against it.

"Tell me about the beetle broach." I smiled at the insect on her chest.

"What?" Emilee chuckled. "Abe, you've probably heard that story a hundred times. You really wanna hear it again?"

"Yup. Spare no details."

"Okay, Mr. Morrison, for the *hundred-and-first* time, this roach was a gift from Mallory. And since you insist on hearing every detail, Mallory is my birth mother, and Nina is the woman she's remarried to now. Got the names straight?" she joked, rubbing her fingers on the golden broach.

I nodded, listening to the orchestra's instruments caress the words on her lips.

"I was three. Mom and I were anxiously planning our first trip to our small town's Forest Faire, an annual old-timey festival in the woodlands. Mallory was a single mom. She worked two jobs and had to juggle her time carefully. One night after her shift at the grocer's, it was getting late, and the faire was almost over, but she still wanted to take me. Once we got there, we made a beeline for our neighbor's distinguished trinket booth. She and Mom were always friends. Like the evening's Forest Faire, her trinket booth was just closing up for the night when Mallory bought me this broach." Emilee paused and smiled. "It was the only sale our neighbor made that day."

Lowering my head, I enticed her to finish the rest of the story, delicately caressing her chin in my palm. "Go on. Then what happened?"

"Abe," she whispered lightly, blushing as she watched my eyes. "You know how this story ends. Why do you wanna hear it again?"

I leaned and kissed her on the lips. "Sorry, babe. I forgot. Remind me again," I teased.

"So, when we got back to the car, my mom opened the door, helped me in, and spoke to me as she fastened the seat belt over my car seat. 'As long as you have this broach, nothing bad will happen to you, Emilee,' she told me. 'You will never have to worry again. I will always be with you.' And from that day forward ... I never go anywhere without it."

She pulled her hand away, and I inspected her beetle broach more closely. It was rather small, maybe an inch or so in size. The first time I saw it, I was freaked out, because it resembled a golden scarab beetle with baby-blue wings, and occasionally it would move—wiggle an arm or a leg, flutter one of its four wings, or even wave an antenna. Emilee's attachment to it was the most adorable thing about it.

"Ooooooooh," Emilee groaned, suddenly hunching over and clutching her stomach.

"What's wrong? Stomach pains?" I asked, kneeling immediately.

"I don't know. Just a ... random surge of pain. Probably hungry."

"Yeah, alright. Maybe you are. I'll just ... uh ... find somethin' small for ya. That okay?"

"Actually ... I'm gonna go grab some punch. So, you get the food, I'll get the beverages. We'll meet back at this pillar before the First Dance starts. Sound good?" Emilee answered, now easily rising to her feet.

"Yeah, deal." I smiled, kissing her forehead.

Walking around the edge of the marble dance floor, I pulled back the psychological restraints and let my mind loose. Telling Emilee that Kiku was the only concern on my mind was just a façade, sadly. All I could truly think about was that stupid raven! I've been seeing that carved idol everywhere: the beaked plague doctor masks shapeshifting into the raven's head, a barn owl mask's strange fluff looking eerily similar to its dark purple feathers ... Even the yellow trim around Emilee's eyeholes glared back at me like the hollow black eyes of the raven.

No one else can know about it, though. From the moment I'd touched it, its image was branded in my brain. Like it was ... Like I was cursed even just knowing it existed.

No, Abe. You gotta think about something else. Otherwise, you'll go stir crazy.

I squeezed between mages and exited into the grand foyer. An ugly gray-gold carpet stretched across the floor. With its scattered chandeliers, the giant room was incredibly bright—somewhat blinding compared to the dimly lit ballroom. Of course, being homeschooled, I had never actually attended one, but I could imagine it. Images of a younger, nerdy Abe wearing glasses and hugging the wall filled my head as giggling and gossiping couples passed by. One thing was for sure:

This bold satyr-themed mask boosted my confidence greatly in comparison to those introverted adolescent years of my life.

Black suits and black dresses awakened more sightings of the raven. That stupid bird was popping up everywhere. Luckily, I had another item on my agenda.

In keeping with tradition, the Masquerade Ball hosted a special moment where mages could meet the previous Pit's winning Elder. Put up like a character meet-and-greet at an amusement park, Kai had been given a corner of the grand foyer to sign autographs on paintings, sculptures, or anything that shared his likeness. Trust me, there was no one who loved Kai more than Kai.

Turning to the corner, I brushed by Phoebe, Solomon, and Baffy, who were heading into the ballroom. I squeezed through a line of traffic and bumped into a short purple-haired girl. Probably not even 5', she wore a matching lilac tea-length dress accented with gray heels.

"Oh, terribly sorry," I stammered, backing away to find Kai's line.

"Hi!" she shrieked, bubbly voice sprouting from a wide grin. "Anxious to meet Kai, too?"

"I am, yeah. This is the line here?" I asked in surprise, pointing.

"Yup!" She nodded vigorously. "I'm Raven. Nice to meet you, Abe! I'm a first year, so it's okay that you have no idea who I am." Her eyes, wide and eager like a kid in a candy store, looked into mine, perfectly disregarding the horned mask.

Of course her name is Raven. Go figure!

"Hi, Raven. How ... uh ... how do you know who I am?" I asked, taking a step forward behind her.

"Really, Abe?" Raven chuckled. "You're a Pit contestant now! Everyone knows who you are. The five of you are pretty famous already!"

"Great," I answered cynically.

With the line cutting into the room, I was nearly thirty people from the front. Mixed conversations swirled around Raven and me as mages flowed in and out of the Masquerade Ball. I was last in line—too far away to hear anything Kai was saying. Trying not to look like a total fangirl, I leaned left and right to catch a clear view of him. Some obnoxious students attempted to force their way to the front before being promptly escorted away by his two orbiting satellites of protection.

Spiked platinum hair, effortlessly styled. Fierce silver eyes, ensnaring anyone who stumbled upon them. With the energy of a jackrabbit, Kai captivated the room. He could enthrall an audience with a simple gaze before needing the charm and charisma. A crown made of conductive metals and harnessed lightning complemented his endearing smile while showing off his wicked genius in the fields of science and engineering. Kai wore turquoise dress shoes, each adorned with a sapphire. His top and bottom were that of a fairy-tale prince: sleek, black slacks cuffed into the shoes, a powder-blue dress shirt with brass buttons, and a stopwatch tucked in the pocket. The final piece of the ensemble was a turquoise fur coat with gold accents and white fluff around the collar. To cap off his egotistical appearance, he had a pair of magic orbs swirling the air around to protect him.

"You like Kai, too?" Raven added, digging around inside her satchel. It was plastered with stitched emblems and badges of sea life: seals, dolphins, fish, coral, manatees, whales ... You name it, she probably had it on her bag.

Raven pulled out several playing cards with the Elders drawn on them. She inspected their craftsmanship and tidied each one as it came out.

"You make those?" I smiled, nodding to the cards.

Her mask had blueish-black feathers glued all over it, some of which stuck up from the crest over her hairline. A glistening silver beak protruded from below Raven's kind eyes.

"Absolutely! These are my homemade Elder trading cards!" She flipped through them, cycling and showcasing each one. "I've done a lot of research during my short tenure here. I'm hoping Kai will sign his. That would be ... next level!"

"Super cool." I nodded, sounding unimpressed, which was a lie. "So, who's your favorite? Which trading card do you like best?"

"KAI!" she shouted, nearly tripping backwards as we followed the line. "As a steam mage, it's my dream to meet him! But I'm not coming off as obsessed, am I? 'Cause I'm not!"

"Little bit. But it's alright. I'll let you in on a little secret: I am, too."

I held up a hand to conceal my smile for only Raven to see. A charming smile grew across her face, too. It was endearing to see her so enthusiastic to meet an Elder—such a treat for a young novice mage.

"So, you're a third year, and even you've never met him?"

Roughly twenty-five people ahead of us now.

"Fourth year, actually. But nope, never." My tone invoked mystery and anticipation.

"Wow. So, this is a cool moment for the both of us, dude!"

Two more mages joined the line.

"Yes, it is. Now, if you don't mind my asking, what are your ... gloves for?"

"Oh ... Coral magic erupts from my skin, like tentacles or vines," Raven replied solemnly, voice quiet, as her head dropped to look at her hands. "The gloves contain my magic ... or my curse, as I call it. It shoots out of my hands chaotically, overtaking anything I touch, like algae. All kinds of strange things I don't understand. I can't control it on my own yet. But once I can, I won't have to wear these anymore! And that day can't come soon enough."

Sadness fell over her. I could tell it was traumatic for her to talk about.

"Hey, hey," I said gently. "This ability means ... that you technically have two kinds of magic within you. If you ask me, I'd say that's a pretty unique gift. I wouldn't call it a curse at all. You're gifted, Raven. Think of it like a superpower—one in a million, something no one else has. Especially not *two* of 'em!"

Raven lifted her head up and looked at me. The glint in her eyes and the vibrancy of her purple hair returned, as did that sweet smile of hers. "I'm rooting for Aaron to win, of course! But if it has to be someone else, I hope it's you. Speaking of Aaron, you haven't ... uhhh ... you haven't seen him, have you? I thought he'd be here at the ball, but he's not. I'm just worried, that's all. You know ... as a fellow water mage."

"Thank you. But no, I haven't seen him either. If I do, though, I'll let you know." I grinned and asked to see her trading cards. I shuffled through them and admired her artwork. "These are brilliant, you know? Truly. Sounds to me like you have more gifts than even magic can offer."

"Just tell him Raven says hi. We're friends ... I think? Wait ... Abe, you like my cards? You're not just saying that?" she answered shyly.

"Yeah, I'll tell him. But oh, definitely." I handed them back to her and pointed to the Kai card at the top of the stack. "I also know he's going to love this one."

"I think so, too." She smiled.

Nineteen people left before our turn. I inched closer to Raven, ensuring that my voice whispered directly in her ear. "You know, Raven ... I have a unique gift, too. I'm a plant whisperer. I can hear what any plant or flower or tree thinks and feels. When I first came to the college, everyone thought it was weird and freaky and different. When I walked by, people would judge me, point and laugh, or simply ignore me altogether. Well ... at least, they used to, because now that 'plant-boy freakazoid' is competing in one of the greatest honors on campus. You may think of your hands as a curse, Raven. Like with me, people may crack jokes or get under your skin. But just remember that it stems from their own insecurities and jealousy. You are more special than they'll ever be. So, wear those gloves with pride, not fear."

Her eyes cheerful at my kind words, she chuckled as we moved closer to Kai. "Maybe you're right, Abe. Maybe I should be more—"

"Can we keep this line a-movin'! Step it up, people!" shouted a drunken voice behind me.

Raven went silent and immediately turned forward, embarrassed and ashamed.

Ignore it, Abe. Big target on your back already. Don't make it larger.

Seventeen people ahead.

"C'mon, guys! Not that hard. One foot in front of the other!" he yelled again, probably cupping his hands over his mouth for an echo.

"Cool it, pal," I snapped, spinning to confront him. "We're all in line here. Gotta wait your turn."

"Brave boy you ... *hic* ... you are. Bold and brash, aren't we?" the heckler shouted—before noticing it was me in front of him. A hefty round of drinking clearly added to the delayed reaction. "Wait—you're Abe? Like, chosen-for-The-Pit Abe?" He shoved the rest of his toasted bread in his mouth, wiped his hands on his suit jacket, and held one out for a handshake.

I scoffed at it and mentally critiqued his outfit—a cheap-looking gray suit with an ugly wolf-style mask, hard like a turtle shell, and brown like ... Well, I think you can find the proper comparison for that one. I may have been a high priority in the eyes of every student here, but I didn't take well to jerks or instigators anymore.

But suddenly, he dropped the anger in favor of a genuine smile. Then the wolf boy pulled out an orange handkerchief and a permanent marker before shoving them in my face, wobbling forward as he did.

"Name's Joseph. Sorry to be a jerk before ... Hey!" he shouted, burping the smell of toast and beer in my face. "Can I get your autograph, bro?!"

"Uhhh ... sure. Yeah." I shrugged, taking the stuff from his hands. I signed my name on the handkerchief and handed it back to him. "There you go, man."

"Sick, bro! Thanks!" Joseph smiled, shoving both items in his jacket pocket. "Really, I appreciate it."

"Why do you want my autograph, though?" I asked, curious whether he was simply drunk or genuinely wishing me luck in the tournament.

"Probs gonna be worth money in the future. You know ... when you die!" *BLURPP!* "Blood mages for Olivia! Woo!"

Yup. Stupid, naïve Abe. You're too nice to the worst people. All you did was stroke his ego, smiling as you did it.

"Lovely. What a saint you are, Joseph," I scoffed, shaking my head in disbelief at his blatant disrespect. I pretended to brush off bread crumbs from my cheek and checked my own breath against the palm of my right hand. "But yeah—nope. That nasty breath is all you, man."

"Nasty breath?!" he grunted, obnoxiously blowing more of it in my face. "I oughta give you more of it then, *pal*. But ... it ain't worth wasting my breath on a guy who literally just signed his own death warrant. I got your autograph in my pocket,

Abraham. Like, honestly? You're a smart guy, right? How could you be so dumb that you'd think I would *root* for you? You're a wimpy earth mage, tree hugger! Like, OOOOOOH, I'm shaking in my ficus!" Joseph mocked.

"You're a gem, Joseph. A true gem of a person. You're the complete package, *pal*." My voice came out louder than I intended. But the only person I was embarrassed for at this point was Raven, whose excitement level had plummeted in the wake of his outbursts. "Great look for the void community as well. What, you're a nurse, right? I pray to Terra that I don't end up in your hospital bed. I'm doomed if I do."

"You won't end up in my ward!" he shouted, patting his pocket with the handkerchief. "Olivia is gonna have a fuckin' field day with you. You'll be *begging* for ol' Joseph to bandage your wounds by the time she's done with you. That chick is mental! You're gonna need all the publicity and good luck you can muster, but I'll be laughin' and clappin' from the stands!"

I paid no true attention to his drunken slurs. This fool wouldn't last a minute in that arena.

Twelve people left in line. Kai's voice boomed across this portion of the room, thankfully drowning out most of Joseph's unwarranted shouting.

"Lot of arrogance for a man who can barely stand on his own two feet right now. Why are you even in line to meet Kai, anyway? Why would an Elder want to deal with this pitiful mess? Lose-lose for you, honestly; he'll degrade you into nothing. It won't be a pretty sight—but I'll be watching the train wreck with bated breath when he does."

"Wait—this line is to meet Kai?" he stammered, eyes flapping in an imaginary breeze, a petrified look on his face.

"You should see your face right now. I wish I were an echo mage so I could show you your own stupid face in a reflection. YES! This line that you attacked for barely moving is to meet an Elder. Didn't you see the banners?" I pointed to a large banner hung above Kai. Old canvases were temporarily hung on the wall, and painted art on easels flanked him. As he waited for the next person in line, Kai posed in the same position as his artwork depicted.

"Ah, crap! I thought this was the line for those little burgers. You know what I'm talkin' about—super small, fit in your hand?" He unnecessarily mimed eating a burger.

"Yeah. This isn't that line, pal." I laughed as we moved within ten people of the esteemed Water Elder.

"Oh, well. Good chatting with you, plant boy. And good luck with The Pit—you're gonna need it!" Joseph snickered and slapped me on the back before strutting away. He drifted into the crowds and thankfully vanished.

Just seven students ahead of us now.

Raven twirled from side to side, holding the trading cards behind her back and anxiously tapping them with her fingers. Now with the obnoxious Joseph gone, the quiet returned to Kai's corner, with only the Water Elder's voice carrying through the room.

"Feeling excited now?" I whispered to Raven.

"Is it that obvious?" She chuckled, nervously spinning around with eyes wide in panic.

"Hey, I don't blame you. This is a big deal. Enjoy the moment. He loves attention as much as anyone, so talk him up and play along with his ego. He'll love it!"

"Yeah, thanks. Now it's all left to ... the uhhh, nerves at this point ... right?" Raven replied uncertainly, taking a shaky step forward.

"Only four ahead of you now. Don't sweat it, Raven. Remember, he loves people, especially water mages, and he loves himself. So, again, talk about him, and you'll do just fine. Just be yourself. Plus, you have those trading cards. Show him those. He'll go nuts."

"Yeah ... Yeah, you're right. Just gotta ... PHEWWW ... keep it cool."

Her feet were tapping in rhythm with her fingers. Kai posed like a Roman statue as the next student approached. Boisterous and masterful, he captivated the attention of the gossiping guests nearby. Even mages just walking past were caught in his trance as they strolled into the Masquerade Ball. And as my turn was nearing, I fell victim to Kai's charisma as well.

I watched him interact with the next few mages. Despite seeing Kai at the Pit Ceremony earlier, observing him in person was a different experience. He could hold an audience with simple words and casual conversation, intense yet inviting at the same time. It was frankly terrifying to meet an Elder ... like the people of Athens talking with Zeus. Most of us thought it was a pipe dream, a fantasy, but this was happening. So, I nerded out for a moment as my opportunity approached.

Kai then turned his focus to Raven, his manner poised and proper, hers anxious, as her foot jitters kicked into overdrive when their eyes met. Kai looked elegant among the painted canvases on easels surrounding him.

"What a spunky color we have here!" he cheered, pointing to her purple hair.

"Yeah ... Yes, yes. It *is* very purple, thank you!" Raven laughed nervously.

"Love the mask, too. You a fellow water mage?" Kai asked, adjusting his fur coat.

"I am, yeah. My name's Raven. I'm a ... a steam mage. First year." Her tone jumped up an octave to quirky and energetic, as if she were trying to surpass his.

"What you got there?" he teased, gesturing to the cards held tightly in her hands.

"These are ... my trading cards. I designed them myself," she answered, pushing closer to Kai and timidly handing them over.

His smile widened, and a glimmer appeared in his eyes. He shuffled through them, admiring and nodding at each card before fanning out the stack on a small white table between them. On it, Kai had individual headshots in your typical model poses, some with wisps of magic painted around him, and others showing him in front of a dark background to enhance his bright facial features. I leaned around Raven and watched the Elder, who picked up a glossy gold pen and sat to sign the first card.

"I really love these—especially the one of me! You somehow managed to capture my dazzle and perfect pearly eyes in a single drawing. Very impressive, Raven. I make some glorious works of art myself, but these ... these are something special." He winked at her and started signing the bottom of his trading card.

Raven was elated, her smile wide and animated as she intently stared at Kai's hand scribbling across the card.

"Thank you! Kai, that means so much to me ... You have no idea!"

"I know. I'm ... kind of a big deal." He chuckled. "But my trading card here—is that what you called 'em?—is tremendous. You are a very talented artist. You captured the twinkle in my eye, a hint of my biceps, my sense of fashion, and my ... *je ne sais quoi* ... Seriously, Raven, these are impressive. I mean that! Now, hopefully you're as good a steam mage as you are an artist." Kai was now in full charm mode, and it was certainly working on Raven, who started to twirl the ends of her hair.

"Thank you, sir. You have ... no idea how much it means to me to hear you say that."

He finished signing his own trading card, a sleek and shiny *Kai* scrawled along the bottom like calligraphy. Quickly, he flipped through Marrick, Eliza, Magnus, and Terra and scribbled the three letters of his name huge across their photos, too, covering the entire cards. Adding a signed photo of himself, he pulled them all together and handed the stack to Raven with a beaming grin.

"Wait? Why ... why did you sign all five?" Raven asked, reluctantly reaching for her cards.

The orbs jumped into gear, frantically orbiting above his head like a moon when she gestured.

"Oh, don't mind them. They're like little guard dogs," he began, brushing off the orbs. "Of course I signed 'em all! When is the next time you'll see another Elder up close and personal? Look, I signed them because I can. I apologize if you don't like it." Kai's laughter was subtle yet condescending. Raven's expression immediately turned sour, though it wasn't angry or irritated. As Kai spoke, his charm managed to turn that frown upside down. "But now, you've got five signatures from the mega powerful Water Elder, rather than just one. Can do whatever you want with them."

"Maybe you're right ..." She nodded, gingerly tucking the cards into her leather satchel. "I have five Elder signatures now. I could frame yours, maybe ... hang it up. Plus, now I can remake these cards and make 'em even more colorful and detailed. Yeah ... Yeah! That's what I'll do!"

"That's the spirit." Kai winked. "Those are great. But I can't wait to see what you create next time we meet, yeah? Think you can do that?"

"You ... you think we'll meet again?" Raven stammered, her voice cracking. Her hands jumped up instantly to cover her mouth. "You really think so?!"

Rising to his feet, Kai straightened his slacks and faced her across the table. "If I have anything to say about it, Raven, yes. We'll meet again ..."

I felt a slight pause in the corner of the room, as if time had frozen. Raven's legs bounced up and down like a track star stretching before a marathon. Kai's kind eyes and eager smile looked back at her from a couple feet away as the two chrome orbs floated in graceful arcs above his head like overprotective parents. The dancers in the ballroom and the orchestra music fell silent, along with everyone else in the room.

"Ah, ah, ah!" Kai said discouragingly as Raven reached around the table for a hug. "Not so fast, little girl. I've dealt with crazed fans before, so I don't think you'll be getting anywhere close with these bad boys swirling around. They sense everything. Nothing is just a precaution. Silly novice mages ... sad and disappointing sometimes. And on second thought, forget ever meeting again. I hope we never do, Ms. Raven."

Suddenly, the scene resumed as Kai's guardian orbs swooshed down in front of him and fluttered like hummingbirds in the air. At the small girl's approach, they bounced off one another and created multiple copies of themselves. Panels sprang out and connected the balls, encasing Kai in a protective dome, completely guarded from the rest of the room. A light mist then trickled out of this shield and evaporated into the ceiling. Once it vanished, the many orbs disappeared along with it, except for the remaining two, which quickly launched themselves into the ceiling. Kai was gone.

"Wait—did Kai disappear? Like, inside that cloud thing?" Raven muttered to me in shock, her arms still open for an embrace that never came.

I laughed cynically, humoring myself at the irony.

"Now I gotta wait even longer to meet an Elder! The suspense continues ..."

I dusted off the awkwardness, spun away from the rest waiting in Kai's line, and moseyed over to the hors d'oeuvres table. If my unspoken side quest crashed and burned, at least I could return to Emilee with her promised food tray.

OLIVIA V

"Come on, Olivia," Tarik whined. "It'll be fun. Doubt it'll even be ten minutes. You just walk in, stand with the other competitors, make a couple disgusted and irritated faces at me, and wave to your fellow void mages like a pampered princess. Quick and painless!"

"God, you're gonna make me vomit." I gagged.

"C'mon, Olivia," Tarik pleaded again, batting his puppy dog eyes at me.

"Nope. No. I'm not going. You can't make me," I stated bluntly.

Standing on the balcony, I watched the ballroom fill with students and professors. A sea of colorful dresses covered the marble floor, backed by the ambient music of the orchestra. Suited counterparts joined their dates shortly after. It was an obnoxiously perfect display of everything I hated about big school moments: fake perfection, ignorance, and plastered-on smiles.

Look at these gluttons—some wobbling in drunk, some hiding in the corners (riddled with anxiety), some flirting their way from girl to girl or guy to guy. Yup, I'm gonna throw up. I'm gonna blow chunks down on the dance floor like a hailstorm.

"You're cute when you're wrong." Tarik blushed, playfully nudging my shoulder.

"Fine. Alright," I sighed. "I'll go. But only because I *have* to—not because you gave me those stupid puppy dog eyes again."

"Hooray!" Tarik beamed, kissing me on the cheek. "We just need to primp you up a little bit before we go down."

"I know I kissed you when we were leaving Azuma Shores, but please don't let it go to your head. I stand by my threats. You know, I was probably possessed by a kinky spirit in that graveyard. So, that's who really kissed you. But keep pushin' your luck—see if I don't open up my Pandora's box of pain on your sorry behind."

"Hello, everyone!" shouted Jax, parting the bronze statues as he arrived on the main stage. "How are we doing tonight? Having fun?"

His question was answered with an uproar of applause. It looked like the majority of the student body was in the ballroom by this point, which filled me with dread. I gulped a little and felt my stomach sink. Half of these mages had mocked me or called me a freak or a "broken witch." But now, Jax and Tarik expected me to parade myself in front of them—and do it with a smile? Harder than it looked, boys.

Tarik chuckled to himself and reached into his pocket. I was afraid he was going to reveal some tacky piece of jewelry or something, but instead he pulled off the single black rose from his suit jacket. He slipped it into my hair, tucking it behind my ear.

"Are you serious?" I glared at him as he stepped back to admire.

"Hey, I'm your biggest fan, Olivia. You know that. But today and for this First Dance, we ... *you* need to represent our element. Your appearance should be a celebration of void magic. I think this little touch of Marrick's will show that. Might win you some brownie points after you freaked out on him a couple days ago."

"This rose smells like sulfur and lies, Tarik. You love to shoot yourself in the foot, don't you? First, you try to boost my spirits, when you know I love darkness and gray skies. Then you surprise me at my place, vaporize my hairdresser, and take me on a date to make it up to me. We go to a fun graveyard, blow away some ghouls, and earn a bit of gold in the process. That's when you finally get me to kiss you on the lips. And now you place that black rose by my ear before I'm paraded through the student body like a prize? Back to the doghouse, Tarik, sorry."

"Woof woof, Olivia! Your back-and-forth about me is adorable, 'cause I know you love me deep down." He winked, leaning over the railing, still looking at me.

"But it's so far down, you might as well call it Tartarus. I'm warning you: Any sweet boyfriend looks or waving at me like giddy parents at the playground, and I will flip the script and glue that doggie door shut so you can't get out. Got it?" I sneered, eyebrows arching.

"Bark!"

"Good boy," I scoffed, rolling my eyes and letting a small grin sneak across my lips.

"That's my girl." Tarik nodded, adjusting his suit and cracking his neck a little (something that he knew irked me).

"I'm gonna head down with the other vultures now. But here," I said, handing him my black jewel-encrusted purse. "Keep an eye on this 'til I get back. Bandages, antivenom serum, spyglass, and heirloom dagger. Anything goes missing in there, and I'll know where to look."

"Olivia," he began warily, "why do you need a knife?"

"Every girl needs her accessories when she attends a ball, dear."

I patted him on the shoulder and darted a simmering glare into his soul before I spun towards the stairs. Laughing at the baffled look on Tarik's face, I appreciated his all-black suit. He looked rather handsome in it. And I should hope so, too—I had helped him pick it out last week! He'd originally worn Marrick's rose as a corsage before putting it in my hair. The mask, however, was all his doing, and it was a surprisingly good choice, at that: a hard matte black one with a beautiful skull pendant, eyeholes painted crimson, on the crest.

"I would like to call all of our new Pit competitors to the dance floor! It is now time for the traditional First Dance, in honor of the 248th Pit Tournament! Abraham, Olivia, Aaron, Kiku, and Kamaul, please join us at center stage."

Clapping and hollering ensued from the lower floor. I turned the corner, running my fingers down the railing while I spun around the pillar. Like hawks, the peering eyes of judgement from teenagers and young adults barreled at me. I shrugged them aside and powered through the massive crowd, making my way to the center of the masquerade. With masks hiding their faces, every mage I passed seemed like a total stranger.

I looked up to see Abe and Kiku on the stage by Jax's side. He had made the announcement mere seconds ago, and these two were already here, as if they'd preemptively waited for it.

Should've assumed those two would arrive first. A pair of Goody-Two-shoes. Teacher's pets, if you ask me.

"Hello, Olivia," Abe addressed me coolly, buttoning his suit jacket as I passed.

Kiku, meanwhile, scanned the sea of masks, caution in her every move.

Get used to it, kid. You're famous now. Join the club.

"Hi," I muttered softly to them under my breath.

Kiku didn't hear me, and honestly, it didn't matter if she did. Tarik said I needed to put on a good performance and present myself accordingly. So, might as well act the part, right?

Taking my place to the right of Kiku, I fixed my dress and looked out at the crowd. There were too many unknown and hidden faces for me to care about. And I knew they would feel the same way about me now, with the mask on, as they would if I removed it. The fear and disgust in their eyes would tell the story, no words needed.

For now, though, I scanned the dance floor and balcony for Tarik, assuming he would be visible somewhere, cheering me on. While I knew it would set off my blood pressure, seeing his support would be nice.

The three of us stood on stage with Jax, waiting for the last two to arrive.

Playing to his image and audience, Kamaul emerged from his posse and raced towards the stage. He bumped into a bunch of students and nearly fell over two or three times as he ran, but he made it. Needing a helping hand up to the stage, Jax grabbed ahold of Kamaul and ushered him to my side. With an insincere "thank you" and drunken smile, Kamaul leaned over to see the entire stage.

As we waited for Aaron, the obnoxious slag mage stepped forward and began instigating the crowd. He managed to get many brutish boys jumping and cheering (clearly fans of his) and aroused other bored students to refocus on the stage. Kamaul's presence was commanding, no doubt about it. Yet I now knew his weakness: the undeniable desire for attention wherever he could get it.

I overheard Jax talking to his assistant near the group of musical statues, who were tuning their instruments during the downtime. He was talking about new floral wallpaper and wondering where Aaron had run off to and how to keep the show moving. Frustrated, Jax spun away, shooing her away to search for the missing mage. A scowl shifted back into a fake smile as he retook center stage in front of the anxiously waiting audience.

Jax addressed the crowd. His voice carried through this room much easier than it had in The Trench—no enhancement spell needed. Once he positioned himself ahead of us, I finally found Tarik's face in the background, smiling between a vulture mask and a bright blue tulip one. A smirk of my own slipped out at the sight of him.

"Seems Aaron has let the excitement get the best of him tonight. No matter, though! The First Dance will continue without him. I will fill him in later on what he missed," Jax began, pacing from side to side. "I now invite The Pit competitors to perform the traditional First Dance. You do not necessarily have to dance, ladies and gentlemen, but the floor is yours if you choose to."

Jax pointed at the orchestra, which summoned loud, peppy music behind us.

Not one to deny the spotlight, Kamaul immediately leapt off the stage and took to the dance floor. His dancing was ... not charming or cute in any way. There was a lot of floundering and swaying, like a dying fish, though it was enough to lighten the mood and have a small circle form around him. A few of the rowdier students joined in and mimicked his "dance moves."

Much like me, Abe looked unamused by Kamaul. Kiku stayed close to his side.

"Nice to see all of you getting along," Jax whispered to the three of us.

"If you call this 'getting along,' Jax, you need to see a therapist." I snickered.

"Love that carefree attitude of yours, Olivia. I admire it."

"Bite me," I hissed, winking at Kiku's horrified face. I stuck my tongue out at him, which got a few chuckles from the mages listening nearby.

"This camaraderie between you all is beautiful, and only events like The Pit can make it happen. Save all that energy for January. Now, let's put on a great show!" Jax yelled, acting like a high school musical instructor.

"You say that like you're gonna be in there with us, Jax," Abe added as the maskless dean vanished backstage.

"You wouldn't last ... *hic* ... fourteen minutes in the ring with me, sir! Don't be ridiculush!" Kamaul hollered from below, trying to sound threatening. This poor, drunken soul loved the spotlight, but the moment was not treating him kindly. King Kamaul looked weak and unnatural, like an ugly weed in the garden of more sober dancers.

"Dean's gone, Kamaul. You can go back to ... whatever it is you think you're doing," I said.

"I'm dancin', fool!" he shouted back. "Havin' a ... *hic* ... having a ball at this ball!" Many simpletons laughed along with him, mostly talking through the alcohol fueling their systems. I shook my head and gave him a final dirty look before stepping offstage.

I knew mages wouldn't flock to me like they did for Kamaul, yet I would be lying if it didn't make me laugh inside. Whether I had a mask on or not. Whether I was a Pit competitor or not. Whether I was a product of their college or not. These other students never paid any attention to the girl in the giant obelisk. They were so conditioned to ignore me, to forget that I even existed, that even when I was paraded in their faces like a pig for slaughter, these heathens barely batted an eye. All of this led me to one realization: Whether I lived or die in The Pit, this college would not miss my existence.

"Pretend the freak girl doesn't exist. Pretend she doesn't have feelings!" Well, jerks and imbeciles, I do have feelings; thus, I will continue to feel nothing for you, as you do for me!

A single tear dripped down inside my mask. It was an ornate black one with frilly golden trim. Attached to the corner of my right eyehole was a paper-mâché rose with gold paint splashed on it.

Distracted by my weak sadness, I bumped into a younger girl wearing a pink dress and a brown mask, Columbina like my own.

"Excuse me," I mumbled, putting a hand on her shoulder to spin her around. "Sorry, I didn't mean to bump into the both of you. Clumsy me. Congratulations, by the way." I tried to laugh off the awkwardness, but this other girl was not having any of my forced charm.

"What the ... *What* did you just say to me?" she demanded, her voice soft but commanding. She grabbed me by the arm and peered at me with cold, careful daggers in her eyes. They were scared and frightened, but also very confused. I did not know who she was, nor did she recognize me.

Yanking me along, the girl in the pink dress moved the two of us off the dance floor, past the lounge sofas, and headed backstage. She was poised either to punch me, kick me, or fall into my arms crying; it was anyone's guess at this point. The music and the sounds of the crowd died out around us. Alone and hidden, she kicked aside a couple empty cans and garbage bags, then looked up at me again. "What did you mean, 'the both of you'? Why did you congratulate me?!" she asked sternly.

"I just mean ... the both of you? I apologize, but ..." I answered uncertainly, cocking my head to the side, perplexed.

"WHAT ARE YOU TALKING ABOUT?!" she demanded in shock, clenching a hand to her stomach.

"Well, I can feel it. When I ran into you, I felt something ... else inside of you. So, I assumed you're ... pregnant."

"There's no way!" she insisted. "Abe and I are so careful. I mean ... you can't possibly know that! It's so early ... I don't know if it's real or not, and ... and ... and what if you're wrong? Oh no! How do I tell him? How do I even bring it up?" she stammered, more softly this time. Fear and shock were clearly racing through her mind as she started twirling a strand of hair. Her eyes never broke from mine. "This cannot be right! I don't know who you are, and you don't know who I am, but I *can't* be pregnant. There's just no way."

"Just my assessment. This is new to me, too." I raised my hands in the air innocently.

"I need to see your face. I need to see the mage who sensed another person inside me. You must be incredibly gifted to feel ... Please, remove your mask."

Hesitant, but not wishing to anger a pregnant woman, I honored her request. With hands still raised, I untied the band around my head and dropped my mask.

She must have recognized my face instantly, because her brown mask with the little antenna poking out fell to the floor immediately.

"Emilee?!" I said, stunned and speechless.

"Olivia?" She giggled nervously. "How did you ...? I was ready to drop spiders down your throat, or like, stick leeches under your dress! You scared the shit oughta me! Wow, okay ... I'm actually somewhat *relieved* that it's you."

"Yeah ... uhhh ... Feel free to do that stuff anyway. I suppose I could unleash some insanity in your brain, if that makes it more interesting." I nodded uncomfortably.

"Yeah, no thanks ... So ... why do you think I'm pregnant? Honestly, as a friend of sorts, I need to know, in case I do find out for myself ... for real." Her pink dress was gorgeous and fit her so well, but terror clouded her eyes.

"Wouldn't use the term 'friend.' You work for me, and I give you stuff. But sure. Anyway, I work for the school. Side projects, mostly. They use me as a weapon to separate unstable revenants from their human hosts. So, I have this ability to ... perceive more than one entity inside a being. Elementals inside humans. Shadows in the Bad Place. And now, you can add humans inside of humans to that list. Guess this is a thing now ..."

"If you are *correct* that I am with child, is it noticeable, then? The bump?" Emilee muttered, placing both hands over her stomach.

"Sure? No? Honestly, my assessment here could be totally wrong. Probably is. You're not showing at all. This ability is brand new—like, discovered *right* now. So, take everything I'm saying with a grain of salt."

"I will find out for myself. But you absolutely cannot tell Abe."

"I'm, like, seventy percent sure I'm right. But no, of course not. Why would I even talk to him?"

"I mean it, Olivia. Swear to me that he won't find out!"

"Okay, okay, I swear! But you'll need to tell him at some point if you are."

"And I will. I will. But it has to come from me. Not you! Got it?"

"Crystal clear, Emilee. No one will know unless you tell 'em. I got it."

"Let me handle that part on my own."

Then Emilee's frightened look shifted as a subtle smile bloomed across her face, her eyes brightening into a more gleeful expression. The Emilee I knew looked back at me now.

"So, you really think I am with child?" she asked.

"Yup," I replied gauchely. "So, you and plant boy, huh?"

"Yup. Me and plant boy. It just ... feels surreal to hear it out loud—I'm pregnant."

"Congratulations," I stuttered again as Emilee squeezed me in a tight hug, the sequins of my dress pressing up against the pink lace of hers. She held me for a few moments. I stayed frozen and didn't really hug her back; it felt too strange. This insect girl had one tight grip, though, that was for sure.

"You're hugging me now? Okay, this is getting weird," I muttered, clearing my throat and lightly pushing away from Emilee.

"Right, yeah. You're not one for sentimentality or sharing feelings. But thank you, Olivia. Thanks for ... uhhh ... letting me know. Just gotta find out how accurate this new ability of yours is."

"Any time." I smiled gingerly, reaching up to retie the mask around my face.

"Now I just have to find the right time to break the news to Abe." She laughed. Emilee retrieved her mask from the floor, dusted it off a little, and tied it over her face. "Keep oughta trouble, will you?" she added as I started to walk away.

"Nah. No thanks. Think I'll pass on that offer." I snickered, turning the corner towards the dance floor. "And hey, don't think this forgives your late deposits, Emilee. You still owe me the wings of a supersonic butterfly, three Jergoli eggs, and whatever plants you can scour from Abe. I'm gonna charge interest if you keep prolonging this!"

"Delightful, Olivia. I'll get right on it." Emilee followed after me, then banked right towards Abe at the main stage. She wiped tears from her eyes and smiled at him.

Ignoring the dancing and drinking and partying, I slipped around the pillars and ventured back up the staircase to the balcony. Elbows over the railing, I stopped to observe the scene below. Bronze statues waltzed and gyrated along the stage, their strings and horns playing a hearty tune that shook the room. Good dancers and poor dancers alike crowded the space in front of the stage. It was so flooded with mages that no one could move left or right without clubbing someone in the head, knocking someone in the back, or shoving them out of the way. It was truly mesmerizing to watch, and I felt like a visitor at a zoo, gawking and laughing at the wild animals caged in their habitats.

Tarik tapped me on the shoulder with my clutch. "Enjoying the view?" He chuckled, joining me at the railing.

"Always. Where were you?"

"Where was I? I was down there. I left to grab a bite to eat. Sorry if I missed your big moment."

"No moment." I shook my head and glared at the sea of colorful bodies. "Just curious is all."

"Ready to head down now, party it up a lil' bit? What do ya say?"

"I'm good up here, actually," I replied, opening my clutch and inspecting its contents.

"*No?* That the word of the day?"

"Yeah, maybe."

"C'mon, O, gotta live a little! Enjoy yourself. Blow off some steam."

"Tarik, I said I'm good. It's my time to scout out the competition and see what really makes these students tick."

"I'm worried about you, Olivia," he added shyly, wrapping an arm around my shoulders.

"Worried about me? Why?" I asked, spinning to meet his disturbed emerald eyes.

"Because of The Pit, Olivia! You're so worried and overwhelmed with what the others are doing or how they act that I fear you've forgotten you're in this thing, too!"

"I haven't forgotten anything. I know I'm the strongest, most resolved, and most intelligent competitor in this tournament. My abilities and the likelihood of death don't concern me. The unknowns concern me—not my strengths or weaknesses, but theirs."

"I think you're being too careless about this. Focus on you, Olivia. Who cares what they do, or how they act, or what magic they know? Use what you know, not what they don't."

"Stop talking to me like a child! You sound just like Marrick right now. And frankly, I don't need either of your input. Are you taking part in this tournament, or am I? Let me handle *my* competition how I want to handle *my* competition. I'm excited for The Pit. I think it's gonna be fun."

"Fun?! See what I mean, Olivia? You aren't taking it seriously! I wish you would."

"And I wish you would leave me alone and let me manage my own stuff however I choose to. You're a carbon copy of Marrick sometimes, and it shrivels my love for you like a prune. Please just leave me alone. Let me spy in peace."

I twirled the vial of antivenom, filled with a hardened liquid like mud inside the glass, between my fingers. After setting it in the bottom of my clutch, I pulled out my spyglass and stretched it to full length. It compacted nicely in my clutch and had three extendable segments. Through the solid brass telescope, my view of the dancing crowd sharpened.

"Fine. You know what? Fine, yeah, I'll leave. Stay up here by yourself, creeping on the student body. I'm gonna go *enjoy* the party and actually partake in it, like a normal human."

"Well, yup. Answered that for me," I scoffed, obnoxiously enough for Tarik to notice. "'Normal human' and 'Olivia' don't belong in the same sentence. I'll be up here, spying on you. Don't do anything stupid, 'cause I'll be watching."

"Yeah, yeah. Whatever, Olivia. See you after the ball."

"Do enjoy yourself, Tarik. I've got my sights on four people already. Making it five would be reeeeally easy." I laughed, scoped into the spyglass like a pirate up in a crow's nest.

Tarik scoffed back at me, snapped silly-looking finger guns (or maybe middle fingers) in my peripheral, and stormed down the stairs. Muttering something under his breath, he turned the corner and disappeared.

I've always been on my own. I don't need him. I don't need anyone else. Never have.

Couples making out. Guys dancing and flirting to capture any attention they could get. Drunk girls and boys passed out on the sofas, leaning on the pillars, or face down on the tables. This was where I spotted Kamaul, a tiger in his natural environment. He was socializing and partying with lots of laughing mages in a corner booth. He truly embodied a weed in the garden.

Buffoon. Easy target. He'll get himself killed before I get the chance to do it myself. Although...? I could just take him out now. Doubt anyone would see it happen. But do I want the panic, or the fire school showing up at my tower, armed with pitchforks? A bunch of Kamaul-hungry, vengeful mages after me? Nah, not yet, I don't.

As he sloshed himself around a group of girls, I never saw the smile fade from his face. It seemed cemented there, pearly whites gleaming in the golden lights. Kamaul embraced the crowd in his corner and made himself the center of any conversation he could. He almost appeared to float from one person to the next, not missing a beat, chatting up as many people as his vocal cords would allow.

I shifted my spyglass back towards the dance floor and accidentally zoomed in on one earth mage's glossy eyes.

"Eww. Not a good look, sweetie," I muttered to myself as I panned across the scene like a sea captain searching for land.

Then I thought about Aaron.

I didn't know where the image of him came from, but it popped into my head—probably sparked by the trio of young mages ogling photos of Kai. I knew he was at the event, but a glorified, has-been fashionista dressed like a prince did not interest me. Plus, I see an Elder constantly—more than I actually wanted to! So, if these novices wanted to witness an Elder's so-called glory on a daily basis, they were welcome to take my place anytime they wished.

Elders? Pffft. Seekers ask me *to extract revenants, not them. Marrick's more annoying and overbearing than anyone else I know.*

Moving the spyglass, I spun from pillar to pillar in search of another Pit competitor. I found nothing except for a professor or two making a mockery of themselves on the dance floor. However, after swinging my scope, I noticed one couple slow dancing to the upbeat music. I retracted my telescope down a segment, zooming out to get a better view. I caught sight of Abe's horned earth mask and Emilee's butterfly one as they swayed together. With her head on his shoulders, the pair waltzed beautifully in sync. It was nauseatingly cute—one of those images you saw that was so adorable and so sweet that you felt the desire to dunk your eyes in a vat of acid.

My insect supplier and my new rival are having a child together. Huh? What a headline that would be! Guess I found Abe's weakness—and an additional ability of mine at the same time. Abe's weakness is his heart. I know exactly how to attack that ... and it will be simple.

I watched the two giggle and whisper in each other's ears. Holding her close, Abe linked their hands, weaving his fingers between Emilee's.

Wonderful. So I get to watch more of this lovey-dovey shit for the next six months? Yippee. Get fucked. Okay, Olivia, you know his weakness now ... yet you are still watching them? It's been a steady five minutes, and your sights are still locked onto a single dancing couple. It's becoming creepy and perverse, much as Tarik feared. Please move the fuck on.

I retracted my spyglass and held it by my side as my eyes readjusted to reality. Having to wear a mask for the entire duration of the ball was horribly uncomfortable and impractical. Frankly, I don't blame Kamaul for ditching his.

No sign of Aaron, though. The balcony held maybe ten mages, and the lower floor was packed with the rest of the student body, yet our water competitor was nowhere to be seen.

From the railing, I kept an eye on the couple to my left. The pair of guys were sipping on flutes of champagne, their free hands clasped together. They looked to be laughing and jiving to the music, and occasionally judging the outfits of those below. (My kind of people.) Sadly, I was not focusing on them, per se. What I was more interested in was their shadows on the floor.

I closed my eyes briefly and whistled for their attention. I watched the dark shadows slide across the tile and arrive next to my own. Commanding the three of them now, I whispered some nightmarish incantations and sent the trio of shadows away.

Find Aaron, I instructed them. *Search the campus top to bottom. The place is empty right now, so this should be simple. And make it snappy! I have other things to deal with.*

I resumed my people-watching. The shadows moved along the ceiling, then jumped into dark corners, and eventually left the room. My usual fear with using the shadow trooper spell was that they often got distracted by nonsense like baby squirrels and dead dandelions. They were remarkably simple, moronic creatures, but they got the job done.

Digging through my clutch, I pulled out the dagger. No real reason; I just wanted to look at it. I was still not sure how my parents had come across this magnificent artifact. As I inspected it, the beige gargoyle-bone dagger felt heavier than usual. After my loving mother and father left it for me in Russia (before they bailed on me, of course), I had carried it with me every step of the way. From foster homes to orphanages, this little beauty had traveled the unfortunate world as I did—a trusty sidekick, if you will. While every kid cowered in horror as I walked past them, my dagger served as a healthy reminder that they were right to feel that way. Today, I rarely left my tower without it. And now, facing a bigger threat to my safety than I was already accustomed to, thanks to The Pit, the dagger easily became the first thing I threw in my clutch.

Wanna hear a funny story about this family heirloom? Eh, who am I kidding? Course you do! I giggled to myself, carelessly mage-spotting from above like a boozed-up sailor.

One time ...

Think it was your master year? No, maybe junior ...? Oh, it doesn't matter.

One time a couple years ago, I had been assisting Tori with a lesson in horseback riding. She made me laugh in many ways, sometimes intentionally, but often by accident. Her western American accent was thick and would inadvertently get a giggle from me, no matter what came out of her mouth. All things considered, Tori was a hoot! Anyway, being from Wyoming and working at a place called Yellowstone (somewhere in Wyoming; don't know if that's right), she loved riding horses and missed it now that she lived in the Midwest. For that day's lesson, Tori needed me to conjure an elemental similar to the stature, attitude, and look of a horse. Simple enough, right? Wrong! You see, horses don't exist in the Bad Place, and since I worked specifically in that department, I summoned the closest creature I could find.

Of the fourteen journeyman mages in her Elemental History class, the daring teacher probably regretted my involvement. I brought a Tuvis into the room via a shadow portal. Those things were terrifying! A Tuvis is a four-legged hoofed creature made of maroon clay, with exposed flesh in lieu of skin. It had the unique feature of two mouths: one at the end of its muzzle, like a horse's (a decoy for aesthetics), and one gaping hole of teeth (for actually consuming food). Where a horse had a mane, a Tuvis had a single ram's horn curving back over its neck. Where a horse had large ears, large pupils, and two nostrils, a Tuvis had no facial features and instead relied on slits along the side of its head to hear like a bat. As you can see, a Tuvis was not quite the mustang Tori was anticipating.

Wow, girl, that dress is hideous and unflattering. Bright red is a bold choice when your skin is fair like porcelain. Go with a lighter color next time, dear.

So, I had pulled the gargoyle-bone dagger out and used it to kill the Tuvis on the spot, tossing it back into the oblivion from which it came. Thankfully (or disappointingly, if you ask me), the elemental did no damage to the classroom or anyone in it. However, a handful of students had to seek weekly help from the school's therapist to get over the PTSD the incident brought on. I guess the dagger and the life-threatening beast were enough to instigate persistent trauma. Tori was understandably upset with me for months, until she came to her senses, and we eventually had a good laugh about it. She told me I needed to see the school therapist as well, to help me "better understand what is okay and what is not okay to show young students." It was what it was. I never ended up going, regardless. Got a lot of flak about it from Marrick and others.

That mask is too ugly, hon.

Short story long, this dagger had been with me through thick and thin. I placed it back in my clutch and returned the spyglass to my eye.

Eureka! There she is.

I had managed to spot a sneaky Kiku lingering in the back of the room. She kept close to another mage with blonde hair and vibrant blue ballgown. Kiku appeared glued to this girl's side, attached at the hip. The air competitor wore a unique white kimono with black lotuses stitched along the bottom. It was bold and adventurous, which I admired, but it ultimately brought on a lot of extra opinions. While the other girl waved and smiled at various mages on the dance floor, Kiku stayed motionless in the corner like a wallflower.

Her timid nature and fear of everything will be her downfall. While I do feel slight pity for her, I can't take it easy on her. She's still an opponent. It did seem, on stage and at the ceremony, that she's close with Abe, which should work in her favor. He's smart and talented. *Perhaps some of his intelligence and magical knowledge will rub off on her ... or perhaps Abe's ignorance of his own limitations will get them both killed. Who knows?*

I'd had no word or sighting of the shadows for a bit, so I tucked the spyglass away and whistled softly to gather them. Tapping my fingers anxiously, I spun around to face the darkness on the floor and waited for three more shadows to appear.

Come on, boys. When I said "snappy," I meant fucking snappy! I don't want to be here much longer. Hurry up.

I tapped my foot like a discouraged mother waiting to yell at her son for coming home too late. Watching over the railing for the three shadows, I figured they would be obvious to spot and might startle a few mages along the way.

I rotated to the far side of the balcony and brought out the spyglass again, chuckling when an appalled couple stopped kissing each other long enough to breathe and ran off to somewhere else when I overtook their spot. Yes, there were other open spots available to scout from—but I wanted their spot. It was clearly the best vantage point.

Hee hee hee ... What a tragedy. Now you have to go suck face in public downstairs.

Suddenly, as my patience was wearing thin, the trio of shadows slithered up the stairs and arrived at my feet. In a jumbled mix of growls and gibberish, they gave me some answers.

"Mistress," they stated in ominous unison almost as a single, scratchy voice, "the boy has gone below the surface of the lake. His heat signature disappeared. The world around him was dark and empty. It was the perfect hunting ground for us and for you, but we imagine the boy will not enjoy his new home."

"Interesting," I sneered. "Okay, that'll be all."

Well, well, well, would you look at that? Guess that is one down. Three to go.

The shadows left my view and glided along the floor back over to the two boys. They returned to their original positions, like nothing happened, and those champagne-sipping gentlemen were none the wiser.

For my last hurrah, I brought out the brass spyglass again, extended it, and scoped out the dance floor again. Kamaul was currently being held up by his partner in crime, Dahir, and another goober, Atlas. Kiku clung to the wall like a painting and hid behind who I assumed was her roommate. Abe and Emilee were dancing the night away, swaying to the string instruments, without a care in the world (well, for now, at least). And Aaron had apparently gone on a little excursion.

Retracting the spyglass, I dropped it back in my clutch, slung that over my shoulder, and beamed a unique smile at the masquerade downstairs.

"Hope you're ready for me, Kira, because come Sunday morning, I'm walking in like a blood-thirsty vampire in a cattle yard. The real fun has officially begun."

Trigger Warning

The following chapter contains a detailed depiction of a character's suicide attempt, including the thought process, mental health struggles, and the method they intend to use. Please take care of yourself while reading, and consider skipping this chapter if these topics may be triggering for you.

AARON V

"WONDER IF THE OTHER Pit students fought off demons today, too?" I teased myself.

After leaving Luke's apartment, I headed straight for my dorm. The euphoric sounds of loud music and bright colors cascaded from the festival nearby. An empty campus was the perfect and equally awful space for my disordered thoughts, which festered and simmered in my brain like the overflowing laughter and obnoxious noises from the celebrations. Luke wanted me to go to the Festival of the Elements, too. Would I secretly deep down have liked to go? No—not even slightly. And even if I were considering a visit to the carnival-circus thing, I needed to situate myself before doing so.

On my quiet walk around the gazebo, the gravitas of my situation was beginning to sink in. In searching like a lost child for my Mentor only to have him rescue me from signing a deal with a demon in his own home, I realized I had done nothing to help my own cause. Despite Luke's ambitions and ideas to look beyond my personal shortcomings, I could not help but think of them. The further I pushed those bad thoughts away, the faster they returned, with a vengeance. It felt like every weakness had a crippling grip on my well-being. They had become beasts of their own, performing for their own agendas and leaving other thoughts to rot.

There was one final flaw, however, that plucked itself from the rest: the fear of disappointing Luke. After today, I already felt like I'd let him down. He'd seen my struggles in his Intro to Magic class, and had he been at the ceremony, he would have seen the definition of dread painted on my face. Then the demon stuff in his apartment! Judging from the way he speared it through the chest, he clearly did not like the idea of me signing that contract. Sadly enough, I kinda wish I had done it. What a scary realization that is ...

I closed my eyes with a heavy sigh and unlocked the door to my dorm. Whether in shock or denial, I almost glazed over the ribbon-wrapped blue box sitting on my doorstep and an envelope with my name on it.

"What? Why? What is this, now?" I sighed, mind immediately racing to the worst-case scenario.

Praying my roommate would not be there, I stepped inside. Probably due to the festival, the apartment was empty. I threw the gift box on a chair and sat on the coffee table. Staring at the name written on the envelope brought back the horrible feeling of seeing my name scripted in blood on the snow. The handwriting was eerily familiar as well. Looking at it gave me a mixed sensation—part anticipation, part dread. This was the first letter I had received from my father since accepting the college's invitation, but it was also the first letter any family member had sent me in nearly four months, and that alone left a queasy feeling in my core.

Before the exaggerated panic took over, I flipped over the envelope and broke the seal. The feeling of dread consumed me now, and my hands paused before I touched the letter.

"Please be good news. Please be good news. Please be good news ..." I murmured, unfolding the yellow parchment. I recognized the handwriting and smiled as I skimmed over my father's sketchy penmanship. That is, until I began reading his letter ...

Dear Aaron,

I don't have much time. I would first like to apologize for not writing to you sooner, but things in our little town of Dunnmore have become dire over the recent months. Something horrible has happened.

It started so simple and innocent. A new traveler came to Dunnmore and sold rare red flowers to the townspeople. So beautiful and vibrant, they were able to grow and flourish, despite the frigid winter temperatures. They appeared all over town. There wasn't a household without a red rose perched in their window. But everyone who bought one ... died a tragic death. Bleeding from every orifice, their flesh eroding ... Truly awful, grotesque sights, Aaron.

Having lived to tell the tale, those who escaped its fate now call it the Plague of Roses.

This is where condolences are due, Aaron. I am so sorry ... Your mother and sister were two of these people affected by the roses. Once our village discovered how deadly the flowers were, I tried to save them. I tried every possible way to reverse the curse and stop the bleeding. But it was too late. There was nothing I could do.

I have a plan. Though ... I don't have much time. Son, I am afraid for my life. They're after me. I don't know who it is or what they want from me or why exactly I'm a high-value target. The authorities? The Citadel? Whoever it is, I'm on the run now. After Mary and Caroline passed, accusations flourished around town left and right—a bunch of "he said, she said." Many people escaped from Dunnmore, myself being one of them.

I'm sorry to overload you with so much information in one letter. I'm sorry for not reaching out to you sooner. I'm sorry for the news of Dunnmore and our family. But I needed to tell you in the only way I knew how. This may, after all, be the last letter I'm able to send. You are strong like me, Aaron. Stay strong, and believe in me. I am going to avenge their deaths and fix this. Whether I caused the problem or not, I am going to fix it. And I have a plan for how to do it ...

Wishing love and fortune,

Dad

The letter floated slowly to the floor, my heart dropping with it. It was the first correspondence I'd had from family since the semester began, and he had just told me ... that a plague of some kind swept through our town, killed my mother and sister, and forced him into hiding, where he was also on the run from the authorities. Or worse, The Citadel, Penumbra's opulent yet ominous capital. And now I, a student recently doomed to participate in The Pit, probably needed to compile my emotions in a positive, healthy way, right? Quite the opposite, obviously! Why was this happening to me? At this point, I was even worrying about my worrying, because it seemed like thinking hard enough about something bad might accidentally manifest it into reality.

I feared going out in public as one of the chosen five and having every beady pair of eyes staring at me like a zoo animal. I feared Sunday morning, when Luke would clearly determine I needed both magical and physical assistance beyond comprehension. I feared that first week of training, the first month of it, the first Elemental Rite, the competition with the other champions. I feared looking at my father's letter again and rereading the horrible news. I feared for his life, and not knowing what was really happening in Dunnmore or who was to blame for the tragedy.

All my life, I had pushed my happiness to the wayside in order to please someone else. I had been so selfless and altruistic my whole life. Was all of that good will coming back to haunt me? Was this some ... some kind of deep-rooted karma, sent to punish me? I'd believed doing right by other people would make me right in someone else's eyes, but I was starting to think I was wrong. Since arriving to The College of Adarius, very few positives have come out of my experience.

I felt nothing, numb. My mind fell blank with nothing to focus on. An engulfing wave of fear and depression painted itself across the canvas. Tears dripped from my eyes onto the letter. My mind was too heavy to carry right now; it felt like the globe Atlas held on his shoulders. Only in my case ... I wasn't strong.

Walking over to my bedroom, I pushed open the door and approached the window. I slid the curtains aside and peeked at the world outside. It was a beautiful evening with the setting sun's glow sinking into the frozen lake, a lovely reflection of the festival and Market Square stretched brightly across it.

There's one great place I like to go and think. The only place I feel happy—the only place I feel like Aaron Dirge anymore. Most everywhere else, I'm a dead man walking, I thought, releasing the curtains over the window. *The gazebo.*

Then I saw the framed picture—the photo of Matthew and I beachside last summer. I thought about him and his family ... whom I'd left in Dunnmore. Several unpleasant ideas raced through my mind at the possibility of this Plague of Roses infecting them, too.

I pleaded my case to the empty dorm. "Please don't let whatever this—this rose thing happening in town—be happening to Matthew or his family, or anyone else close to me. No more dead friends or family. Please ...?"

I only seemed to know two words today: "please" and "sorry." I had said them so much over the past six to eight hours, or however long it's been, that I was doubting my own sanity. It was hard to believe I was sitting clueless in the stands before watching my name spill in blood. It seemed like it had dragged on for a year. I was simply ready for it to be over, but I needed somehow to calm my nerves. Unfortunately for Luke, that meant the Festival of the Elements and any subsequent parties were off the table. Did relaxation and peace of mind exist today? I was starting to think those were delusions of the mind ...

I forced an unconvincing smile at the photo and removed myself from my bedroom. I grabbed the letter off the floor, folded it, placed it in my pocket, and threw a random sweater on. Turning the doorknob, I left my dorm quiet and dark and headed for the staircase.

The outside world was colder than it had been earlier. Chilly air nipped at the hairs under my clothes. With my hands tucked in my pockets, I walked across the gloriously empty sidewalk. I fiddled with the letter, feeling the deaths of my mother and sister on the tips of my fingers and the rush of my father's writing scratching across the page.

I needed to get away. Now.

I thought about sprinting for The Stables and hijacking a griffin or dragon to fly myself off campus. But there was no way I would make it even a hundred feet without someone sniffing me out.

"Aaron Dirge," Jax's voice suddenly echoed in my head.

"I don't stand a chance against these other mages," I answered.

Water had always been calming to me—a soothing escape from life. I lived in the middle of the woodlands, so the beach and coastlines were dream destinations. My family could never afford a vacation there, however, so those dreams had stayed just dreams. Thunderstorms terrified Caroline, but I found them comforting and provocative. Perhaps my branch of storm magic made more sense than I realized—which, in turn, made my lack of skill in it more heartbreaking.

The lake on campus was like this—this touch of Penumbra in a sea of unfamiliarity. It was large and broad and took up plenty of space between the elemental courtyards. Now that winter had come, the water lilies and lotus flowers could not withstand December's temperatures. Dark, cold ice capped the still water.

Regardless of the season, though, the untouched part of the campus's lake was the boardwalk and gazebo built directly in the center like the look of a young sunflower.

"Aaron Dirge," the voice echoed again.

I strolled slowly onto the snowy wooden boardwalk. A brief sense of calm swept over me as I breathed in the cold, quiet lake air. Its soothing effect lasted mere minutes until the feeling vanished, melting away like light snow under the hot sun.

I took in another deep breath. This time, no soothing feeling accompanied the cold air.

I closed my eyes tight and tried another. Yet another gasp of nothing.

I did this exercise until I was dizzy. I could feel myself starting to hyperventilate. My breathing was staggered and labored. I needed to calm my nerves and slow my rapid heartbeat. There seemed to be no reprieve from the panicked state I was in.

Running my hands over the icy banister, I stopped and leaned over it. I just stood there, not moving and not feeling. My skin was numb to the touch. Even as I watched my fingers hit my arm, I couldn't tell if they were making contact or not. Alone in the gazebo, I wished away the anxiety and slumped against the wooden barrier as the frozen water lay dormant below. I wished the numbness of my skin could be felt on the inside—an equal serenity of deafened worries. Thinking of what I was going to do, I took another shaky breath.

"What's going to happen?" I asked the voices in my head.

Oh, I know! exclaimed one of them. *We're going to get massacred by mages stronger than we are in a sadistic game for the college's pleasure!*

It'll be a fun spectacle for them, chimed another. *I can see the article now ... "Lowly water student succumbs to the pressures of The Pit!"*

"NO!" I snapped. "Calm thoughts, Aaron! Calm thoughts. Ignore those voices. Think of ... think of family, and home. Raindrops. Matthew, and building sand-castles on the beach." It was easy to yell to myself when the festival's noises muted the shouting.

I paused for a second and managed to smile at the ice. But, much to the beat of today, that smile quickly became a frown.

"Calm thoughts!" I shouted gently. "Happy thoughts, Aaron! Try to see the light at the end of the tunnel, huh? Popular, powerful storm mage, victor of the tournament, admired by my peers, a ... a real social butterfly ..."

But my inner voices and I both knew the truth. That was all a dream—a distant reality too far-fetched to be believable. My ... family? Or what was left of it. My mother and sister were dead, and my father was on the run from who knows who. My home? Ravaged by an infection of deadly roses, so it was anybody's guess what type of wasteland Dunnmore had turned into. Raindrops, water ...? My supposed salvation from the outside world was now my greatest magical downfall, as I was crippled by the inability to understand magic or spellcasting. Matthew and the others? Odds were that they, too, had succumbed to the flowers' plague. Were there any real diamonds in the rough here?

After a series of exaggerated deep breaths, I knelt onto the cold wood and did a few yoga poses to clear my head. Mara's words reminded me to think happy thoughts and filter out the negative headspace. But my inner voices overpowered the downward dog and snake poses like a conniving demon. Their incessant demeaning of those happy thoughts beckoned me to my failures like a gong.

You are going to die, a voice whispered in my head. *You will never see your family again, and they will never see you again either. But you already knew that, didn't you? Your life has an expiration date, just like the rest of your family. It's over. It's done. So ... why wait to die?*

The voice was so loud in my head that I jerked upright and looked around to see if someone was actually speaking to me. Of course, no one was nearby—not a single soul. I was alone in the cold in the gazebo on a frozen lake while thinking about killing myself.

The entire college was enjoying the Festival of the Elements, but I was here.

Do it. End it. This is the only way ... the only way to escape your miserable life.

The voice, sounding more like my own, hit me like a brick.

Why waste time and face the humiliation? If you do this now, no one will know. If you do this now, you control the narrative and the way Aaron Dirge will be remembered. I could control my own death versus being killed in the ring by the odds. *They never noticed you before, so why would they notice you now? This would make them notice you.*

Was this right? Had I just found my own way out of all this? Had anyone selected for The Pit ever done it before? Was this the way to escape my fate? Was this my answer to finally take control of my life?

"Well ... here's to being the first," I whispered, spacing out at my reflection in the ice.

"I wish I had some paper to write a note," I muttered.

No need. They would figure it out soon enough.

I remembered the story of a young boy about Caroline's age who had fallen through the ice on a lake in Calonia. He was playing hockey with some friends but slipped and fell through a crack in the ice. His body sank to the bottom of that lake as his friends panicked and cried on the surface. When my father shared this story with me, he had told me that the freezing water would numb the whole process, so the boy did not suffer.

I thought about my family, my loved ones, and Luke. Everyone I knew either let me down, or I let them down. Luke, for instance, had let me down. When I needed him to be at my side like the other Mentors, he wasn't! As for my family and loved ones? I had let them down and wouldn't even be able to make it up to them. They were in a better place, though. Me, however ... one quick instant and I'd be able to see them again, to make up for all the mistakes and lost time in my life!

But my mother and sister are not in Dunnmore anymore. They aren't alive anymore. My father's letter made that clear, and the fact that he is now on the run means you will never see him again either. What kind of family is there really left for you to return to?

Atop the railing, my muscles were already flexed to jump ... when I realized I couldn't do it.

Suddenly, my conscience interjected. *Luke had a valid reason to miss that ceremony, and he did save my life, after all. What would my mother think if I did this? What would Caroline think? My father? Do not do this, Aaron. There are no take-backs.*

Suddenly, I didn't have the guts to go through with it. I flailed around frantically, trying to undo my mistake.

There was a crash. My head hit something hard.

Gong.

The next thing I knew I was falling.

Then, cold—SO much freezing cold water! With numbness and darkness all around, the last thing I thought of as I sank deeper was that my father had clearly fucking lied to me about this being painless. The lake was so frigid and black under the ice I could not tell if I had already died or was stuck in an Arctic purgatory. Breathing immediately became more and more difficult.

Wind chimes rippled their echoing sounds underwater.

I listened to the calm water. It was totally serene, everything becoming tranquil. The voices softened. My worries waned and my thoughts weakened. All of it. Then my heartbeat slowed, echoing the pulse in my ears. I ... was starting to feel free. Was I doing the right thing?

For the first moment in my life, I finally felt relieved, eyelids heavy as potato sacks.

Gong.

The world went cold and silent. I was free.

Then I blacked out.

If you or someone you know is dealing with some shit, just know that you are not alone. You are special, you are brave, you are validated in those feelings, and you matter. Healing is a journey, not an overnight destination. Here are some links and websites to help begin your healing process.

www.988lifeline.org
www.adaa.org
www.thetrevorproject.org
www.samhsa.gov
NAMI Helpline: 1-800-950-6264

Acknowledgements

I have been wrong about many things before and will be wrong about plenty of things in the future. But I nailed it on the great people I assembled to bring this book and the world of Penumbra to life. Often, it has been a rollercoaster ride of heartbreaks and breakthroughs, where the hurdles felt endless. This team both personal and professional, however, joined to help surmount it like the Avengers. There is a wild journey ahead of us, and I am incredibly blessed and honored to share it alongside you.

Thank you to my mom and dad. I love you both dearly. I can never repay you for the sacrifices you've made to provide the life that I have nor the opportunities you've presented for me, but I can try to make you proud. I have lofty expectations for myself and even higher ones to match what you have both done for me. I will never stop trying to live up to them. Thank you to Savannah for keeping my head on straight. You are such a powerful and profound woman, someone I model my female characters after. Between marathons of The Twilight Zone and horror flicks, I can always count on you to lift my spirits and be my closest ally. Our bond has no limits.

Thank you to my copy editor Robin Fuller and proofread editor Aly Owen. Each of you gave brilliant advice and feedback. Thank you for tolerating my multiple threads of messages and discussions and your patience as I navigated this new world for the first time. You facilitated my manuscript to become its best version. All mistakes left behind are mine to own.

Thank you to My Lan Khuc for this magnificent cover and the exterior artwork. You are a true talent. Thank you for the extensive tweaks, mockup concepts, and feedback that helped illustrate my vision. Thank you to Tanner Yurchuck for drawing and map illustrations. After peering over your shoulder as you sketched other characters, I knew there was no better person to be my map cartographer and artist. Our discussions of adapting my crude Sharpie drawings to your masterful inked hands were some of my favorite.

Thank you to Jaycee DeLorenzo for formatting and designing this book's layout. Your expertise and diligence is admired, and it only looks as good as it does because of you. Thank you to Olivia for being one of the first readers of this story. You saw a version very few have and assisted me in making it much more digestible. I hope all your writing dreams come to fruition as you have helped mine to do.

Thank you to Kim Bouchard for guiding me throughout the entire journey. Your advice and assistance is invaluable. Not a single aspect of this book's existence would have been possible if it weren't for your kindness, understanding, and direction. I felt lost in the woods when I first began, but you showed me the way to make my dreams a reality. You are the Yoda I do not deserve, and the Pit Mentor I never knew I needed.

Thank you to Adarius for taking care of my mental health. When we met, I was a lesser version of myself and a shell of who I truly am. Therapy is paramount in my life and you are the shining example of that. I wish Aaron had someone like you.

Thank you to Allison, who showed me what a healthy relationship is. You are the support when I need it, the loving hand when the future seems uncertain, and the missing piece in the puzzle. Your compassion and generosity are second to none yet don't even scratch the surface to prove how special you are. Meeting you has infinitely changed my life and redirected it on the right track.

And finally, I need to give a quick shoutout to Red Bull and their flavor editions. I look forward to all the new releases like an unofficial holiday. Many writing days and editing nights have been fueled by cans of Red Bull. Penumbra is a fictional place, but Red Bull helped give Sonnet her wiings.

About the Author

Enthralled by fantasy as a child, Garrett Kosis often wrote short stories, fan fiction, and graphic novels for fun. Those years set the stage for the debut of his first novel, *The Pit: Part One*, a labor of love for the genre and a project roughly five years in the making. To fight off writer's block, he can be seen enjoying theme parks, sporting events, and the occasional play. Garrett was born in Pittsburgh and now lives in Orlando with a goofy dog named Jasper and his cat sidekick named Mowgli.

Scan the QR code to enter the digital world of Penumbra and uncover more details about The Pit. Watch for upcoming installments and new releases on his website: www.thepitnovels.com.